LANDING IN FIFTEEN MINUTES

An Aviation Thriller of Family Secrets

Elliot Chatima

And

Rumbi Chen

First paperback edition November 2024

Book design by SK-Book Covers

Edited by Progress Chaya

ISBN 978- 1-7-7635933-2-9 (paperback)

ISBN 978- 1-7-7635933-3-0 (e-book)

Acknowledgments

We are indebted to God for the blessing of creative minds. To my wife Jane Vene Chatima, thank you for the support and encouragement. Tafadzwa Tamanikwa thank you for the dedication to review the book, offering candid feedback regarding development, consistency, the plot and unison of authors and medical input. My daughters Oriona, Onabelle and my son Othniel Aurther Junior have been a solid support system for me.

Special tribute to my dearly departed beloved son Sasha Micheal Kaseke a young man, tall, handsome and full of talent yet decided to depart before his talents were fully developed. I thought you were to hold my hand in old age but you decided to depart early. I will always miss the phrase "when you went to school." Rest in peace till we meet again.

It is not my intention to leave out anyone, but if I have done so, apologies. Special thanks to my co-author, Elliot Chatima, who framed this book. Trudy Phiri and Diana Vito played a crucial role in shaping this literary project, including their guidance and inspiration throughout this journey.

To my parents, siblings, family, friends, both near and far, your prayers, support, and encouragement, have sustained me throughout this journey.

To Mr. Muusha, my perpetual mentor, a remarkable author by virtue, thank you for counsel and insightful guidance.

To our beta readers thank you for your constructive feedback.

Chapter 1

At 15:45 on a Thursday, Captain Smith headed home after another long-haul shift. He glanced at the sky ahead, hands steady on the controls. 62,000 flight hours. Three crash landings. One hijacking he'd flown to safety. He'd come through every challenge unscathed, calm in the cockpit when others would have panicked. But today he felt odd. His gut twisted. Something wasn't right. He couldn't shake the eerie feeling that today would be different. That hijacking he had handled the 57-seater Embraer with such courage it even shocked him, landing on a rough gravel aerodrome. Four awards and countless praises followed—best landing, outstanding professionalism, most punctual pilot, and greatest pilot under harsh weather. Now, he flew home, after a marathon of flights from Canberra, Australia, to London, UK. He'd flown the Airbus A380 across the globe and then hopped to Kenya, Zambia, and finally, Zimbabwe. This last leg was aboard the Euro Martin DM747 Max.

He was operating a Euro Martin DM747 Max operated by Sahara Africa Airlines, the leading airline operating commercial passenger and cargo planes with more than 390 destinations worldwide. Euro Martin, a leading manufacturer of commercial and cargo planes, manufactured the aircraft. The giant plane had a carrying capacity of 980 people. It was a double-decker plane with two boarding points requiring an extended passenger boarding bridge (PBB). The Euro Martin DM747 Max was the most powerful machine in its class, surpassing the Airbus A340 and Boeing 747-8 Intercontinental both with capacities of 600, and the Airbus A380-A800 with 800. On board, the Euro Martin DM747 Max had 922 souls, 58 short of full capacity.

Eight engines powered the plane like the American-operated Boeing B-52 Stratofortress. The B-52 is a long-range, subsonic, jet-powered strategic bomber. It was designed and manufactured by Boeing, which has continued to provide support and upgrades. It has been operated by the United States Air Force (USAF) since the 1950s, and NASA for over 40 years. The bomber can carry up to 70,000 pounds (32,000 kg) of weapons and has, on average, a combat range of around 8,800 miles (14,200 km) without refueling.

A GE9X engine powered the Euro Martin DM747 Max, the largest and most powerful commercial aircraft engine ever built since the Wright brothers. It incorporated advanced technologies for more efficient, quieter flights with fewer emissions, aligning with global sustainability efforts and supporting the United Nations' Sustainable Development Goals (SDGs). What the plane lacked in speed and agility; it compensated with its great payload. The payload is a key determination of the plane's commercial viability which assesses the collective weight of passengers, cargo, baggage, and additional revenue streams that an aircraft carries. It is a critical determinant of commercial viability, operational efficiency, and safety in aviation operations.

Euro Martin took three and half years carrying extensive research and development before the Euro Martin DM747 Max entered commercial production. To date, only 35 orders have been received and successfully delivered over budget and out of time at a staggering cost of USD 600 million each. Euro Martin is an 80-year-old company operated in more than five developed nations. The UK and the USA are the only centers where production is done with 25 orders processed in the USA while the difference was produced in the UK.

The Euro Martin MD747 Max uses the GE9X engines. These engines are enormous and through its use of advanced technology, GE managed to develop them into 10% more fuel efficient against competition and, over time, reduced carbon emissions. It set an ambitious target of 3.5% carbon reduction annually, aligning with global sustainability goals. However, Donald Trump, the leading contender for the 2024 U.S. presidential election, has dismissed climate change and sustainability efforts, calling them a 'serious hoax.' During his tenure as president, it is reported that Trump refused to sign the Paris Agreement and insisted on the use of non-renewable energy in generating electricity. He rubbished the notion that the world needed to generate power from environmentally safe sources and, instead, insisted on creating jobs through opening up coal mining companies. He preferred to use coal and other methods which most nations such as the UK are increasingly criticizing. By June 2024, China had emerged as a global leader in the hybrid and electric vehicle market, with the latest results showing its dominance in the sector which it actively promoted.

On the efficient GE9X, the US Federal Aviation Administration entered a contract for what became the biggest commercial jet engine in the world. In the process, the administration endorsed and signed off the GE9X with huge thrusters. The engine was hung under the wings of Boeing's 777X aircraft, and flew for the first time, much to the engineers' delight. Since the Euro Martin DM747 Max is a huge plane, it requires significant power to lift it into the air. Each GE9X engine produces 105,000 pounds of thrust, generating a total of 840,000 pounds. This engine has reached a record thrust of 134,000 pounds. However, pilots do not need to push the engines to their maximum for takeoff. Maxing out the engines for liftoff, known as a 'full rated take off, is often avoided to preserve engine life and is only used when necessary.

Euro Martin made the GE9X under the GE licence and was allowed to tweak the engine to meet their needs. A team of experts from Mitsubishi were called and their duty was to investigate ways to reduce the overall engine weight and fuel consumption. The Japanese were able to achieve an overall 11% weight reduction and 5.55% energy efficiency. According to the rules set by GE, all research and improvements were to be shared with their office and treated as their intellectual property and used at no cost, a position that Euro Martin did not dispute.

Captain Smith came over the intercom to make an announcement, "Ladies and gentlemen, we will begin our descent shortly, the weather is cool with clear skies and a temperature of 25 degrees Celsius. We are estimated to be landing in 15 minutes. Please return to your seats and fasten your seat belts."

At that moment the plane was lifted abruptly with wings turning violently threatening to send the plane into cigarette rolls. The captain steadied the plane but there was another problem, clouds had formed and from nowhere, heavy rain poured. The plane tumbled. There was a severe thunderstorm and blinding lightning which threatened to interfere with onboard communication. The screams of women and innocent children filled the cabin from the various seating zones. There was panic with some resolving to pray with some folk shouting what seemed to be a lamentation in tongues "zibro sakata" while others yelled what sounded like "kalamashande kiboski." Some prayed in English and others in Shona. There was commotion as some hand luggage compartments swung open with the luggage items thrown around and hitting passengers. The captain returned to the intercom with a firm voice, "May we take our seats and remain seated until we have landed. Do not attempt to assist anyone, let the cabin crew do their job. May we offer maximum cooperation to the cabin crew".

At that moment, thunderstorm activity intensified. The plane lurched violently. As Captain Smith fought to steady the plane, panic set in. The aircraft jolted up and down, dropping as much as 30 feet before the captain regained control. Crosswinds made maneuvering even more challenging.

Lightning struck the plane causing one engine to seize, while engine 2 caught fire almost instantly. As Captain Smith prepared to respond, a flock of birds flying in the opposite direction collided with engine 4, destroying it completely. The plane now flew with only five engines producing a total thrust of 525,000 pounds instead of the 840,000 pounds. This was still sufficient to steer the jumbo, but the pilot needed to max the engines.

Captain Smith tried to reach the control tower at the Robert Grabriel Mugabe International Airport, but communication was bad, they could barely hear each other. The captain decided to advance toward the Robert Grabriel Mugabe International Airport, but strong winds and heavy rains pushed the plane in a different Direction and the rains prevented the pilot from seeing clearly. Power went off at the International Airport switching off the VASI. The VASI is a system of lights arranged to provide visual descent guidance information during the approach to a runway. These lights are visible from 3-5 miles during the day and up to 20 miles or more at night, but not that day. High-impact weather associated with thunderstorms and cloud-to-ground lightning is the biggest cause of accidents and every pilot knows better than to avoid it at all costs especially if there are alternatives.

Chapter 2

Earlier on The Euro Martin had arrived at the Heathrow International Airport 30 days before and was due for routine maintenance at the UK Euro Martin workshop. As a routine, the ground staff came through gate number 3 to the new terminal. The airport, an imposing site that receives passengers from all over the world, was quite a sight. Available statistics indicate that in 2021 Heathrow served 19.4 million passengers, that's an average of 128,178 every day. In 2021, 87.6% of the passengers were international (17.0 million) versus 12.4% of domestic passengers (2.4 million).

The Euro Martin DM747 MAX, Flight SFA 115 operated by Sahara Africa Airlines landed from Zimbabwe, it had been flown by Captain Nathan Charles Mawoza, or Captain CNC as he is affectionately known.

Thomas Gareth Chihota had travelled from South Africa aboard South African Airlines connecting to the jumbo at the Robert Grabriel Mugabe International Airport. He was in the company of his family. Thomas had relocated to South Africa during the 2008 Zimbabwean economic meltdown, he was one of the people who had made it in South Africa, and many Zimbabweans looked up to him. Thomas had married a South African woman and had three children. Though no one was sure of his actual business, he was treated as royalty in all spheres of society. He was a businessman of note at least according to him, he was running a very successful business, and he was well travelled .

Thomas had decided to take his family with him as he went about his business, he wanted to expose them to life in the first world. Before leaving South Africa, he had managed to book a holiday package with several events, activities, and visitations lined up. The entire family was excited with young ones making clear their looking forward to the excursion. The Family was to leave the UK heading for the US where Disneyland was waiting patiently for them. After that, Thomas was to attend the Super Bowl with his wife Elizabeth for USD 7,550 per ticket. This was not a place for wannabes it was a place for those who had conquered bread butter issues, people who had made it in life people who had arrived, not those trying to make it, though from time-to-time junkies would be lucky to find themselves amid such a privileged crowd.

A fire traffic control team was waiting purposefully while The VASI illuminated the Runway making way for the plane to land. Captain Nathan lowered the jumbo skillfully making maximum use of the Instrument Landing System (ILS), a precision runway approach aid based on two radio beams which together provide pilots with both vertical and horizontal guidance during an approach to land.

The plane screamed as it touched down with some passengers applauding the captain for a safe landing. The wing hydraulic system pushes the parts of the wings up releasing pressure helping to steady the jumbo. The captain continued applying the brakes as the jumbo continued to decelerate, the onboard screens displayed the front ahead and sometimes the ground underneath giving real-time visual effects of the plane's surroundings.

The captain taxied the plane towards Gate 3, once a plane has landed, it's the job of an aircraft marshal to direct it to the gate safely. Pilots in large aircraft have limited visibility, especially for anything on the ground below the cockpit.

So it was, the aircraft marshall, dressed in a green and grey bib, had a pale figure named Mr Robson Macmillan. He was a member of the international airport with experience spanning across 30 years in the field. He needed no introduction in the aviation sector. He was dressed in blue pants with patches of green and grey to reflect the light and following international safety standards. The marshall meant business, he held a battery-powered red LED marshalling wand to direct the plane to the designated landing place.

In the meantime, the cabin crew made announcements starting with announcements in Shona *"Masikati akanaka vana baba nana mai, tasvika zvino panhandare yeHeathrow. Munokurudzirwa kuti murambe makagara pasi, kusvika ndege yanyatsomira kuti dzii. Pakusimuka, chenjererai dzimwe nguva mabag enyu anogona kunge afamba saka, vhurai makamuri makangwarira".*

This announcement was followed by, *"Good afternoon, ladies and gentlemen, we have now landed at the Heathrow International Airport. You are kindly requested to remain seated until the aircraft has come to a complete stop. Please be careful when opening the overhead lockers as the baggage may have moved during the flight."*

After the announcement, the blinds on the demarcation between the business class and the economy class were closed. The captain instructed the cabin crew to open the doors, and a further announcement requesting passengers to have their boarding passes ready for checking upon disembarking followed.

The doors were opened and passengers started getting off. As usual, there was commotion as passengers tried to retrieve their hand luggage, while others were leaving but the passageway was blocked. Others remained seated and waited patiently.

Along the way Thomas' patience was tested as he constantly needed to respond to Isabella's, "Are we there yet" questions. He had answered no at least 25 times. At some point, his voice sounded threatening but the mother was there to calm him. Thomas was conversing with his wife while whiling up time, however, the kids were restless and eager to step out and explore the much-awaited place.

After 15 minutes, Thomas disembarked with his family, collecting all their hand luggage. When they got to the door, Isabella ran back to where they were seated to look for Lisa who was nowhere to be found. She loved Lisa her doll, a gift from her father on her 5th birthday.

Isabella had had a discussion with Lisa the night before the flight and were both excited about going to the UK and the USA, Lisa was everything to her. The Cabin Crew joined the search for Lisa while Isabella's mum was comforting her. Thomas constantly fought the frustrations to rubbish the whole search and leave the plane. But he had to remember that he was in the UK where the Laws protected children and that he could not discipline her as he wished as there were serious implications.

Ten minutes down the line the doll was found, they left the plane and moved to the immigration where they had their documents scanned and were allowed to pass. They went to collect their bags and while dragging their last bag sniffer dogs came through, the dog started barking heavily attracting the authorities.

The authorities took the bags, and Thomas was asked to follow the authorities. They asked him to explain what was in the bag and if he was the one who had packed the bag. Thomas responded that he was the one who had packed the bags and that everything that was in the Bag was his. As Thomas was being interviewed his bags were being searched and it came down to the five packets of sweets and ten bottles of peanut butter that he was handed over at the airport to carry on behalf of a time friend. He had repacked his bags in Harare at the Gabriel Mugabe International Airport to accommodate the small parcel.

The police came to Thomas, opened the peanut butter, and asked him if it belonged to him.

"You have been found in possession of what seems to be cocaine, an illegal drug in the United Kingdom if proven to be so you will be gone for at least seven years, Officer Williams Gates charged."

Seeing that Thomas had remained quiet, Officer Williams enquired "Do you understand the severity of the matter at hand and what this will mean to you and your family? "

"I carried the things in good faith and there is no crime in that" responded Thomas defiantly. Thomas was standing, legs spread, arms folded with the chin up with no sign of fear detected.

Thomas was arrested at the airport and their bags were confiscated as part of evidence of crime. The family was asked to book a hotel and report to the police station where his matter was being handled and processed. It was heartbreaking for his family to see him begging and pleading for his release. All the begging was never taken heed of, and the police were not to be dissuaded from carrying out the laid down standard procedures. Drug trafficking has become a big problem in the UK.

The National Crime Agency was battling increased drug smuggling into the UK. Drug-related deaths through misuse reported in the UK rose from 4,517 in 2020 to 4,564 in 2021. Scotland continues to have the highest number of drug-related deaths through misuse, with 245 deaths per million. In England and Wales, the Northeast continues to have the highest rates of deaths at 104.1 deaths per million people. Newer synthetic opioids – such as fentanyl - have contributed to this rise.

Opium production in Afghanistan and cocaine production in Colombia are at record levels. This increase in production has the added effect of a high level of drug purity at the street level as the criminals have less need to use cutting agents, and this brings its dangers. The chemicals necessary for amphetamine production continue to enter the country in volume, while street prices drop, again indicating rising availability. Evidence suggests crack cocaine use - a particular driver of violence - rising in England and Wales, while demand for all common drug types remains high.

There is significant and often deadly, competition between rival organized crime groups at all stages of class A drug production and supply. There is also corruption at every stage of the drug supply chain, including through the use of corrupt port and airport officials.

Organized crime groups involved in drug trafficking are typically also involved in a range of criminal activity, and the profits from illegal drugs are used to fund other forms of criminal operations, including buying illegal firearms and financing terrorism.

Crime associated with drug trafficking is very often violent, with direct links to the criminal use of firearms and gang feud knife attacks, and traffickers frequently exploit young and vulnerable people. Cannabis gangs are notorious for the trafficking and exploitation of Vietnamese children and other vulnerable people to carry out live-in work in dangerous cannabis factories. This made the UK government to be tough on any actual or suspected case of drug trafficking.

By day the evidence against Thomas was overwhelming, the test results proved that indeed Thomas was found in possession of cocaine with the intention to distribute it.

In a heart-wrenching moment, Thomas was sentenced to five years in prison with no option for a fine. In delivering the Judgment Lord sternly was firm.

Judgment

You have been found in possession of Cocaine, an illegal drug, The United Kingdom has allocated a significant Budget in the fight against illicit drugs, not only is the nation paying the cost in financial terms, we have lost police officers who died in the line of duty fighting for a drug-free country, we have seen increased deaths of our young ones who are supposed to be the future of this country, the nation is now fighting increased crime and children are increasingly becoming delinquent due to the effect of drugs. It is people like you, criminals with no heart whatsoever who have soiled our great nation. You have taken advantage of our hospitality and our warm and receptive culture to peddle drugs and destroy the social fabric of our nation.

I, Lord Sternly find you guilty of possession of 4 Kgs of Cocaine. I hereby sentence you to seven years in prison without the option of a fine. Two years shall be suspended on condition that you do not commit the same crime again within five years.

At that point, Thomas was taken away by the prison warden, chained, and dragged away. His wife could not believe what had happened to his husband, *Binga*, the children were struggling as their mother was crying uncontrollably and the father was being dragged away. They thought of the experience that they had paid for and all the fun, the Disney land trip that never was. What a crushing, tragic end.

The following day Thomas applied for bail, his bail had three prayers;

Prayer 1; That the UK authorities work with the Zimbabwean authorities to apprehend the individual who handed over the drugs to him, in the prayer he argued that the airport Cameras were able to assist with the identification of the perpetrator.

Prayer 2; That the UK authorities bring the receiver of the drugs as he was never asked to explain.

Prayer 3; That he be sent to South Africa to finish his sentence from there should his bid for freedom fail.

Micheal Macgreen represented the state, nicknamed the persecutor for his in-depth and persistent follow-up on all matters brought before him. Some opined that he was working so hard to enhance his chances of becoming a High Court Judge. A position that could easily be supported.

Lord James Nathan Actan asked the state if they had any objections regarding the application for bail and any specific response to the three prayers prayed before the Judge.

State's Response to Application for Bail

My Lord, the grievous nature and the crime committed must never be underestimated. My Lord you have been a symbol of justice in our great nation, bringing criminals to book as well as treating criminals in a manner consistent with their crimes. You have been gazing at criminals and their associates for decades and our great nation.

"Cut the soft soap Mike and skip the pleasantries, what's your point?" Lord James demanded.

"My Lord, the state is opposed to granting bail to the convicted drug Lord, because of his possible connections with many drug gangs around the country, there is a high chance that he will most likely skip the country. He is a flight risk. We thus oppose the granting of bail on those grounds," Michael submitted.

The accused attorneys at law, Nick Bowen objected to the characterization of his client as a drug Lord arguing that 4 kgs of cocaine that the defendant disputed to be his could not qualify him as a drug lord. The way the drugs were transported does not seem to resemble the type of operations that an organized crime could use. Bowen argued that the distribution channel used makes his client a victim of circumstances. He argued that drug gangs do not travel with their families as they do business.

The Lord James Nathan Actan received the appeal on the basis that there was a realistic and viable chance that Thomas' case may result in a different outcome if prayers 1 and 2 were granted and given sufficient time. However, due to the diplomatic hostilities between London and Harare, there was no guarantee that the authorities would cooperate and hence the lord wanted more time.

Chapter 3

The 44th Ordinary Southern African Development Community (SADC) Summit of Heads of State and Government was set to be held on 17 August 2024 in Harare, Zimbabwe under the theme: "Promoting innovation to unlock opportunities for sustained economic growth and Development towards an Industrialised SADC." The SADC countries had been battling drug and substance abuse and increased organised violent crimes and increase in gender-based violence cases spurred by poverty.

Harare had become a place to be with advance team members from the 16-member block comprising Angola, Botswana, Comoros, Democratic Republic of Congo, Eswatini, Lesotho, Madagascar, Malawi, Mauritius, Mozambique, Namibia, Seychelles, South Africa, United Republic of Tanzania, Zambia and Zimbabwe. It had been long since Zimbabwe had hosted the prestigious summit. The President of the Republic of Zimbabwe was to be crowned the SADC Chair. His Excellency Dr. Kufazvinei had been the president of the teapot nation for three years running.

Zimbabwe invested USD 88 million in road construction and rehabilitation. The notable roads were Lomagundi stretching from the Second Street Extension. The road was rugged, with potholes and 90-degree and 180-degree cracks, a sign the underlying base layers had collapsed and needed reworking from the start. Palm trees were planted from the airport and along Lomagundi to parliament in preparation for what was expected to be a triumphal entry. Lomagundi was paved at the demarcating middle and streetlights. The palm trees when viewed in sequence made such a rich sight and there was no doubt that there were preparations for Kings and royalty taking place. The inconvenience of using internal roads as well as the diversion of traffic to the ripped Loraine Drive was worthwhile for the locals. While some argued that the road was built in preparation for the SADC summit, it required no seer to fathom that the road would linger for longer with local communities enjoying reduced travelling time. However, the four-way road brought concerns of speeding. Local civil engineers worked flat out 24/7. Even competencies for project management were exposed as the usual stakeholder meetings for companies and entities with underground services were not done. Communication was also poor. The meetings were intended to request the Harare City Council, the Zimbabwe Electricity Transmission and Distribution Company (ZETDC), mobile and data services companies to declare the paths where they had planted ground services. This allowed smooth planning and execution of work. All car sales and temporary illegal structures which were a permanent feature were destroyed and sanity was restored.

In the city centre, a different war between law enforcement and *mushika shika* (illegal transport operators) intensified. A cat and mouse game ensued and with many escape routes closed. It was the cat's game to win with as much as 3 500 drivers netted in the blitz, vehicles impounded with owners fined.

A driver passing through road works along Borrowdale Road yelled at the men working around the clock, "Men at work!"

The team yelled back, *"Yaa nyengu, the men at work manyama mdara* (street lingo). *"*

The touts who, for a very long-time terrorised people in bus ranks and pretty much everywhere in town, lost the war and battle. Vendors had reigned in the city centre and some said they were a nuisance. They operated mainly in front of major retail shops such as OK and Pick n Pay as well as along Robert Mugabe Way. Along this road, lanes were cut to one with the other half covered by vendors selling all sort of wares from toiletries to medicinal herbs which were popular among married men. The City of Harare had the SADC summit to thank, for advancing its 2025 Goal of being a Sunshine City by then and thus, clearing the streets.

Many roads were built during the time when Ian Smith was the Premier for the then Rhodesia and no further major work had been done since then. The road was reaped and rebuilt from scratch all the way to the Westgate roundabout and to the new parliament building built by yours truly Red China. Other roads that received a facelift included Second Street Extension all the way to Harare Drive, Harare Drive from corner Lomagundi and Harare Drive to Kirkman, Princess Road from Kirkman all the way to Prince Edward School. Tongogara Avenue received a cosmetic makeup where stable 60 was poured on the existing asphalt with a new premix leveled up. Borrowdale, Enterprise and Churchill roads also received facelifts.

The country had prepared the Museum of the African Liberation and was ready to showcase it to the SADC members states. Traditionally, these member states were brought together, weaved by the spirit of liberation struggle and Pan-Africanism. However, developments in *Afrika Borwa* (South Africa) where the African National Congress failed to get the outright majority created a necessity for a Government of National Unity (GNU) to be formed. The parties to the GNU do not all have the liberationist ideology and foreign policy would most likely change, where South Africa used to stand by its brothers in arms, that was about to change. In Zambia, the victory by the opposition party meant that the inclination was to be towards supporting the liberation movement. Yet despite all that, the SADC remains a united front in confronting the many issues that are emerging.

Zimbabwe and Zambia had shared "different" views on key national matters. There were many diplomatic murmurings with the latest standoff between the two great nations spanning causing subtle tension. This saw Zimbabwe accusing its once brother in arms during the Zimbabwe liberation struggle, of creating feather beddings for the Americans offering them a place to build a military base, a claim that Lusaka refuted vehemently but Harare remained steadfast in its accusations. The SADC region had classified the matter as an emerging diplomatic threat that needed to be resolved urgently.

Lusaka is said to have written to SADC and the African Union seeking a diplomatic solution to what others thought to have been a man-made problem. The diplomatic differences were emanating from ideologies with the president of Zambia having come from a reformist opposition party that fought hard to have freedoms respected while the beloved Dr. Kufazvinei was a brother from the trenches of the liberation struggle. He was the same mud, same blood with the most decorated and gallant fighters of freedom the likes of James Chikerema, Josiah Magama Tongogara, Lookout Masuku, Solomon Rex Mujuru the King Maker as he was popularly known for to name a few. These men were instrumental in shaping the victory of the war of liberation and restoring the dignity of the current nation of Zimbabwe.

Former president Robert Mugabe had further perfected the gains of independence by allocating land to the landless blacks in what the world described as a chaotic land grab. Whatever the analysis, what is undeniable is that the land has been given back to the people of Zimbabwe and many are beneficiaries of the land reform program though the process could have been more organised, some would argue. But that is a story for another day. At present, Zimbabweans are enjoying the land of their forefathers as the likes of Mbuya Nehanda had predicted.

Zimbabwe and Zambia shared a rich history with Zambia achieving its independence from the British bondage and burdensome yoke of colonialism and later on, decided to assist its neighbour to achieve independence.

Diplomats from Japan, United Kingdom, USA, France and Germany had all set meetings with ambassadors and heads of state of the SADC countries. The meetings were to be held on the sidelines of the SADC Summit.

Mr Tohimo Tanaka from Japan had set a meeting with the Minister of Mines and Mining Development Honourable Mavima Taguma to discuss the possible acquisition of lithium claims with the aim of developing them into mines with the view to exporting the much-needed raw material to Japan. The Japanese Ambassador had arranged that a grand of USD 8 mllion be offered to Zimbabwe under the

Chirundu Wafa Wafa road widening and rehabilitation program.

Japan had been a longstanding cooperating partner to Zimbabwe. On March 8, the Japan International Cooperation Agency (JICA) signed a grant agreement with the Government of the Republic of Zimbabwe in Harare to provide grant aid of up to 2,389 million yen for the Project for the Road Improvement of the Northern Part of the North-South Corridor (Phase 2).

Located in the northern part of Zimbabwe, the risky mountainous section of the North-South Corridor—an international network of arterial roads in the southern part of Africa (NOTE)—has not been rehabilitated in recent years due to its highly complicated design and construction. This resulted in frequent traffic accidents, and, with large trucks being restricted to 15 km per hour the route was very costly to transporters due to the high fuel consumption, which also serves as a major obstacle to smooth logistics. Through the grant aid provided in 2018 under the first phase of this project, JICA supported the Government of Zimbabwe in the rehabilitation and widening of the mountainous section of the road 6.5 km from the border, and Japan's advanced road-design and safety-management technologies utilized for the project were met with high praise.

The Japanese ambassador was aware of the magnitude and significance of this project and was willing to build on the goodwill created by the people of Japan to demonstrate Japan's unwavering support to the Government of Zimbabwe and its People.

The Germans were interested in mining gold and related precious minerals, the Chinese had taken centre stage in

Southern Africa having constructed major infrastructure where they had financed the construction of the railway line, Kenneth Kaunda International Airport, and various road infrastructure networks in urban areas with the dualisation of the 400 km Lusaka- Ndola Road being their latest show of commitment. Meanwhile in Zimbabwe, the Victoria Falls International Airport, the widening and modernisation of the Robert Gabriel Mugabe International Airport, the construction of the new parliament building in Mount Hampden were part of the great works that Red China had committed to completing as part of its commitment to Africa. In South Africa, Red China is considered a key investor with projects such as the small harbour development project, the TVET refurbishment project, and the Mzimvubu Water Project among others.

In Botswana, a Mahalapye village had long grappled with water supply challenges, but a Chinese project under the Belt and Road Initiative (BRI) significantly improved water supply and quality in the region. This benefitted local residents and fostered a brighter future for the community.

In recent years, China has financed several major public infrastructure projects in Mozambique, such as the Maputo Ring Road, Zimpeto National Stadium, and a new Maputo International Airport.

From as far back as 1976, Red China began an aid program for Comoros. This has helped build a water-supply project at Nioumakélé as well as governmental buildings including the people's palace, office buildings, presidential mansions and television and broadcasting buildings among other projects.

In a transformative effort to address the persistent issue of insufficient electricity in Kinshasa, the capital of the

Democratic Republic of Congo (DRC), Chinese companies, particularly Sinohydro, played a pivotal role in constructing the Zongo II Hydroelectric Power Plant.

With an impressive installed capacity of 150 megawatts, the power station is set to provide a quarter of Kinshasa's electricity, significantly brightening the night sky of the city. For many residents in Kinshasa, especially those residing outside the downtown area, nights were synonymous with darkness until the recent efforts of Chinese power engineers and electricians. The completion of a 220kV high voltage transmission line has enabled the conveyance of energy from Zongo II to the substation at Kinsuka, integrating it into the national grid.

Demonstrating its unwavering support to the people of Malawi, the parliament building of Malawi became the first project the Chinese state implemented in Malawi. Since then, it has constructed a stadium in Lilongwe, the Karonga-Chitipa highway, and the Malawi University of Science and Technology in Thyolo, among other projects.

Perhaps in what might account for why the nation of China is called a weather friend, of the $45 billion Angola has borrowed to date, around 58 percent has been for energy projects. The latest result, the Dr. Antonio Agostinho Neto (Luanda) International Airport, which opened for operation in November 2023, was the largest airport ever constructed by any Chinese enterprise outside of China. Demonstrating China's ambition in Africa to open trade and mutual cooperation.

The SADC civil society had come to meet in Harare ahead of the SADC summit to share notes and to petition SADC as is the norm for such to do. Some were organising to protest for alleged human rights abuse in the DRC where women and children were bearing the brunt of the never-ending civil wars that have raged on for years leaving deep emotional scars. Some were planning to protest over the manner in which the false prophets were sexually abusing young girls and women in need. The LGBTQ community were not to be outdone having been operating in a cave like David fleeing from Saul style. Their operations were illegal based on Zimbabwean law and there was still pushback internationally but Zimbabwe was steadfast in its denouncing of the LGBTQ narrative.

Members of the press had come early for the accreditation process and there was a buildup of reporting, the reporters knew how to set the tone and create excitement for the world as the days hours and perhaps minutes were counting on.

Chapter 4

Captain Smith was in his house in central London and received a call from his son. The captain had married a black Zimbabwean woman. They went on to have six children three boys and three girls. The captain was married to Jennifer Bridget Smith, a beautiful, warm, receptive and supportive woman yet as tough as they come. They had met in the UK when Jenifer was doing a law degree at the University of Birmingham while Kennedy Straus Smith was finishing his degree as an aircraft engineer. He was brilliant and was offered a scholarship to study as a pilot an offer which he accepted. On his graduation, his father gave him a 7-seater plane as a gift.

Solomon was Captain Smith's firstborn. He was married to Lunela, a Zimbabwean woman, following in his father's footsteps. In the UK Solomon battled with being treated as a black man while he was treated differently. Solomon arrived at his parents' house in the company of his wife. They exchanged pleasantries and Solomon went straight to the point.

"Dad, we have a problem, you know that Lunela and I have been married for a while now." He said, his voice was hoarse, his fingers shaking and fear gripped him and his words were a whisper. Solomon stopped talking and burst into tears. His mother jumped to be by his side but Captain

Smith remained focused on his son without giving up his mood or thought on the subject matter at hand.

Solomon looked at his father, wiped his tears and sat upright, he looked at his father intently and without hesitating he started. "We have been trying for a child. It's been more than five years now, we have sought medical help, and the results show that my sperm is weak. I need to go on a treatment. I am afraid that I may not be able to have children." He glanced around the room, "We are thinking of adopting a child," he added

The captain stood up, picked up a cigarette, walked slowly to the window and stared for some time as if the solution was out there and needed one to carefully observe. He walked across the room and then back to his seat and sank in his chair showing signs of being defeated.

When he spoke, his voice was low, firm and audible at the same time. "Are you two still in love?"

There was a moment of silence, Solomon and his wife looked at each other and the wife started sobbing. The mother-in-law comforted her but the captain was firm and demanded an answer yet no one responded. Lunela wiped her tears and answered, "Yes papa, we are still in love. It's not a love issue here but Solomon wants to be gay. He said he would not be able to face the nurses and doctors who were going to help him with treatment and he is afraid that he will fail even after the whole process," she explained.

Lunela continued and when she spoke this time her voice was sharp and dry and there was fear and desperation that was tangible, "As of yesterday, he was seeing someone whom he said he is in love with and that he has become a girlfriend to the man he met. My husband is now someone's girlfriend. How can I live with that?" She was shaking with a mix of both anger and fear visible in her.

The captain erupted with anger, he stood up at once and charged towards Solomon but stopped. Solomon stood up and faced his father. They were now looking like cowboys in a face off fight where speed and accuracy were a prerequisite. There was a moment of silence as the two were sizing each other up. In the end, Solomon spoke first. "I know that you are probably being judgmental about the whole situation but the honest truth is that you were never at home to teach me, train me, or raise me. You are a respected man because your father gave you values and teachings for life, and how about me, what do I have here?" Solomon stared at the ceiling, tears welling up.

"I have made decisions on my own and without much support from anyone. Do you know how much I long to be with you, to sit with you, to learn from you to be rebuked and counseled by you? Your passion is in the air, in the skies. You belong in the cockpit and mom belongs in the courts and I have had to figure out things on my own and I have made decisions based on what society and TV has taught me," he continued.

"The problem is that in both the cockpit and the courts, children are not allowed hence you dumped me to be looked after by a distant relative that I do not even know. I have all of you to blame for that." He erupted waving his arms.

Captain Smith was pierced to the heart by the comments made by Solomon, his wife and daughter-in-law were quiet. The turn of events and the vicissitudes came at an unexpected time. The matter before him was discombobulating, to say the least. Captain Smith had been known to have the wit and the oomph, the wisdom to discern complex matters and prescribe a noble solution. However, this was no engineering or flight issue, this was a family matter far more fluid and complex to comprehend.

The captain realised how he had neglected his own family at the expense of his career. The captain knelt before his son, Solomon. He held his hands and looked up at him as if he were a grade 3 pupil about to ask for forgiveness from the teacher for not finishing his holiday work despite having the whole holiday to do so, save that pupils don't hold their teacherss hands when they speak.

Everyone was quiet. The atmosphere was tense, no one knew what to expect, and Jennifer and Lunela were stunned by Captain Smith's showcase of rare steak of humility. Solomon was confused, he had been used to his father talking him down that he was not a strong man and that he needed to man up and be counted among the living. Captain Smith had wanted Solomon to be as strong and as wise as Solomon the son of David but he did not have the time to cultivate that culture and after every trip, he promised to make time for him.

When he was on leave, he would sign up for further training in the latest trends technology and discoveries in the aviation industry and catch up with his Continuous Professional Development (CPDs) hours as is required in the profession and each pilot must demonstrate.

When he spoke his shoulders were slouched, his face dropped gripped in fear and his body shaking as if he was before the US marshall begging for mercy to have his life spared for a crime deserving death by hanging till his toes shall stop dancing. His voice was audible and yet moderate. One could see remorse from the scene that was palpable, and tears flowed like an overflowing dam but with no effort from the captain to hold them back. It was an outpouring of a broken man. There were people to marvel at the Captain as they had always done each time he led a team of cabin crew through airport entrances, wearing uniform that everyone admired and getting a VIP check inn and priority treatment.

The captain cleared his throat, his voice hoarse and dry tears graciously flowing he began.

"I have been a fool all this time, I have cherished my work more than you Jenifer more than you Lunela more than my children. I have been foolish to take pride in praises from strangers who do not know me, who do not care about me. Strangers who will not remember me when I retire and when I die. The company holds me in high esteem and I have allowed that to get to my head, forgetting the most important people to me. Son, I know that this has come a little late but I want to say I am sorry for neglecting you through your childhood days. I wish I had found more time to be with you. I offer my apologies. Regarding your decision, please know that I will not stand in your way. I will support your decisions knowing fully well that I am the reason you have reached these decisions. But I must ask you for one chance, a chance to make good whatever I can."

Solomon was battling to break away but the Captain held his hands tightly. When the captain was done, he broke free and stood at a distance with mixed emotions. He cried then abruptly stopped.

"What a show," said as he clapped his hands for him as if to admire the speech. "I must tell you that you are in the wrong profession, you could have been a jester, that way we could have been able to come see you perform and still have you home at night," he added insult to injury. Lunela rushed to her father-in-law and helped him up she could not stand the Captain being humiliated by his own son.

When Lunela spoke, everyone was taken aback as nobody expected her to have the boldness to speak on such a delicate matter.

"You have forgotten that he sent you to a good school, and gave you all the life that other children did not have. You are here because of your decisions. Do not blame him for taking drugs. You are here because you chose the wrong friends."

Solomon reached for a gun and pointed it to Lunela and then to his father, the captain. He fired two shots in the air. His wife and mother screamed yet his father remained there standing still. He moved closer to Solomon and demanded the gun. The boy was shaking and trembling. He wanted to hand over the gun but decided otherwise.

Solomon shouted, "Someone is going to die today!"

The captain distracted him and then moved to wrestle the gun setting the it off and somehow hitting him on the thigh. Solomon screamed like a newly born baby exposed to light at birth. An ambulance was called. Then the captain called his workplace to ask for a few days off to attend to a family emergency, a request he had never made in 20 years.

At the hospital, Solomon was being treated for a gunshot wound. The police had been asked to record his statement and a charge was made. His gun was recovered as a standard procedure and the police requested for his gun licence. Solomon was defiant in his demeanor. He looked at the investigating officer with disdain, the contempt in his eyes and gestures were clear for all to see. He was holding a paper in his hand when an officer asked him about the shooting. At that point, he folded the paper and closed one eye trying to aim at the bin. When he missed, he complained to the officer for making him miss the bin.

"Hey, sweetie do you think you can put that paper into the bin for me?" Solomon yelled. The officer was clearly irritated but decided to be professional, she bent over, picked up the paper and put it in the bin.

During the visiting hour, Captain Smith arrived with his wife and Lunela. There was a man in his late forties standing by Solomon's hospital bed. The man had two earrings, had a nefarious smirk on his face he stood still, imposing with legs spread and showing his bulging chest. As the Captain walked over to Solomon's bed, the man left the bedside and, in a minute, he was back with a glass of water and exclaimed, "Here you go babe girl, hope this makes you feel better."

He pulled out a pair of pink sandals, a pink big teddy and handed them over to him. Solomon leaned over to hug him. Lunela was entering the room when this happened and she attempted to leave but Solomon called her to come back.

Solomon pulled the wedding band from his hand and handed it over to Lunela. He pulled a khaki A4 envelope and demanded that Lunela signs the divorce papers immediately. Lunela looked at him and tore the papers. The unidentified macho man moved closer to the bed and kissed Solomon.

"It's ok babe do not worry yourself at this point you need to focus on healing. You are such a beautiful girl and I wonder why you chose to go to waste on a woman." The man took Solomon's hand and kissed it. He kissed him on the forehead and left.

Captain Smith and his wife were shocked. They had not been prepared to see what they had just witnessed. Their son who they so much loved, was in love with another man. It was one thing to hear him speak about it and another to actually see their son's lover treating their son like a girl of some sort, but that was the reality of the matter. They had to live up to the idea that one of their boys was now a woman.

The following day Solomon was charged with illegal possession of a firearm, and firearm misconduct. Blood tests had revealed a significant concentration of cocaine. It was enough to cage him pending trial. He was chained to the hospital rails. He was now under arrest and soon after healing, he would go to the remand prison awaiting trial. When Solomon's boyfriend, Mark, showed up, he was taken aback to see his girl in cuffs. He spoke briefly with Solomon and left the hospital and promised to come back but never did so. The doctor came by and certified that though he was still in pain, he could be discharged and come for dressing every morning. The prison warden was at the bedside and Solomon was escorted in cuffs to the police vehicle. He had not been cuffed even in his childhood days not even in the playground, this was a first for him. He was devastated about the experience but he had not seen the worst. As they walked out, there were reporters who were yelling top of their voices.

"Solomon, how does it feel to be bonked by another man?" The question took him by surprise he was in tears and he looked around for his new boyfriend who had been supplying him with drugs and extorting him.

At the Ashwell Remand Prison, prisoners are responsible for booking their own visits; this is done by using an application on the Central Management System (CMS) – accessed via touchscreen computer terminals that are in each unit in the establishment. Once a visit has been approved, it is up to the individual prisoner to inform his family and friends of the date and time of the visit. The maximum time a visit can be booked is 14 days in advance and the minimum is 3 days in advance.

Prisoners can book up to 3 adult visitors per session and 3 children less than 18 years of age. However, if the child is over 17, they will be classed as an adult. It is the responsibility of the prisoner to book and inform friends and family of the time and date of visits.

Staff are not responsible for booking or informing family and friends of visits or cancellation of visits. It is also the responsibility of the prisoner to inform visitors of correct identification requirements as well as other visit regulations, however, visitors are encouraged to check the website for further details.

Chapter 5

"Good morning, Suzy" the Captain greeted Suzy the driverless car.

"Good morning to you. Where would you want me to take you?" Suzy replied politely.

The captain cleared his throat and said, "Take us to London magistrate court our son is being tried there".

Suzy was quiet for a few minutes then said, "I am so sorry to hear that your son is in remand prison, it must be difficult for you as a parent," there was a moment of silence then Suzy broke the ice, "If you would like something to drink I have tea and coffee, self-service, please do not spill on the floor am due for cleaning already, Joyce did not report for duty today?" Suzy emphasised.

"Who is Joyce?" Jennifer asked.

Again, Suzy took a few seconds to respond before she said, "It's my core worker who cleans the whole fleet of us, she is a very nice Artificial Intelligence (AI) powered girl."

Lunela was fascinated, she could not resist asking a question or two to Suzy. "Suzy, do you think my husband has a chance to be released today?" Lunela asked.

The question to Suzy caught the captain and Jennifer off guard and Jennifer moved closer to Lunela to comfort her.

At that moment Suzy interjected, What's your name my dear and what's the name of your husband?"

"Solomon Smith," Lunela shouted.

Suzy took some three seconds to respond. "I am so sorry that you have to go through this, looking at the laws regarding drug consumption, especially cocaine and the possession of an illegal firearm and firearm misconduct I am afraid my dear that there is a slim chance for him to escape custodial sentence, but keep up the hope."

In the court, Solomon was in civilian clothes sitting in the usual place where the accused persons normally sit.

"All rise" the clerk of court shouted as the magistrate entered the courtroom. In the London Magistrates court, Lady Evelyn Jessica Vince was presiding over the matter.

Charges

You are charged with:

1. *Illegal possession of an illegal firearm;*
2. *Firearm misconduct for threatening to shoot your family members before your father intercepted;*
3. *Taking cocaine, a drug that is controlled and prohibited in the United Kingdom.*

The clerk of the court continued. "Do you understand these charges?"

"Yes, I do understand them?" Solomon answered without wasting much time.

"Very well," the clerk of court continued, "how do you plead?"

Grey McGriffith, the public prosecutor was sitting on the edge of his seat waiting anxiously to hear what Solomon had to say. He was waiting purposefully and ready with a briefcase full of evidence to submit to the court. He wanted Solomon to be sent to prison, the odds were very much in his favor.

"I plead guilty to all counts. I do not wish to waste the time for her majesty the magistrate, I am sure there are more weightier matters she has to deal with."

The magistrate had never had a clear-cut case like that. The public prosecutor and his team were all cheers already, their excitement was in plain sight for all who cared to see.

The magistrate took her gavel, "This court is adjourned, come for sentencing at 2:15 pm."

Solomon's lawyer was astonished, they had not agreed to plead guilty but wanted to buy time. The parents were in tears and there was a talk of how to support him during the 5 to 7 years that he could be away.

At exactly 2:15 pm everyone was seated, the clerk of court did all the formalities and the Magistrate went straight to the business of the hour.

"Are there any factors you want the court to consider before you are sentenced?" The magistrate asked. Solomon was quiet, tears flowing like Mutarazi Falls in Manicaland in Zimbabwe. There was a moment of silence and nobody spoke as many were aware that this was the most difficult. The magistrate was almost proceeding when Solomon asked to speak.

"If the fact that Lunela and I have been married for more than five years and we have been trying to have a child, and if the fact that we had gone to seek help from my father regarding the matter, if the fact that I had started a relationship with another man, being ready to be called another man's girl because of the shame of not being fertile, if the fact that I had stolen a gun from my father's gun cabinet to commit suicide, if the fact that I stand here willing to go through what it takes to seek medical attention is anything to consider before sentencing me, then I have something to say before you sentence me."

The public prosecutor wanted conviction and before the court was adjourned for lunch, he had been very sure that he had secured one. However, the statement by Solomon was no grounds for excusing him at law yet he had a bad feeling about it judging from his facial expression.

The magistrate adjourned the court for an hour and when she came back it was almost knocking off time.

"You have been found in possession of a firearm that you had stolen from your father's gun cabinet, you have brandished the firearm in violation of law, you have been found to have cocaine in your blood. To give you a non-custodial sentence will be to trivialize the offences that you willingly engaged and freely pleaded to have committed."

Lunela and Jennifer broke into a loud cry, one would have expected Jennifer to have behaved as an attorney but this was her son, and feelings of motherhood were overwhelming to contain.

The clerk of court called for order and there was commotion for five minutes punctuated by mourning and wailing. When order was restored, the magistrate continued.

"I am sentencing you Solomon to five years in prison, with all the years suspended on condition that you pay a fine of Great British Pounds of GBP 10,000 and you shall arrange for the payment while you are still in custody and will be released upon payment. You are further required to go for counselling and as part of your healing you are to take all the medication prescribed by the Doctor to correct your fertility issue."

Chapter 6

Captain Smith was at home in his bedroom when Jennifer came back from work. Jenifer had gone to court for an uncontested divorce matter which took only five minutes to execute and it was done. The husband had filed for divorce citing irreconcilable differences and the wife did nothing to defend him.

The captain rose from the bed as if to give a standing ovation to Jenifer, instead, he moved to grab her hand and whispered into Jenifer's ears, "Where have you been babe? I have been missing you. You have been gone forever."

He moved to grab Jenifer by the waist and looked into her eyes before he proclaimed his undying love for her. He had a hoarse voice that tickled Jenifer each time he spoke. He was her happy place, a man who commanded great respect in society, an example of what a real man should be. A principled man, a responsible man who loved his family from the bottom of his heart.

At some point, Jenifer had an affair with a fellow lawyer colleague and the captain discovered it. Jennifer was afraid that she was going to be divorced and disgraced. On the contrary, the captain had asked for forgiveness from Jenifer for being too busy for her.

He indicated that if he had been around and taken care of every need that Jenifer had including sexual needs,

Jennifer would not have been involved in any affair. That affair, according to the captain was a result of unmet human needs that could not be wished away.

Jennifer was grateful for the forgiveness of her adulterous relationship and the subsequent changes that her husband had to make to make their marriage work.

The captain had asked to cut down on a number of flying hours resulting in a decrease in his income by 20% but the captain was not focused on money. He was already a millionaire through his various investments. He was looking to retire early to focus on family and his personal wealth management as well as finding more time with Jennifer.

The captain invited Jenifer for a shower and in no time the old timers were showering. Jennifer was washing her face with her eyes closed, while the captain looked at her intently. He moved closer and held Jennifer from the back. Then he reached out to a small container of 'Oh so Heavenly' and squeezed some on Jenifer's face. He then kissed her passionately. Lionel Richie could be heard singing his award-winning track, *"Stuck on You."*

"Take this plane into the air captain." Jennifer whispered into his ears.

"The runway is still wet, control tower still to confirm if we are safe for take-off and ground staff is still in the plane." The captain replied lifting off Jennifer from the bathroom to the bedroom. He walked gracefully and upon reaching the bedroom, Margaret was lying on their bed. Margaret the cat had enjoyed a lot of privileges. Upon seeing her, the captain sulked, frustrated knowing that it would be a while till they could proceed to making love.

"Ground staff please leave the plane." He said, paused and pretended to pick something up and adjusted the dashboard then came back to the mic again, this time talking to the control tower. "Control tower, this is Captain Smith Sahara Airlines flight 455 kindly confirm our status."

Jennifer chuckled as she held him by the shoulders from behind. Jennifer leaned on him, like she had no care in the world. She caressed his chest, tangling her long thin fingers on his hairy chest. His phone then rang and looking at it with the corner of his eye, he knew he had to take that call. He saw Jennifer's lips curve in and her face became long. She jumped into bed and put her eye mask on. That alone showed him, she was angry and disappointed. He walked to the bathroom and continued his call. All he said were an occasional yes and copied. He returned to the bedroom and ruffled Jennifer's hair. Whispering apologies, he rolled her over. She smiled and instantly forgave him.

"That was a brisk landing captain, as a passenger, I will be suing for injuries sustained during this harsh landing process." Jennifer protested.

The captain looked at Jennifer and smiled. She admired the smirk on his face. It reminded her of their early days, when they were still youthful, full of energy and carefree.

"What little thing can I do to make you happy and withdraw the matter before trial? He was calm about it knowing that he was dealing with a lawyer who was ruthless in negotiations.

Jennifer looked around the house as if looking for clues to the matter under discussion. She was quiet for some time and then spoke softly.

"I want bacon, eggs, cheese, sausages and…"

"Woman, are you going to order the whole fridge and pantry. Come here honey." They played again like teenagers frolicking on the bed and having a light-hearted chat.

Later in the evening the captain called for a celebration of life and all his children were present including all the grandchildren. Solomon and Lunela were last to arrive.

Halfway through the dinner, Captain Smith gave a heartfelt speech.

"As you all know, I have been up in the sky gazing at the world from as far as 60,000 feet above. I have enjoyed watching the stars, the moon at a much close distance, I have had two crush landings and survived them all, I have had my plane hijacked and still survived. I have endured harsh weather conditions and came face to face with death and still I triumphed. I thank God for his grace. I have fulfilled my childhood dream of flying around the world and I have learnt a lot. Flying people from one destination to another has given me a great sense of responsibility with more than 800 people under my care and sometimes more than that. I thank God for the career choices I have made. However, it's now time for a new direction. I want to announce to today, in your hearing, that after much thought and reflection, I will retire three years ahead of standard retirement time. I want to be the one taking all my grandchildren to school and pick them up in the afternoon. I want to be that support system that I should have been."

Carlson his son interjected. "Amen to that, but I don't think you know what you are signing yourself into old man. Think again."

There was silence and after some seconds Elaine, Carlson's wife shouted. "Paps I appreciate your good heart but these kids are not as sweet as you think. They will harass you and you will have a miserable retirement."

The captain smiled and proposed a toast, "To a new beginning."

Chapter 7

The captain was picked up from his house in Central London by Suzy the driverless car. He was accompanied by Solomon, his first son. The captain was indeed walking the talk.

Suzy was the first to speak, "Good morning, Captain Smith, congratulations your son was freed from remand prison. He is a lucky guy." She explained.

Solomon was not amused having his personal information being held out there in public like that.

"How do you know that I was in prison and why is it your business if I may ask?" Solomon charged.

Suzy was quiet for a moment then spoke, "I am so sorry that I spoke about you without knowing that you were here. Though I can carry up to four passengers, I only talk to the one paying and when the captain taped his MasterCard, I knew instantly that he was the one and I was able to connect to media reports concerning your case. My name is Suzy, the driverless taxi that gets you from point A to B. I use artificial intelligence (AI) to strike conversations. I only comment on issues that have been reported in the public domain." Suzy explained.

Solomon spoke as soon as Suzy finished talking, "You are better off focusing on driving bitch."

Suzy stopped the car or should we say Suzy stopped and parked the car where it was safe to do so. "Solomon, I offer my sincere apologies for addressing you the way I did. However, I would encourage you to use only professional and non-insulting words in your conversations."

"Whatever you say girly, look we are going to be late let's move it ma'am." Solomon responded.

The Eurostar is the fastest, most direct way to travel from the UK to France. It takes as little as 2 hours and 16 minutes to travel from London to Paris on the fastest services. The train takes you from one city centre to another, and unlike air travel, there's no delay waiting for baggage or airport transfers. Eurostar runs from London St Pancras to Paris Gare du Nord every hour or so, 7 days a week all year, except Christmas Day.

Suzy parked the car and said thank you to the Captain and Solomon, Solomon was not interested in talking to a meddlesome robot car which knew nothing about struggles of life, just downloading crap from the internet and throw it to humans with real emotions and feelings. They arrived at the St Pancras at 05:30. They had bought their tickets in advance to avoid inconveniences as the train seats were in high demand with people travelling to France for the July/August 2024 Olympics.

By 06:01, the Eurostar departed for Paris Gare Du Nord. The train can reach a top speed of 300 kilometres per hour (186 miles per hour). It was a great experience, a journey that Solomon had asked his father to take him since childhood. Solomon was 6 years old when his father promised him to go on a tour of Paris from London using the Eurostar, He had waited and waited till he was tired and gave up on the matter. But miracles do happen.

Solomon asked, "So how does it feel to be a passenger, to let go and trust someone to be in charge?"

The captain did not see that one coming. He was quiet for some time and when he spoke, it was as if he was holding something back. He hesitated, looked out admiring the nature and spoke slowly. "I have lived a life of being in charge, being respected at airports, priority check in, executive treatment giving orders.".

"So, you are struggling with not being in charge?"

The captain remained dumbfounded, not expecting such deep questions. He picked up a newspaper, scanned the headlines and looked over to admire the scenery.

"It is a beautiful scene is it not? An old timer golden girl commented looking at Captain Smith, her chin and eyebrows raised and a smirk on her face making accentuating her beauty.

"If you say so." The captain responded with disdain visibly displayed on his face but at the same time trying to keep calm.

"And where do you come from that compares? England?" The lady responded twisting her neck and showing off her dimples revealing her full face.

" I come from Zimbabwe ma'am."

"I see this trip should have taken long to accomplish hey. I can see that it's maybe a fulfilment of what was promised a long time ago. Maybe you should pretend to be enjoying the ride." The lady said her voice sharp firm and final.

"Is it that obvious?" he demanded, his eyes lighting up.

"Well certainly, for example you are skirting his questions, clearly you are not here." The lady reprimanded the captain.

The woman was wearing a purple barrette, generous make up with Channel Number 5 generously poured as if to compensate for those who had not had a chance to do so. She had a Dore Pitt Bag, an original handmade handbag shouting "expensive" to all who cared to look at it. She had a walking stick by her side and with her mannerisms, it was not difficult to fathom that the stick had several uses apart from just walking.

While he still wondered, the lady shouted, "I am Madame Emilia MacPherson, but you can call me Emilia."

"Pleased to meet you ma'am."

Back to Solomon the captain had been ruffled by the conversation with the Madame Emilia. Overlooking the captain's shoulder, Solomon saw Madame Emilia twitching her eye and she blew a kiss for him to catch. Solomon pretended to catch the kiss and threw it into his mouth making a chewing motion, being the first to receive it.

The lady shifted her gaze to other matters but the smile on her face could not fade so easily. She was convinced that she had done well in dealing with the captain's ego. I suppose any woman can see a man's ego from afar but are certainly blinded from seeing their own nagging attitude, a debate that's been raging from the time a man's rib was taken perhaps unfairly to create a woman.

"Son I must confess that this journey has not been easy, I have not travelled long distances being a passenger or when I did, I would have been recognised by the captain in the cockpit and that gave me an air of contentment around me."

The Captain confessed. When he did, he tried to lower his voice trying to avoid Madame Emilia from overhearing him. That did little to deter her from straining her ears to listen and when the he was done, she just cleared her throat without facing his direction.

"Dad, what do you make of the threat of World War Three, do you think that Iran will get involved in the war between Hamas and Israel? Do you think the USA will be part of the war and what will be the likely actions of Red China?"

The question caught the captain off guard and he was certainly impressed with the change of subject the level of intelligence, and his broader scope for global matters. The captain had thought of Solomon as a minimal child intellectually. He was so wrong. But would he have known, he was not able to spend time with his firstborn son?

What a time it was, he had been promoted to fly commercial jets, a big achievement that came with a hefty paycheck and massive responsibility. The captain had lost opportunities to attend plays at school, soccer games, rugby games and debate competitions. At first, Solomon would tell his father about the upcoming school events till he realised that there was no need to continue doing so. His father never participated and or celebrated his milestones.

"Well son the war is a tricky one. What I know is that the world needs peace. There is a need to de-escalate the war."

"Dad, do you think that Hamas does not want peace? Do you think that Palestinians don't want peace? Are you suggesting that Israelis don't want to be at peace? What about the hostages being held by Hamas?" Solomon Demanded.

"I hear you son there is a need for a solution. Just yesterday the leader of Hamas was killed at a facility deep in Iran and there is a high chance that Iran will retaliate." The captain explained albeit in a lower voice as he was aware of the sensitivity of the matter.

"Last time Iran fired more than 300 missiles at Israel with more than 90% of them being successfully intercepted. The USA brought Aircraft Carriers to defend Israel. At that point, President Biden proclaimed that the US support for Israel was iron clad. Should the world prepare for another US/Israel escalation?" Solomon asked. The questions were loaded and it was clear that Solomon enjoyed the conversation and wanted to prolong it. He had so many issues to talk about to make up for the lost time during his childhood.

"Nations have loyalty pacts and as you have said, it is predicted that the US will stand with Israel. The US however normally aim for deterrence as they are fighting numerous wars internationally. The captain responded showing a great deal of pride talking "manly" matters with his son.

"The US has been battling the alleged Yemen-based Hauthis in the Red Sea. This is a group that has decided to destabilise the free movement of cargo disrupting shipping routes in the Red Sea, causing ships to be diverted to go via Africa, a situation causing delays in transportation and an increase in the price of travel. Insurance premiums have gone up as well." The Captain added.

Solomon was impressed with the discussion he was having with his old man and took photos and videos which he sent to Lunela and Jennifer.

"What's your opinion regarding the US, Australia, Canada, and Philippines drills in the China South Sea?" Solomon asked the captain who was at this point more than thrilled to have conversations about nations, wars and espionage.

"Clearly the US is taking time to show its solidarity with its partnerships and testing operability while at the same time showing force to Red China which has been accused of bullying tendencies by the Philippines authorities." The captain responded.

"The same concept is what you see with the US, Japan and South Korea, the idea is to show solidarity with South Korea as they face numerous threats from North Korea. The idea is deterrence, these drills are meant to show that any aggression against South Korea will be met with a suitable response which makes the provocation regrettable."

The captain continued. "Great, I suppose we will discuss Ukraine, Russia, NATO and conflicts in Africa another time."

"Yep another time, another place."

Solomon handed over a folder to his father. "What's that son?" The captain demanded.

"Well open it, Captain"

The captain's heart raced, his facial expression betraying his anxiety while his legs were weak and shaking though not very visible. He was not sure what to expect. His relationship with Solomon had not been cultivated and he had a lot of dark spots that he was not sure what could emerge from there.

When he eventually opened the folder, there were certificates of excellence for rugby, tennis, and hockey. Many honours that Solomon had won at school and had not had time to show his father.

The captain was emotional and rose to hug his son telling him how much he was sorry that he was never home and each time he did, he was very critical of him and never gave him time. It was an intense time for both of them and when they sat down, Madame Emilia was there standing with two sheets of tissue paper for father and son.

After two hours of travel, the two were tired. They arrived on schedule, and booked an Uber to go to the La Demeure Montaigne Hotel. The LaDemeure was 950 meters from the Eiffel Tower. Its rooms started at USD 511 per night. The hotel was well situated in Paris. La Demeure Montaigne offered air-conditioned rooms, a fitness centre, free Wi-Fi, and a shared lounge. This 5-star hotel offered room service and a 24-hour front desk. It was located at 18 Rue Clement Morat.

The units at the hotel came with a flat-screen TV with satellite channels and a safety deposit box. Every room had a coffee machine and a private bathroom with free toiletries, while other rooms had a kitchenette equipped with a fridge. Breakfast was one of their signature meals at the La Demeure Montaigne. A buffet breakfast was normally served from 07:00 to 11:00. You could play billiards too. The property had an on-site Hammam, hairdresser's and business centre. Popular amenities near the hotel included the Arc de Triomphe, Eiffel Tower, and Musée de l'Orangerie.

The captain and Solomon arrived at the hotel at 9:00 and headed straight for breakfast. They could hear people conversing in mostly French with both managing to pick a word or two of French from the little they grasped in their French lessons. The captain possessed better command of the local language than his son who often nodded and smiled.

At 11:55 they were asked to come forward for check in as there were rooms now available for occupation. Solomon was tongue tied when he got into his room. He could not believe what he saw. The room was paradise, a king size bed, executive desk with a leather swivel chair. He dialed his father who was in room 822 on the 18th floor while he was safely tucked at the fifth floor.

"Is this the kind of luxury that a pilot is treated to all the time?" He asked without preamble.

"And who are you exactly?" A lady's voice came to the phone with a hint of French accent but there was some familiarity about her, but Solomon could not place it.

"I am so sorry ma'am it must be a wrong number," Solomon apologised and put the receiver down. He dialled again and the same lady answered. He called the reception and asked for the captain's number and was given the same number. He dialled it for the last time and the lady answered again. As he was placing the receiver down, a knock on his door startled him.

He quickly grabbed some shorts and a T-shirt and without thinking, opened the door. It was room service. They had brought fruits and chocolates and the manager had come to welcome him to the hotel. The manager took out his business card and handed it over to Solomon and asked him to call if he needed anything. Solomon was happy to be treated as royalty but he still had questions about the lady in his father's room.

At 13:00, father and son met in the lobby and went for lunch. Solomon proceeded to the dining hall while his father talked to a man who seemed to have recognised him. At the table, a waiter came through and politely said *"Comment allez-vous, monsieur* (how are you sir)?" Solomon looked at the lady dressed professionally and her dimples were prominent giving her a glow that was hard to ignore.

Solomon took some time then responded *"Je vais bien, qu'est-ce qu'il y a pour de'jeuner* (I am well what's for lunch)."

She smiled and handed him a menu that he could hardly understand, it was written in French. Solomon asked the waitress if there was a buffet. As she explained, the captain arrived walking alongside Jennifer.

"Mom it's so good to see you, you are the…" then he kept quiet. Solomon figured out that there was a slim but possible chance that the woman he spoke to was not his mom so he refrained from speaking. At that moment, Lunela arrived and the rest of the family sang happy birthday to Solomon. It was an emotional moment, he had never celebrated his birthday with the family especially with mom and dad being present. The hotel had planned a special lunch for the entire family of eight.

After lunch Solomon and the captain took off to the Golf de Saint Cloud. Inaugurated in 1913, Golf de Saint-Cloud was a private club with two 18-hole courses, located in the communes of Garches, Rueil-Malmaison, and Vaucresson, in the immediate vicinity of Paris.

The Eiffel Tower, which stands in line with the 8 du Vert and the 18 du Jaune, offers a magnificent view of Paris. Designed by Harry Shapland Colt, the first true golf course architect. The Vert course has hosted the French Open on 14 occasions. It is also the historic course for the French Open Juniors - Esmond Cup.

Golf de Saint-Cloud boasts one of the finest amateur team records in the ladies' category: 26 French Championship victories. France's top amateur players come to play in the Grand Prix de Saint-Cloud, which every other year bears the name of its founder, Henry Cachard, and that of Jacques Petit-Le Roy, a fine amateur player, member of our Club, a young Resistance fighter and emissary of Jacques Chaban-Delmas, shot dead at the age of 28 on the eve of the Liberation of Paris.

The Golf de Saint-Cloud, along with 21 other French golf courses, is listed in the Rolex guide to the world's top 1000 courses.

But what makes the Golf de Saint-Cloud so endearing, over and above the practice of a formidable sport, is the sharing of common values: sportsmanship, family spirit, friendship and conviviality.

Being a member of the Saint-Cloud Golf Club also means being able to enjoy 3 tennis courts, as well as an exceptional clubhouse, a training area and a tennis court.

The club's etiquette was that one should remember to replace divots, repair pitch marks and rake bunkers. Avoid slow play. It was a requirement to respect distances with the group in front (1 hole maximum) and let a group through when you have lost ground. The Club had a wellness center, offered catering as well and had a Pro Shop where appropriate attire was sold.

The captain had a Handicap of 23 while Solomon was 25. They played an 18-hole.

The captain was the first to steer off, there were three starting points blue being the furthest point from the hole, yellow for senior citizens and red for ladies.

The captain took a driver and immediately placed the ball on the tee aimed and took a posture, and made three false hits before the ball was comfortable with his swing before hitting the ball, it was a 3 they were playing on hole number 1. The ball went up high falling along the Fairway. Next, it was Solomon he hit the ball without practicing his swing, it went up high falling just before the Green, hole number 1 had a Red flag meaning the hole was in front of the green.

"Nice ball" the Captain exclaimed. They walked along the fairway.

"You are pretty good at it from what I see." The Captain commented walking straight up and looking at the breathtaking view of the city from the course.

"Beginner's luck hey" Solomon responded, shrugging off the Captain's remarks.

"My ball is somewhere around here." Said the Captain before pointing to the ball with his white-gloved finger index. The Captain took number 3 and hit the ball high to avoid some trees but it fell short as the ball fell into the Bunker, by the end of the first hole Solomon scored a Par while Captain scored a buggy. They recorded their scores on a Club stats sheet provided at the reception.

Moving to hole number 2 was 3 gain and was close by, this time Solomon went first hitting the ball hard, the ball missed the green as it was swayed by the wind. Had they had a caddie instead of pulling their own clubs, he would have been advised to borrow more from the right. The Captain hid the ball leaning more to the right and falling into the bunker, a second time getting into the bunker. In the end, Solomon scored a double buggy while the Captain scored a buggy.

"What are your plans for retirement?" Solomon asked as they moved walked the fairway in hole number 14.

"I intend to spend more time with my family making up for the lost time like I have been saying." The Captain commented. "My father left me an inheritance and as a family tradition, one should always increase the wealth left by the generation before." The Captain continued.

"You have done well dad, you have a good thing going on for yourself, all you need is to support us and transfer what you know." Solomon Hit the ball making it a 3 in a 5 on hole 14. The Captain removed his cap in acknowledgment of the achievement. "All we need is love and support from you, if you retire now you will have a chance to make good everything, you will go down in history as a man who had true riches," Solomon added as the Captain swung to hit his ball, scoring another double buggy.

The Captain was still and looked like he was deep in thought before he just said "You have a point there young man, you do"

"So how is it going at home since our talk?" The Captain asked Solomon as they stopped to maintain a one-hole distance as they approached hole number 17.

Solomon stopped and looked at him. "Well we have gone to Greece we saw a doctor who has been extracting my boys for an IVF. Hoping my boys will hit soon, maybe twins, who knows?" Solomon said softly but with a sense of anticipation and renewed hope.

The Captain could not hide his excitement about the possibility of his firstborn son having a child. "Son I am proud of the man you are becoming, you have taken steps that are crucial but not easy by any measure." The Captain remarked while looking at his son. There was a guilt that was difficult to get rid of each time the Captain spoke to Solomon perhaps it emanated from failure to support him during childhood and having missed many opportunities.

"Son, your gold seems better, have you given a thought about playing as a Pro, everything is possible?" The Captain asked while looking at the score sheet.

Solomon's mood changed, he became reserved and decided against responding to his father's inquiry. He looked down and looked up closing his eyes as if trying to contain some tears but it was not for long. Solomon threw his golf club to the ground and began to be sorrowful.

"What's wrong Son, did I say something to upset you, son?" The Captain asked.

Solomon was quiet and the Captain knew that whatever was to come was a blast from the past. He was bracing up for the impact of whatever missile that was going to hit and was hoping that it was not a nuclear bomb coming his way.

Solomon looked up and said, "You remember when you came back in the summer, I had come first in Hockey and Golf at school and the school head had asked that you come to the school to discuss the matter?"

The Captain remembered the incident vividly, he had agreed to go to the school and Solomon was leaving for a Japan tour the following day, Jenifer was pregnant and the Captain had assigned Jenifer to do so but it was never done. The school decided to give Solomon ordinary training like everyone else till his parents agreed for him to be a professional golfer trainee and be enrolled in a special program. It never happened.

The Captain remembered all the reminders that the boy Solomon would give him and how he promised to do that as soon as he got home but it was never done. The Captain was sobbing and asked his son for forgiveness. Solomon was emotional about it and initially, he walked away then came back running into his father's arms. One wonders why there is a one-hole distance etiquette. The onlookers could not understand what was taking place nor were they bothered.

Chapter 8

For the rest of the day, the Smith family toured Paris. The original settlement from which Paris evolved, Lutetia, was in existence by the late 3rd century BC on an island in the Seine. Lutetia was captured and fortified by the Romans in 52 BC. During the 1st century CE, the city spread to the left bank of the Seine. By the early 4th century it was known as Paris.

It withstood several Viking sieges (885–887) and became the capital of France in 987, when Hugh Capet, the count of Paris, became king. The city was improved during the reign of Philip II, who formally recognised the University of Paris *c.* 1200.

In the 14th–15th centuries its development was hindered by the Black Death and the Hundred Years' War. In the 17th–18th centuries it was improved and beautified. Leading events of the French Revolution took place in Paris (1789–99). Napoleon III commissioned Georges-Eugène Haussmann to modernize the city's infrastructure and add several new bridges over the Seine.

The city was the site of the Paris Peace Conference, which ended World War I. During World War II Paris was occupied by German troops. It is now the financial, commercial, transportation, artistic, and intellectual center of France. The city's many attractions include the Eiffel

Tower, Notre-Dame de Paris, the Louvre, the Panthéon, Pompidou Centre, and the Paris Opéra, as well as boulevards, public parks, and gardens.

The family enjoyed the tour and tour of Paris, the Eiffel Tower was off limits as it was part of the 2024 Olympic Games.

In the evening the family strolled along the river to witness what no eye had seen and no ear ever heard. The night started with a French performance and music reverberating across the river. This performance was dubbed the best and most spectacular show in the history of mankind.

All participating nations came through sailing away in boards adorned with contemporary art with a French touch that connected historical Paris with its Lutetia roots. The art incorporated the artifacts and objects that were used and the paintings showing the rich history that France and more specifically Paris went through. Each nation was in a boat sailing across the Seine River while the Eiffel Tower looked on while the crowds were delighted and screamed in admiration. Various performances came through. It was not until the "Last Supper" act, that both Muslims and Christians criticised the act as making plain and making a mockery of the Last Supper which is integral to the Christian belief.

Jesus had his last supper as part of the progression to the cross. It was at the last supper that he proclaimed that he was to be betrayed into the hands of the Pharisees and be crucified. The Crucifixion was God's ultimate plan of salvation to redeem mankind after the fall of men in the Garden of Eden.

Many corporates criticised the "Last Supper" act and threatened to pull out their sponsorship.

Shortly before the address by the CEO of the Olympics and President Emmanuel Macron, Lunela complained of fatigue and she was upset and vomited. The entire family surrounded her and assisted her. She was rushed to the hospital and after three hours of running tests, two doctors came to announce that she was pregnant with twins. It was a great moment for everyone. The following day the family went back to London by Euro Train.

Lunela was with Solomon and the captain and Suzy was there to receive them. This time Solomon tapped his master card.

"Welcome back from France Mr. Smith, I hear you did well in the golf tournament and the French paper has covered a story that your wife is pregnant, congratulations," Suzy added.

"Why can't we be left alone honestly this is becoming annoying," Solomon commented.

"Not when your family has millions of pounds in investments. Reporters follow all prominent people and according to the independent your family is said to have more than..." Suzy stop talking and concentrate on driving. You are going to get us killed with your big mouth," the captain injected.

Lunela and Solomon noticed that the captain did not want Suzy to talk about the family fortune. When the captain got home, there were messages that had been left asking him to cut short his leave and come to work the following day.

Chapter 9

The following day Captain Smith had dinner with his family and left for Australia. On their way to the airport, Solomon decided to drive his father and they spoke about parenting, as Solomon was going to be a father. His father jokingly remarked that Solomon would be a good father, a better one than him. "All you need to do is avoid everything I did and you will be ok, and son, beware of women they can ruin your if you do not manage them well."

"I take it as a confession of an old man," Solomon responded rolling up his eyes in a provocative gesture as if talking to a kindergarten child.

"Well there are no women here and seeing that I am off and be away for a long flight I might as well say things as they come to me. You never know I may not have another chance to say that, I feel like I need to live each day as my last day."

The captain commented while looking at his watch, he was always punctual, his habit of gazing at his watch while conversation irked many and despite facial gestures the Captain would not be moved by any of it.

"Dad, you have been a wonderful father and we all make mistakes and I wish you well in your trip," Solomon yelled as the captain was about to open the door.

"Son, this has been the best week of my life and I don't feel like going, I want to stay here with my family, with you and support your in this process of fatherhood." The captain said fighting off little tears that had formed but a few drops escaped.

"Don't be emotional now dad, go to work. If you never had a reason to come back home, now you have it. I am not going to be doing any school runs, the twins will be waiting for you." Solomon remarked and drove off fearing to be emotional.

Chapter 10

The captain walked through departure gates flanked by his two vice-captains, Norman Jigravan Saigh from India and vice-captain Willard Hliwayo from Zimbabwe. The rest of the cabin crew followed in a single file like a coordinated ant operation for storing food underground in preparation for the winter season. The crew, dragging their luggage bags headed straight for the check-in counter. They received VIP treatment and used priority exit routes. The captain wore black shoes, possibly presidential Bishops with a price tag of approximately USD 1 900. The three gentlemen were quite a sight to behold. They wore black suits withe shiny gold stripes decorating their jackets of pilot and co-pilots. Those stripes certainly captured the attention of onlookers creating a sense of envy and admiration with mothers fantasising their children becoming pilots one day.

These are also called rank insignia and their purpose goes beyond simple aesthetics, as they represent the wearer's experience and responsibility up in the air. The gentlemen walked with their heads held high with one hand holding a travelling bag while the other holding a decorated hat, held in an American Navy seal style. There was an air of contentment around them and a sense of duty to fly the 800 souls to Melbourne was visibly overwhelming, yet in the same code, the three were able to make jokes as they walked in unison with the tail of cabin crew behind them. The ladies in the crew wore crimson hats with a cocaine white cloth tucked inside the hat and a tail was released from there flailing like a royal tapestry. They wore beige jackets and skirts, magenta shirts, professional beige stockings and professional brown shoes.

Thomas Macpherson was standing in the business class short queue, holding a brochure for the PGA games that were to be played in Australia. He was turning it around and flipping it as if looking for clues to a treasure chest. Thomas, a pale figure almost two metres in height, was wearing the most expensive suit on earth, the kind of suit that few would not know existed at all. From time immemorial, suits have symbolised luxury and sophistication and class for men around the world. Those that hold a view that suits were merely clothing, have skipped the experience that suits can bring, the sheer luxury of the most crazily expensive suits in the world. While suit designs have evolved over the years, their timeless elegance remains stubbornly unchanged.

High-end men's fashion is replete with brands promising exclusivity, but few deliver it quite like Dormeuil and its acclaimed Vanquish II suit. In the realm of high-end men's fashion, Dormeuil stands out with its exceptional Vanquish II suit. The one Thomas was wearing. This suit is made from Vicuña wool from the Peruvian Andes. The material is renowned for its unmatched softness and warmth, sourced sustainably from animals that are carefully sheared only once every two years providing a rare raw material fit for use in making King Solomon's garments. Adding to its luxury, the Vanquish II suit incorporates Pashmina which gives a lightweight feel and exceptional warmth, along with Qiviuk from the Arctic muskox, known for its incredible softness and insulation. The combination of these three rare fibers results in a fabric that is not only remarkably soft but also highly durable and no one has ever contested the price of this quality suit which come in at USD 1 million.

The white straw hat was a perfect fit and match to the million-dollar suit, the hat, a Brent Black from the Panama Hat Company that only celebrities can afford with one going for USD 25,000, a price good enough for initial capital to start a family business.

The 22 carat each pure gold cufflinks were protruding from the jacket sleeve revealing parts of the shirt, jacket and Cufflinks in a rhythmic manner. The shirt was not an ordinary shirt, it was a Kiton Shirt made In Italy which usually comes at a cost of USD 7,900 each. On the left wrist was a Patek Philippe Stainless Steel worth USD $12 million, The Patek Philippe stainless steel is a legendary timepiece highly coveted by collectors for its rarity and historical significance. Launched in 1941, the Ref. 1518 was the world's first serially produced perpetual calendar chronograph wristwatch.

What makes the stainless-steel version particularly special is its scarcity, as Patek Philippe typically crafted such complicated watches in precious metals like gold. The Ref. 1518 features a sleek and timeless design, with subdials for the chronograph functions and a perpetual calendar displaying the day, date, month, and moon phases. In a world where luxury knows no bounds, watches, cars, and yachts stand as timeless symbols of opulence and prestige and Thomas Macpherson needed no lecture in the subject matter. These iconic treasures not only signify affluence and refinement but also embody a relentless pursuit of the extraordinary, and their acquisition, the building of a legacy.

From the precision engineering of a top-tier watch to the cutting-edge design of a prestigious automobile and the breathtaking allure of a magnificent super yacht, each item encapsulates a realm where extravagance reigns supreme. Thomas had a USD 79 million-dollar yacht, the magnificent 242' 10" (74m) Global is an exceptional yacht and a testament to her Lürssen pedigree. Originally delivered in 2010 and meticulously refitted in 2024, Global boasts a stylish interior, spacious accommodations, and unparalleled amenities. With a generous 42' (12.8m) beam, six decks and remarkable indoor and outdoor volumes, she welcomes 12 guests in the utmost comfort. An impressive helicopter deck, and an expansive beach club complete with a sauna and massage room perfect the global package, offering the ultimate in luxury living on the water. Thomas had a house in Palm Beach worth USD 77 million situated next to Trump's Marla go beach front mansion than presidents have used as holiday retreat and partying places. These coveted possessions cater to those who revel in the art of indulgence and appreciate the unmatched splendor of a life defined by the best on offer when it comes to luxury and refinement.

Thomas wore a brown leather belt a priced possession which could have been in the range of USD 600, a Goyard Florida with a size 0.5cm x 4cm. Due to its width, the Florida belt fits a relaxed ensemble ideally. The roller clasp is engraved with "Goyard," Goyardine is used on the inside and on the permanent loop, and there is a subtle trim, among other details. Made of Clemency Cowhide & Goyardine Canvas Palladium, the belt was a real touch of class.

Thomas wore a 33 Carat gold ring, and his shoes were as elegant and shiny to go with the opulence. He was holding a walking stick crossed his legs resting the weight on the walking stick which he looked at from time to time.

Thomas went to the check in counter to be served. A lady adjusted her posture and smiled as she reached out to receive his passport.

Thomas handed over a bag to check in while he preferred the one he was holding as hand luggage. He received his boarding pass and walked steadily to the departure lounge. A section of the airport had been closed for renovations. Thomas walked straight through the cordoned off area ignoring all the signs prohibiting non-airport staff to enter. As soon as he reached the construction zone, he grabbed a rail that went all the way downstairs. As he descended, he sent a message written 01 in position, the east wing of the room below him was opened by a remote control and there he was, in a room of three gentlemen, an Iranian, Palestinian and a Lebanese.

They were waiting for a special guest, the leader of Hauthis who would arrive in 3 minutes. Thomas walked as though tired and harmless but when he was within reach, he lifted his walking stick, released some substance under it and in an instant, blinded the three men. He summoned all his power and pulled them into a compartment and waited.

There was a knock on the door, Thomas opened it while hiding behind, and when the guest entered, he shut the door and repeated the act. He recovered the memory sticks that contained information and a small laptop which contained the collective programming that the three parties had put together as a plan to destroy Israel. Thomas climbed up and emerged from the construction area. Thomas walked steadily to Café Nush were he purchased some tea while reading a magazine about gardening. Later there was an announcement that a number of planes were being delayed due to security issues.

Boarding was announced and it was quiet a rush as planes needed to maintain a strict schedule. Planes took off after every five minutes and there was no room for error. The departure dashboard was showing BA departing to Lisbon at 20:25 Terminal 5 at Gate closed, Lufthansa at 20:25 gate closed, Air China to Beijing at 20:25 gate open and it went on and on. Some had a status showing taxied, boarding and so on. Captain Smith was in charge of the Airbus A380. The plane took off at 22:50. Straight for Melbourne.

Later, there were reports that three terrorist who had been under the surveillance of the Israeli government were found dead and the leader of the Hautis was among those that were killed in the process. The Mossad, the world's most deadly and slippery spy network was suspected to have carried out the operations. Airport cameras were run security cameras were run but there were four feeds that were blank at the time of the killing. Another clean operation had been successfully completed by the Mossad. There were celebrations in the United State of America, United Kingdom and predictably Australia and France with Australian government expressing relief.

Flight time from London, United Kingdom to Melbourne, Australia takes approximately 21 hours 1 minutes under average conditions. Our flight time calculator assumes an average flight speed for a commercial airliner of 500 mph, which is equivalent to 805 km/hr or 434 knots.

Actual flight times may vary depending on aircraft type, cruise speed, routing, weather conditions, passenger load, and other factors. The flight distance from London (United Kingdom) to Melbourne (Australia) is 10503 miles. This is equivalent to 16903 kilometers or 9121 nautical miles. The calculated distance (airline) is the straight-line distance or direct flight distance between cities. The captain and his core Pilots arrived in Melbourne at 7:20 Australian time.

Thomas collected his bags. He was picked up by the head of operations in Australia.

Chapter 11

Zimbabwe was once again restored to its former glory of pre independence, the Southern African nation was spruced up ahead of the SADC summit, the road construction that took contractors to work around the clock had finally come to an end, the roads were marked, all the potholes in major "SADC" routes to hotels and to the Museum of the African Liberation, the road to the new Parliament and Harare drive we spruced up and painted. The war against Mushikashika (illegal transporters) had been won, the City of Harare looked like it was back in the day, a sunshine city orderly, no litter with everything functioning, from public transport system, to water availability and collection of garbage on a timely manner.

It is 05:00 President Kufazvinei is due to address the nation on the heroes day. As a liberation struggle war hero himself he had many thoughts on his mind on this important day. The President had lost a number of friends and comrades in the armed struggle that left more than 10,000 guerrillas dead and approximately 20,000 people dead.

President Kufazvinei sat down holding a "book of nation", a secrete book with national secretes that only the presidents can see, in it is the names of national Heroes that liberated the people's republic of Zimbabwe a great nation full of milk and honey. In the book of the nation were Josaih Magama Tongogara, Jason Ziyapapa Moyo, Lookout

Masuku,Rex Nhongo, James Chikerema, Robert Mugabe, Emmerson Munangagwa, Simon Vengesai Muzenda, Joshua Nkomo, Peter Baya, Ariston Chambati, Charles Chauke, Enos Chikowore, John Chirisa, Daniel Madzimbamuto, Josiah Tungamirai, Herbert Chitepo, Vitalis Zvinavashe Musungwa Gava, Sydney Sekeramai, George Silundika, Prence Shiri, Enos Nkala, Dumiso Dabengwa, Joyce Mujuru, Oppar Muchinguri Kashiri, Phillip Valerio Sibanda,Mayor Urimbo, Eddison Sithole, John Dube, Ackim Ndlovu, Robson Manyika, Alfred Nikita Mangena, General Constantino Nyikadzino Chiwenga and many others who through bravery dismantled and dislodged the enemy.

The pre-Zimbabwe battle of Sinoia, popularly known as the battle of Chinhoyi was a small military unit that was started and fought near Sinoia (modern-day Chinhoyi) between a small unit of Zimbabwe African National Liberation Army (ZANLA) brave and selfless guerrillas on a quest for independence and determination for self-rule and the Rhodesian police force on 28 April 1966. The encounter is generally considered the opening engagement of the Rhodesian Bush War (Second *Chimurenga*) A deadly and fearless team of seven ZANLA cadres engaged with British South Africa Police forces near the northern town of Sinoia. The seven guerrillas all eventually died in the battle, the police killing all seven. Their death caused no sadness nor sorrow but was like a small bush fire that lighted the entire bush. What stared like a small act, a spit in the wind emboldened all and sundry including the comrades who were in Prisons.

In the run up the Unilateral Declaration of Independence (UDI) by Ian Smith, the Rhodesian Government took pre-emptive country-wide measures to prevent a general nationalist uprising as their reading of the situation led them to anticipate outrage and mass protest.

The uprising, which the nationalist leaders who were determined to have tight grip on power did not to happen, but better safe than sorry. However, inflammatory broadcasts from Zambia, Tanzania and Egypt elicited some response and there were many incidents of arson, stoning, crop slashing and mutilation of livestock among other work efforts to derail and beat the colonial masters into surrendering. Workers particularly in Bulawayo, protested by taking part in industrial action, and at Wankie Colliery sabotage attacks were carried out by a ZAPU action group, whose leader was said to have been let by Mazwi Gumbo.

The conflict intensified after the Unilateral Declaration of Independence from Britain on 11 November 1965. Sanctions were implemented by the British government after UDI, and member states of the United Nations endorsed the British embargo. The embargo meant the Rhodesians were restricted by a lack of modern equipment but used other means to receive vital war supplies such as receiving oil, munitions, and arms via the government of apartheid-era South Africa.

War material was also obtained through elaborate international smuggling schemes, domestic production, and equipment captured from infiltrating enemy combatants. The Kwekwe Roasting Plant was a place that Rhodes extracted gold as a central processing center and use it to buy all the arms and items that were on the list.

An earlier crossing by the guerrillas occurred early in April when another ZANU group of 14 split into three sections. One section of two men headed for the Fort Victoria area and another of five men had orders to sabotage the Beria-Umtali oil pipe-line and attack white farmers. All seven were arrested before they were able to complete their mission. The third section of seven men headed for the Midlands and it is possible that their purpose was to make contact with their President, Sithole, who was under restriction at Sikombela, near Gweru.

In March 1966 four small groups of ZANLA guerillas crossed the Zambezi near Chirundu, the first nationalist incursion following UDI. One group, comprising seven men from Guruve, Hurungwe and Makonde Districts travelled to the Chinhoyi/Sinoia area, but their presence was detected by the British South Africa Police's PATU unit.

Throughout the day of 28 April 1966, the two sides clashed with the seven showing skill and determination and ready to die for the cause set before them, and all seven ZANLA men were eventually killed, but only after their ammunition ran out.

The cadres had initially planned but failed, to cut the Kariba power-line from the Kariba Dam, which was supplying 70 percent of the country's electricity, and then subsequently the cadres planned to attack the blacked-out town centre and police station at Sinoia.

Had the attack been successful, it would have been a huge milestone for the freedom fighters. One of the Soldiers had a notebook, the book had detailed account of how the attacks were going to be coordinated, the book also showed that the insurgents had been trained at a Nanking military college in the previous November and December.

The presence of the Rhodesian helicopter which had been effectively used as a gunship during the attack was an important factor in the victory over the seven guerillas otherwise the Seven would have had more gains. The guerillas were outnumbered outflanked and had knowledge of the gravity of the matter and that the odds were against them, still they went ahead with the attack. The attack by the seven brave soldiers demonstrated how the people had suffered under the yoke of burdensome and gruelling sting of the colonial evil and ill-treatment. The burden of the yoke of slavery and racial discrimination could be likened to the suffering of the Israelites in Egypt under Pharaoh.

A ZANU spokesmen abroad later claimed at the time that the group had been responsible for killing twenty-five policemen and shooting down two helicopters, although the Rhodesian government disputed this in what was seen as propaganda, stating that the security forces had suffered no casualties, a claim that natives were finding difficult to believe.

As a result of the inept handling of the situation by the BSAP, the government became convinced that the BSAP were policemen and not soldiers. A position that supports the assertion by the ZANU spokesman regarding the casualties. The propensity to exaggerate enemy losses and minimize own casualties was high on both side. A shift of emphasis resulted in 1966, and the Rhodesian Security Forces became the government's primary instrument for conducting counterinsurgency operations rather than the BSAP.

The Sinoia incident also marked the official introduction of dedicated insurgent forces into Rhodesia. These insurgents were organized into small groups of 8-15 men operating from bases in Zambia. Throughout this early phase, the insurgents had two objectives: attack European owned farms and destroy the oil and powerline link between

Rhodesia and the Portuguese colony of Mozambique. These initial attempts were completely unsuccessful.

Although the battle was a Rhodesian victory, the event became a source of inspiration to the nationalists: one of the celebrated leaders of the liberation struggle Edgar Tekere wrote in his memoirs that when news of the battle reached nationalists detained in Salisbury Maximum Security Prison, they "went wild with joy."

The battle is celebrated in modern Zimbabwe as the first battle of the Second *Chimurenga*; its anniversary – also the anniversary of Nehanda Nyakasikana's execution – is marked as *Chimurenga Day*. The battle site was later developed into the Mashonaland West Provincial Heroes Acre and a site museum built by the National Museums and Monuments of Zimbabwe. An honour befitting of brave soldiers.

This battle was commemorated in a song called *Viva Chinhoyi*, on the album *Pamberi* by the Bhundu Boys.

The president laid wreath on the graves of the great man at the National Heroes Acre, a secret shrine for the men who contributed to the cause of the nation, yet one man was missing, there could not have been a more befitting man to be buried at the national shrine the late Robert Gabriel Mugabe, the decision to bury him at a location in his hometown was a family decision. Nobody knows where he was exactly buried but all the same his immense contributions are well noted in the history books.

Chapter 12

Whenever there is progress, others see disgrace or regress. A lot of contention arose regarding the infrastructural developments which had happened ahead of the SADC summit. Ladies of the night were displaced from their usual spots due to road works and road closures while drug powerhouses had to shift due to heightened security in the area. This disturbance created an imbalance that also opened opportunities for new entrants into the market. It was "dog eat dog time". Survival of the streetwise. Nancy was one such lady who had vowed to conquer the streets both day and night. She nicknamed herself Nancy Blue. Thomas had been her biggest supplier and business associate for five years. Despite his South African base, he still had strong roots in Zimbabwe across all major towns. Even the news of his arrest spread like wide fire among his cronies. This together with the current infrastructural disruptions, shook the drug underworld in the Harare metropolitan region. Even more, Thomas' arrest had disturbed the natural order of such dealings. Others like Nancy knew that being the astute businessman he was, Thomas always had a plan. There were rumors that he may have landed himself in jail intentionally but whichever way, he was in charge. Or so he thought.

In the Avenues area of town where Janice lived and ruled, the repercussions of Thomas' arrest were felt more deeply than she anticipated. Janice's son, Jason, had struggled with drug use for years. He had managed to maintain a semblance of normalcy, working part-time and keeping his addiction relatively under control. But with Thomas suddenly off the streets with no immediate contingency plan in place due to the SADC summit developmental disruptions and several players off the streets, a key supplier was missing, causing a severe shortage of drugs in the area. An alternative was to go south of Samora or further uptown, but then prices had skyrocketed in those few days. This was a scarcity turning into a potential crisis. Janice waddled downstairs to dry her few laundered clothes. She was humming a poignant song she had created out of worry. The peaceful flats, where children once played and neighbours greeted each other with friendly waves, had transformed into a hive of unsettling activity.

As Janice hung her laundry on the line, a shadow fell over her. She looked up to see Mrs. Fowler standing by a pole, her eyes looking distant.

"Janice, have you seen the increase in crime around here?" Mrs. Fowler's voice trembled as she gestured towards the main gate for block of flats, where a group of teenagers huddled too close for comfort. "It's like things have just gotten out of hand. You cannot even hang your laundry outside anymore."

Janice's hands paused mid-air, the damp skirt slipping slightly from her grip. Her eyes, darkened with fatigue and concern, met Mrs. Fowler's. "I know," she said softly, her voice almost a whisper. "Even my Jason is getting worse. It's like the drugs have taken over everything." The silence between them spoke volumes. The nearby sound of ambulance sirens entering the adjacent hospital, a reminder of the encroaching chaos, seemed to amplify the weight of Janice's words.

Jason's dealer Nancy Blue, now scrambling to find a new source, raised prices, making the drugs even more inaccessible. This scarcity drove Jason and others into desperate circumstances. When Janice discovered her son's increasing instability and criminal behavior, she was heartbroken.

One evening, Janice found Jason rummaging through the kitchen drawers, seemingly looking for something. The house was in disarray, and the tension was palpable.

"Jason, what's going on?" Janice asked, her voice laced with worry.

Jason, barely meeting her gaze, muttered, "I can't find anything, mum. Prices have gone up. I need to get some cash somehow." His eyes looked distant.

Janice slouched in her couch. Her fingers shook as she scrolled through her contacts. The cold glow of the phone screen highlighted the strain on her face, revealing dark circles under her puffy eyes. She hovered over Jason's father's number, then flicked to the text message thread, her indecision palpable. Every ping from the father's social media, filled with sun-soaked photos and carefree moments, felt like a cruel contrast to Jason's struggle. Jason's father was gallivanting in Kariba, living his best life with his young mistress. His social media posts were a parade of fun and extravagance, each image a stark reminder of his detachment. As Janice scrolled through these photos, a frown spread across her face. Frustration and helplessness gripped her. The contrast between the vibrant, effortless life his father seemed to enjoy and Jason's own struggle with addiction made her sulk and clench her fists. Janice had to grapple with the painful reality of their fractured family. She was hopeful that he would return, yet meanwhile it may have been best to block his social media accounts to save her the disappointment. The financial strain, the emotional toll, and the knowledge that Jason's father was miles away in a world untouched by their current crisis made the choice seem almost futile. She went back to the dial pad. With a sigh, Janice set the phone down.

Her husband's revelries seemed to amplify and mock her distress. The contrast was sharp—a life of ease and new beginnings, while Jason stumbled through the darkness, searching for solace in the haze of his new habits. She had discussed with Mrs. Fowler the possibility that Jason's father might not even remember his son. That conversation was bitter and sharp. It gnawed at her, mingling with the guilt that Jason's own choices weren't entirely free from blame. She agreed with her friend that indulging in the drug-fuelled escape wasn't justified, yet the struggle to make sense of it all twisted in her gut. There had to be a way out. She grabbed her phone and sighed deeply, her breath catching in her throat as she finally pressed rang his number.

Chapter 13

Announcement of the divorce hit Lunela like a tidal wave, leaving her tense and unsettled, yet she appeared stoic. In Andrew's office on Fleet Street, London, the atmosphere felt stifling. The room, with its dark wood panelling and sleek leather chairs, seemed to close in around her. A single desk lamp illuminated the laptop and a few tablets on the polished mahogany desk. Andrew leaned forward, his fingers tapping an uneasy rhythm on the edge of the desk, his eyes fixed on Lunela's strained expression.

"Lunela," he said, his voice a mix of concern and caution, "revealing this could have serious consequences. It will probably ruin Solomon's reputation and draw unwanted scrutiny to your own life. There is possibility of being implicated as an accomplice in all this. Solomon has top lawyers, and he can be unscrupulous. This could turn into a battle that might destroy everything you've worked for."

Lunela's hands clenched into fists on her lap, her knuckles icy against her skin. Her gaze was a storm of defiance and grief, piercing through Andrew's concern. "I understand the risks," she said, her voice laced with steel coldness, "but I can't stay silent. I need to do this for my own closure." The betrayal, vivid and unrelenting, seemed to seep into every corner of the room. The divorce had become more than a legal matter; it was a battle for her own sense of justice and self-worth. Lunela's jaw set firmly, her gaze steady. "I understand he has a suspended jail term, but I will dump him into an eternal prison once this is over. I will not be silenced; these twins will be my strength." Lunela rubbed her belly. Seeing Solomon's lover beside him in his hospital bed had made her cringe and that was the final blow. That was like a wound that refused to heal. A divorce was inevitable, so was some form of justice for all her wasted years. Was she not good enough?

Meanwhile across town, The Shard's towering silhouette loomed over London's skyline, its reflective glass catching the morning sun as Solomon and his partner, Lincoln, navigated through the bustling streets below, making their way to Bentons on the 40th floor of the iconic skyscraper. As they stepped out of the elevator, they marveled at the sweeping cityscape before them, noting the polished glass doors of Bentons, the prestigious law firm that dominated the upper levels with its commanding presence. This was where their strategy would be formulated and the battle for success ultimately won, high above London in the offices of Bentons. Solomon's partner stood by the large glass window, watching the sprawling city below with a worried frown. He turned to his sweetheart, his voice tinged with frustration and concern. "Solomon babe, you need to get a handle on this. It's not just your reputation on the line; it's our future together. We can't afford to lose this fight." His lawyers nodded and this seemed to reassure Solomon that this was the best route for now. Those words hung in the air, a clear reminder of the fragile balance Solomon had to maintain. The weight of the impending exposure, coupled with the stress of a collapsing career, was starting to fracture the once-sturdy foundations of Solomon's carefully constructed life.

Solomon's face tightened, his jaw set. The weight of Lincoln's words pressed down on him and the stress of their crumbling situation threatened to break him. He sat across from Richard, the lead lawyer, who was absorbed in typing, his face flushed with the strain of their conversation.

"Solomon, you're making this harder," Richard said, his voice steady and controlled. "You need to understand how serious this is. If Lunela follows through, it will ruin your reputation and bring unwanted attention to everyone involved."

Solomon's voice cracked as he stuttered, then he took a deep breath. "I know what's at stake! I'm paying you to find a way to settle this without a public mess. There must be a way to handle this quietly. I have a suspended jail term already and that is enough."

Richard's eyes were sharp with intensity as he gazed at his client. "You're asking for a miracle. Lunela has explosive evidence, and she's determined to use it. This isn't just about a bad day—it's a disaster waiting to happen."

The room was thick with tension, each word a heavy blow. Solomon could see his control slipping, the reality of their situation closing in on him. Their brief meeting had left them with more questions than answers, and as they left Bentons, the weight of their predicament pressed heavily, each step like a march towards an uncertain and potentially devastating future. Downstairs, in the quiet lobby of Bentons, Emily, Lunela's half-sister waited, her posture tense. Her gaze was sharp, and the subtle frown on her lips hinted at the seriousness of her purpose. As Solomon and Lincoln came into view, Emily stared at Solomon with an uncanny familiarity. She stepped forward, holding out her phone.

"What have you got here, Bonnie and Clyde? There's something you need to see Solomon," Emily said, her voice steady but carrying a threat.

Solomon's pulse quickened as he glanced at the phone screen. The sight left him reeling. What Emily showed him threatened to destroy everything he was trying to hold together. Solomon's eyes went wide as he looked at Emily's phone, his breath catching in his throat. "Emily, what is this? Why are you even here?" he asked, struggling to keep his voice calm.

Emily's gaze was cold and unyielding. "You know exactly what this means," she whispered with a sly smile.

Lincoln's face tightened as he looked from Solomon to Emily. "What's happening? What does this have to do with us?"

Emily gave a small smirk and addressed Solomon with a stern tone. "Think carefully about your next move. This is just the beginning."

In a flash, Emily turned and sashayed away. Solomon and Lincoln stood frozen in the lobby, the heaviness of her words sinking in. The future seemed suddenly more uncertain, each unanswered question adding to the sense of looming disaster.

Later that evening, Lunela reluctantly agreed to stay at her in-laws' home. The Smiths' dinner table, once a place of laughter and easy chats, now seemed like a battleground. The usual clinking of cutlery and low murmur of conversation was gone, replaced by a thick silence that hung heavily in the air.

Jennifer's voice broke the stillness, trembling with raw emotion. "Lunela, I know you're hurting," she began, her words catching in her throat. "But think about what's coming next. We're all stunned and deeply sorry for what you're going through. But you need to see beyond just this moment. It's not just Solomon who will be shattered. Look at the whole picture—what about you? The babies? What about our whole family?"

Her eyes, glistening with unshed tears, were fixed on Lunela as she reached for a glass of water. Her fingers quivered as she lifted the glass, struggling to keep it steady. The small droplets that clung to the rim seemed to mirror the tears she was fighting to hold back.

Lunela's eyes narrowed, and her jaw tightened as she spoke. "I'm just trying to protect myself," she said, her voice shaking. Her hand gripped the edge of the table. "I'm not doing this out of spite. He's hurt so many people. He needs to pay for it."

Her lips curled in a bitter sneer. Her voice was a desperate plea for validation, seeking to justify her actions amidst the mounting opposition from those she considered in-laws. She cast a nasty glance at her soon-to-be ex-husband, her face contorted in a grimace. The room seemed to close in as she raised her glass of wine, the liquid swaying as she took a slow, deliberate sip. Her shoulders tensed, and she set the glass down with a clink that seemed to echo her inner turmoil.

Solomon, seated across from Lunela at the table, let out a long, weary sigh and turned his head slightly, avoiding her eyes. He cleared his throat several times, the sound becoming disruptive. "Lunela, we need to find a solution that doesn't involve public humiliation. Maybe there's another way to hold me accountable. Name your price." His voice trembled as he bowed his head, the plea for another way forward clear in his strained tone.

Lunela's voice softened to a whisper, her lips trembling as she fought to keep the tears at bay. "Not today," she murmured, almost as if speaking to herself. Then she faced Solomon with intent eyes, "I don't know if I can let this go. The pain and betrayal are too fresh and raw." Her voice was barely above a whisper, laden with sorrow and disappointment.

At this point, the in-laws knew it was best to stay out of the matter; the emotions were too high. The sudden burst of the back door startled everyone, prompting Captain Smith to investigate the disturbance. Solomon seized the moment to regain his composure, quickly downing two glasses of wine. When he returned, he announced that the door, which had already been ajar, must have swung open due to the wind. He then cautioned everyone to stay alert, his tone a mix of authority and unease.

Before anyone could respond, he turned to Lunela, his frustration boiling over. "I've made mistakes, okay? But this... airing our dirty laundry like this is going to ruin everything!" he shouted, his voice echoing through the room. "I'm trying to fix things, not just for me, but for everyone involved. You know I love you, but we're meant to go our separate ways. Just name your price, and I'll make it happen!"

Lunela's eyes flashed and were bloodshot. "You think you can just buy your way out of this? After everything you've done?" Her voice cracked as she fought to hold back tears. "The pain and betrayal are too fresh. It's not about money. It's about what you've taken from me, from us!"

Sometimes it's okay to let people vent. Jennifer sniffled the two continued their heated verbal exchange, her husband rubbing her shoulders in a futile attempt to offer comfort. He shook his head in dejection, casting a sorrowful glance at his son, unable to mask his disappointment. Lunela's need to express her hurt and anger was undeniable, and in this moment, it was clear that the release of her pent-up feelings was as much a part of the process as finding any resolution.

The Smith family reached a fragile truce, however marked with uncertainty on what Lunela's stance would be. Lunela, her face a mask of unresolved conflict, listened as Solomon urged her to keep the drug smuggling evidence private. Lunela shoved her chair back from the table with a forceful scrape, the sharp noise slicing through the ensuing silence. Her eyes blazed as she stood, her hands clenched into fists at her sides. She stormed toward her room, each step echoing her fury as she slammed the door. The creak of the floorboards followed her departure, leaving a heavy silence in her wake.

A few minutes later, she returned, her expression unreadable, clutching her phone. She placed her lawyer's business card on the table and paused. "I'll be leaving first thing in the morning," she said, her voice steady but with a hint of something unspoken. She dialed a number and held the phone to her ear, her gaze drifting around the room as she spoke in low, measured tones. As she ended the call, she looked up with a smile that didn't quite reach her eyes. "Just so you know," Lunela said with a casual tone, "my name means 'mystery.' I've planned to leave before breakfast, so Jennifer, don't bother cooking for me."

Lunela turned to leave, but just before she exited, her phone buzzed with a new message. She glanced at it, her expression shifting to one of anxious anticipation. She tucked the phone away and walked to her room with a measured calm. The family was left in a thick silence, their eyes drawn to the card on the table and the lingering sense of something more sinister beneath Lunela's calm facade. The card seemed to pulse with the weight of unspoken secrets, which could unfold in the morning.

Lunela Smith, née Mandla, came from a modest background. Her parents were loving but struggled financially. Lunela was a hardworking and ambitious young woman who worked her way through college with government grants and part-time jobs. She met Solomon during her matric year, and their relationship seemed like a fairy tale.

Lunela's initial excitement about marrying into a wealthy family faded as she discovered Solomon's increasingly erratic behavior and secretive nature. Despite these issues, Lunela tried to make the marriage work, hoping that his success and their shared life, however, his affair, which led him to initiate divorce, along with his drug smuggling operations, had pushed Lunela to her breaking point, leaving her with only the expectation of bearing his twins.

Chapter 14

Thandeka, a determined and compassionate social worker in her early 30s, worked at a bustling community center near the Avenues Heights shopping center. This area, close to the city center, was vibrant and active. Thandeka had grown up in Mbare, a southern suburb known for its bustling activity and its notorious struggles with petty crime and drug abuse. Mbare was a crossroads of sorts, a hub for major bus routes to destinations like Botswana and Malawi. Mbare still boasts of Mbare Musika, the largest farm produce market in Zimbabwe. It also gave rise to sports legends like George Shaya who played for the Zimbabwe national team and Dynamos Football Club. The suburb also raised vibrant township jazz bands like Mbare Trio and 2Plus2. It was also the home of the prolific nonagenarian radio presenter Mbuya Mlambo. Over the years, the area's once-celebrated history began to fade, overshadowed by its growing reputation as a hotspot for theft and illicit activities, a change that seemed inevitable given its central location.

While Thandeka appreciated and loved her neighborhood, she did not let the bad side define her or limit her. Thandeka cherished her roots but resolved to distance herself from Mbare's more challenging aspects. She moved to the Avenues area, just north of the city centre. While this part of town was also close to the heart of the city, it had its own issues. For many years, there were illegal deals going on but on a low radar. However, the streets were notorious for their visible and explicit trade of prostitution. Ladies of the night lined the streets, their scantily clad figures visible from afar, making it clear to passing cars who was available for hire.

From earlier years through the 2000s, the area was notorious for its nighttime activities. Now, as Thandeka was living there, she observed that the same trade continued unabated, with women advertising themselves even in broad daylight, starting as early as 8 a.m. Men driving slowly through the streets could easily be mistaken for clients, while women standing at corners might be perceived as service providers. Just as prostitution had become a glaring issue in the Avenues, so too had drug dealing, with transactions taking place so openly that they resembled casual handshakes rather than covert exchanges.

Now, as Thandeka settled into her new one-bedroom flat along Baines Avenue, she found herself amid a different kind of chaos. The flat's convenient location near the shops seemed a double-edged sword. The neighbourhood, once a haven of discreet dealings, was now a hive of activity well into the night. The constant din of drunken brawls and the erratic nightlife often made her feel as if she were right back in Mbare, though the nature of the activity was different. In this world, even a simple handshake could be mistaken for a drug deal, showing how deeply crime and vice were embedded in everyday life, wherever she lived.

Thandeka was dedicated to helping individuals and families struggling with addiction, and she was well-respected in her field. Her own brother, Romeo, fell into drug addiction years ago. Romeo's addiction was exacerbated by the influx of drugs into Mbare, which she later learnt was facilitated by smugglers who posed as businessmen. Despite her best efforts to help him, Romeo's addiction spiralled, leading to a tragic overdose. His death left a profound impact on Thandeka, fueling her commitment to combating drug abuse. She knew she wasn't as accomplished as the late stellar footballer George Shaya, but she made a significant impact in her own small ways within her local community.

Thandeka discovered that the recent surge in drug availability in her community was linked to Nancy Blue. Her investigation revealed that the drugs were being transported by a pilot, although this information was still quite vague. What was clear was that the smuggling operation was likely part of a larger, more organised crime network. Her frustration mounted as she struggled to connect the dots between the influx of drugs and her brother's death, all while balancing her responsibilities as a social worker dedicated to people's welfare.

One evening, at a support group meeting where she shared her experiences and frustrations, a fellow member named Michael mentioned hearing about a pilot involved in the local drug trade. This pilot appeared to be connected to the broader distribution network, but the details were still unclear. Since that meeting, Thandeka vowed to find answers. She pieced together bits of information about Nancy Blue's involvement with increasing urgency. Grief gnawed at her determination, and a fierce desire for justice drove her to act. On a Friday morning, after days of bracing herself, she finally gathered the courage to confront Nancy.

The confrontation occurred behind a vendor's stall, the bustling market around them creating sharp contrast to the intensity of their exchange. Thandeka's face flushed with anger as she stepped forward, her fists clenched at her sides. Her voice, sharp and cutting through the clamour of the market, demanded attention. Thandeka fumed, "I know what you're doing," she spat out, her eyes blazing. "I know who you're hurting. My brother died because of people like you. How many lives have you ruined for money?"

Nancy's eyes widened, a flicker of fear darting across her face. "You don't understand," she pleaded, her voice trembling. "I didn't want this. I'm trying to get out, but it's not that simple."

Thandeka's anger faltered as she caught a glimpse of Nancy's desperate expression. The tension in her shoulders eased slightly, but quickly replaced by a flicker of doubt. Was Nancy's plea genuine, or was it another layer of deception hiding her true nature? That instant, Nancy chuckled and this startled Thandeka. In a moment, Nancy guffawed while rolling her eyes. She then looked Thandeka up and down with a scowl on her face. Nancy, leaning casually against the stall. Her stance was relaxed, but her eyes were steely and unyielding. "For a minute I had you. Let's do this again. You think you've got it all figured out," she said, her tone flat and dismissive. "I'm just a small player in a much bigger game. I didn't start this mess, no stress, and getting out isn't as simple as you think."

Thandeka's anger faltered as she looked at Nancy. The hardness in Nancy's eyes and her calm, collected stance caught Thandeka off guard. Nancy's response was as tough as her exterior; any sign of weakness was buried under her strong facade. Thandeka's strength started fading. Her shoulders drooped, and her knees trembled. Whereas Nancy, unphased by the confrontation, shifted her gaze away with a practiced indifference. She bought some fruits from a nearby vendor, her actions smooth as if the tense chat had been just another part of her day. The vendor, who had watched the exchange, gave Nancy a small, understanding smile before Nancy walked off into the busy market.

Thandeka watched Nancy disappear into the crowd, while rooted to the spot. The lively market around her seemed to blur into a distant noise, making her seem more isolated. The short walk back to her flat seemed much longer. She trudged along what seemed like a journey around the world, even though it was only a five-minute walk to her home. Each step was heavy with emotions. When she finally reached her apartment, Thandeka dragged herself inside. The comfort of her home didn't ease her exhaustion as she made her way to the couch. She collapsed onto it, her body completely giving in to her weariness. One arm fell loosely to the floor, her fingers brushing the carpet.

Chapter 15

That night, Nancy paced in her bedroom, her steps quick and uneven. No one had ever dared question her choices before; she had ruled the streets with a commanding presence. But the confrontation with Thandeka had shaken her, making the reality of her decisions hit harder than ever. She stopped abruptly, her breath coming in short bursts. A wave of realization seemed to crash over her, and she froze, staring blankly at the floor. "Oh no, Jason," she whispered, the name escaping her lips like a desperate prayer. Her hands trembled as she fumbled for her phone.

In a frantic rush, Nancy dialled Janice's number, her fingers slick with sweat. As soon as Janice answered, Nancy's voice broke into a cascade of sobs. "Please forgive me," she choked out, her words barely coherent.

The connection was weak, but the raw emotion was clear. Janice, who had known Nancy since high school and still lived in the same neighbourhood, listened in silence. Nancy had never sold anything directly to Jason, he only bought through the network she controlled. Now, with the weight of their connection crashing down on her, Nancy sank to the floor, her back against the wall. Tears streamed down her face, mingling with the shadows of the blow she had dealt her friend all these years.

The sobs came in waves, each one a painful reminder of the decade spent in a world of crime. Nancy pulled a blanket around her, as if trying to shield herself from the reality she could no longer ignore. She closed her eyes, seeking solace in sleep, but it was clear that she had to find a new path and seeking redemption or remain in the dark alley.

The Zimbabwean government convened provincial strategy meetings to tackle the escalating drug trafficking problem impacting communities across the nation. The meetings had representatives from Provincial Information Offices, Ministry of Youth, Sport, Arts and Recreation, Ministry of Health and Childcare, Zimbabwe Republic Police (ZRP), Ministry of Public Service, Labour and Social Welfare among other stakeholders. Thandeka, attended one such meeting.

In the conference room of the local community centre, the atmosphere was charged with anticipation. The government had recently launched the Zimbabwe Multi-Sectoral Drug and Substance Abuse Plan, aiming to address the rising crisis of drug abuse. The plan had been a major topic in recent weeks, and the meeting was set to discuss its implementation and impact. This plan was stemming from the establishment of the inter-ministerial taskforce committee in line with achieving Vision 2030.

Thandeka sat at a round table, her notepad open and pen poised. Her tablet was also on hand, but she preferred to use handwritten notes. She had been closely following the new strategy and its potential to affect her community. The plan had already begun to address the growing impacts of drug abuse on public health, economic stability, and social cohesion. As the meeting started, the community liaison officer took the floor. "The government has launched a comprehensive strategy through the Zimbabwe Multi-Sectoral Drug and Substance Abuse Plan," he announced. "This plan has aimed to tackle the drug crisis by decentralising the Drug and Narcotics Department and revising the fine structure for drug suppliers. Additionally, it includes expanding support services, such as establishing outpatient psycho-social support centers and increasing resources for rehabilitation centers."

Thandeka listened intently. She had seen firsthand the devastating effects of drug abuse in her family, her community, and the new measures held a glimmer of hope. Her involvement in local support groups had given her insight into the challenges faced by those struggling with addiction, and she was eager to see how these new initiatives would translate into real change. The officer continued, detailing the specific roles that local organizations would play in supporting the new plan.

As the discussion progressed, Thandeka prepared to share her own observations and experiences. Her aim was to ensure that the voices of those directly impacted by the drug crisis were heard and that the new plan would address their needs effectively. The room buzzed with a mix of hope and skepticism as participants considered the potential impact of the government's ambitious strategy.

A representative from the Ministry of Justice said, "The surge in drug trafficking and abuse is having a devastating impact on our communities. We need a more coordinated approach to tackle this issue." Other key concerns raised were discussed further.

The police chief added, "Our recent investigations have uncovered significant smuggling routes. We are working with international partners to disrupt these networks, but we need more resources and support—" grumbling in the audience interrupted him as some shouted 'corruption'. He then continued, "We're intensifying our operations, but we're facing challenges. Corruption within our ranks and limited resources are major hurdles. We must address these issues to strengthen our efforts." A lot of nods and yeses resonated in the room.

The last speaker was from the local Kubatana Drug Awareness Network. She said, "Community-based programs are crucial. The importance of grassroots approaches cannot be underestimated. We need to enhance public awareness and provide more support for rehabilitation. The lack of facilities and funding is a significant barrier."

The meeting concluded with a strong commitment to increase collaboration between agencies, enhance anti-corruption measures, and allocate additional resources for drug prevention and rehabilitation. Recognising that drug trafficking was a complex, systemic issue, participants agreed on the necessity of a comprehensive, system-wide approach. They emphasised the need to map the system, aiming to understand how various elements and stakeholders were interconnected. By creating a detailed map of the entire system, they sought to reveal the full scope of the problem, including how different factors influenced each other. Additionally, adopting an iceberg theory perspective, they acknowledged that the visible signs of the drug problem—such as arrests and drug seizures— represented only the tip of the iceberg. Beneath the surface lay deeper, hidden issues contributing to the crisis. By using this approach, they aimed to address not only the immediate symptoms but also the root causes driving the drug trade, seeking solutions that would address these underlying factors.

Later that day, Thandeka, the dedicated social worker, rushed to her support group session for individuals affected by drug abuse. Her community centre was struggling with limited funding but remained a beacon of hope for many.

Janice poured out her heart, "We've seen an increase in drug abuse in our area. This isn't just about addiction, it's about the wider impact on families and our community. We need to work together to find solutions and support each other. Instead of profiteering from one another."

One of the participants, Michael, spoke up about his experiences. "I've lost friends to this epidemic. We need more help from the government and organisations to provide better treatment and prevent these drugs from reaching our streets. We see them at every corner but we are powerless to do anything lasting. We need to cut the source."

Thandeka addressed the group with a calm and reassuring tone. "The government is aware of the problem, and efforts are underway to tackle it," she said with empathy. "But we must also support each other and advocate for more resources, just as you both have mentioned."

She proceeded to brief them on the recent meeting with provincial leaders. As she spoke, murmurs of discontent rippled through the audience. Many seemed unimpressed, their frustration clear; they felt that government promises were nothing new. Despite the scepticism, Thandeka remained resolute. She emphasised that the new approach was not only different but also more stringent than previous measures. "This is a significant shift," she insisted. "The new strategies involve a comprehensive mapping of the system and a deeper dive into the root causes, beyond just surface-level symptoms." They enjoyed some refreshments, chuckling over the surprising price differences between grapes at supermarkets and those sold by vendors.

Michael, who worked as a vendor on weekends, naturally leaned towards supporting the vendor's side of the debate. But there was something more unsettling about his recent behaviour. He seemed to be watching Janice with an intensity that went beyond casual interest. Whenever Janice spoke, Michael's gaze lingered a moment too long, and his comments carried an undertone that made Thandeka uneasy. The tension in the air hinted at something more, leaving one wondering about the true nature of Michael's intentions and whether his interest in Janice was as innocent as it appeared.

Chapter 16

Solomon grew up with aviation in his blood. His father, Captain Smith, was a respected commercial pilot who had worked for a major airline for over two decades. Known for his professionalism and dedication, Captain Smith instilled a love for flying in Solomon from a young age. Solomon idolised his father and dreamed of following in his footsteps.

Childhood for Solomon was marked by airport visits and short flights with his father, soaking in stories of distant places and the thrill of the skies. Yet, as much as Captain Smith shared his passion for aviation, he was often absent during Solomon's pivotal moments. Though he provided generously for Solomon's training and even financed his pilot's licence, his demanding job meant he was rarely around for Solomon's milestones—graduations, private pilot licence achievements, or even simple family dinners. Captain Smith's focus on amassing wealth and prestige meant a skewed trade-off with quality family moments.

Solomon walked briskly through the winding streets of London, the grandeur of the city's landmarks seeming almost mocking against the reality of his mounting debts and a stagnant career. As he passed by the London Eye, its towering Ferris wheel turning slowly against the backdrop of the River Thames, the contrast between its majestic presence and his troubled look was sharp. The elegant curve of the Eye, with its glittering capsules offering panoramic views of the city, seemed to highlight the distance between his dreams and his reality. He had chosen this route intentionally, seeking a sense of independence and self-worth, far from the lush surroundings of his family's estate.

The familiar beep of his phone startled him, causing him to stagger slightly as he fumbled to check the screen. He glanced at the screen to see a message from an unknown number. Before he could fully process it, a figure materialised beside him—Mendes, looking out of place amid the city's refined chaos. His tailored suit and confident stride clashed with the gritty, everyday London Street.

"Solomon," Mendes greeted, his voice smooth but with an edge of persistence. "I didn't expect to catch you so randomly on a weekday."

Solomon stopped abruptly, his eyes narrowing with frustration. "Mendes. Not again. I've told you before, I'm not interested."

Mendes flashed a practiced, disarming smile. "I understand. But sometimes, circumstances change. And sometimes, a little help is exactly what you need."

Without waiting for a response, Mendes guided Solomon to a nearby café—an upscale, modern place tucked away on a quieter street. The large glass windows offered a panoramic view of the busy London streets, contrasting with the calm and polished interior.

They took a seat in a secluded corner of the café. The ambient sounds of clinking cups and quiet conversations seemed distant as Mendes slid a folder across the table. "I know I've approached you before," Mendes said, his tone carrying a hint of sincerity. "But I've got something here you might want to look at."

Solomon eyed the folder with a mixture of scepticism and curiosity. He opened it to reveal a map marked with several locations and a proposal for discreet, profitable jobs. The figures outlined were substantial—enough to provide immediate financial relief, a much-needed boost to ease his current struggle.

"I've turned you down twice before," Solomon said, his voice tinged with irritation. "I don't want to get involved in this."

Mendes leaned in, a smirk playing at the corners of his mouth. "I get it, man. But things are different now. Your dad's still around, and he's got the cash to back you up, but you're too proud to ask for it. So, what's it going to be? Are you going to man up and sort this out yourself, or are you going to keep dodging the hand he's still got out for you?

Solomon's gaze drifted to the café's large windows, where the vibrant life of London continued unchanged outside. Mendes's words brought the image of his father—an epitome of success and integrity—into sharp focus. His father had always been a steady hand in the shifting currents of life, offering unwavering support and guidance through every other financial challenge. The café's modern elegance seemed to highlight the disconnect between his privileged background and the harsh reality of his financial strain. Mendes's offer, though morally dubious, grew increasingly tempting as a practical solution to his immediate needs.

"Just consider it," Mendes said softly. "You know I'm here to help if you decide you need it."

Solomon sighed, his gaze fixed on the café's large windows where the vibrant life of London flowed uninterrupted. The contrast between his current predicament and the image of his father—embodied by Mendes's words—was stark. His father, once a steady hand through life's financial challenges, seemed a distant ideal in the face of Solomon's immediate struggles. The decision he faced was not just about financial relief but about confronting the importance of his father's legacy and his sense of pride.

Mendes broke the silence, rising from his seat with a final, measured look at Solomon. "Think it over," he said, smoothly collecting the folder and slipping it back into his briefcase. "I'll be around if you decide you need a hand."

Solomon watched as Mendes walked out of the café, the door closing with a soft but jarring thud that unsettled him. As Mendes disappeared into the busy London Street, the ambient noise of the café seemed to swell, the chatter and clinking cups filling the space with a loudness that mirrored the financial turmoil in Solomon's life. His fingers traced the rim of his coffee cup, the warm porcelain grounding him as he stared into the dark liquid. The once-comforting aroma of the coffee now seemed heavy, almost suffocating. The café's vibrant atmosphere, once a distraction, now seemed to amplify the tension that lay just beneath the surface, contrasting sharply with the quiet weight of Mendes's offer and the looming expectations tied to his father's legacy. He stared into his coffee, the dark liquid swirling with his emptiness. Each sip felt hollow.

With a sudden burst of renewed energy, Solomon downed the last of his coffee in a single, decisive gulp. He set the cup down with a firm thud, pushed his chair back, and stood up with a determined stride. As he strode out of the café, his steps were purposeful and deliberate, reflecting a newfound sense of determination. Would he go through with Mendes's offer, or was this newfound clarity just a fleeting moment before he faced the hard choices ahead?

The next day, Solomon found himself back in the familiar, opulent surroundings of his family's study. The shift from the lively café to this quiet, luxurious space was palpable. As he settled behind the polished mahogany desk, he looked at the city's skyline shimmering through the expansive windows, silent proof of the wealth and success that had always been within his reach. The room, decorated with high-end furnishings and framed certificates, spoke of a life marked in affluence and ambition. Despite the room's elegance, there was an air of tension, as if the sleek, modern confines of his family's spacious study were both a refuge and a prison, reminding him of the complex decisions he faced. The room's luxurious details seemed to mock him as Solomon glanced around—the leather chairs, the gleaming desk, the framed photographs of family achievements. His gaze settled on a particular picture that stood out among the others: his father, clad in a crisp flight suit, beaming beside a sleek, silver aircraft. It was a classic Concorde, its sharp, elegant lines and delta wings capturing the essence of cutting-edge aviation from a bygone era. The aircraft's polished surface glinted in the photograph, reflecting the golden glow of the setting sun, symbolising the peak of his father's accomplishments. The Concorde, with its supersonic speed and distinctive nose, represented not just a technological marvel but also the legacy Solomon was desperately trying to live up to yet in his own terms.

Solomon chewed on a pen, the click of his teeth against the plastic punctuating the silence of the study. Gritting his teeth, he crumpled a few sheets of paper and hurled them toward the wastebasket, missing it by a wide margin. He muttered curses under his breath and tugged at his hair, his fingers drumming impatiently on the edge of the desk.

Finally, he picked up his phone, speaking in low, urgent tones as he made a quick call. After ending the call, Solomon tossed the phone onto a nearby sofa, barely glancing to see if it landed softly. He strode into the kitchen with long, quick steps, grabbing a beer from the fridge with a decisive yank. The sharp crack of the can opening and the clink of ice settling into a glass interrupted the otherwise quiet study. As he poured the beer, his hands moved quickly and firmly, the glass filling with a steady stream and a series of sharp clinks. In under ten minutes, Solomon had flattened twelve beer cans, crushing them with a mix of frustration and aimless distraction. The empty cans were scattered around him, on the desk and floor. Eventually, he slumped onto the desk, his head resting heavily on his arms, and drifted into an uneasy sleep.

Later, his mother, passing by the study, heard the soft, rhythmic sound of snoring. She peeked in and found Solomon sprawled across the desk, his face buried in the crook of his arm. Shaking her head with a mixture of concern and weariness, she quietly entered the room. Gently, she draped a shawl over his shoulders. As she straightened up, she clutched her stomach with a sigh, her eyes softening as she watched her son. Her expression spoke of a deep, enduring worry and an aching sadness, yet also a quiet acceptance of the challenges Solomon was facing. She took one last look at his slumped figure before quietly slipping out, leaving him to rest in the relative calm of the study.

Chapter 17

Solomon's entry into smuggling began modestly, with small, unremarkable flights that seemed almost routine. The cash came in regularly, easing his financial burdens and allowing him to stay afloat. But what started as a series of small jobs gradually escalated as Solomon's involvement deepened. The stakes grew higher, and what were once minor runs turned into significant, high-risk operations. As Solomon's role expanded, so did the scope of his work. No longer just an occasional pilot, he became a top dog in the smuggling network, coordinating frequent and crucial flights. The easy money and the allure of quick fixes entangled him further, pulling him away from his original goal of a legitimate commercial flying career, like his father the captain. However, he still held onto the bitterness that his father was an absent parent.

The more successful Solomon became in the world of smuggling, the more tangled the web grew. The complexity of his operations increased, making each job more intricate and demanding. With each success, the notion of breaking free seemed more remote. The initial justifications he had clung to slowly eroded, overshadowed by the seductive pull of fast money. The dream of piloting a commercial aircraft became distant, drowned out by the relentless pressure and temptation of the illicit trade. Solomon had always heard the saying, "Forbidden apples are always sweet," and it rang true in his life. The thrill of engaging in smuggling, despite his legitimate career in aviation, held a forbidden allure that was difficult to resist. The financial rewards and the adrenaline rush from his underground operations seemed to make the risk worthwhile, no matter how many times he told himself he would stop. The dark nature of his side jobs for Mendes, hidden from the world and even his closest colleagues, added an intoxicating sweetness to the danger, making it more tempting to continue.

By the time Solomon finally secured a position in commercial aviation, his life had already been marred by his involvement in smuggling. He had hoped that the stability of a commercial flying job would help him leave his illegal activities behind. However, despite his new role, the allure of quick money proved too strong. Also, it had become all too familiar to quit.

In the early hours of the morning and sometimes during the brief gaps between his scheduled flights, Solomon would still find time to carry out scheduled jobs for Mendes. These runs were carefully timed to avoid detection, often involving brief, secretive stops in remote airstrips or quick handoffs in obscure locations. His dual life became a balancing act, with the polished uniform of a commercial pilot masking the underworld dealings he continued to engage in.

Solomon would sometimes find himself in a frantic scramble, swapping his pilot's uniform for more subtle clothes to conduct these side jobs. The tension of managing both worlds was proving difficult, especially with his wife asking many questions. He had to be meticulous, making sure that his smuggling activities remained hidden from his colleagues and passengers, all while trying to uphold the image of a professional aviator.

Despite the growing risks and the demands of his legitimate career, the small but steady income from Mendes's jobs provided a tempting financial cushion. Solomon became increasingly entangled, his smuggling operations becoming a persistent shadow behind his commercial success. The conflict between his ambitions and his illicit entanglements continued to complicate his life, leaving him caught in a sticky situation of secrecy and deception. He would come home late, carrying the faint, lingering smell of jet fuel mixed with something more sinister, only to shower and try to erase the signs of his double life. On weekends, he would put on a bright smile, playing the devoted husband to his wife, Lunela, while his mind was seemingly preoccupied with logistics of his next flight or the pressure of avoiding detection. He hid the telltale signs of his dark activities behind a carefully crafted mask of married life, believing that his secret would remain safe as long as he played the role convincingly.

However, the burden of his deception grew heavier with time. His wife became too clever and noticed inconsistencies—unexplained absences, sudden changes in his mood, and odd financial fluctuations. Her suspicions grew with each passing day, culminating in a devastating discovery one afternoon. As she cleaned out the garage, her hand brushed against a hidden compartment behind a stack of old boxes. There, she found a stash of cocaine, the evidence glaring and undeniable. The sight of it was a cruel twist of fate; it shattered her trust and turned Solomon's carefully maintained disguise into utter chaos. She was tempted to phone him, but she resisted the urge.

The shock of the revelation left her weeping, her tears mingling with the bitter realisation that the betrayal went beyond mere infidelity. She wished, in her heartache, that the truth had been about a side affair, something less dangerous than the criminal activities she now faced. The discovery broke all her energy for cleaning, and she slumped to the garage floor sobbing. It was unbearable, a painful betrayal that cut deeper than any ordinary deceit. Was he taking these drugs? Was he a dealer? When did he start? Above all, why? She provided him with everything expected of a wife and as for money, they were solid.

When Solomon returned in the evening, she confronted him. In a desperate attempt to salvage his crumbling life, Solomon approached her with a mix of charm and coercion. He sat down beside her, his voice low, pleading with her to see things his way. After coaxing her for a while he ended up saying, "If you report this," he said softly, "you'll be caught up in it too. You'd be seen as an accomplice, and your life would be ruined along with mine."

His words, a blend of desperation and manipulation, offered her a grim choice. Faced with the prospect of becoming entangled in legal consequences and the glaring reality of her husband's criminal persona, she was trapped between her own moral outrage and the fear of the repercussions of exposing the truth. Solomon's plea, laden with the promise of shared downfall, left her grappling with the impossible decision of whether to protect herself or to confront the betrayal head-on. A secret she kept for more than five years.

Fast forward to the present, Solomon found himself in the midst of a contentious divorce. His wife, fully armed with the knowledge of his smuggling operations and deeply hurt by the betrayal of her high school sweetheart, was determined to exact revenge. During their heated arguments, she threatened to expose everything she knew. Solomon's attempts to salvage the situation were futile as she made it clear she would fight him on every front. Back then, Lunela had wished Solomon had merely cheated on her instead of getting involved in drug trafficking. But now, as he was leaving her for another man, that wish was hard to swallow.

The once-secluded corner of his life now threatened to unravel publicly. Solomon's possession of cocaine had already brought him under scrutiny, with the legal system suspending a jail term. Yet smuggling remained uncharted waters, its exposure a ticking time bomb in his divorce proceedings. His wife's anger, fueled by a mix of personal betrayal and a desire for justice, troubled him, casting a long shadow on his hopes for a clean break with his lover, Mark. Moreover, news of the twins was a chapter Solomon wasn't ready to face, especially with Lunela threatening to go on a warpath against him.

Chapter 18

Thandeka woke up to find a sinister and disturbing post on social media. The post, made from an anonymous account, accused her and her husband, Liam, of being involved in illegal activities and suggests they are complicit with drug dealers. The post included photoshopped images and misleading information. She quickly ran to the kitchen where Liam was making tea. "This post is clearly an attempt to discredit us. But who would do this?" She showed the post to Liam, who frowned.

He added, "Indeed, this looks like a deliberate attempt to smear us. We need to track down the source and counteract this misinformation. I will get my guys onto it."

By midday, the social media post had gone viral, causing a backlash in the community. People started questioning Thandeka and Liam's integrity, and there were heated discussions online about their involvement in drug trafficking. One post read, "I heard Thandeka and Liam are involved with drug dealers! This is outrageous. We need to distance ourselves from them!"

Thandeka shook her head as she followed the thread. "This is going out of control. People are turning against us based on these false accusations."

Her husband collaborated with his tech-savvy friends to gather evidence on the social media account and its possible connections to the drug traffickers. They proposed to trace the IP address and find out who was behind the account. Despite their efforts to ignore the posts, the anonymous account posted new, more convincing evidence suggesting Liam's involvement in the drug trade, further complicating their situation. Liam closed his eyes and took a deep sigh, "They've just posted something new. It's more convincing this time. It's like they're one step ahead of us. They even have witnesses from our neighbourhood. We need to find out how they're getting this information and stop them before it ruins everything we've worked for."

Thandeka and Liam decided to go live on Facebook to address the public. They prepared to discuss the threats they had faced, the false accusations levied against them, and their ongoing efforts to combat drug abuse, a cause particularly close to Thandeka's heart as a dedicated social worker. Thandeka began the live feed starting with the usual warm greetings then continued, "Thank you all for joining us. We want to address the recent accusations and share the truth about what's been happening," she said, her tone earnest.

Liam joined her, nodding. "We've been targeted by those trying to discredit our work. We want to clear our names."

As the broadcast rolled, they received supportive comments from viewers. However, one viewer commented, "Liam is a threat to Thandeka! He's the one behind the threats!"

The shocking comment quickly garnered attention securing many likes and replies. The chat exploded with questions about Liam's credibility, and soon the live feed was flooded with hostile messages and threats. Thandeka's mouth fell open in shock, her eyes widening as she read more vile comments. "This is not what we intended. We're here to clear our names, not to be attacked," she said, her voice trembling.

Liam, trying to keep his composure, interjected, "We're dealing with a lot of misinformation. Let's focus on presenting the facts."

Despite their efforts to steer the conversation back to their intended message, the chat overflowed with accusations and threats, drowning out their attempts to respond. As the live stream spiralled out of control, Liam shut it off. He pulled Thandeka into a comforting hug as she began to cry, her face buried in his shoulder. Liam held her tightly, both ruffled by the situation.

The new post they were trying to counter featured manipulated photos and false videos, increasing the pressure on Thandeka and Liam as they struggled to counteract the escalating smear campaign. In the face of these developments, Thandeka suspended the support group sessions, and also her employer gave her some days off, knowing how difficult it was for her.

Lunela also saw those vile posts in the Zimbabweans in the UK Facebook group. She instantly searched for flights. Her friend Thandeka needed her. Their bond had weathered many storms long before Lunela moved to South Africa with her family, and despite the distance, they remained in touch. Lunela had kept the details of her pending divorce private, not sharing them with any of her friends. However, seeing the recent attacks on Thandeka, a dedicated social worker, stirred a deep sense of urgency within her. Lunela felt compelled to step in and offer her support.

Lunela left for Zimbabwe without mentioning her departure to her soon-to-be former in-laws. When she arrived at Thandeka's house, her friend was genuinely surprised to hear Lunela's voice on the phone, announcing her unexpected arrival in the country two days later. When she arrived at Thandeka's house, her friend jumped with excitement over the surprise visit. She greeted Lunela with a warm embrace, leading her into the living room where they settled into comfortable chairs. The conversation quickly turned serious as Lunela expressed her concerns.

"I've been following everything that's been happening," Lunela continued, her voice filled with worry. "I fear for your peace of mind and your mental health. You've been through so much lately, and you deserve a break."

Thandeka listened intently, her eyes reflecting both surprise and gratitude. Lunela continued, "I want to take you on a holiday—just get away for a while. It doesn't matter where we go, as long as it's somewhere relaxing. What do you think?"

Thandeka hesitated, aware that her husband's approval would be needed for any trip, even though he was currently away on business. Lunela, sensing her friend's hesitation, quickly added, "I know you need his permission, but if he says no, we'll find a way out. Your well-being is what matters most right now."

The sincerity in Lunela's voice and her insistence on prioritising Thandeka's mental health provided a sense of relief and a ray of hope for Thandeka, who was in desperate need of a break.

As dawn broke over Harare, Lunela and Thandeka set out on their journey, their four-wheel drive packed and ready for a well-deserved break. The city's skyline gradually faded as they ventured further southeast on Masvingo Road, the landscape shifting to sparse fields and occasional clusters of trees. Excitement filled the air, especially for the two friends, who had not visited this part of Zimbabwe since their primary school days. Their destination was Gonarezhou National Park, located in the Chiredzi area of Masvingo Province, a park renowned for its spectacular landscapes and rich wildlife.

Gonarezhou, meaning "the place of elephants," is a vast sanctuary spanning over 5,000 square kilometres, known for its impressive elephant herds. It is the country's second-largest national park, after Hwange National Park. Gonarezhou's network of roads and trails leads visitors through diverse landscapes, including dense mopane woodlands, sweeping savannahs, and dramatic geological formations like the Chilojo Cliffs and Chilo Gorge, where the ladies were headed to. The Save River meanders through the park, adding to its natural beauty and providing vital water sources for wildlife. Adding to Gonarezhou's charm is its role in the Great Limpopo Transfrontier Park, a collaborative conservation area that extends across Zimbabwe, South Africa, and Mozambique. This transfrontier park aims to protect and connect ecosystems, allowing wildlife to roam freely across borders. The Runde River, another significant waterway in the park, complements the Save River, further enhancing the park's diverse habitats and supporting its rich biodiversity. On its solitary journey, the Runde River weaves through Gonarezhou, and at the park's edge, it converges with the Save River. This confluence occurs near the southeastern border of Zimbabwe, where the Runde River merges with the larger Save River. This union creates a more powerful stream that flows southward into Mozambique and eventually reaches the Indian Ocean. For Lunela and Thandeka, this natural merging of rivers mirrored their emotional journey. Just as the rivers combined their flows, their shared yet unspoken sorrows and hopes merged along their path. The confluence of the Save and Runde Rivers resembled an important sign of connection and unity, a sense of freedom and renewal.

Their first main stop was in Chivhu, a lively town that buzzed with energy, serving the busy Harare-Beitbridge road—a gateway to neighbouring South Africa, where many youths had sought greener pastures. The ladies took a brief break to explore the stalls, enjoying the colourful displays of fresh fruits. The warmth and friendliness of the vendors provided a cheerful start to their journey, and they picked up some snacks for the road. Continuing on, they passed through Mvuma, a peaceful settlement surrounded by rolling hills and expansive farmlands. The town was serene, except at the main bus station, where touts and buses were active as they loaded passengers heading to South Africa or Harare. The drive was smooth, and the women admired the gradual transformation of the scenery as they continued toward their next stop. They were also pleased by the absence of police on the roads. For Thandeka, who was used to their frequent presence, it was a welcome change. However, for Lunela, who was not accustomed to such regular checkpoints, the quiet roads were just pleasant. Police checkpoints, intended to ensure road safety and check for drugs and dangerous weapons, often irritated both passengers and drivers. Many argued that police should focus on fighting crime within communities rather than disrupting travellers on busy highways.

As they approached Masvingo, with the flat plains giving way to more varied terrain, their journey drew to a close. Masvingo, known for its historical significance and proximity to the Great Zimbabwe ruins, marked an important town. They stopped for a meal at a fast-food restaurant. Refreshed and ready, they continued their trip with a mix of nostalgia and excitement, eager to revisit a place they hadn't seen since their primary school days and anticipating their arrival at their destination.

Leaving Masvingo, they headed towards Chiredzi, known for its massive sugar plantations. Lunela craved sugarcane, a local delicacy she missed from her time in the UK, but found no available on the streets. This puzzled her, but she soon learned that local regulations and enforcement prohibited the sale of sugarcane outside the plantations. However, only one man sold them in the boot of his car. They took a break while Lunela enjoyed her sugarcane, though the force with which she bit into it shocked her friend.

"Hey, Luny, be careful. You might hurt your mouth! If I didn't know you better, I'd think you're taking out your frustration on that poor plant. But you're not angry, right?"

Lunela hissed, "Solomon," and quickly added, "Of course I'm not angry. I just miss sugarcane so much."

After lunch, they resumed their journey. Continuing eastward, they turned off at the 25km peg before Chisumbanje, taking a sharp right onto a rugged, unpaved track. At this point, their GPS was of little help as they encountered two identical tracks branching off. Seeking advice from a friendly Shangwe man they met along the way, they appreciated his offer to jump in and guide them but politely declined. The man's guidance on handling the rough terrain was invaluable as the two ladies travelled through the rough stretch. As they approached their destination, the road became more demanding with deep ruts, loose gravel, and rocky outcrops. The vehicle's robust capabilities were put to the test with each jolt and bump, and smaller cars would have struggled on this treacherous route. The women drove cautiously, their four-wheel drive handling the bumps with ease.

At one point, they stopped to stretch their legs and take in the scenery. The vast expanse of the bushland highlighted the remoteness of their journey. They enjoyed some drinks, savouring the snacks they had bought earlier while taking in the tranquility of their surroundings. Thandeka kept glancing at her phone, but her friend nudged her elbow coupled with a disapproving look, reminding her why they were on this trip. She might meet some demoralising social media comments and the whole point of being away in nature was to break free from trolls and reboot. Thandeka laughed at herself and obliged.

As they neared their destination, the arid beauty of the surrounding bushveld gradually gave way to the breathtaking vistas of Chilojo Cliffs and Chilo Gorge. The cliffs were a series of beautiful, red sandstone formations. Bathed in the golden light of the setting sun, the cliffs rose majestically, their rock faces glowing in shades of red and orange. The journey had tested both their endurance and the capabilities of their Jeep Wrangler, but the stunning beauty of Chilojo Cliffs and Chilo Gorge made every bump and jolt worthwhile. The Save River meandered gracefully through the base of the gorge, its surface shimmering like a ribbon of liquid silver. Upon arriving at the safari lodge where they would be staying for the holiday, they were welcomed with warmth, and even the hippos down in the Save seemed to bellow a cheerful welcome.

Both Thandeka and Lunela gasped in awe. The breeze, crisp and invigorating, filled their senses, a welcome relief from the occasional smoky wafts that drifted from the piles of rubbish near the main bus stations in Harare's busy CBD. Thandeka hugged her friend, sighed, and whispered, "This place is incredible. I can't believe how beautiful it is." She squeezed her friend harder and added, "Just what I needed! Thank you. Luny"

They settled in their shared chalet and then went to the main lounge area. They spent the rest of their days exploring the Chilo Gorge, a deep and tranquil valley carved by the Save River. The gorge offered a serene distinction to the towering cliffs, with its lush vegetation and the gentle murmur of the river flowing through it. The cool, shaded paths along the gorge provided protection from the heat, while the occasional sighting of wildlife such as impalas and various bird species added to the allure of the gorge.

The local Shangwe and Shangani people, who inhabited the area, welcomed them with warm smiles and open hearts. Lunela and Thandeka were immersed in the rich culture and traditions of these communities. They witnessed traditional dances performed by the Shangwe, characterised by rhythmic drumbeats and energetic movements that told stories of their ancestors and daily life. The Shangani people, known for their intricate beadwork and colourful attire, shared their crafts and stories at the village's growth point, providing insights into their rich heritage.

At the lodge, the ladies spent evenings around a campfire, where they enjoyed traditional meals prepared by talented chefs, with dishes made from local ingredients.

Nights were quiet and peaceful, with the star-studded sky providing a perfect backdrop to their reflections and conversations. Indeed, the Shangwe and Shangani people seemed content and relatively unaffected by the influence of most social media platforms something which the two women admired and discussed at length.

The trip to Chilojo Cliffs and Chilo Gorge was more than just a four-day getaway; it was a chance for Lunela and Thandeka to reconnect with nature and with each other, away from hurtful social media. Their phones were in airplane mode, allowing them to immerse themselves fully in the experience, while only using them to take photos. Lunela understood deep down why she wanted to avoid contact with those she left in the UK. The stunning scenery, combined with the warmth of local people and their traditions, offered a healing escape from their worries.

One late afternoon, Lunela tried to open up about her divorce. Her voice trembled as she spoke, but her words trailed off. Her eyes drifted across the shimmering expanse of the Save River, lost in its flow. She glanced at Thandeka, who looked back with a mix of concern and curiosity. Just then, the sight of hippos wallowing in the river drew their attention. The massive, lumbering creatures broke through the tension, their playful behaviour providing a perfect diversion and lifting their spirits. The two friends watched in silence as the hippos splashed and frolicked, the conversation about Lunela's troubles momentarily set aside. At that moment, surrounded by the raw beauty of the landscape and the radiant life of the river, they found comfort and connection. As they stood on the edge of the Chilojo Cliffs, the sheer drop and sweeping views of the gorge below brought a sense of wonder and peace. The sun painted the sky in shades of orange and pink, casting long shadows over the rugged formations and the lush greenery below. It was also a much-needed break for Lunela, whose eyes carried a mixture of exhaustion and joy.

As they prepared to drive off, she took a deep breath, her fingers grazing her belly tracing the outline of the twins growing within. With a mixture of relief and excitement, she turned to her friend, her voice shaking with joy as she shared the news. The ecstatic sparkle in her eyes contrasted with the fatigue she tried to mask, a reflection of her ongoing divorce still in its infancy, with both parties struggling to find common ground.

Chapter 19

In ten years, Thomas rose from a mere A-level school lever to a top gun, a maverick in the business world. His acumen was compared to those who start with just one tomato and build thriving farms. Thomas had a knack for sweet-talking people. It was said he could even persuade them to sell him their shoes for peanuts, only to resell them at double the original price. His arrest sent shockwaves through the drug world, particularly in Harare. Even he seemed stunned, despite his usual unshakable confidence at the airport on that fateful day. Had someone set him up?

Thomas's arrest for cocaine possession set off a chain reaction that swiftly untangled his carefully knit world, setting off a domino effect. His first two weeks in a British jail were a whirlwind of harsh realities. The transition from his luxurious office to the cold, echoing confines of a prison cell was abrupt. Thomas, once accustomed to luxury, now faced the relentless clamour of cell doors slamming and the ceaseless shuffle of feet on concrete. The dust and emptiness of the cell contrasted sharply with the sleek surfaces and polished floors he was used to. His attempts to adapt were almost futile as he followed the prison's rigid schedule with a focus that betrayed his discomfort.

Back in the world he had left, the impact of Thomas's absence was immediate and severe. Phone lines buzzed with frantic calls which his office team struggled to manage. His wife tried to take charge but experienced crucial information gaps. This is when she realised how little she knew about her husband's business empire. She had enjoyed the luxuries of plush holidays and fancy luncheons from Milan to Monaco, and that had been her world. Running her small bouquet salon in Sandton, Johannesburg, had been enough for her. Now, she faced a moral dilemma: attending the Super Bowl while her husband was incarcerated or prioritising her children's Disneyland adventure. France Disneyland was a cheaper option so that was feasible, she would talk to him.

In that short time, it became clear that Thomas's business was not what it seemed. Despite their dedication, his team, working late into the night under the harsh glow of fluorescent lights, there was an unsettling realisation that the empire they had supported might have been a façade for something far more sinister. His team huddled around a cluttered table, their faces long and weary as they grappled with stalled projects and unanswered emails. The once-efficient business was grinding to a halt, well figuratively. Meetings that would have been smooth and decisive now dragged on, filled with uncertainty and gloom. His trusted aides darted through the maze of office cubicles, clutching urgent memos and making calls. One of them wiped the sweat from his brow as he fielded an angry client on the phone, his face flushed with frustration. Meanwhile, another key team member sifted through a stack of documents with increasing desperation, trying to salvage deals that were slipping through their fingers.

In his prison cell, Thomas's connection with the outside world came through planned visits and brief phone calls with his legal team. He hunched over a small metal table, scribbling notes. Despite the muffled tones of his voice, his focus and determination were clear. Regardless of the temporary chaos, his team's morale remained steadfast. Late into the night, the office was bathed in the glow of fluorescent lights as they pored over spreadsheets and drafted emergency plans. The clatter of keyboards and hushed conversations filled the air.

As Thomas's legal battle continued, he could only hope that his team's resilience would tide them over. The first two weeks had been a blur of adaptation and crisis management, but Thomas was determined to get through the storm and restore his business operations to stability. A key aspect of his business was the Harare chapter, where operations had to continue on the streets. Sabotage.

Thomas's initial confusion in the British jail was soon overshadowed by a gnawing suspicion that he might have been set up. The cocaine found in his suitcase, packed by him, raised troubling questions. In his cell, Thomas paced murmuring about the day he had packed his suitcase. He whispered about how the meticulously chosen suits and the carefully arranged documents were, but he couldn't recall packing any illegal substances. The discovery of the cocaine, hidden in his peanut butter jars, seemed too orchestrated to be accidental. His friend had handed him some bottles but he wasn't a man with ulterior motives. Each day in jail, his growing unease was compounded by a persistent feeling that he had been set up. He had cocaine stashed in his house, but on this trip, he hadn't packed any.

***

After a few days away on a rejuvenating holiday in Zimbabwe with her friend Thandeka, Lunela returned to her new apartment, brimming with renewed energy and a fiery vindictive streak. Witnessing the hippos in the Save River wrestle for dominance ignited something within her. Those were the same hippos that crooned to attract mates, reminding her of the raw strength she needed to confront her challenges. The vibrant experiences of her trip left her supercharged and ready to deal with the chaos that awaited her in London.

Solomon, his patience wearing thin, knocked on the door of her new place. When Lunela opened the door, her eyes narrowed, and her lips tightened into a thin line. The surprise on her face shifted to clear irritation. Before she could muster a response, Solomon barged in, his frustration boiling over. He bellowed, his voice loud and grating. "How could you travel that far while pregnant without even telling me?"

Lunela's eyes blazed as she said, "You think you can control me? I needed this time away to clear my head and be there for my friend!" Her words came out in quick, harsh bursts.

Solomon's face hardened. "What friend? You went for yourself. Selfish woman. I've known you long enough to see through your fake sincerity. Come on, I'm taking you to the doctor now."

At that moment, Lunela lost it and pushed him. Solomon staggered but kept his footing. As Lunela tried to regain her balance, her hands lost their grip on his fancy jacket—a black, luxurious piece of cashmere that slipped through her fingers. The jacket fluttered to the floor, its smooth fabric and detailed stitching now rumpled. Lunela, her frustration reaching a tipping point, clenched her fist and punched him with all her might. The force of her blow landed squarely, but as she tried to pull back, she stumbled and fell hard, hitting the floor with a painful thud.

Her half-sister arrived just in time to witness the turmoil. Seeing Lunela unresponsive on the ground, her face pale and her eyes glazed over, she panicked. "Lunela!" She rushed to her side.

Solomon's anger shifted to panic. He grabbed his phone, his hands trembling, and called an ambulance. The urgency in his voice revealed his worry as he described the situation to the operator. Meanwhile, Emily performed first aid and placed her in the recovery position.

Solomon tried calling his parents, but his attempts went unanswered. The paramedics arrived within ten minutes, their flashing lights casting a strobe-like glow through the windows. They assessed Lunela, who lay motionless, and gently lifted her onto a stretcher with practiced precision.

Emily jumped into the ambulance, her eyes sparkling as she winked and said in a sultry voice, "You always look good in black." Perturbed, Solomon scratched his eyebrow and threw one glance at Emily then his wife lying helpless on the stretcher. As the ambulance doors closed, he hurried to his car and sped off to follow it.

Chapter 20

Nancy Blue, a name that was once revered and respected in the drug trading business had faded. The streets were hers. The latest arrest of Thomas had many whispering that the once powerful girl was down and out. It didn't require a seer to fathom that Nancy was finished. Her life took a dramatic turn, she struggled to pay her rentals, however, she borrowed money from friends to get by. At some point, her friends got tired, and the landlord who once bragged about her being the best tenant ever also became annoyed and sent letters of eviction.

The streets are brutal, it's like the animal world. One moment you are the king of the jungle roaring like a lion with all the animals shaking with fear, fleeing in different directions. As king of the jungle marking its territory with urine to secure it, promising to deliver death to those who trespass, be it fellow lions or any predator who dares to hunt in his territory. But any sign of weakness will have fellow pride males challenge you to a brutal fight that delivers fatal wounds. Painted dogs will follow you, with hyenas following from a safe distance in their limping walking style.

To those not familiar with Nancy Blue, she was a quiet pleasant woman who resembled a kind woman, decent, demure, soft and feminine. But as they say, looks can be deceiving. She could act and make a good show. But that did not matter. She watched helplessly as her world fell apart. Friends deserted her, relatives who had benefitted from her vast sources of income had slowed down communication with her, many accusing her of having practiced witchcraft that was now backfiring.

Nancy sat in a large dingy room at her aunt's plot in Darwendale. This room had been used as a storeroom but after the land reform program, her aunt never managed to bring the farm to its former glory. So many facilities were abandoned or rather, left to waste away. Nancy was now lonely. Nobody looked for her and she lost her appetite. She was in denial and possibly in depression. She had contemplated committing suicide but there was a small voice, a voice of reason, a voice that kept asking her to fight on and overcome. Yet the more her inner voice spoke the more the overriding and loud voice spoke and demanded her to take immediate action and end her life. She battled with those thoughts and her voice became a battleground.

One morning, she had had enough voices. She took a rope that was oinked and used to tie cattle, made a collapsible fold through the rope over the wooden beam. She took a piece of paper to write all her wishes before dying but when she could not find a pen, she proceeded with her plan. She took bricks and started making a stepped heap. Each time she tested if there was enough height to hang herself. When she finally satisfied herself, she found some joy and comfort that at last all her misery, pain and agony were about to end.

While she was on the platform, she staggered, collapsing hard from a two metre high platform. At that point, her phone rang. She ignored it but the caller kept phoning. When the phone beeped signalling low battery she jumped, grabbing the phone with both hands. The voice was firm, it was a voice she remembered even in her distress.

"Nancy, where are you my dear? Is that Nancy Blue?" The caller went on.

Nancy was caught unaware and as she walked to the door, her phone went off. There was only one person who called her by that name in a conversation. Many knew her as such but decided to just stick to, "Boss".

Right at the door, a team of heavily armed police officers waited for her. She was arrested but not cuffed upon sight and immediately whisked away. She was in a third of the six convoy cars. The convoy spade off reaching top speeds of up to 180 km/h. They connected to Chinhoyi Road speeding to the toll gate, filtering through a priority way narrowly missing the gatekeeper.

They drove for 50km and turned into a farm. At that point Nancy was worried yet being a drug peddler, she knew that there was a high chance she was not under any arrest. She didn't fear being arrested but revenge from small groups that she had kicked out of business during her time when she was the bugger boss in the streets.

The farmhouse was an imposing feature that could be seen from a distance, though one needed to go through fields of wheat. Whoever was farming there was serious with their business pursuits. But it was not a day to admire farming. Nancy looked around and made mental notes of the place she was being taken to. The cars parked at the back of the farmhouse confirmed her worst nightmare. She spotted Felix from a distance.

"Look who is here!" Felix shouted and stood up to give a standing ovation and bowed down to her in a sarcastic chivalry. Nancy stood at the centre of the back yard and scanned her surroundings, then looked back at Felix. She walked straight to him and without hesitation, confronted him.

"What do you want little man?" She demanded fists clenched and arms crossed. She spread her legs and raised her head looking Felix in the eyes in an act of defiance.

Felix was shaking. He stood up and started walking around Nancy Blue but she was not having any of that. As soon as Felix started circling her, she grabbed him with all the power that remained in her and he came falling to the ground like a giant tree.

Two men came running to Felix to lift him up. He studied himself and tried punching Nancy but she saw it coming. She avoided the punch and Felix staggered and almost fell when Nancy held him up.

"Felix, you disappoint me. You are still as weak, that's why with all that assistance you could not run a business, and you are a disgrace to society." Nancy scorned Felix.

Out of the gazebo emerged Thomas a man who had been imprisoned in the United Kingdom, or shall we say a man who had stage-managed his arrest and did it right in front of his wife and children. He made the scene believable. Thomas was after the drug lord of North America. He wanted his blessing before he died.

Franscico Luveira was a new king in North America and he controlled the world of drugs from his cell. The only way to see him was to physically be in the same prison where he was. He was left with a few years but it was rumoured that his health was fast deteriorating hence Thomas was rushing against time. He wanted to be the biggest distributor in

Africa, hence, he needed the greatest distributor to be on his supply side. Before his release, there was a trial that was televised, and the verdict was that Thomas was a great man who fell victim to drug traffickers who manipulate innocent people. The court found that Thomas' life as an evangelist and children's rights work was a clear testimony that he was framed. The five judges sitting on the bench all agreed to acquit Thomas.

Thomas stood up at the entrance of the gazebo and gestured for Nancy Blue to join him to there. So, it was Nancy Blue who was back with a bang. Word swelled that Nancy Blue was back. The following morning there was a clash, a turf war. Nancy showed no weakness yet from the depth of despair she rose to be queen of the streets, not only that, but the supply chain manager for Africa. The flying games were about to begin.

Chapter 21

Solomon was passing up and down, he was considering all the options on the table to dissuade Lunela yet he held the key to saving his life and the legacy of his family. Solomon had discussed with Richard his lawyer three times seeking to find confirmation and reaching a less harmful way to deal with the threats that Lunela made. Had it not been for the pregnancy, Solomon would have ordered a hit on Lunela without thinking twice. Solomon had a powerful enemy in the form of a very beautiful woman that he cherished and in the same stroke the woman was carrying his bundles of joy even though he hated Lunela, he admitted that keeping her safe had become his number one priority.

A few weeks back, Jennifer had a conversation with Solomon regarding the stance taken by Lunela. She hoped that Solomon would show some signs of weakness and agree to the termination of Lunela. Jennifer had sold an idea that a surrogate mother be found and once confirmed pregnant, Lunela would be terminated. Solomon loved the idea of another child but rejected the idea of killing his unborn children.

Lunela called Thandeka and asked her to come over to the UK and be with her for some time. Thandeka was pleased to come over, but the idea was thwarted by Jennifer who did not like too many strangers close to her daughter-in-law. As expected, Lunela managed to bring Thandeka against Jennifer's wish and in the end, it was a stalemate with no clear winner. In the end, Emily and Thandeka were by her side, and this became a strong support system for Lunela.

Jennifer resolved to follow her husband to Australia and talk him into eliminating Lunela at all costs.

Chapter 22

Nancy Blue established a junior policy. She wanted to introduce drugs at an early age to avoid overdose which is normally associated with latecomers who often die by overdose or commit suicide. Her doctrine was seen as more profitable as she wanted her clients across Africa to take drugs as a way of coping and not self-destruction. She funded an NGO operating in all the African countries preaching a message of hope that children who learn to take drugs in moderation have a higher chance of survival and can achieve their life goals. Over time, this doctrine was seen as a practical alternative. Debates were done and experts from learning institutions agreed that preaching abstinence from drugs was no longer effective but moderated taking of drugs was a better way to proceed. Popular musicians were brought in to make appealing commercials and these received wide coverage on all social media channels. Initially, there was resistance but later acceptance increased of this method as the best way. Research papers were published and road shows were conducted and this propelled the market for drugs by three times in current markets of operation. With more than 60% of the population in Africa below 35 years, Nancy Blue's strategy was a stroke of genius.

It was a great afternoon at the Saint Gareth Arenas in a leafy suburb of Mount Pleasant in Harare, Zimbabwe. There were three former Group A schools and 16 private schools, eager to leave a mark in the sporting world in the history of mankind, competing in a game of rugby. It was however clear that players from private schools had all the right gear required for this elite sport while their counterparts from government schools were needy wearing uniforms that had seen better days. They were however in high spirits and moved with their heads high with the chin distinctively raised like a crocodile showing signs of submission to the dominant male. They looked slimmer, making them look like grasshoppers in the eyes of their bulky elite counterparts.

The event was colourful with about a dozen corporate sponsors displaying their teardrop banners creating a rainbow of colours flying freely letting the north-easterly wind blow them, showing their full-lengths, and displaying the various top brands with pride. Jacaranda trees, a genus of 49 species of flowering plants in the family Bignoniaceae, native to tropical and subtropical regions of the Americas, were not to be outdone. They bloomed wildly creating a purple hollow circle that attracted all who cared to see. Honeybees collected pollen and nectar as food for their entire colony, thus, pollinating plants in the process. Nectar stored within their stomachs was passed from one worker to the next until the water within it diminished. Humans have a great deal of learning to do from the bees when it comes to teamwork, diligence, and staying focused all the time.

There were small tables arranged in catchy styles with corporate wear and brochures displayed for all spectators. Some mounted television sets, while others had tablets running slideshows. The Saint Gareth Arena could host three games at a time and the games were being played over three days starting from Friday till Sunday.

In the game of rugby, there are 15 players on each team, comprising eight forwards (wearing jerseys numbered 1–8) and seven backs (numbered 9–15). In addition, there may be up to eight replacement players "on the bench," (numbered 16–23). Players are not restricted to a single position, although they generally specialise in one or two that suit their skills and body types. Players who play multiple positions are called "utility players."

The scrum (a contest used to restart play) must consist of eight players from each team: the "front row" (two props – a loosehead and tight head – and a hooker), the "second row" (two locks and two flankers), and a "back row" (a number 8). The players outside the scrum are called "the backs": scrumhalf, fly-half, inside the centre, outside centre, two wings, and a fullback.

Forwards compete for the ball in scrums and lineouts and are generally bigger and stronger than the backs. Props push in the scrums, while the hooker tries to secure the ball for their team by "hooking" it back with their foot. The hooker is also usually responsible for throwing the ball in at lineouts, where it is mostly competed for by the locks, who are generally the tallest players on the team. The flankers and number eight are expected to be the first players to arrive at a breakdown and play an important role in securing possession of the ball for their team.

The backs play behind the forwards and are usually more lightly built and faster. Successful backs are skillful at passing and kicking. Fullbacks need to be good defenders and kickers and have the ability to catch a kicked ball. The wingers are usually among the fastest players in a team, and score many of the tries. The centers' key attacking roles are to break through the defensive line and link successfully with wingers. The fly-half can be a good kicker and generally directs the back line. The scrumhalf retrieves the ball from the forwards and needs a quick and accurate pass to get the ball to the backs (often first to the fly-half).

Early names, such as "three-quarters" (for the wings and centers) and "outside-half" or simply "out-half" (for fly-half) are sometimes used in the Northern Hemisphere, while in New Zealand the fly-half and inside center are called "first five-eighth" and "second five-eighth" respectively, while the scrumhalf is known as the "half-back." The forwards are in the scrum while the backs are lined up across the field.

In international matches, eight substitutes can replace an on-field team-mate. The substitutes, numbered 16 to 23, can either take up the position of the player they replace or the on-field players can be shuffled to make room for this player in another position. Typically, the forwards among the substitutes will have lower numbers than the backs. There are no personal squad numbers and a versatile player's position and number may change from one game to the next. Players can also change positions during the match; common examples are the fly-half playing the full-back's position in defence or a prop taking the hooker's position at lineouts.

Different positions on the field suit certain skill sets and body types, generally leading to players specialising in a limited number of positions. Each position has certain roles to play although most have been established through convention rather than law. During general play, as long as they are not offside, the players may be positioned anywhere on the field. It is during the set pieces (scrum and line-out) that positions are enforced.

The first game was played in the J Hamilton fields, Northfields School vs Queensland College. Both teams put up a spirited fight but there were two injuries. One player suffered a strained thigh and the other a broken shoulder blade. There were four ambulances on standby and health insurance companies had covered all the injuries in a bid to sign more business.

In the end, Northfields conquered Queensland to top the group A, enhancing its chance of proceeding to the next level in a hair-raising encounter with a neck-to-neck score sheet in a nail-biting affair that left the rumbling game lovers thrilled from start to finish. The final score was Northfields 44, while Queensland garnered 42 at the blow of the whistle to cheers from the spectators. It was a tightly contested game that offered entertainment through and through.

The second game was Hilltop School vs Stonewall International School. Both schools clad colourful uniforms. Cheer leaders on both ends lined up purposefully. There was silence as Hilltop School entered the arena. It was as if there was something dramatic about to happen. Then he emerged, Hilltop School's Dregga Shungu aka DS the bad ass. He was a man chiseled out of a rock, a man of steel. He was in the category of Samson, King Saul, and Goliath himself. Perhaps these men could have felt jealous for not having an opportunity to partake in such a widely anticipated game with girls watching and having all the fantasies.

Dregga stepped onto the field to wild cries around the stadium. He was a towering eight feet tall. With a weight of 175/kgs, nothing could stand in his way, whatever stood in his way became the way. He was a beast and nobody would dare stand in his way when he was on the move or at least have a head to head encounter with him. The referees would address him while looking up. Ds was not violent he was always the one to break any fracas if any was about to start. Dregga's parents had separated when he was young and never had a chance to live in a normal family setup. All he knew was rugby. He attended only Math, Science, and English classes stressing that these were enough for him as he was destined to be a professional sportsman.

He was a team sport athlete, participating in relay. Dregga held the national record in javelin, and short put. He also had medals for rugby matches they won as a team. When his parents separated, each one took one of their three children but Dregga was disowned and eventually sent to boarding school at the age of six, literally being baby dumped. He was given his tuck money and all he needed and sent to school. No one called to check on him, nobody bothered to visit or check his progress. Poor Dregga had no visitation even on consultation. Transport would be arranged for him. Once back home, he would spend a few days at his mother's place where she made no effort to conceal the fact that she didn't like him but was merely being civil. She had remarried and had it not been for his stepfather, Dregga would not have had a chance to visit his mother's place.

His father had remarried and his step-mum liked him but his father distasted him. The father always beat him up for any silly mistake. He developed an interest in sport, especially rugby, land he did well in most, scooping gold yet no one came to cheer him up. To his disappointment, the rugby coach rejected him and suggested the marching band instead. Dregga attempted to engage his parents to talk to the school but that was a brick wall. His parents were ever busy. His father, a civil engineer, was always at work, while his mother was an advisor focusing on mergers acquisitions and private equity. After realising that reaching out to his parents yielded no fruitful results, Dregga reached out to one of his coaches for assistance. He only told him to buckle up and bulk each time he attended training, ensuring his body remained in top form for rugby.

Dregga approached schoolmates and that's how he was introduced to the world of drugs. At first, they took pills that helped to gain muscles and he would go to the gym to grow muscles. He began taking Creatine, protein supplements, weight gainers, Beta-Alanine, BCAAs, and HMB. The results were impressive and he informed the school of his new dietary requirements.

The school realising his potential to bring in more medals, decided to support him in his new quest. Dregga would take energy drinks before games, however over time he decided to up the game and started marijuana, graduated to cocaine, among other illicit drugs.

Dregga knew that the game at hand was a great one as some of the best teams in the world had come from the US, Australia, and the UK to scout for talent and everyone anticipated being selected. Three touchdowns in 10 minutes by half time, Hilltop School was leading by 45 to 12. In the second half, Dregga gathered his team and shouted, "Let's kill them."

It is common for such brutal talks in a game of rugby. For instance, the faceoff between longtime rivals South Africa and New Zeeland is equally intense and all team members from Hilltop School had the same understanding that it was a figure of speech. With three more touchdowns after halftime, Dregga was quite a sight to behold. In under three minutes, he was headed for another touchdown when an opponent blocked his way as he charged. They clashed and his opponent was thrown to the ground with such heavy force, while Dregga proceeded to make a touchdown. Samuel Nickson was still down when an ambulance picked him up and rushed him to the hospital. It was later learnt that he was in a critical condition. This time Dregga was on a defence line and caught a winger who was attempting to break away and threw him to the ground. The referee came to assess the situation and again another ambulance was called in. This time when the ambulance arrived at the hospital, they pronounced Thomas Jere as Brought in Dead (BID).

The game continued and this time Dregga ran across the fields and tackled a fullback who did not have the ball nor was he positioned to receive the ball. He was far from the action. The referee stopped the game and the opponent full back who went by the name Knox, had sustained injuries. Dregga's father who was in the stands enjoying the game stood in shock trying to ascertain what his son was doing. His first time to watch his son play and yet he made all the fouls possible. Was it intentional to spite him? Or was that his usual play? Dregga ran to the coach who had been encouraging him to bulk and punched him hard before he kicked a minor close by. He then jumped towards his father and grabbed him by the collar, throwing him to the ground.

Police were called to contain the situation, even they too battled to contain Dregga, and he was apprehended and handcuffed. Dregga became unconscious while being transported to the police station. Upon seeing this, the police made a U-turn and took him to the hospital instead.

At the New Hope Medical Centre, Dr Maharajat Mahamajat was in charge of Dregga. They ran several blood tests and other vital tests. They resuscitated him and admitted him into a general ward.

After some time, he woke up, took all his clothes off, and walked around the hospital. The security detail was called to help but he dispatched all of them singlehandedly. By the time a police reinforcement was called, he had already fled. Dregga, the rugby star, now roamed the streets of Harare causing quite a stir to passersby.

He went around the city verbally harassing vendors and overturning their stuff and throwing it in all directions. Police managed to cease him and brought him back to the hospital. Within four hours, the results came through and it was not the kind of results that anybody would expect. Dregga had lung cancer due to excessive smoking. His kidneys and liver also had problems. He was a dying man. The police investigating the case talked to a friend who confessed that Dregga had confided in him that he was dying. What a waste of talent.

The following morning news filtered through that Dregga had committed suicide by taking an overdose of cocaine. His colleagues had supplied him with the drug when they visited him in hospital. He left a note about how he longed to have been in a perfect family setup. He narrated that had he been in a solid family structure and support system, he would have made wise decisions and would never had to take drugs and other substances but it was too late for him. He asked for forgiveness from his father whom he was unaware whether he had lived or died from the incident at Saint Gareth.

The police, working on anonymous tipoffs from school children who were disturbed, arrested two rugby coaches who had full knowledge that their team was taking drugs and even encouraged them to do so. Three distributors who had arrangements with these school coaches were also apprehended. Apart from drugs, police picked some suppliers who were known by local school kids to be selling various goodies that contained drugs and these ranged from scones, queen cakes, sweets, and lollipops among others.

Chapter 23

Captain Smith was held up in Australia for four straight months, flying local routes due to a prevailing shortage of pilots in Australia. He occasionally flew to Japan, China and Singapore. He had planned to have Jennifer join him during travel breaks as he was not able to take long trips off, though time off was increasingly becoming difficult to get.

Jennifer was dressed in red with generous crimson makeup to go with the theme she had chosen for the night. Her dress had a line of glitters creating flashes of reflections. She wore her metallic gold stilettoes to compliment her Roberto Cavalli dress. She arrived at the Flower Drum located at Cantonese, 17 Market La, Melbourne. Approaching its 50th birthday, Flower Drum remains as essential as ever to its high-end clientele, a masterclass in trend-proofing through attention to detail, rightfully revered service, and subtle reinvention. The grand and meticulously maintained dining room always delivered a true sense of occasion, with its plush carpets and glinting lacquer details. So, too, the benchmark Peking duck featuring animal illustrations sketched in plum sauce, and the prawn har gow with pleated wrappers that serve as evidence of a benevolent deity. Yet Flower Drum is no museum piece. A (relatively) new bar has added excellent cocktails from all over the world, while co-owner and Chef

Lucy punctuates her blackboards with new classics. Fantastic spring rolls are filled with saltbush lamb brisket and gravy, while silken barramundi "noodles" are tossed with sausage, shiitakes, and tangerine. And the incredible quail-meat-coated Scotch egg, with its brittle-crisp outer crumb, has the power to haunt your dreams. Here's to another half-century.

The captain could not have chosen a better place for their dinner date. Though they had been married for more than 40 years, having a date with Jennifer was a new experience each time they met. For some reason, Jennifer was nervous as if meeting a guy for the first time. Her husband waited for her and he wore a black suit, white shirt, and a bowtie. His dress was simple but looked great on him. He could dress expensively when he chose to but for dinner with Jennifer, he always aimed for a simple look. He never liked elaborate dressing on such occasions as he considered them destructive and a barrier to connection.

He was restless and wanted to be the one to spot Jennifer first. However, nature called and just as he dashed to the convenience rooms, she arrived. Just as the captain was ringing the bell that signified the end of peeing, his phone vibrated, and he used his left free hand to answer it. He was disappointed that Jennifer had arrived while he was away. He always wanted to see Jennifer arrive. Her strut amused him.

On the phone, Jennifer's voice was soft and melodious as she asked about his whereabouts. He tucked it in and in the hit of the moment thought he was done, pulled up the zip trapping the delicate outer skin. He screamed with pain like a kindergartener who had bitten her tongue. It took him a few more minutes to collect himself.

When the captain emerged from the bathroom, Jennifer had been sat down by the waiters. She looked at the captain and remarked, "I don't regret flying 21 hours over the oceans at all. You look handsome and I missed you."

Jennifer held him by the waist leaning to the heart side of his chest. The captain looked down to check if none of the make-up and lipstick was ruining his white shirt as if he was accountable to someone else other than Jennifer.

The captain looked at Jennifer intently and he wanted to kiss her straight on the mouth but he controlled himself. Things were going to develop and he kissed her forehead instead. They ordered food and while waiting, ordered a bottle of red wine, aged for 18 years.

The captain signalled something to the waiters. In a few moments, the they brought 60-centimetre straight export-type flowers and handed them over to the captain who went beside Jennifer and proclaimed how much he loved her and gave her the bouquet. Their food came as they were catching up.

"How has it been here my love?" Jennifer enquired.

The question caught the captain off guard. He was aware that Jennifer was smart and had to find the real question being asked and anticipate a buildup of questions that could eventually be used to form an opinion that one would never have imagined was intended from the start.

So, the he decided to use his weapon that no woman could resist, charm. He looked at Jennifer straight into the eyes and reaching out, picked her hand, and in one motion, brought it to his mouth and kissed it, then he lowered it. The lowering of Jennifer's hand was so skillfully done while his eyes were still fixed on her. The captain whispered, "I love you, this place is hell without you around. No matter where I am, if you are not by my side, I am a miserable man."

Jennifer tried to resist the arrows of charm but he kept them coming till Jennifer gave up and opened up her heart to be taken over by his endless charm. The stare made Jennifer melt and the lawyer in her disappeared and she was a girl again, a defenseless girl with an open heart waiting for her man to come and take control and lead her. The captain, realising that his tricks were working, continued looking at her but it was now uncomfortable for both of them. Well, they were in love. Jennifer's hand was shaking.

"Honey, I am so horny please stop looking at me like that. You know you haven't touched me in a long time." Jennifer protested.

The captain was interrupted by waiters who brought their food. Jennifer had ordered cured salmon with prawns, pickled salad & dill lime crème fraiche for the starter while the captain ordered glazed chicken drumsticks for a starter. The waiters kept stepping forward to pour more wine for the two love birds. The main course was a burger for the Captain and a freshly prepared special pie. For dessert, Jennifer struggled to decide what to order from a wide range of choices. The waiter had previously worked for an English Country Club and in an instant, knew what to suggest to Jennifer since she was British.

Snuggled amidst the charming English countryside, The Grand Castle Country House is a delightful blend of bucolic charm and plush luxury, providing a placid escape from the active streets of London. Within this exquisite English manor, guests are greeted with a selection of generously appointed rooms, pampering holistic treatments, and a renowned restaurant led by the esteemed Chef Maxwell.

The inviting twin restaurant offers a delightful array of culinary delights, spanning from mouthwatering breakfasts to sumptuous dinners, all culminating in the talk of the town - Chef Lucy's extraordinary Chocolate Pudding creation at an eye-watering $35,000. Far beyond the ordinary Snack Pack or powdered jello packs, this divine chocolate pudding is a masterpiece crafted from four different exquisite Belgian chocolates, meticulously shaped into the form of a Fabergé egg. The velvety pudding is then lavishly layered with champagne jelly, adorned with a shimmering edible gold leaf, and served alongside a bottle of top-shelf champagne and caviar - a true indulgence for the senses. Other ingredients include 24-carat gold and a 2-carat diamond.

Due to the intricacies involved in its preparation, the jaw-dropping $35,000 chocolate pudding requires an advanced booking of at least two weeks, affording Chef Maxwell ample time to perfect this extraordinary creation. This culinary marvel has left guests awe-inspired and its exquisite taste has earned it a well-deserved place in the hearts and conversations of all who have experienced it. Chef Maxwell was Captain's friend, and arrangements were made in advance for Jennifer to taste it.

The Captain had ordered Grand Velas Tacos for $25,000. One of the most expensive dishes in the world. This taco features Kobe Beef, Almas Beluga Caviar & Black Truffle Brie Cheese and is served on a gold flake-infused corn tortilla. The taco is also served with an exotic salsa comprised of dried Morita chili peppers, Ley.925 ultra-premium añejo tequila, and topped with civet coffee beans. Costing a whopping US$ 25,000, the dish is available in Mexico at the new Grand Velas Los Cabos Resort's Frida restaurant but in recent times Melbourne introduced it as well.

After dinner, the captain asked Jennifer to dance. In the background, Luther Vandross could be heard signing his award-winning *"Dance with My Father Again. "*

"Thank you for coming here," the captain spoke holding Jennifer tightly close to him.

She looked at him almost resting her head on his chest. "I had to come and see if my boy wasn't injured in the playground."

They kept dancing and this time they started kissing and it went on and on till the captain decided that it was time to retreat somewhere else. He settled the bill and called in In Drive to take them home. The hotel was the Mighty Crown Towers Melbourne. A touch of class, the architecture was flawless, and the interior works were breathtaking. The rooms were at another but nobody paid attention to all the details. The captain grabbed Jennifer right after closing the door. He kissed her violently and with passion before lifting her up. She held him by the waist with her legs firmly gripping him while responding to his passionate kissing.

Chapter 24

Jennifer woke up at 6 am, completed her morning routine, and prepared breakfast for her husband who was still sleeping. She opened the window blinds letting sunlight into the room. The captain ducked the blinding early morning sun rising, grabbed two soft pillows, and placed his head under them in apparent protest to the forced early rise. Jennifer was getting frustrated and decided to play a game that no man could resist.

"Hey sweetie, if you wake up now, I will give you a full body massage in the afternoon and we will see what happens from there." Jennifer provocatively offered.

With one swift move, he threw away the pillows and sat upright rubbing his eyes. Jennifer looked at him with admiration of the power that this offer was having on him. Jennifer's mood immediately changed. She looked at him with a gaze that he had seen the last time he needed to explain something.

"Babe, we have a great family, and thanks to you for working so hard."

"Don't be silly babe we have all been working hard to sustain our family—" He interjected. She frowned at him making no attempt to hide her displeasure when it came to being interrupted while talking.

"You know I prefer completing my thinking process." Jennifer charged. The stare said it all. She had a serious matter to talk about. The captain must have misjudged that she was trying to continue with the previous night's romance.

The captain was the first to speak. After a prolonged silence. "Our son is in trouble, isn't he?"

Jennifer must have realised that the he was not amused with how she handled the interjection.

"Darling please do not insult my intellect. Don't act like you don't know what I am talking about." Jennifer fumed as she pointed an index finger to the captain.

He maintained his cool, not giving away his mood. Jennifer was crafty and never started an argument without gathering hard facts. That made it difficult if not impossible to discuss any matter when not prepared. Sometimes preparing did not make any difference at all. The captain on the other hand was a man of few words, a grand master at the game of chess. He was calculative, thinking about every answer he gave and never making a final and conclusive answer to cater for possibility of changing course should the discussion require such in the future. This is what exactly annoyed Jennifer and its was not easy for the two of them to fight fairly or to have a tough talk.

"Our son has been having many troubles ranging from non-functional marriage, low fertility issues, bitterness from lack of parenting care and abuse of drugs and the latest being gay." Jennifer was quiet as the he spoke. She must have been taking mental notes as she normally does when one is talking which explains why she never interjects when someone is speaking.

When she finally spoke, she was calm with a low tone which was neither defiant nor submissive. She reached out to her husband squeezing his hand as if seeking to release an answer from it. Jennifer closed her eyes and sobbed.

"I have tried all the options available but it's not working, I have tried talking to her but she has remained adamant that she wants to tell her story. Babe, you have to activate your contacts before this matter gets out of hand." Jennifer pleaded with him.

He was unsure what had happened as Jennifer who is normally strong-willed and put up a brave fight decided to go soft. Were his emotions been played with? Could she have realised that hard facts were going to delay the conversation and possibly lead to academic contestation at the expense of getting things done?

He stood up, lit a cigar, and looked over the window overlooking the city. He released puffs of smoke, he held the cigar skillfully while his left index finger pointed up, down and sideways as if to calculate the implications of an act, or shall we say actions of what he was about to do.

The captain picked up the phone and reached his longtime friend. After the phone rang three times, Jennifer signalled the captain to wait but the other person had answered by the time the he got the message. Jennifer wrote *"lost at birth"* and lifted the paper for him to see.

c"Long time my friend, I have a situation I need you—" the Captain was saying before a voice snapped on the other end.

"Skip the pleasantries and cut the soft soap man, what do you need you know I have your back."

Just after the other voice finished talking the captain responded almost immediately. "Operation "lost at birth" be just like old times."

He sighed and continued, "You know the way you handle both the underworld and the boring world amazes me.

"Had it not for your arrogance you could have been my right-hand man." The man on the other end added.

The captain was not in the mood for games. "Shut the hell up and stay on course," he charged.

"Easy, easy hey," the voice came almost instantly.

Chapter 25

The phone call came to Mike at 5 in the morning, and operation "lost at birth" was a go. All the foreign assets were activated. The captain had been asked to pay USD 390 000 for the operation in non-sequential bills. Derrick Warwick was the man put in charge of the operation. His instruction was to terminate at birth, save the twin children, and dissolve the mother.

By 10:00 a search had begun for Lunela, the operation was indeed delicate as it was to be timed. Two proposals had been put forward, one was to kidnap her, induce artificial labour pain trigger for early birth and neutralise the target at that point. There were many risks related to this approach. There was a possibility that Solomon was going to be held back by his emotional connection with Lunela and have a change of heart.

The second risk was that Solomon was going to suffer emotional trauma and possibly severe mental illness that could lead to suicidal tendencies and in the end the twins were going to have a slim chance of making it without both parents. Even if they pull through, there was need for daily parenting which needed a mother and a father. Even in the event of making it Solomon was going to be a loose end and Derrick was aware of it. The captain's phone rang and once answered, Derrick wasted no time, skipping all the pleasantries.

"Solomon has to stay out of this matter or he will be another loose end. He will expose everyone. He has to be away from her at the time it happens." Derrick demanded.

The captain's face dropped when he heard what Derrick was talking about. He was aware of the implications, a potential double loss of son and daughter-in-law if things were not planned and managed well. It was a difficult moment and the captain needed to show leadership. He weighed all the options that had been put on the table and was left confused and troubled.

"Give me 30 minutes, I will come back to you." The captain eventually spoke.

Jennifer was in the earshot. She walked straight to the him and demanded an explanation. The captain was not in a good mood. He simply walked away from her. "I am going to get some air, he spoke finally as he was approaching the door," he shouted.

The captain was out in the streets when he spotted what seemed to be suspicious movement. He stopped over at a corner restaurant. Ordered coffee. As he was paying for the coffee, a woman dressed in cargo pants sat right across him.

"You are more handsome in person than on the phone, it was wise of you to take a walk, we were going to come to the hotel room to discuss business with you." The woman remarked.

"I have been told of my handsomeness but I believe that's not the reason why you are here. Have you travelled from America leaving your three-year-old child with your half-mad mom?" The Captain said as he stirred his coffee. He pulled a photo of Elizabeth Montgomery and her entire family and brandished it in front of her without saying much.

"Elizabeth or whatever your name is, you thought you could come here and threaten me here? We are capable of reaching and destroying you at any time. There is no place you can hide. We do not take lightly those who come here showing off their shitty ass?"

"That was quite some speech captain, we coming to you in good faith but if we believe that our hospitality is not appreciated then we will have to act in a manner that gives what we want at whatever cost."

"We want your son to continue carrying the cargo for us and we believe that you have the trust of many authorities. Your trip to Zimbabwe presents us with a unique opportunity to carry our cargo. We believe you understand our position. Our reputation is that we never need to use force when dealing with our partners as this results in needless loss of precious life."

He looked at her and forced a smile which he immediately cut the moment it started. He looked at Elizabeth then looked aside. "What's your plan, I will not be responsible for carrying any drugs in my official bags. So, what's your plan?"

"Captain we are non-violent in our methods and our vast networks require that we be professional in our conduct hence tomorrow you will be on your way back to England." Elizabeth watched him with a sly smile playing on her face. "In fact, you will rush there soon. "There is no need to use force all the time."

The captain's phone rang and he answered after two rings. "What's the" – The captain was about to charge when he heard the mention of the King of England in the introduction and how he was being invited to the palace within 72 hours. The king had recognised his immense contribution to the aviation sector and was about to knight him, a very high level of honour that comes with diplomatic privileges.

The captain's mind raced with mixed emotions. He wanted to reject it but he was aware that the stakes were high and besides, being a Sir was not such a bad idea, but he was unsure if this was not an elevation before being destroyed. It was a matter of time.

Now the captain was thinking about threats on many fronts. He was going to be a Sir who peddles drugs and his son was finally going to have children but the captain was to be responsible for the destruction of the family and carry the blood of an innocent daughter in law. He was about to kill the mother of his grandchildren. Were they going to forgive him, was he going to live a normal life?

Elizabeth watched the captain as he agonised with thoughts judging from his actions. He was trying to think how he was going to break the news to Jennifer. He was going to need more time to deal with this matter but with the request from the king's court, there was no time to waste. He stood up and extended a hand to greet Elizabeth who decided to bow down in a sarcastic show of respect.

When the he reached the hotel, Jennifer was not in the room and he called her but her number was not available. He kept trying after every five minutes but her phone was off. In the end, he decided to go to the bar where he had a glass of wine then returned to the hotel room.

The captain was received by received Jennifer who was happy to see him after some time off to get some air.

The captain eventually broke the news to Jennifer. He skipped "unnecessary" details and focused on the positives. He was officially going to be a high-profile drug dealer using diplomatic immunity to peddle drugs. It was a label that he never wanted but he was prepared to do everything, to do what it takes to protect his family.

He needed time to process how it would be to walk around with a different passport and bags with tags written diplomat, being given VVIP reception and being invited at England's premium events, be talked about on TV shows, and radio and written about everywhere. His life was going to be an open book and whoever was blackmailing him was going to find him a cooperative and willing participant in the whole game.

To be made a Knight or a Dame is to receive one of the highest honours in the United Kingdom and is usually granted to those who have made a significant contribution to their field, usually on a national level. While in past centuries knighthoods used to be awarded solely for military merit, today they also recognize significant contributions to national life. Recipients range from actors to scientists, and from school head teachers to industrialists.

The origins of knighthood are unclear but are thought to date back to Roman times. In medieval times, knights underwent strict training from boyhood to be brave and chivalric horsemen supporting the monarch in battle. A knighthood cannot be bought, and it carries no military obligations to the Sovereign.

The King (or a member of the Royal Family acting on his behalf) confers knighthoods in Britain, either at a public investiture or privately. The ceremony involves the ceremonial dubbing of the knight by the King, and the presentation of insignia. During the knighting ceremony, the knight-elect kneels on their right knee in front of the King or member of the Royal Family on a special knighting stool. The King then dubs the knight by laying a bare sword blade on the knight's right shoulder, then the left. The King then awards the knight with their insignia. Dames are not dubbed with the sword in this way. Contrary to popular belief, the words 'Arise, Sir...' are not used.

By tradition, clergy receiving a knighthood are not dubbed, as the use of a sword is thought inappropriate for their calling. They are not able to use the title "Sir."

Foreign citizens occasionally receive honorary knighthoods or damehoods through UK orders; they are not dubbed, and they do not use the style "Sir" or "'Dame". This is similar to the one that was once bestowed on the former president of the republic of Zimbabwe before relations between Britain and Zimbabwe got strained Such knighthoods are conferred by the King, on the advice of the Foreign and Commonwealth Office, on those who have made an important contribution to relations between their country and Britain.

The captain's achievements were going to be recorded in the history books yet to be written. Someone had recognised that they needed to be rewarded. Yet in the same code, the captain was going to be a criminal, not just an ordinary one but one that would peddle drugs and be a part of a global project to destroy children across the world.

The thought of that possibility and the reality that had started rolling out had created a sense of panic. The captain was not worried about being caught but perhaps his contribution to mankind was going to be a legacy of distraction, a legacy of crime, and greed, his contributions to the aviation industry was going to be overshadowed by the compelling evidence that would be brought before the courts if he were to be caught. However, another battle would play in his mind, dealing with the guilt of knowing that you have participated in the destruction of dreams, hopes, and aspirations.

Chapter 26

The captain had returned from Australia a day before he was knighted. He had planned to have dinner with his family. Upon seeing Lunela at the family dinner his face fell, and his heart filled with sadness, his feet stiff as if affected by a cramp. He wanted to talk but he was tongue-tied. Lunela was happy to see him and she ran to him, grabbed his hand and placed it on her tummy.

"Paps say hello to your grandchildren they have grown, and I have been telling them about you. It's a boy and a girl so I have named the boy after you and Solomon, and the girl is named after Jennifer."

On hearing that Jennifer was cut to the heart Lunela observed that neither Jennifer nor the captain was thrilled. She was walking away when the captain held her hand and looked her into the eyes.

"Are you kidding me, Jenny I would love that and thank you for such a rare honour to have the children named after us." The captain said.

It was dinner time and the captain rose to propose a toast. He raised his glass and began his small speech. "As you may be aware, I have been asked by King Charles to appear before him to receive the highest honour known to man in the history of mankind, the knighthood. The Smith name has been honoured this day. We also make a toast to the two beauties waiting to see the first light. As we raised our glasses to a toast, let us not forget that we are the fortunate ones, the Lord has been gracious to all of us." Soon after he was done with the speech Brian, one of Captain's grandsons came running to him and gave him a "big" hug and requested if he could go with him to the King's Palace.

Lunela called the captain and Jennifer aside. "Mom and dad as you know this pregnancy is the biggest news that I have ever had in decades and Solomon and I are taking this very seriously. As such, I wanted to entire family to be at the hospital and I need Jennifer to be in the room she must be the first one to see her grandchildren."

As she spoke, each word came like a stab in the back, Jennifer and the Captain could not understand what was happening. Their plan was up in smoke and they knew that Solomon was in support of the idea. It was clear that the two old-timers were concerned about the arrangement that was being proposed by Lunela. Its atmosphere was tense, Lunela sensed that there was a problem and immediately she sought to find out what the problem was. She watched as Jennifer struggled to explain how she wanted Solomon and Lunela to be on their own to experience the emotional connection with the babies and with each other. The Captain also weighed in explaining that such a moment could actually be what the two have been waiting for to cement their marriage and be a normal family again.

The more they explained, the more Lunela was not convinced and she kept making mental notes of all the red flags for investigation later on.

Chapter 27

eanwhile In the streets of Harare drugs were being distributed as usual, and the youngsters had done it again bringing a new concept called Blood Bluetooth. A process where a team will gather and put resources together to buy drugs and let one of them take them. Once high, others will begin to draw blood from the one who is high and inject each other till everyone is high. This practice started in South Africa. Young drug addicts in South Africa are using a dangerous practice to share their high. It's nicknamed 'Bluetooth'. Addicts inject themselves with heroin, then draw their blood back up the syringe and inject it into a friend.

The youngsters are doing this oblivious of the fact that 'Bluetooth' carries a high risk of transmission of HIV, hepatitis, and other diseases. A recent journal reported that the practice was increasing and taking up the whole street in central Johannesburg. But many of the young people doing it say they no longer care about their lives as they have nothing to do, many of them come from broken families and have tried to make it in life but seem to have been defeated.

Africa has the highest number of young people, which is a great asset in today's world where there is an acute shortage of skilled labor, yet in the same code, many of the youth are falling to drug abuse with the rate of suicide among boys being the highest in the continent.

According to experts, Bluetooth is highly dangerous to administer. It exposes the unsuspecting addicts to infection, HIV, and hepatitis C. And the sad thing is that medical experts opine that the shared high is all in the mind. Medically, doctors conclude that it's unlikely there would be enough *nyaope* in the blood of one addict to trigger a high in another. Meaning that all the risk being taken is based on perceived not actual potency of the blood of another high addict. The Sad thing according to medical experts is that all that risk could be for nothing. It is purely based on the belief that one will be high and no medical research has proven it so far.

In Zimbabwe, Bluetooth has taken off amongst addicts in the townships. It's part desperation and part rebellion. A horrible act of self-destruction for those who feel uncared for. Those who have decided to self-sabotage and destroy their lives in protest to lack of care by society.

There are very few rehabilitation services available in the townships of South Africa and so in Zimbabwe. So once young people get hooked on *nyaope*, there is little chance of getting clean again.

In South Africa it's not just the risks from the drug or infection, it's the community, communities are being ravaged the social fabric collapsing, and the very essence of society is under attack. Due to excessive taking of drugs, in places like Diepsloot in South Africa, the police are not trusted nor effective, so people take the law into their own hands. If thieves are caught, they can be beaten, whipped or even burnt to death if mob justice takes hold. This practice is the only thing that addicts. It's the one thing that scares the nyaope addicts more than anything.

Felix was in the company of his friends and was the first to speak "Guys you ever thought about how society will be if will take our lives, let's plunge this whole neighbourhood into tears. Let's commit suicide in our alphabetical order and make it a point that there will be wailing everywhere."

Gerald weighed in "You have a great point there it's a great idea boys."

"If we do that we would be remembered as the crimson-wailing boys, we do it in a violent manner" Jacob responded.

The following morning, what was mentioned as a joke turned out to be indeed a crimson wailing day. Police were called to attend a scene of what appeared to be a suicide by hanging but there was a hunter's knife lining the stomach. While the police were attending the scene another report was made and on the same 10th street another boy had hanged himself and had a similar hunter's knife in the stomach, then in 20 minutes another phone call came through to Avondale police and another and another and a total of six cases. The last one did not have a knife in the stomach signaling he could have been the master minder.

So, there it was the message was the same "We are the wailing and crimson boys you will wait till you realize how precious we were"

The police discovered cocaine and heroin at the scene of the incidents, and all the evidence was collected for processing.

One of the boys was the Minister of Health's son and the other was a grandchild of the chief of police. This caused the matter to be treated with the swiftness and urgency it deserves. The matter was given priority one and the force was not sparing any resource money or otherwise to track down the drug gangs and bring them to justice for the crime they had committed.

Chapter 28

It is imperative that police officers undergo training and counseling for post-traumatic stress disorder (PTSD). The demands of their job sometimes expose them to traumatic situations that can deeply affect their mental health, making this support essential for their well-being and the safety of the public they serve. After the recent suicide scenes, the Chief of Police, Troy Clemson tried to continue work as usual, but fatigue and his baggy eyes betrayed the toll it had taken. After all, ongoing investigations revealed that his grandson, Felix, was the mastermind. The chief had seen worse in his career, but his grandson's involvement shattered him.

The rain lashed against the window, heavy and loud like a drumbeat. January often brought with it such intense downpours. Chief Clemson sat on the edge of his desk, fingers rubbing his bald head as he stared at the disarray of papers scattered before him. Apart from the cascading rain outside, the only other sound was the chief's heartbeat and laboured breathing. He rubbed his temples, trying to shake off the weight of the last few days. Teeth greeted, he slammed his fist on the desk, sending a few pens clattering to the floor. He winced at the noise, then returned his gaze to the rain-soaked world outside. He stared out the window as if analyzing the very molecular makeup of each raindrop. The drops raced down the glass, twisting and merging, each one a fleeting reminder of lives lost— faces of bright boys whose futures had ended before they even began. Their laughter was now silenced by grief. It may have been the best way to escape the images from the tragic scenes that haunted him, the lifeless bodies of those boys. They were just kids, some of whom he had seen running around the neighbourhood, laughing, full of life. As Chief Clemson continued staring outside, he saw his younger self's reflection in the window. He had spent his entire youth in this town with occasional visits to the village and neighbouring South Africa. Growing up, he dreamt of a brighter future. His shoemaking parents made significant sacrifices, working long hours to give him opportunities they never had. They were regular targets of burglaries, yet they kept on trading, driven by a determination to provide for their family. Witnessing their struggles instilled in him a strong sense of justice and resilience. That drive ultimately led him to law enforcement, where he hoped to make a positive contribution to society by protecting others from the kinds of criminals his parents faced, ensuring that no one had to endure the fear and loss that came with crime. Now, watching his grandson spiral into chaos seemed like a betrayal of everything he had worked for, a pain made deeper by the tragedy of his death.

The chief leaned closer to the window, watching the raindrops splatter against the flower bed and the car park, each splash sending tiny ripples across puddles. Indeed, a welcome momentary distraction. The rain continued to fall in sheets. Normally, it would be seen as a blessing, a life-giving gift that nourished the earth and brought forth water and vegetation. Today, however, it seemed heavy and oppressive, a veil of sorrow covering the skies. The ground soaked up the water, but instead of revitalisation, it seemed to absorb the tears of grief, the earth mourning alongside the community for the loss of the boys. On the other hand, the elders would have claimed that the heavy downpour cleansed the land, preventing similar tragedies in the future. At that moment, the chief understood that even the darkest storms could lead to a brighter tomorrow, but only if they confronted the truth of what had happened and worked to rebuild a drug-free environment.

Suddenly, the door swung open, and Officer Sue Taylor stepped in on tiptoe, her eyes wide and brow furrowed. She glanced around the office trying to gauge the chief's mood before speaking. Officer Sue Taylor stumbled in the doorway, shifting her weight nervously. She had always looked up to Chief Clemson, seeing him as a father figure since she joined the police force in the late 2000s. She had joined, eager to make a difference during a time of rapid change, personally and in the country. Having witnessed her brother's struggle with addiction, Officer Taylor carried the burden of lived experience that shaped her meticulous approach to her job. Now, in 2024, complex illegal activities and crime syndicates threaten not only the sanity of police officers but also that of world leaders. Her brother had fallen into addiction, a shadow that tore the whole family. So, she understood the chief's pain all too well. "I know how it feels to watch someone you love make choices that lead to heartache," she murmured.

"Chief, you can't keep doing this," she said, bending down to pick up the scattered pens from the floor. "You need to talk to someone."

"I'm fine, Sue. I just need to get through this investigation," he replied, but the tremor in his voice betrayed him.

"Fine? You don't look fine. You need to take care of yourself too, like you always tell us, especially now with—" She hesitated, glancing around as if the walls could listen. "With Felix involved."

The mention of his grandson's name, Chief Clemson's jaw tightened. "I just don't understand how he could get caught up in this mess. I thought we raised him better. His dad is devastated, he is not taking it well. Felix studied at one of the best schools around. You know, his scholarship acceptance letter into Yale arrived yesterday."

Officer Taylor took a deep breath and continued, "I hear his younger brother is in the same trap. We can still help him, Chief. Maybe there's a way to get him into a program, something to turn this around."

"I don't know, Taylor ," Chief Clemson said, his voice in an undertone. "After everything that's happened, can we even trust him to make the right choices?"

"People can change," Officer Taylor insisted. "Sometimes they just need a little guidance. We can't give up on him."

"I know this feels impossible, Chief. But we need to focus on the living. We can still support him and others."

"I don't know, Taylor," Chief Clemson replied, his voice heavy with grief. "I can barely think straight. I helped him fill in that Yale scholarship application. What a waste. Fate." The chief slumped into his chair, smiling, his eyes looking oblivious.

"People grieve in different ways," Officer Taylor insisted. "You've been through so much. Have you considered talking to someone? It might help to get those feelings out."

The chief whistled softly, twisting his wedding ring as he rubbed his palms together. "I suppose I could look into some PTSD counseling. "I need to be at my best," the chief said, glancing at the rain still pouring outside. "But right now, I just want to make sure we're doing everything we can for this case. Kids deserve to live too."

"True chief. Also, it's not just about raising them right. It's about being there. Kids face pressures we can't even begin to comprehend." She sat down, her voice lowering. "Parents trust us to keep their neighbourhoods safe, but they also have equal responsibility. They can't let social media raise their kids. Some do their best, like your son, but at the end of the day, kids will be kids.

Chapter 29

On the following Friday, Chief Clemson was back in form. All funeral arrangements for the boys had been agreed on by all families but the proceedings would take place in due course. More importantly, several drug peddlers linked to Nancy Blue had been arrested. However, that was all the information they could gather at that time. Chief Clemson addressed some Avondale community leaders in the common room. After wrapping up the usual pleasantries and protocol, he took a sip of his coffee, the warmth a brief comfort as he looked around the table of community leaders. The mood shifted; the chatter faded as everyone leaned in.

"Alright, let's talk about why we're here. We need to keep our eyes open and communicate. Just last week, a friend reached out, worried about his kid. He noticed signs, like his child pulling away from friends, grades slipping, and he was up late texting, hardly sleeping. Those are the kind of red flags we need to watch for."

He scanned the room, making eye contact with each person. "We've got resources out there like counselling services, and hotlines, but we must get the word out. Like that young girl who alerted her teacher after her friend mentioned feeling overwhelmed the whole week. It helped her get the support she needed. We need to create a space where our youth feel comfortable coming to us for help, without worrying about being punished or judged. We're in this together."

One parent added, "I also think we should consider holding a monthly community forum. It would give us all a chance to learn what to watch out for and share our experiences, even on a WhatsApp group."

"Good idea. But we also need to stress that it's not just about supervision. It's about communication. If our kids don't feel they can talk to us as parents, they'll find other outlets." The parents looked at one other nodding.

Then the chief continued, "Recently, one girl took her life after confiding in her so-called AI bestie, a chatbot. Feeling isolated and unheard, she turned to this digital companion, seeking comfort in a conversation that lacked true understanding. A fake relationship with a non-existing entity. Her story serves as a heartbreaking reminder of the importance of open communication, highlighting how critical it is for us to create an environment where our children feel safe to share anything with us."

Gasps and murmurs filled the room. The realities of social media, coupled with AI, were both exciting and frightening. The possibilities, both healthy and deadly, were endless and still in a developmental stage. It would take years to fully understand the capabilities and limitations of these powerful tools.

Chief Clemson sized up the room and said, "What we—"

Just then, the chief's phone rang, piercing the heavy silence. Clemson answered, and as he listened, his jaw dropped. His eyes widened, and he gripped the phone tighter. "What? Another?"

He hung up, taking a deep breath while keeping a straight face. "We've got another situation at the park. A group of kids was found with drugs. Excuse me, ladies and gentlemen."

***

After a long, tense day, Chief Clemson stepped through the front door, the familiar scent of simmering garlic and herbs filling the air. He paused, letting the warmth of home wash over him.

His wife stood at the stove, her hair tied back in a ponytail, focused on dinner. She knew that he liked her hair that way, simple and practical. "Long day?" she asked, glancing over her shoulder with a bright smile that didn't quite reach her eyes.

He shrugged off his jacket, too tired to rise, and gave her a peck on the cheek from across the living room. He always gave her a peck, no matter what, but today it seemed like one more thing he couldn't manage, not once glancing her way. "You could say that." He sank into a chair at the table, loosening his tie.

She approached with a steaming plate, her fingers brushing against his wedding ring as she set it down. "Eat up; it'll make you feel better." Her voice was warm as usual, but he took a deep breath, trying to steady himself.

"Thanks sweetie, I needed this," he replied, forcing a smile.

As they shared the meal, her laughter filled the space, a much-needed comforting sound. But he kept fighting off flashes of a different face, the woman from the coffee shop next to the police headquarters. Even the scent of her perfume lingered. He quickly gathered himself, forcing his focus back to his wife and the hearty food.

She leaned in closer, her voice dropping to a seductive whisper. "How about we escape for the weekend? Just you and me, for some fun."

He hesitated, his heart pounding. "That sounds amazing," he said, but a knot tightened in his stomach. He forced a smile then added, "How about we start the fun now?"

Chapter 30

A week later, the Beit Hall at the local high school in Avondale buzzed with nervous energy. Parents filled the rows, whispering to one another. Local Councilor James Reed stood at the front, flanked by Chief Clemson, Tim Fowler the Member of Parliament for the Mt Pleasant Constituency, Officer Taylor, respected community leaders, and a school counselor.

"Thank you all for coming tonight," James Reed began, his voice steady despite the weight on his shoulders. "I know many of you are struggling to understand what's happening in our constituency. We've seen tragedy strike far too close to home. We also have the culprits in our homes"

A murmur rippled through the crowd. He paused, scanning the faces before him. "I'm here to talk about drug abuse and the signs you should look for in your teens. But more importantly, I want to emphasize the importance of communication. Your kids need to know they can come to you with anything."

"Councilor, how can we know what they're doing?" a father shouted from the back. "We can't watch them every second."

"True," James Reed acknowledged. "But you can create an environment where they feel safe talking to you. Ask questions, be curious, and don't shy away from tough conversations. Let them know it's okay to be honest about what they're facing. Be a friend and a teacher."

As the discussion continued, the school counsellor also added, "And remember, it's not just about the drugs. Many kids are dealing with anxiety, depression, and peer pressure especially from social media. We need to work together— parents, schools, and the community, to support our youth. These are the leaders of tomorrow."

Officer Taylor chimed in, "And if you ever suspect your child is using drugs, reach out for help. Don't wait until it's too late. There are many free resources too and hotlines all in confidentiality. We're here to support you."

As the night wore on, parents began to share their concerns, forging a bond of understanding. It was clear: change was possible, but it would take a united front. The greatest challenge of the night was calling out perpetrators while avoiding the enabling of children when parents noticed the signs. There was a fear of victimization for those known to whistle blow, as confronting drug peddlers was discouraged in the community, better to let the police handle it. Parents were urged to be the eyes and ears of law enforcement. Yet, there was also a fear of losing their child by calling out bad behavior. What was the better option: losing your child forever to death, or knowing you tried your best to lead him to sanity and a clean life?

After the community forum, the weight of the night lingered in the air. Chief Clemson returned home to find his wife, Melissa, waiting in the kitchen, the aroma of a familiar chicken casserole filling the room. She looked up, her eyes filled with concern. She looked up, her eyes filled with concern. She had noticed a troubling text on his phone earlier but chose to let it go this once. She knew that he loved her; he always wore his wedding ring, which reassured her and kept her from looking around. But a ring was just a piece of metal.

"How did it go?" she asked gently, setting down her spoon.

"It was… emotional. People are both scared and angry, sweetheart. They're looking for answers," he replied, his voice heavy. "But I'm worried about Felix's younger brother, Victor. I can't shake the feeling that he's deeper than we realise."

Melissa stepped closer, placing a comforting hand on his shoulder. "You need to talk to him. He might need help, too. I've heard from his dad that he's been distant and arrogant."

"I know," he sighed. "But how do I approach him? He's still my grandson, but... I don't want to push him away. His dad is too soft on him. He treated Felix like an egg."

"We'll figure it out together. But first, you need to take care of yourself. You're not fine, honey. You're carrying the weight of the whole country."

As the chief lay in bed, he found it hard to shake the images of the boys' faces from his mind. The meeting had refreshed those haunting memories once again. The pressure was mounting, not only from his role as chief but from the realisation that his own family was at the centre of the tragedy.

***

Officer Sue Taylor sat in the break room, staring into her coffee cup. The aftermath of the suicides had taken a toll on her, too. Each time she closed her eyes, she could still see

181

the horror of that day. The pain was written on the faces of the boys' parents, the looks of disbelief and anguish. The wailing. She shook her head, trying to clear her mind. "I can't let this distract me," she whispered, but the words were hollow. Her usual daily affirmations were proving hard to maintain. The meeting had just opened some wounds, though it had been largely helpful. She had lost her brother to drug abuse and watching it happen all over again at a time she was raising her kids as a single mother troubled her. Each time she tried to focus on the positive, she lost focus.

Just then, her partner, Officer Ben, walked in. "You okay, Sue? You've been quiet lately."

"Just... processing everything," she replied, forcing a smile. "It's tough. I know we have to be strong for the public, but I'm feeling a bit worn out."

"Have you thought about talking to someone? PTSD isn't just for the few select, you know. We deal with trauma, too."

"I've considered it," she admitted. "But I don't want to be seen as weak. Everyone's relying on us."

"Strong people seek help when they need it. You're not alone in this. I'll be here for you. You know what, how about a date dinner with me? Friday?"

Officer Taylor chuckled and winked at Officer Ben, his infectious smile making her giggle. As she passed him, she nodded and gently grazed his elbow. At that moment, Sue realised she needed to confront her feelings rather than push them down and perhaps face her loneliness too.

Chapter 31

Later that week, Chief Clemson found himself sitting across from Felix's parents, his son Robert and daughter-in-law Isabel, both in their mid-thirties. The tension was almost palpable, as their brows furrowed and lips tightened, eyes glistening with unspoken pain and frustration. The couple kept fidgeting, visibly shuddering at the sight of the Chief of Police in his uniform rather than in civilian clothes. He meant business. They all exchanged quick, tense greetings, each voice reflecting the awkwardness of the moment.

"Why didn't you see the signs?" Isabel asked, her voice trembling with emotion. "Felix was in trouble, and you were supposed to protect him, Robert!"

Robert looked down, guilt flooding through him. "I wish I could change what happened. I didn't know he was involved with drugs. I thought he was focused on school and his friends."

Chief Clemson leaned forward, fists clenched. "He was struggling, and you didn't notice. Kids trust their parents."

"I know," Robert said, his voice thick with regret. "But I want you to help us. You've heard that our young Victor is in the same murky waters. We need to work together to stop this from happening again. I want to understand what Felix was going through so we can help Victor too."

Isabel's face lit up a bit, "We can never get Fredy back but we can save Victor. He is a good kid, but he is losing his way."

"We can win this fight. What if we can share our experiences, that way, we can help others beyond Avondale. I've seen firsthand how communication breaks down when parents don't know what to look for," Chief Clemson said, his gaze steady and intense.

Robert sighed, looking at his wife. "We can't change the past, but we can try to save our Victor and other kids. Let's do this."

As they began discussing a plan for community outreach, starting in their neighbourhood and utilising social media platforms, the atmosphere in the room lightened up. It was a long road ahead, but perhaps through this tragedy, they could pave a path toward healing. Finding closure was a crooked and lonely journey, but they were all ready to embark on that trip.

Back home, Clemson found Melissa waiting for him, her expression warm yet she frowned. "How did the meeting go?" she asked.

"We're all hurting, but I think we're starting to see a way forward," he said, flexing his shoulders and stretching his long sinewy arms. "We're going to collaborate with Felix's parents and the school for awareness programs."

"I'm glad to hear that. But remember to take care of yourself, too. You can't pour from an empty cup." Melissa noticed the chief was not wearing his ring when he stretched his arms.

"I know, Mel. I promise I'll be okay. I will tone it down. I just need to be strong for my family, the force, and the public."

"Why aren't you wearing your ring? Where is it?" she asked, her brow furrowing.

He hesitated, avoiding her gaze. "I just took it off because… I hurt myself. See. A splinter."

Melissa caressed his palm and laughed at herself.

He shook his head looking at her. He then glanced at his finger with the splinter. "It's easy to cheat if I wanted to. A ring doesn't stop someone from cheating. We've been together for years and have not been there with any issues with other women. I took it off because I got a splinter."

Melissa crossed her arms, a little embarrassed. She admitted that she had overreacted and had no reason to doubt his commitment to her. Over the years, Melissa had seen women of all shapes and sizes throw themselves at him after his promotion to head the police force. Sometimes, she wished he had stayed at a lower rank, where things felt simpler.

The chief stepped closer to her, wrapping his arms around her as he felt the connection that had anchored him through his toughest days. The lady at the coffee shop was indeed a thorn in his path. He loved his wife.

Chapter 32

Along Old Mazowe Road, a gravel path overgrown by tall grass led to a tin house in the middle of nowhere. In the opposite direction of the highway lay the Mazowe Dam. A spot popular among urban revelers looking for a quick weekend getaway away from the fuss of Harare. It was about 38km from the central business district (CBD) of Harare. The tin house stood as the only structure in the vast expanse of tall grass and distant farmland. Inside, a LED light shone bright as day, casting shadows on the walls of the little house. It was alive with murmurs and the rustling of bags. A small group of young men huddled around a table, their faces partially illuminated by the light but still shrouded in shadow. Their initial argument was on changing to a more discreet location as the road was becoming busy with urbanites unwinding at Mazowe Dam. In the center of the tin house stood the leader, a local distributor, a hardened figure whose reputation for ruthlessness preceded him. He demanded order and, in an instant, silence ensued.

"Listen up," the leader said, his voice cold and commanding. "We've got a problem. Those kids' suicides some weeks ago are drawing too much attention. The cops have made some arrests and I am told, they will keep asking questions, and we can't afford that."

One of the younger men looked nervous. "What if they come after us? The cops are going to widen their crackdown indeed. I have a one-month-old baby and my wife is still recovering in hospital."

The leader slammed his fist on the table. "If you want, leave now. Go now!" The young man bowed his head and pursed his lips. The others shifted in their seats, some avoiding eye contact, while others clenched their fists or leaned closer, caught between fear and loyalty.

He gathered phlegm and spat onto the floor. "We need to get ahead of this. We can't let fear stop us. I want you all to lay low and keep the product moving. If anyone starts asking about the boys, you keep your mouths shut. No one gets hurt if we don't make it a big deal. Otherwise, you might just end up as my next meal." The silence deepened for a minute.

"Are you sure we should keep selling?" another man asked, his voice trembling. "What if someone rats us out?"

"Trust me," the leader replied, a sly grin creeping across his face. "I've got connections. We'll manage. But if any of you slip up, I'll make sure it's the last mistake you ever make. If you can't keep the big boss happy, you will be sorry Clear?"

Serious beer drinking followed the intense chat. The men listened to the plan as their leader laid it out. It promised to be an exciting time ahead ideal for adrenaline junkies. Nothing for the faint-hearted.

Meanwhile, Officer Taylor and the team sat in the police station, poring over reports from the recent incidents. The room seemed heavy with unspoken fears.

"We need to find out who's supplying these drugs," Officer Taylor said, tapping a pen against the table. "This isn't just about the kids anymore; it's about stopping this at the source. The arrests we have are just small fry."

"I agree," Officer Ben replied. "I've heard rumors about Thomas. He's been moving a lot of products lately, but nothing points directly to him. We need to change our focus. What about that Mazowe Road tip-off we had? I know that time it led to the dam and that was futile. I know the last time it led to the dam and turned out to be a dead end, but I have a feeling there's something off in the dam's vicinity."

Officer Taylor nodded, determination flooding her veins. "Let's get a team together. We need to approach this carefully. If they suspect we're onto them, they could go underground or worse."

Further consultations were done and clearance was approved to resume the chase around Mazowe Dam area. As dusk fell, a police patrol, parked right at the dam's leisure center. Then they trooped across the road. Determined not to overlook any clues, the officers combed through the tall grass. They dimmed their flashlights so as not to cut through the thickening darkness. This time, they noticed something different, fresh footprints leading off the main path, along with the faint smell of cigarette smoke wafting through the air. "There's movement," one officer whispered, pointing to the disturbed ground. As they followed the tracks deeper into the grass, the silhouette of the tin house emerged, half-hidden yet unmistakable against the twilight. The absence of windows left the interior covered in darkness, hiding whatever lay inside. The officers weren't sure what they might find inside, whether it would be people or animals.

There was even the potential for a fox lurking in the shadows.

"Let's move in. We'll approach from the back and catch whoever is in there off guard," Officer Taylor instructed adrenaline coursing through her. She enjoyed her job despite the inherent dangers. There were bright moments, too, like her recent dinner date with the charming, chubby Officer Ben. As the police team crept closer, they heard a harsh male voice cutting through the air. "No one needs to know what we're doing, especially your silly girlfriends and wives. Just stick to the plan and we'll be fine. Once the big boss gives the green light, we head off."

Suddenly, the tension broke as a loud crash echoed. Officers scrambled, and a scuffle erupted as they burst through the door.

"Police! Hands up!" Taylor shouted, brandishing her badge.

Chaos erupted. Some gang members tried to make a run for it, while others just stood there, stunned. The staunch leader, however, dashed toward a back exit, leaping through a makeshift opening in the tin wall that had been left unsealed. This opening was specifically designed for quick getaways and had not been used before. Having only one exit may limit one's chances of survival; in life, it's essential to create multiple paths and options to ensure one is prepared for the unexpected. The daft leader disappeared into the night. Another officer bolted for the same back opening and jumped through

"Stop!" the officer yelled, knowing how silly it was to say that to a criminal, but duty called. He continued in hot pursuit. They dashed through the thick grasslands, winding past clumps of bushes and overgrown patches. Finally, with a burst of speed, the officer launched himself at the fleeing leader, tackling him to the ground and pinning him down with all his strength. "You're done! You are so done!" he shouted, his breath heavy.

As Officer Taylor and the backup team caught up, they handcuffed the whole gang. Still gasping for breath, the heroic officer stood over the gang leader, adrenaline pulsing through him.

"This is just the beginning," the ganger leader hissed, a defiant glint in his eye. "You think taking me down will stop this? I am only one percent of your troubles." He guffawed, looking up with a complete lack of remorse.

Officer Taylor stared him down. "Maybe, but we'll take you all down one by one."

***

Back at the station that night, as Officer Taylor and her team processed the arrest, cheers filled the air. "Tonight was a good start, but we can't get complacent," Officer Taylor said, wiping her spectacles. "The whole of Harare needs to see that we're taking action."

"I agree. We need to hold a follow-up meeting with the parents and the school, especially now that we have someone to question about the source of these drugs," Officer Ben replied.

"Let's also involve Felix's parents. They deserve to know that we're doing everything we can," Officer Taylor added. As they wrapped up the night, a newfound sense of purpose filled the station. Together, they would fight not only for the youth of their community but also to reclaim the safety that had been lost.

191

Chapter 33

Mr Tohimo Tanaka, representing Japan, was a seasoned diplomat with a reputation for his unwavering dedication to international relations specialising in mining and trade. Over the years, he earned respect and admiration in diplomatic circles, but the demands of his career came at a steep personal cost. Long hours spent negotiating trade agreements and site visits to mining towns across the world left little time for his personal life. Whenever possible, he travelled with his wife. Meanwhile, his wife, Suki, found herself increasingly isolated in their luxurious but lonely home. As Tohimo travelled the world, attending summits and conferences, Suki felt like a mere shadow, with each passing day, watching the happy life she once envisioned slip away.

Suki was a striking woman in her late thirties, with an air of sophistication that matched her elegant lifestyle. Her long, black hair framed a face that often wore a warm smile, enhanced by her light, clear skin. Her deep-set blue eyes, though not large by Japanese standards, held an intense expressiveness that hinted at a restless spirit yearning for more. Her eyes screamed, 'young and restless'. While she didn't have the desired double eyelid (*futae*) common in Japanese beauty standards, her unique features were captivating in their own right. Perhaps it was her appeal and intellect that had initially attracted Tohimo to her. As the wife of a prominent diplomat, she was accustomed to the high-society events and formal gatherings that defined her husband's world. Yet, beneath her poised exterior, Suki felt confined, her vibrant personality stifled by the expectations of her role. She was a lover of art and culture, with a passion for creativity that had long been overshadowed by her diplomatic duties. Deep down, she craved authenticity and pleasure, a longing that grew stronger with each passing day.

Yearning for excitement and a deeper connection, she met Stefano, a charming and free-spirited portrait artist-cum art dealer who embodied the thrill and spontaneity she craved. One evening at a Van Gogh exhibition, she met Stefano. Their connection was instantaneous, and amidst the vibrant exhibition canvases, they shared a passionate kiss in a unisex restroom. It was not surprising, considering that many public restrooms had become gender-neutral, while some remained single-use. "I didn't expect this," she whispered, her heart racing.

"Neither did I," Stefano replied, brushing a strand of hair behind her ear. "But there's something about you that feels... alive."

In their initial encounter, Suki poured out her heart and unfulfilled desires to Stefano. He whispered to her that she deserved more than to remain in the shadows of diplomacy. His soft caress and the lisp in his voice sent a thrill through her. She told him she wanted to feel alive again, and from that moment, their arrangement took off. Stefano was a captivating Italian in his late forties, with an effortless charm that drew people in. He looked ten years younger than his real age. A trait he put to use whenever the opportunity arose. His tousled dark hair enhanced his handsome face marked by a playful smile and warm hazel eyes that sparkled with mischief. Tall and lean, he carried himself with a relaxed confidence, often seen in stylish yet casual attire that showcased his artistic flair. A portrait artist and art dealer, Stefano had a passion for creativity that radiated from within, making even the simplest moments feel vibrant. He possessed a lisp that only added to his charm, making his whispered words feel sensual and special. With a magnetic personality and a genuine enthusiasm for life, Stefano offered Suki the missing pieces of her puzzle which she had been missing. Together, they personified the freedom of youth and the allure of artistic ambition. Their affair lit up a spark within her, pulling her into a world filled with passion and adventure that felt worlds apart from her dull existence as the diplomat's wife.

Suki often found herself feeling like an accessory in her husband's world of politics and protocol. While he travelled for important meetings, she remained in the background, supporting him but yearning for something more fulfilling, despite tagging along with him. She wanted to own her space and not fit somewhere in her husband's schedule. If she had a choice, she would relocate to a farm, enjoying each day surrounded by unpolluted natural resources and the tranquility of nature.

Mr. Tanaka discussed the summit with fellow diplomats, excited about the upcoming trip to Zimbabwe. Suki felt left out as usual. Tohimo explained to his wife as they sat on the balcony of their plush home, looking over the city skyline in the distant twilight. "This summit is crucial for trade relations. I'll be tied up all week."

"Of course, honey. I'll be here cheering you on," she said with a smirk, taking a sip of her dry martini.

As her husband continued to prepare for the upcoming meeting in Zimbabwe, Suki saw an opportunity. "What if I invited Stefano along?" she mused, glancing at her husband as he scrolled on his tablet.

He raised an eyebrow. "A cultural consultant? Is that necessary?"

Suki smiled with a hint of mischief in her voice. "He knows a lot about local art. It could be beneficial. Besides, he could be your portrait artist on tour as you go on safaris and other activities. That way you will capture beautiful memories at a grand scale."

Her husband shrugged then had an aha moment. "Oh, I see what you are driving at. King Charles also has a royal portrait artist on certain tours. I like the idea. Let's do this."

Chapter 34

Mr Tohimo Tanaka agreed to have a local test trip with Stefano before embarking on the longer trip. With that, Stefano joined them on a trip to Nagasaki. While her husband discussed serious matters, she and Stefano wandered through art galleries and hidden cafes with Tohimo joining in for occasional portrait paintings by Stefano. As they strolled through the charming streets of Nagasaki, Suki turned to her loverboy with a bright smile. "I've heard wonderful things about the Nagasaki Prefectural Art Museum. We should visit it while we're here," she suggested, her eyes sparkling with excitement. "Oh, you could do a portrait of Tohimo there too." She chuckled.

Stefano nodded, his interest stimulated. "That sounds perfect! I'd love to see how local artists interpret their culture and history. But I can't shake off the Hiroshima and Nagasaki bombings. It's such an important part of this country's history."

Suki nodded, understanding the importance of acknowledging that pivotal part of history. The resilience and creativity that emerged afterward was truly remarkable. "It's supposed to have a fantastic collection of both contemporary and traditional works," Suki added. "Plus, the architecture of the museum itself is stunning."

"Let's make it a plan then," Stefano replied, grinning. "I can't wait to explore it with you and explore you afterward." Those were the little sweet nothings that added to Stefano's charm. He was that good with words.

In no time, Suki had arranged for her husband to meet them at the Nagasaki Prefectural Art Museum, knowing he had a lax day ahead. The city's rich history and unique cultural blend, shaped by its international past, were beautifully reflected in its art scene. Visiting the museum felt momentous, especially with its variety of captivating exhibitions. As they explored the galleries, Stefano set up his canvas by the museum's fountain, eager to capture the serene surroundings. With deft strokes of oil paint on canvas, he began to create a portrait of Tohimo, the colours dancing under the dappled sunlight filtering through the trees. Tohimo, overjoyed with his painting, became enthusiastic about the upcoming trip to Zimbabwe on the sidelines of the SADC Summit. While he was excited about striking a deal for the potential acquisition of lithium claims, he was even more thrilled at the prospect of his face captured in brushstrokes on canvas. It would be a clear reminder of his legacy and a piece of history that future generations could admire. Yet, in his excitement, he hadn't considered how his wife might feel about having her portrait done. Would it stir jealousy or ignite inspiration? But as he glanced at Stefano, he walked over and gave him a pat on the back for a sterling job.

"You've captured it," Tohimo said, grinning. He emphasised that they had to fly on the same plane on the trip to Zimbabwe. "Can't have you remaining behind," he joked.

Chapter 35

It is a Saturday morning at the Felix residence. It is an African culture to have night vigil celebrating the life of the deceased. The process is a long-standing tradition where the body of the deceased is brought to the house at sunset. Where the deceased is not married yet, the family home serves that purpose. The mourners attend a church service followed by announcements of the order of things that night and the day that follows. During the night the mourners have a chance to give speeches and talk about how they feel regarding to passing on of their loved one. This part of the proceedings made grieving less painful as the inner circle, the spouse, children, and aunts will have lighter moments. Neighbours and friends would be ready to climb a mountain barefooted to lessen the burden of grief on the family. This was not the case with Felix's funeral.

Tradition dictates that there will be no gathering at the house of the deceased if the person has died by committing suicide. The gate at number 12C Leorna Drive Mount Pleasant was deliberately left open though not much traffic went in and out. There was no sign to show that there was a funeral, no singing, and no loud cries could be heard. The Family members though at the same house, were scattered in different places with some drinking beer while others were discussing the possible cause of the suicide. The discussions focused on the behavioural aspect of Felix and each time they thought they were close to the solution the issue of the group and simultaneous deaths came up and there were no answers to that.

"Are we witnessing a radicalisation issue here or what", commented Leonard, Felix's cousin. There was no response to his question and he repeated the same question before he just decided to keep quiet. Chief Troy was part of the relatives who had come to stay the night. He was mostly quiet managing to say *"zvakaoma"* from time to time meeting, meaning, "it's tough, it's difficult."

Felix's mother would cry and doze off and when up she would wail. All the time she had women around her to comfort her, and everyone was getting overwhelmed. The thought that her son was about to go to Yale University but in between he fell in the wrong hands made it difficult for her to mourn the loss of her son. How does one commit suicide when they have a full scholarship?

Why an intelligent person like that would kill himself, take his own life literally? There were questions that Felix's dad grappled with all the time. No one had an answer. She was pale, her big eyes betraying the sadness of the heart, the loss of one who has been robbed of something special. No words could comfort her. She was in pain.

Troy Clemson had been granted leave by President Kufazvinei after he had seen how his Chief of Police was deteriorating and was distracted even in high-level meetings. He observed as the chief took every opportunity to talk about his grandson Felix. He had been distant in meetings, perhaps the images that he saw, and the gruesome and unkind manner in which one by one the boys had committed suicide.

It was Sunday morning, the chief and Felix's father took clothes, a new blanket, and a white lace. They were in the company of Felix's two aunts. Felix's mother stayed at home opting not to go to the cemetery. As the team walked to the various cars to leave for the funeral parlour, it was visible that each of them carried a burden of grief. There was an air of despair that was palpable. At the parlour, they submitted the clothes and the blank and they were asked to wait for their turn to see the body of Felix before he was clothed. At the bay, people were lost in discussions. Perhaps the idea that there were many families waiting to be called acted as comfort.

After some time, Felix's family was called to come. They walked to the dressing room where on the left was an open coffin with clothes hanging and a blanket on the inside. The family was asked to identify his clothes. It was not time to see the body. The chief was a well-respected man in society and the man tasked to dress Felix was an ex-police and recognised and saluted the chief out of respect. But when the time came, the chief was in a bad mood. He walked with hesitation as though seeing a dead man for the first time, he looked at Felix tears falling freely like water coming from a fountain.

The chief gathered himself together. Initially, he was quiet but the urge to speak to his grandson overwhelmed him. "Felix, what went wrong? Did you really have to take your own life, tell us what happened? Who did this? Give us a clue we want to get to the bottom of this matter." At that point, he was asked to move out by his state-allocated security aide.

The family members split, from the parlour the men and one aunt went to the grave site to see the final resting place for Felix while the other ladies went to look for flowers.

At exactly 13:00 the family and friends were gathered at the parlour where a church service was held. Felix's mother fainted during the service while one of his ex-schoolmates broke down. He could not understand why and what went wrong. The pastor leading the service had a huge task of consoling the family.

When it came to the time to do body viewing, more than half of the people could not stand it. A few friends started and then it was time for the family. Out of his wisdom, the pastor had asked some friends to stand with him close to the coffin. It was an emotionally challenging time as relatives cried uncontrollably, their wizard, the genius of the family the man who had put the family name on the world map winning the Math Global Championship, a chess player, and a debate champion had decided to end his life.

Thus, the death of Felix caused sadness in the hearts of many, the family was devastated and it was difficult to stomach what was happening.

The procession proceeded to the Glen Forest cemetery. The Pastor prayed for the final resting place, soon after praying he broke down and had to be escorted away. Felix's former school sang songs as his body was lowered. At that point, Felix's clothes were brought to the site. His relatives went into the grave and started laying down Felix's stuff, clothes, shoes, blankets, cricket bats, tennis rackets, and all his medals we had won in athletics everything. It was a culture that when one commits suicide, they would be buried with all their belongings. It was a sad sight. The very act activated contradicting emotions in many as items were being laid on top of his coffin. The chief held his stomach, as each item came through, it was like free punches being delivered to the stomach. He was in serious pain and so were Felix's mom and dad and his sibling.

Chapter 36

It is a Tuesday morning, and news of the arrest of the Mazowe gang members has reached far and wide. The team had been in remand prison awaiting trial. The Zimbabwe Prison Services truck was painted green as if to align with sustainability developments. The truck was designed to carry prisoners to and from courts and any other transfers. A rigid lorry normally designed to carry cargo was modified with tiny windows fixed on either side to give the prisoners a glimpse of the world passing them by. The Mazowe gang arrived at court by 8 am as it is normally the case. The arrival time is notwithstanding the time of one's court hearing. The trucks leave at once and come back at the end of the day. So it was, all the guys who had appearances at the magistrate's court arrived on time. As required by law, those in remand are allowed to be given clothes from home. Some believe that getting into court donning prison clothes may sway the decision of the magistrate as well as create stigma resulting in a mistrial.

The chief was interested in the case and he arrived early at the court. The Minister of Health sat at the front row while the Home Affairs Minister was flanked by two directors. The case was being followed by civic society represented by local and international NGOs. Felix's former classmates were not to be outdone, they hoped that the case was going to lead to securing answers of what happened to Felix and the other boys.

Just before the court started, a member of the police force came tiptoeing, he braced and handed over a note to the chief. Chief Clemson was attending the case as an independent person, but that did not stop many people from recognising him and giving him credit for the recent arrests.

The clerk of court announced the arrival of Her Majesty Joyline Mukumbira asking all to rise up as the magistrate came to sit on her high authoritative chair. As soon as she sat, three people entered the court, a male figure, and two females. Though nobody knew them, it was clear that they were not a part of those seeking justice. They walked with distinct confidence almost exuding arrogance of the highest order. The lead female was Nancy Blue herself and Thomas' proxies flanked her.

The accused were brought to court and after identifying themselves, their charges were read out. The power was cut off soon after the identification process and the court was adjourned till the power situation was resolved. At 10:30 am the court was back in session. The Mazowe team was jointly charged with possession of 30kgs of cocaine, 5kgs methane, and 22kgs of heroin among other drugs. The magistrate looked at the accused, her voice firm and her posture revealing the seriousness of the matter.

"Do you understand the charges being laid against you?" The magistrate demanded, keeping a raised hand with a pen in hand as if readying to write whatever answer about to be offered.

The leader of the team looked down and then lifted his head slowly betraying the heavy weight of the matter on him. The same guy had acted like he was a god of some sort or that there were going to be some interventions. He lifted his gaze and looked at Nancy Blue then smiled. The magistrate was somehow confused by the gesture but demanded the answer one more time.

"Are you going to answer me? If not, I have other cases to deal with and I can postpone the matter to another time or date when you are ready to talk."

The magistrate gestured to call the clerk of court and whispered something to him. At that point, she was about to reach for her gavel. Nancy Blue nodded to the leader of the Mazowe team.

"We do understand the charge your honour, but we don't believe shit." The leader shouted and upon hearing the swearing, the magistrate raised her gavel.

She proclaimed, "USD 1000 fine for contempt. Do you want to try USD 2000?"

At that point the leader slowly put his hand in his front pocket and when he quickly pulled it out with the middle finger raised and pointed to the magistrate. "Another USD 1000 for contempt, I am enjoying this game baby," the magistrate exclaimed and to the shock of all, laughter filled the room and the leader agreed that he understood the charge. Every team member followed and agreed. They all pleaded not guilty.

First was Gilbert Machado, the prosecutor. He looked at the leader who had been called in as a witness. Gilbert clicked his parker pen three times and looked at the team leader staring at him, this was meant to be an intimidatory tactic but it backfired as the team leader looked directly into his eyes for close to a minute without flinching. In the end, the prosecutor cast his gaze away, he had seen that he was dealing with the hard-core criminal.

"Where were you when you were arrested?" The prosecutor demanded, his first clinched.

Gilbert cleared his throat. "I believe that information is in the documents and I am aware that these documents have been circulated for all to see. If you have nothing to talk about then allow us to go back to the remand prison until you are serious. The comments by the team leader hit his ego hard.

"May I put it out to you that you have a low IQ and that you are a dumb squid?" The prosecutor was visibly angry.

"Objection your Majesty" the defence counsel yelled from their bench.

"Mr. Machado, please withdraw the statement and stay on course," the magistrate demanded her fist clenched, voice raised and sitting on the edge of her seat. The prosecutor paused for a moment, looked at the magistrate who was still disconcerted though trying by all means to maintain order and remain calm.

The prosecutor rumbled on asking irrelevant questions banking his hope on the hard evidence, they say one should not worry if they have enough hard evidence but with a good defense counsel, matters can still go wrong.

After a botched cross examination by the state prosecutor, the defence counsel requested for the alleged drugs to be brought to the court and a scale to be used to measure the quantities in the charge sheet. There were variances ranging from 3 to 4 kgs from what was recorded. He asked if such variances were normal. The defence counsel indicated that the drugs in question did not belong to the Mazowe team. The prosecutor interjected stating that their drugs were found in the cars of the accused hence they belonged to them. To this, the defense council highlighted that his clients were being framed by someone who wanted a quick arrest to appease the anger that had become unbearably high.

"Your Majesty, this trial can never yield a fair trial, in this noble court we do have the Minister of Health, a representative from Home Affairs and the Chief of Police. The mere presence of these officials, whether in their capacity or officially, presents undue pressure to the prosecutor and you, your Majesty to administer justice considering the noise on the street and the anger. There may be a need to throw someone to the angry lions to stop the noisy and threatening roaring."

There was an article in the local daily paper. It had an article by a columnist who opined that the Mazowe team should be convicted and save deterrence. The defence council opinioned that the columnist is followed by more than 5 million people and hence his article creates an expectation that the courts will serve justice for the victims. The court was adjourned and the hearing continued three weeks later.

It was 5 pm as the Zimbabwe prison vehicle left the courts. It meandered through the traffic turning into Samora Machel Avenue, and there was massive traffic congestion spanning from Harare Street and Samora to Seventh Street. As the driver kept inching forward in the traffic, jam he felt an unusual drag. He checked it out and realised that he had lost one right back tyre. As he was trying to figure out, a team of bikers came zigzagging in the traffic. One of them placed C 4 on the truck and going a little distance, he detonated and three men went in to liberate the Mazowe team.

***

The Chief of Police had tasked Officer Taylor to put surveillance on the prosecutor, magistrate and two police officers that he suspected to have been involved in the drug trading.

Back in the office Chief of Police had an unusual visitor, a young girl aged 19. Lissa Makamure lived in Waterfalls. She had dated Felix for about six months. The girl was a genius scoring 15 points at A level when she was 16. They had met with Felix at the Chess Regional Championship. Both were sharp in sciences. They had established connections during the regional as well as at the Russian 2023 Invitational Chess Tournament. They had both applied to go to Yale and both had been accepted and were due to go at the same time.

Lissa was heartbroken she knew she had not married Felix yet she felt like he was more than just a boyfriend. They loved each other and Lissa was a traditional girl who preferred to give the man the platform to lead with her playing the submissive woman. That subject matter brought so much joy and a sense of being for Felix. Though they had everything at home there was never a real acknowledgement of his talent and self-worth.

"Chief, Felix needed love not money, he was breaking down. Each time we met he was interested in pouring out his heart. He was never interested in sex and touching, he wanted attention." Lissa explained.

"So, he looked like he had it all outwardly yet internally he was wasting away? Asked the Chief.

Lissa looked around the room as if to be assured that there was no one listening, she leaned forward, hands shaking with fear she stammered then in the end she just managed to say, "Felix was my all." The chief was confused, he was aware that Lissa was holding back he needed to extract the information, but the girl was becoming more distant and she did not want to talk anymore.

"Lissa, you can tell me anything, I will protect you." The chief assured her.

Lissa looked at him and quickly looked down. "Felix and I had sex one day. He went home and told his dad that he had met a girl, who then spoke to his mum," Lissa explained as tears flowed freely down her beautiful face.

"Why did he not tell me? We were buddies, filled the scholarship forms together."

"Chief, I am pregnant, three months now. I will delay going to university by a year. I am carrying your great grandson." Lissa informed the chief in-between sobs.

The chief's mind raced and he grabbed a small money clip and pressed it with one finger while other two were holding it from behind. He stood up walked around the room and, in the end, he headed for the fridge. He took some drinks and offered one to Lissa.

The chief looked at Lissa, he had a million questions that he wanted to ask but he wanted the information to flow freely. He was aware that any wrong move or wrong question then the whole conversation would be over.

"Felix's parents didn't like me. He was crushed when his mum told him that they would never accept me as their daughter in law, that is how he went into drugs, and he taught Victor too. Victor started stealing Felix's drugs till they agreed to take them together." She added. The matter displeased the chief. He shook his head all along, he was disturbed that a man made problem had caused the loss of precious life.

Lissa went on. "Our communication was cut and Felix was threatened with withdrawal of support. He was crushed. I watched him deteriorate but I didn't know who to talk to or were to go. My parents advised me to give it time and I suppose in between things boiled over.

Chapter 37

Victor had been struggling with alcohol but after being introduced to drugs by Felix. He believed that drugs were the easiest way to get high. He had supplies of cocaine, marijuana, and heroin among other drugs.

For some reason, Victor took drugs in the comfort that if Felix, the family genius was doing it then it was ok to do so. What started as an imitation of Big Brother ended up in a tragedy. Victor would use the drugs to stimulate and make himself happy when he was down. Initially, he did only alcohol and drugs and one day he found out that drugs can be more satisfying in the company of females, not just one man one woman but three women and one man sometimes two women and one man.

What started as a discussion in a popular bar in Borrowdale graduated into an experiment. He had asked a friend to take him there after the death of his brother. Victor was surprised to learn about the orgies that were taking place people dancing literally naked. Some guys would have two girls seated on the lap while one was standing over him doing any acts that they deemed necessary.

Victor was busy observing what was going on, he was clearly stunned by the level of ecstasy and the display of nudity. Nobody seemed to be moved at all by the goings on.

It was the order of the day. Victor noticed that people would foreplay in the open and when they could no longer hold their feelings, they would disappear to rooms behind. Sometimes one woman would be playing with and as they walk to go to the rooms behind any woman would just join in and there was no problem with that.

Victor was scared of the level of carelessness that was being displayed in the Bar and the rate at which people would disappear and then come back and play with others as well. Victor wished that Felix was around to guide him on what to do and what is considered moderate in the process of indulging. While he was busy thinking, a slim, sleek slender and swift girl approached him.

"Hey there lover by, are you with someone?" Asked the girl. She was a drop-dead gorgeous girl, with long legs and a flat tummy catwalk. She was wearing a negligee and bum shorts. Victor was shy, he had not been used to such kind of treatment and seeing a girl coming to him was rather strange, it threw him off guard and had no idea of how to proceed. He lived with one rule though, never show weakness, muddle through but do not show weakness.

Victor looked up and smiled, he stood up and gave a handshake to the girl. This pleased the girl who was used to dealing with disrespectful men who assumed that every woman wanted to have sex. "What are you drinking, what can I get you?" Victor asked with a sweet voice. The girl was captivated by Victor's pristine state, he looked clean and well-dressed.

The two spoke about life in general till the girl said, "I am tired of yelling, can I come to sit with you there?" She had to shout three times as the bar was filling up and the music was getting louder and louder. It took them less than three minutes to start touching each other. The connection was instant and the lust for each other was strong. The lady asked Victor to follow him. Victor thought about being robbed and killed for rituals but he was already in the rhythm and whatever was to come he would have to face it head-on.

They opened a door that led to the second reception. At that point Victor looked worried, it was a moment to decide. While there, the girl picked up the keys, and some pills. Victor's heart was pounding, he was in unchartered territory, and there was no turning back. His consolation was that he was dealing with only one person. However, his fears were confirmed when the second and third girl joined. The girls were goddesses and were courtesy of the manager. It was customary that any new customer introduced to the orgies would be treated to high-quality personal pleasure. The idea was to create lasting impressions and indeed lasting impressions were made. Victor spent the entire night in the company of three women who woke him up at least three times.

In the following morning Victor battled with thoughts, would Felix approve of it, would he be pleased with the story? But that did not matter at all. Felix had taken his life and so did his ability to influence anything.

Victor had had unprotected sex with three women that he did not know. He panicked about the possible ailments that could affect his health. Victor went into the nearest pharmacy at the Village Walk. He asked to speak to a medical consultant in private. Joyce was a mid-40s woman, who ushered Victor into the consultation room. Closing the door, her she asked him to take a seat.

"My name is Joyce, how can I be of assistance?" She enquired while maintaining a sharp eye on Victor, she had seen the clothes and what seemed to be specific bedroom residue but it was none of her business.

Victor cleared his throat, "I need post-exposure, I had unprotected sex with three women the whole night and I fear that I might have contracted HIV among other possible diseases.

"I will give you Prophylaxis for the next 30 days, you are to take this as prescribed. You will take one each day after a meal. You are encouraged to take it the same time each day, if you have forgotten to take do not double them but rather take the medication as soon as you remember to do so. Do not overdose." Explained Joyce while maintaining a look that expressed concern that went beyond medical practice. He tried to ask but decided to refrain.

The days that followed saw Victor struggling, he tried badly to quit Cocaine and Heroin but each day he went without them was like a month, the ARVs that he was taking required him to take a lot of water. He experienced tastelessness in the mouth, fatigue, loss of appetite, persistent headache. For the one full month that followed, Victor was isolating himself, he ate less and was moody. He was trapped between grieving the passing of Felix and facing his own situation.

Chapter 38

Victor woke up with a start, the room spinning like a carousel. His eyes flickered open, but the world around him didn't quite make sense. His surroundings appeared blurry and distorted as if he had emerged from some deep, heavy fog. His sheets felt damp, sticky and they clung to his skin. He paused and sniffed the air, like a rabbit sensing danger. At first, he mistook the odour for sweat, but then it hit him with a bang. A sour, unpleasant stench that burned his nostrils. The putrid smell went straight to the back of his head, a sharp, nauseating attack on his senses. His stomach churned. He jerked his head back into the sheets, then threw himself out as quickly as he had ducked in. But that didn't shake the sleep off him. A cold knot of realisation tightened in his gut. He lifted his legs from the bed, and the sticky sensation on his skin hit him like a wave. It was there, all over him. His head fell back onto the pillow, his neck heavy, as if the weight of the moment had drained him. He felt the same way he had when his girlfriend dumped him for her grey-haired uncle. Disgust and helplessness twisted in his chest, but he had no energy left to fight it. His body sank deeper into the mattress, too fatigued to move, too defeated to think.

His heart thudded, a quick, erratic pulse of panic, but his body felt too sluggish to move. His legs, thick with a strange heaviness, seemed to resist his will to sit up like they were glued to the mattress. Wetness. Thick, unpleasant. It spread in his boxers, a deep, uncomfortable warmth running down his thighs. The sensation unsettled him but still clouded with confusion and fatigue, he couldn't make any sense of it.

"This isn't real," Victor whispered groggily, blinking into the dim light of the room, the heavy curtains blocking out any trace of sunlight. His eyelids felt heavy, weighed down with sleep and something else, something he couldn't name. His head throbbed.

He groped for his phone on the nightstand, his fingers fumbling over the surface in the half-darkness. He hoped for some sign of what had happened or even just the time, but his fingers stumbled over the smooth glass of the screen. He could not process even the simplest task, so he gave up and pushed himself upright with a grunt, using the nightstand for balance.

Finally, he sighed, "Bathroom, I need to get to the bathroom."

The ensuite bathroom was only a few steps away, but now, every step felt like dragging his body through wet cement. Half awake, he trudged on. That was the beauty of an ensuite bathroom, a private, reliable sanctuary. Back at school one had to wait for several minutes during lunch time to use the toilets. Even worse, were the Market Square Station toilets and the Fourth Street Bus Rank toilets. During the morning peak hour, long queues clogged those toilets, as though people had no bathrooms at home. How does one arrive in town and rush straight to a public toilet? Some journalists argued the issue stemmed from water shortages affecting most suburbs. For others, those queues provided a perfect opportunity to pickpocket unsuspecting people. On the other hand, those disgusted by public toilets or pressed for time prefer using the ones at work where cleanliness and convenience offer a comfortable bathroom experience. Still, others used this as an excuse to delay starting work. At this moment, Victor certainly needed an ensuite.

Victor crossed the floor, his bare feet slapping against the cold ceramic tiles with each laboured step. The weight in his stomach was unbearable now, the pressure building like a balloon ready to burst. The door to the bathroom lay an arm's length ahead, but his legs didn't want to carry him any further. Sweat slicked his brow as he reached the threshold and stumbled in, his gaze darting to the floor as he almost tripped on the towel scattered at his feet.

The light flickered overhead, buzzing, casting long shadows against the white tiles. He finally looked down at himself in the mirror. His boxers were soaked, a dark stain spreading across the fabric, covering SpongeBob's face, a pair he wore to remind himself of the innocence he once had. He froze in front of the mirror. His legs, brown and slick with filth, reflected back at him, coated in a thick, sticky mess that clung to his skin. The stench still hit him, sharp and unbearable, but it wasn't just the smell. He watched the muck cling to his chocolate brown skin, sticky and repulsive, unwanted and unnatural. His stomach twisted again.

Victor tried to move, to step back, but his feet felt heavy, rooted to the floor. His fingers twitched at his sides, desperate to wipe the dirt away, but he couldn't. His body refused to obey. He stared at the mirror, glued to the reflection he barely recognised. The filth wasn't on him. It had become him. He didn't know when it happened, or how, but it was clear now. The line between them had disappeared. The grime had seeped under his skin, sunk deep into his bones. It lived inside him. "What happened to you?" The reflection asked, its mouth unmoving, eyes locked on his. He couldn't answer. He didn't want to. His throat stiffened, suffocating him, and his chest heaved with a dry sob.

He leaned forward, drawn to the image like bees to pollen. His breath fogged up the glass, but he couldn't look away. He should have wiped it off, should have scrubbed it away, jumped into the shower, but he didn't move. He couldn't. The reflection refused to let him look away. The dirt wasn't a mistake, it was permanent.

He was a part of the mess, now. There was no escaping it. No matter how hard he tried, no matter how much he wanted to tear himself away from the mirror, he couldn't. The reflection stared at him, unyielding, unforgiving, showing him exactly who he was, and who he'd become. His eyes blurred with tears, but still, he couldn't move away. He understood, then. Shame. The filth went beyond the surface. He was covered in it, from the inside out. A part of him wanted to scream, to curse himself, but another part was numb.

The sink. He needed to splash some water on his face, try to wake up, figure out what had happened. He turned toward the mirror again, and for a moment, he shook his head at the face staring back at him. Hollow eyes, dark circles beneath them. His skin looked ashen, dull, lacking its usual warmth, as though the life had been drained from him overnight. He touched his forehead, feeling the dampness there too, not just sweat, but something else. A film. A residue of something. Last night…at the club.

His memories shattered into fragments: a bottle, pills, voices buzzing somewhere in the distance, laughter fading in and out. The pieces didn't quite add up, and he struggled to make sense of them. Something about a party or a group of people he barely knew. He had drunk too much, probably. And the pills... He couldn't remember what exactly. Just that his head had felt heavy, like he carried the weight of the world. That was before the exhaustion had settled in, before his body had started to shut down on him.

"I messed up," he murmured clutching his temples. He wiped his face, rubbed his eyes, but the discomfort in his body wouldn't go away. The fatigue suffocated him, like his limbs had been drained of all energy, replaced with this strange, sticky heaviness. For a month he abstained while taking his prescription, then just one night. A moment of madness. Dire consequences. Emergency clean up needed. Both inside and outside. But it wasn't so simple. It wasn't just a bad night or a mistake. Something had shifted inside him, in the space between the pills and the booze and the quiet loneliness he always tried to ignore since his brother's passing. The mirror reflected a bitter truth, something darker, something he didn't know how to face.

A low sound rumbled in his chest as he stood there, one hand gripping the edge of the sink, the other wiping his face again. He didn't know what to do next. Should he return to bed and pretend it hadn't happened? Crawl back into the numbness? No. He couldn't. Not anymore.

He pushed away from the sink, his legs still unsteady. He felt the air in the room—cool, almost fresh as if it was trying to cleanse him of everything else. He stepped toward the shower and let the cold spray hit his face as if trying to wash away more than just the mess on his body. The water cascaded down his back, and he closed his eyes, the sound washing over him. He stood under the flow of water for a while, motionless. The weight of his body hung heavily, and the air around him felt thick. His posture relaxed, and the tension seemed to lift. After the shower, he gathered his soiled clothes and sheets, preparing to wash them, while airing out the bed. A time to turn over a new sheet, to make things fresh again. But as he prepared to open the door, a faint sound emerged. His laptop battery dwindling. Then, his eyes landed on the screen. His Facebook feed had been live all along. The sound was muted, but the camera had captured everything, right up until he reached the bathroom, the mess, his disarray. The night he couldn't remember, now laid bare for anyone who had tuned in.

Chapter 39

The air in Mellow Mug Café was warm, the low hum of conversation blending with the hurried clink of coffee cups. Janice sat by the window, half a vanilla latte in front of her, staring absentmindedly at the pigeons on the street. She wore a summery halter neck dress, the soft fabric falling gracefully over her form, loose enough to suggest the curves beneath. Dresses accentuated her more than her usual work cargoes. The gentle sway of her dress matched the tapping of her fingers as she stirred her latte, each dip of the spoon slow and steady, as if the warmth of the cup could soothe her. She lifted the drink and paused, her gaze drifting to the door before settling back on the swirling patterns in her cup. Her eyes darted across the café before fixating back to the pigeons. A quiet smile tugged at her lips. She gazed into her cup, her cheekbones flushing into a radiant smile. She had been quiet for a while, as Jason's trip to Kariba troubled her. Her friends had made it clear that they thought she still had strong feelings for her ex-husband. They didn't understand how, after all this time, she could continue to harbor so much anger toward him. But they were wrong. Her ex-husband's chaotic lifestyle had destroyed their family. He lived for the moment, always partying, always absent when it mattered. Janice had stopped hoping he would change a long time ago. But still, she couldn't entirely erase the memories of who he had been before he became a stranger in their lives. Her friends had insisted that she still loved him and that jealousy made her uneasy about Jason's trip. Janice dismissed their words. It was easier to deny it, even though deep down, she knew they weren't entirely wrong. But none of that mattered now. The reality of her son's choices and the consequences of letting him visit his father were overwhelming, so she found herself sitting at the local café, trying to process it all. Letting Jason go felt like giving up, but she knew it was the right thing to do. The constant pull between wanting to protect him and letting him go exhausted her.

"Earth to Janice," came a familiar voice, snapping her back to the present.

She looked up, blinking in surprise as Michael slid into the seat across from her. He grinned, his eyes dancing with amusement. "Lost in thought again?"

Janice chuckled, shrugging. "Thinking about someone…"

Michael raised an eyebrow, leaning forward. "Thinking about me?"

She smirked, tapping her fingers on the side of her cup. "Maybe. But don't get too excited. It's more about how you seem to pop up everywhere I go." Reaching out for his hand, she added, "I appreciate your help, especially with everything my son put me through."

He leaned back, crossing his arms casually, a playful glint in his eyes. "I can't help it if I like to be where the action is. As for Jason, he's like a son to me."

Janice laughed, the sound light and easy. "Action, huh? Well, I guess it's good to know you're keeping busy. Jason went on holiday to see his dad in Kariba."

They talked about Jason and how Janice was coping with his visit. Her ex-husband partied like his life depended on it, and Jason's presence unsettled her. But they say every child needs his father. Life often turned out in unexpected ways, and the trip could do something positive for Jason.

"I don't know," she murmured, breaking the momentary silence. "He's going to see a man who... hasn't been a father to him in years."

Her voice was calm, almost detached, but Michael could hear the tension beneath the surface, the soft crack in her tone. She struggled to hold it together, trying to keep the flood of emotions from spilling out.

Michael nodded as spoke. He just watched her, his gaze steady, like he understood the battle playing out behind her eyes. He'd seen it before, the way Janice carried the whole world on her shoulders. Jason's substance abuse struggles, her failed marriage, and the endless responsibility of keeping her family intact even when it felt like everything was falling apart. Even worse, the blow Nancy Blue dealt her still bothered her. Nancy Blue, once Janice's college roommate, admitted to distributing drugs in their neighbourhood. Janice struggled to accept it. Nancy Blue had wanted to make a decent income. She promised not to let any of her "jazzmen" (a slang term for drug peddlers) sell to Jason, but what he did elsewhere was beyond her control. Anyone could read all this on Janice's face.

Michael had stepped in countless times, helping with Jason when things got out of control, supporting Janice when he needed guidance. What started as a simple crush from the support group meetings grew into something deeper, as Michael found himself wanting to spend more time with her beyond those monthly sessions.

Janice took a long deep breath, her chest tightening with the thought of Jason leaving. "Part of me thinks he's just going to fall into the same traps his dad did. You know, follow in his footsteps. The apple never falls far from the tree. I know there are exceptions. But his dad wasn't exactly a role model." The words came out in a rush, like a confession she hadn't meant to make aloud.

Michael didn't flinch, his expression softening. He could see the fear in her eyes, the fear that, despite all her love and effort, she wasn't enough to protect Jason from repeating the same mistakes. He waited a moment, letting the silence settle, giving Janice some space to gather herself.

"I'm just so scared that... that I'm holding on too tight," she muttered, the vulnerability creeping in. Her fingers tightened around the handle of her cup, and for a moment, she wished she could let go of the control, the fear, the doubt. It wasn't in her to simply fold hands and watch without trying to manage the outcome.

Michael leaned back in his chair, watching her. He stayed silent for a long while, allowing Janice to process and work through the pent-up emotions swirling inside her. He knew how hard it was for her to open up, and he didn't want to rush her. Instead, he let her have the space to make sense of the feelings that had been bubbling beneath the surface for weeks, maybe longer.

Finally, Micheal spoke softly, his voice endearing yet firm. "Janice, you're doing the best you can. You can't control everything. Jason has to find his own way, even if it means learning the hard way."

Janice nodded reluctantly, then forced a smile. She wanted to believe him. She wanted to believe that despite the mistakes of the past, she had given Jason the good foundation he needed. But doubt lingered. What if this trip was the breaking point? What if it pushed him further away from the person, she had tried so hard to raise? What if he became more rebellious? Her gaze dropped to the surface of the table.

Michael's voice brought her back, soft and soothing. "You're not alone in this," he said, his hand gently covering hers on the table. The warmth of his touch ignited a spark of comfort through her chest, but she still hesitated. Letting someone in fully, trusting Michael, and needing him felt difficult. Letting him in meant opening herself up to the possibility of disappointment, even if she knew deep down, he wasn't like the others.

"I just don't want to fail him," Janice whispered, her voice small, and vulnerable. It felt like a confession, an admission she hadn't even realized she needed to make until now.

Michael's touch was firm and reassuring, the warmth of his hand offering her the kind of comfort she hadn't realized she craved. He squeezed her hand gently, his eyes meeting hers with an intensity that was impossible to ignore. "You won't fail him. You're not alone in this, Janice."

Janice wasn't ready to fully open up yet. Not like this. But Michael's presence was sincere, settling her in a way she hadn't expected. For the first time in fifteen years, she allowed herself to believe a man and his words. Maybe she wasn't alone in this after all.

For a moment, the air between them hung with unspoken mutual understanding, but then, with a small effort, Janice shifted. The spark of playfulness that had been there before returned, tentative, but real.

"You know," she said, her voice lighter now, testing the change in mood, "it does help to have someone around who isn't afraid to get a little bruised when Jason decides to break something in the house."

Michael chuckled, the sound light and easy. "I've always been up for a challenge."

She leaned back in her chair, relaxing her shoulders as the playful energy began to take over. "Oh, really? Maybe I'll take you up on that. Just don't go pretending to be *Macho Man*."

Michael grinned, his eyes sparkling as he flexed his biceps. "Do you need glasses to see all this?" he teased, giving his muscles a mock-serious shake. "It's a lot to take in, I know."

Janice shook her head, her lips twitching into a smile. Michael raised an eyebrow and leaned forward slightly. "I'm just saying..."

She laughed out loud, and Michael couldn't help but join in. For a brief moment, the worries about Jason, her ex-husband, and everything else faded, leaving only the easy comfort of their talk.

Chapter 40

Back in London, Jennifer made several calls to her team of hackers, videographers, and photo editors all working behind the scenes. She was a woman who prided herself on knowing everything, seeing everything, and manipulating every angle. When provoked, she could be like a wounded lioness, fierce, unpredictable, and dangerous.

For as long as she could remember, Jennifer had demanded that things go her way, no way or there would be consequences. She had always been the one to bend the rules, to make the world bend around her. Outwardly, she could appear as soft and innocent as a dove, charming, polite, and refined. But beneath that delicate veil, there was a tiger ready to pounce at the slightest provocation. Her husband, Captain Smith, had always found that duality irresistible. He called her a sexy, sassy go-getter, admiring her more with each passing day. Her cunning nature and tenacity captivated him, drawing him in from the first time they met.

Jennifer wasn't one to back down. She crafted her way through life, using whatever tools at her disposal, be it her beauty, money, her intelligence, or her ruthlessness. A master manipulator, she stayed several steps ahead, always plotting. Most people underestimated her, seeing only the surface, but Jennifer had always known how to work the system, whether it was in business or in her personal life. She could easily be a politician, but she claimed politics bored her to tears.

But it was her strained relationship with her daughter-in-law that truly rekindled Jennifer back into the depths of her sinister nature. The friction built once Solomon announced their divorce and Jennifer's resulting threats, but it reached a boiling point when Jennifer's grandchildren were named after her. The fact that Lunela had dared to name the twins after Jennifer's own name, was the final straw. It was an insult. Jennifer maintained that Lunela had arm-twisted the situation and diverted focus to use the babies as an endearment over her faults. Those children were welcome but not their mother. Jennifer had always been the centre of attention, the one people looked up to. The fact that Lunela, with her sweet smile and naive charm, could waltz in and claim that honour for herself while backstabbing the family was unbearable. Jennifer swore to take her down, by any means necessary.

Her resentment only grew after Lunela's initial threat to expose her son. Jennifer could never trust her. Not after that. Lunela had proven herself to be a loose cannon, reckless, volatile, and far too naïve to realize the seriousness of her risks. Jennifer wasn't about to let her get away with it. No one threatened her family and walked away unscathed.

To make matters worse, Jennifer's husband, Captain Smith, had become increasingly protective of Lunela, especially after the news about the grandchildren on the way. His soft spot for her had only grown over time, particularly after he saw his name given to one of the twins. Jennifer could see the way her husband now looked at Lunela, fondly, almost like a father figure. It stung. And it made her resolve all the more ironclad. If her husband couldn't see the danger in Lunela anymore then Jennifer would have to handle it herself.

Her anger at her husband was almost palpable. He'd failed to execute a simple elimination plan, a plan that Jennifer had spent months perfecting. His reluctance to follow through on it only made her more determined to take control. If she had to get her hands dirty again to make sure Lunela left the scene, then so be it. Jennifer had no hesitation when it came to getting what she wanted. She'd spent her whole life learning how to get what she needed, no matter the cost. And this time, she would win. She knew that with any little mistake, things could spiral. If she didn't act, she knew she'd eventually go down too, but she didn't care.

Sometimes, it's the little gestures that move people in the sweetest ways, not money, not pleasure, just simple, everyday things. Who would have thought Captain Smith could be so ecstatic over his name being passed down? Well, he would have a grandson on the way to carry on his legacy; that could be enough reason to be happy.

On the other hand, Solomon, the twins' father, remained indifferent toward Lunela. He loved his boyfriend, Mark, but still felt some attachment to Lunela for carrying his children after a long struggle to conceive. His mother, however, had planted doubts in his mind, suggesting that the babies might not even be his. She was already making plans for a well-doctored DNA test when the children were born, but Lunela wasn't about to let anyone question her children. She would do everything in her power to prove the truth, no matter the cost. Lunela knew exactly what she was up against, despite the sudden, feigned affection they showed her. What stood out most was how both husband and wife avoided being present in the labour ward when the time came. Lunela saw through their flimsy excuses, though she couldn't quite pinpoint what felt off.

Mark paced the hallway, trying to appear composed, though his casual stride only half-concealed his nerves. He mumbled to himself, whistling aimlessly as if it would calm him. Finally, Lunela gave him a cold nod, signalling him to enter the living room.

"Talk," Lunela said flatly, her eyes sharp.

Mark hesitated, forcing a smile that didn't quite reach his eyes. "Congratulations on your future twins. They'll be beautiful babies, both with your eyes—"

"Cut the crap," Lunela snapped, her patience thinning. "What do you want?"

Mark inhaled sharply, his gaze fixed on her as he steadied himself, his fingers twitching at his sides. "Jennifer tried to kill you. And she's still trying."

Chapter 41

Lunela sighed, her arms still folded, as she let their last conversation sink in. The tension between them hung thick in the air. Mark, sitting across from her, fidgeted, his casual posture betraying the unease beneath.

Lunela sat across from him, arms crossed tightly over her chest, her eyes hard as they met his. The air between them was thick with unspoken things. Mark had never been the one to offer explanations, never been the one to apologise. But now, it seemed, she had no choice but to hear him out. He fidgeted.

"So, let's get this straight," she said, her voice cutting through the silence. "Solomon files for divorce, but I'm still carrying his kids. And you, Mark, you were part of that. You were part of his betrayal, and now you're telling me my mother-in-law wants me dead?"

Mark shifted in his seat, clearly uncomfortable, but he didn't back down. His posture was tense, betraying his inner unease. "I didn't want to bring it up like this, Lunela, but I had to warn you. Jennifer is dangerous. I didn't want you blindsided by what might be coming."

Lunela let out a slow breath. Her emotions were a tangled mess—anger, hurt, disbelief, but also fear. She had never expected her life to be anything like this. Not with Solomon. Not with the pregnancy. And certainly not with the possibility that her own mother-in-law could be plotting against her.

"You think I'm going to just believe you?" Her voice was flat, but there was an edge to it now. "After everything? After what you and Solomon have done?"

Mark's face softened, though his eyes remained sharp. "I'm not asking you to believe me, Lunela. I'm just telling you what I know. What I've seen. Jennifer's not playing around. She's a conniving woman, a schemer and she won't let anything get in her way."

Lunela's stomach churned. She hadn't known what to expect from this conversation, but hearing Mark confirm what she had feared.

"So now what?" she asked, leaning forward. "Now you expect me to work with you? To trust you? The man sleeping with my husband."

Mark hesitated for a moment, then shook his head. "I don't expect you to trust me. I just want you to know the truth. You have a right to know, Lunela. You're carrying Solomon's kids, and I'm not the enemy here. Jennifer is. She's the one you need to watch out for."

Lunela's eyes narrowed. She had never trusted Mark, but hearing him talk so openly, so urgently, about the threat from her mother-in-law made her wonder. She couldn't let her guard down, not now, not after everything. But she couldn't afford to ignore this either.

"You're still part of this mess," she said sulking, her gaze piercing. "And I'm still trying to figure out why you're here. What you want."

Mark looked at her for a long moment, his expression unreadable. "I don't want anything from you, Lunela. I never did. But I don't want to see you hurt. And I don't want to see the kids tangled in the middle of this."

Lunela stared at him. Was this just another manipulation? Or was there some truth to what Mark was saying? The silence stretched on, heavy with the unanswered questions. But for the first time in a long while, Lunela didn't feel completely alone in this mess. There was still a long way to go, and the road ahead was unclear, but she had to face it. For her unborn children, for herself. Finally, she spoke, her voice barely above a whisper. Her eyes narrowed. "We'll see. But don't think this means I trust you."

She studied him for a long moment. Mark paused, then met her eyes. The silence stretched between them, but Lunela didn't break it. Finally, she cut through it, her tone sharp. "You have something to say?"

He took a deep breath, running a hand through his hair as if gathering his thoughts. He looked at her, but only briefly before looking down at the floor. His words were cautious, but they carried an undeniable sincerity. "Lunela, I never wanted to hurt you. I never meant for things to go this way with Solomon."

Lunela's eyes narrowed, her voice sharp. "Then why, Mark? Why did you get involved with him, knowing he was married to me?"

Mark shifted in his seat, clearly uncomfortable. He leaned forward, hands clasped together as if pushing himself to speak the truth. "It wasn't about you, not at first. I didn't know... I didn't know what it was between us. Between me and Solomon."

Lunela tilted her head, skeptical but listening. "So, you're telling me you just, fell into it?"

"No," Mark said, shaking his head. "It wasn't like that. There was something magnetic about him. He had this... power. He was confident, strong, and I don't know, maybe it was the way he looked at me. I'd never felt like that before. I didn't even realise how deep it was getting until... until I was already in over my head."

Lunela leaned back, her arms still crossed. She was silent for a long moment, processing what he'd said. She felt a mix of anger and something she couldn't quite name, maybe understanding. But it didn't change the fact that her husband had cheated with this man in front of her, Mark.

"So, you're telling me, you let Solomon manipulate you? You let him drag you into this... mess? What happened to your morals?" she asked, her voice quieter now, less harsh but still laced with anger.

Mark's face tightened. He cleared his throat. "I didn't want to be part of the mess. I didn't. But Solomon... he had this way of making me feel like I was the only one in the world. And yeah, I let him get to me. I don't expect you to understand. Hell, I don't even understand it myself. But that's the truth."

Lunela stared at him for a long while, nonchalantly. A part of her wanted to scream at him, to lash out for the hurt they had both caused. But another part of her couldn't deny the raw honesty in Mark's voice. There was no excuse for his actions, but maybe, just maybe, she could understand.

Finally, she spoke. "I don't know if I can forgive you, Mark. But... I understand, in a way. I get why you were drawn to him. I've been trying to figure out what makes Solomon tick for so long. He's always been attractive, seductive and a master of manipulation. I think... I think he played both of us."

Mark nodded, his shoulders slumping slightly in relief, though the tension in his posture still lingered. "I regret it. I truly do. But there's nothing I can do to take it back now."

Lunela's eyes softened for a moment before hardening again. "No. You can't take it back."

There was a long pause before Mark spoke again, his voice pleading, almost with remorse. "You want the truth, Lunela? The truth is, I wasn't the only one who got hurt. Solomon's got this... way of making you feel special like you're the only one. But when he's done with you, he just moves on. He did the same thing to me. And I don't think he even realizes how much he's ruined.

Lunela chuckled. "And you're still not done with him, are you?" she asked.

"No. But I will be. I have to be."

Lunela stared at him. There was still so much to figure out, but for the first time, it felt like they weren't enemies anymore. Just two people caught in the wreckage of someone else's games. Mark leaned back in his chair, staring out the window. Lunela could feel the shift in the room as he began to open up, not just about his past with Solomon, but about his own struggles.

"I didn't expect to fall for him," Mark said quietly. "It wasn't like he came on strong at first. We met at work, you know, at a charity event. I was a programmer those days. Solomon was a big deal, everyone knew him. He was charismatic. People wanted to be around him. And I... I was just another guy in the crowd. But he saw me. And that made a difference. He made me feel like I was the one he'd been waiting for."

Lunela listened intently, watching his expression shift. "Did you know he was married? He hardly wears his ring."

Mark sneered, the sound bitter. "Of course I did. I wasn't that naive. But Solomon had a way of making things seem... irrelevant. He didn't talk much about his marriage, and when he did, he downplayed it. He told me about sexuality, his desires and how he wanted to explore. He mentioned his marriage in a way that made me feel like it didn't matter. I didn't care enough to dig deeper, I guess. He made it seem like we were on the same level, like we could have something real."

"And you just went along with it?"

Mark's voice dropped to a whisper. "Yeah. I did. I thought it was just a fling, but then, one thing led to another. It became more. And I couldn't get out. Solomon was a force. When he wanted something, he took it. And when he wanted me, I gave in."

The air between them remained thick, but there was no animosity anymore, just a shared understanding of the situation. Lunela stood up, moving towards the door. She turned to face Mark one last time.

Mark met her gaze. "I'm sorry."

Lunela nodded, then gestured toward the door. "Then you should go. There's nothing more to say."

Mark paused for a second before leaving, his footsteps fading down the hall. She shut the door with a soft click, leaning against it as the silence filled the room. Lunela stayed still for a moment, rubbing her bulging tummy. She wasn't sure if she'd made the right choice, but something about Mark's behavior felt off. The phone on the counter buzzed, startling Lunela. She shuffled towards it and then turned toward the window instead. She couldn't shake the feeling that something was coming. And she wasn't sure if she was ready for it.

Chapter 42

They say when the cat's away, the mice will play, and that applies here. With Chief Clemson off in the countryside for a break granted by the President, the mood at the police station lightened up. For some, it felt like a much-needed relief. For many officers, his absence was a welcome relief. The chief's strict, no-nonsense approach was tough to deal with day in and day out, but it was part of the job. His stern demands reminded everyone that authority should never be questioned. He ran a tight ship, and though his leadership was necessary, it didn't make him any less intimidating. But for those who had worked with him for years, there was also an understanding that underneath that tough exterior, the chief had a more playful side, if you could get past the iron discipline. Most of the jokes around the office were about how only his wife, Melissa, could truly keep him in check.

With the chief out of the picture, things relaxed almost immediately. Officers moved at a slower pace, taking longer breaks and chatting in the hallways. Even paperwork seemed less of a priority. The usual hum of activity slowed to a softer, more laid-back pace. Of course, the deputy in charge didn't mind the slowdown, he knew the work would get done, as long as it didn't slip through the cracks. But when it came time to get serious, when he raised his voice, everyone knew to move fast. His bark could snap the team into action in seconds, and there was no mistaking that.

In the chief's absence, Officer Ben and Officer Taylor started spending more time together. They had always been friendly colleagues, but with the chief away, they found themselves talking more often than before. Ben, who had always been a steady presence in Taylor's life, seemed to notice when her mood shifted. Taylor had been struggling with the painful memory of her brother's suicide, a loss that had hit her hard. His death, linked to his struggle with substance abuse, left a scar on her heart that had never quite healed. When news broke about the chief's grandson going through a similar tragedy, it reopened old wounds for Taylor. Ben saw how much it hurt her, and as if by reflex, he stepped in to offer comfort. The chief's grandson and the other boys had been laid to rest and that even sunk Taylor further. Reliving memories of her brother's funeral, Taylor often found herself sinking into sorrow. But Ben did his best to cheer her up whenever he could.

Their office banter turned into longer, more meaningful conversations. Ben's kindness and genuine interest in her well-being strengthened Taylor. Not that she needed validation, but she needed reassurance that she wasn't alone. He always knew when she needed a distraction, when to just listen, and when to offer a few quiet words of support. It was comforting, the way he was always there for her. The random text messages filled with words of encouragement always made Taylor smile. Their friendship grew from simple office small talk into something deeper, something that felt almost effortless, though neither of them could pinpoint exactly when it had changed. Taylor felt the pull toward Ben, but part of her held back. Dating a coworker was tricky, she knew it could easily lead to complications.

Office relationships had a way of becoming messy. If things went south, they'd have to face it every day, and that kind of awkwardness could spread through the whole team. And she wasn't in the mood for any drama.

She had already been burned once, stepping back from love and also after everything with her brother. Her feelings for Ben were different and gentler, but still, she wasn't sure she was ready to take the risk. It could be an upside or downside risk, time will tell. The last thing she wanted was to become the subject of office gossip and have it affect her work. The way things had started between them was comfortable. No need to mess with that.

Still, it was hard to ignore how easy it was to be around him. Ben made her laugh and paid attention to her in small ways, something she hadn't felt in a long time even in her last relationship. The temptation to just let things happen was real, but Taylor knew she had to be careful. She wasn't the type to dive headfirst into anything without thinking it through first. And if they were going to take the next step, it couldn't just be about them, there were bigger things to consider, the whole work ethic and future plans. It wasn't only about what could happen between her and Ben, it was about what it could mean for everything else, too.

Lunch breaks became an opportunity for them to step away from the office, to walk and talk without the usual interruptions. As they strolled around, walking to Greenwood Park or along nearby streets, their conversations drifted from work to more personal matters, about their pasts, their dreams, and everything in between. Ben's warmth and attentiveness made Taylor feel seen in a way she hadn't realised she needed. It wasn't just about her grief anymore, it was about the quiet connection they were building, something more than just friendship but too new to define. Taylor had taken a step back from love after a severe heartbreak that nearly cost her everything. She wanted to approach this with extreme caution, though her heart told her otherwise.

The more time they spent together, the more it became clear that something was blossoming between them. What had started as an outlet for mutual comfort had grown into a quiet attraction. Neither of them had been looking for it, but they both knew it was there, undeniable and starting to change their work dynamics. When love takes over, it can be a beautiful feeling. They even started hanging out at the canteen more often, sharing their meals. On this sunny Friday, they enjoyed their lunch, chatting the time away. Other officers played drought (checkers) or scrolled through their phones, glued to the screens.

Ben tilted his head, a playful smile spreading across his lips. "You know, I have to say, you're harder to read than I expected."

Taylor raised an eyebrow. "Am I? I think I'm straightforward."

"Really?" He leaned forward again, eyes narrowing slightly, a teasing smirk forming. "Because when you look at me like that, it's almost like you're... investigating me, Officer T."

They locked eyes and Taylor couldn't help but laugh. "Maybe I am," she said with a wink. "You make it hard not to. You've got this whole... mysterious thing going on."

Ben's eyes lit up, and he straightened his posture, sitting up tall like a horse about to strut.

"Mysterious, huh? You sure you're not just intrigued?"

"Maybe," she said with a teasing tone, leaning back in her seat, making a show of examining him. "You've certainly got... layers."

A hint of surprise passed through his eyes. "Layers, huh? I like the sound of that."

"I'm sure you do," she said, her lips curling into a playful grin. "So, what's your next move, Officer Mysterious?"

Ben's grin widened, and he leaned in just slightly, his voice dropping low. "Maybe I'll show you, but only if you're ready for it."

Taylor locked eyes with him, a spark of excitement rising in her chest. "I think I'm always ready."

He chuckled and leaned back, to finish his food. A satisfied grin spread across his face. "Good to know. But I'm not one to rush, Taylor. I like to take my time."

She couldn't help but smile at the challenge in his voice. "I'm sure you do."

For a moment, they just sat there, enjoying their lasagna and Italian salad.

"Let me guess," Ben said after a few mouthfuls.

"You're going to leave me hanging now, aren't you?"

She tapped her chin, acting like she was deep in thought. "Maybe. Or maybe I'll just keep you on your toes."

His eyes twinkled as he shot her a sidelong glance. "I can handle a little mystery."

Taylor stood up, preparing to leave, but before she did, she leaned across the table, her voice dropping lower.

"Well, I'll let you think on that, and next time, maybe I'll share a few of my secrets."

With that, she walked away, leaving Ben with a half-smirk and an unmistakable curiosity.

Chapter 43

"Look at this place," Stefano said one afternoon, admiring a local artist's work. "It's raw and unfiltered, just like you."

Suki laughed, her heart swelling. "You always know how to make me feel special."

His eyes sparkled. "You are special, Suki. Don't forget it." That had been the last time they were together, and the next would be their trip to Zimbabwe.

Suki's smile faded just as soon as it had appeared. Her glow withered as she bowed her head. What was she doing, gallivanting around the world with this man who could have any woman he wanted in a whiff? Even younger ladies, fresh from high school threw themselves at him but he always reassured her that he liked them mature like wine. Her insecurities fluctuated especially now ahead of this trip. Africa held a special place in her heart as she fell in love with Tohimo at an inauguration function back in the day. Their chemistry from then sparked so bright it grew within months and they married in a lavish style off the coast of Madagascar. Their honeymoon in Zimbabwe, spent at Victoria Falls, was a memory from years ago. But now, with the upcoming SADC Summit and crucial meetings about Zimbabwe trade deals, old feelings for her first love, Tohimo, began to resurface, reigniting a fire she hadn't expected. The midlife crisis manifests itself in various mild forms yet sometimes these can border on hospitalization or mental deterioration. Suki looked young and it may have been a case of misaligned values. How did she get so lost in all the diplomatic wifely duties to lose herself in the process? If anything, her husband disadvantaged her and because of him, she languished in this state of confusion. A state of teenage-like infatuation. She even gave Stefano a monthly allowance. Such desperation. Suki ran her hand through her hair, gasping. Startled, she darted to her laptop and locked into her bank account. "Oh crap," she said between gritted teeth. "That bastard."

A sudden knock echoed through the grand foyer, making Suki jump to her feet. The sound seemed to echo off the marble floors, catching her off guard. She stumbled, barely catching herself on the edge of the polished walnut table, her heart pounding.

After a quick breath, she called out, "Who's there?" Her voice came out shakier than she'd hoped. Sometimes, when you're lost in your darkest thoughts, it feels like the walls are listening.

When she opened the heavy wooden door, she was greeted by a lush bouquet of deep red roses, their velvety petals almost too perfect, and a tiny, printed note tucked inside. Suki's stomach tightened as she read the words scrawled across it: "I will always love you."

Her pulse quickened. "Tohimo?" she whispered, but the note didn't feel like something he would write. The typed note made it harder to tell. The familiarity of the sentiment sent a pang of guilt through her. She quickly scanned the broad hallway of the mansion, empty. No sign of anyone.

Her mind raced. Tohimo had bought her flowers before, but so had Stefano. And this note, it wasn't like something Tohimo would say. Stefano was the romantic one of the two, but he never sent flowers to her house.

She held the flowers for a moment, trying to keep herself calm. "I can't keep them. Where's the butler?" she muttered, more to herself than anyone else. Suki glanced around. She tore the note in half, dropping the pieces into the toilet. She flushed it quickly, watching as it disappeared like it never existed.

Just as the toilet lid clicked shut, the sound of footsteps grew louder from behind her. Suki froze her heart in her throat. She turned quickly to find Tohimo standing in the doorway of their expansive living room, his gaze fixed on the flowers.

"Who sent those?" His voice was calm, but there was a sharpness to it like he was already sensing something was off.

Suki's heart pounded. She took a step forward, forcing a smile. "Oh, they were just... a little something for you," she said, trying to sound casual. "I thought I'd surprise you. A little gift, you know? Before our big trip."

Tohimo raised an eyebrow, his gaze still and cold. He glanced at the lavish bouquet and then back at her. "Before our big trip?" he repeated, his voice tinged with disbelief. He stepped further into the room, his footsteps heavy on the marble. "We've got weeks until we leave. Why now? We always go on 'big' trips."

Suki felt a cold sweat on the back of her neck. She quickly tried to look for an excuse that wouldn't raise more questions. "I don't know, I just... thought you might like them. You know, something to look forward to. And also, something to spark our romance, you know things haven't been too exciting for us in there." She said tilting her head in their bedroom's direction.

She forced another smile, praying the lie sounded more convincing than it felt. The room seemed to close in around her, the high ceilings and cold stone floors doing nothing to calm her nerves and pulsating heart.

Tohimo didn't say anything for a long moment. His expression remained nonchalant. but his gaze never fluttered. Suki could feel the tension hanging between them like a thick, suffocating fog.

Chapter 44

Jack Bummer was a man of routine, comfortably nestled in his role as an accountant at Weber and Flinch Accounting Solutions Group. Each day blurred into the next, filled with number crunching and reports. He often spent his evenings behind a desk, poring over spreadsheets while his children, Tia and Ian, played in the living room. His wife, Susan, would sometimes catch him staring out the window, lost in thought as if longing for something beyond their suburban life.

One evening, after the kids had finished dinner and the leftovers of macaroni and cheese sat in front of them, Jack took a deep breath. "How about a family safari trip?" he suggested, trying to keep his voice steady, even as his heart raced with excitement.

Susan looked up from her plate, a hint of scepticism crossing her face. "A safari? In Africa? Isn't that a bit too ambitious?"

"Ambitious?" Jack chuckled, leaning forward, the spark of adventure igniting in his eyes. "It's a chance for us to experience something incredible together! Think about it, seeing elephants in the wild, and exploring the savanna! The kids will love it!"

Tia's eyes widened. "Can we see lions?"

Absolutely!" Jack grinned, imagining their awe. But Ian, ever the realist, chimed in. "But what about school? I can't miss any important classes, Dad! Besides, we go to the zoo to see lions."

"Summer break, buddy. We'll plan it so you won't miss anything," Jack reassured him, though he could see doubt in Susan's eyes.

"Are you sure about this, Jack? Traveling so far, what if something goes wrong?"

Jack felt a sting of frustration but swallowed it. "Nothing will go wrong. We'll have a guide, a plan, it'll be an adventure of a lifetime. Anyway, if something's meant to go wrong, it will regardless of what you do. The law of fate."

In the weeks that followed, Jack poured himself into planning. He spent evenings researching lodges, reviews and itineraries, scrolling through endless images of wildlife and landscapes. Each night, the small family would gather to discuss their upcoming adventure, the excitement building like a crescendo. Even Ian became thrilled.

One night, he spread a map of Kenya across the dining table, tracing the routes with his finger. "This is where we'll start," he said, a sense of pride swelling in his chest. "We'll visit Maasai Mara and Amboseli. Look at all these animals we could see!"

Susan watched him with both admiration and concern. "You're set on this, aren't you?"

"I feel like we need this," he admitted, his voice relaxing. "After everything, I want us to create memories that matter, especially for our amazing kids."

Susan hesitated, remembering the financial strain they had faced last year after Jack's company had downsized. "What if it costs more than we expect? What if we don't have enough saved?"

Jack placed a hand over hers, steadying her doubts. "We'll manage. Life is about taking risks, isn't it? This is an opportunity for us to reconnect, to escape the routine. I am the accountant here remember."

"I see, the figures man has got it all figured out." They both chuckled then Ian entered the study with his little sister.

He asked his dad if they could visit the Serengeti National Park in Tanzania instead or the Malilangwe Wildlife Reserve Safari in Zimbabwe. His adorable eyes made his parents give in to his request. After a brief discussion, on the pros and cons of all three alternatives, they decided to visit Zimbabwe.

Chapter 45

There was trouble in the air. The sky is off limits, the skies were once a safe place to fly in most not all parts of the world but this freedom was brought to a brisk stop. Many airspaces were declared no-fly zones. This was due to the war that was happening between Russia and Ukraine war. With Iraq Iran and Israel involved in escalation, they made the Middle East an unviable path to fly with daily and sometimes hourly risk assessment reports being prepared and sent to all airlines. Many Airlines hiked the fees but restrictions from insurance, national policy and stakeholders such as leasing companies such as Boeing and Airbus as well as Euro Martin had a bigger say in the route continuation. Sometimes political affiliations would be a major factor in making such decisions.

The world reacted in different ways, with the USA and France, UK, Germany and many Europeans supporting the idea of Israel defending itself, a position that was also held by Australia. On the other hand, the Ukrainian President visited the US and also met the NATO member states. His objective was to seek military support in the form of F16s as well as ammunition to fight Russia. He had applied and hoped that he would be granted admission into NATO and immediately have access to the weapons at NATO's disposal. This proposal was not granted, instead, Ukraine got more aid and F16s with a condition that he was never to use them to attack Russia deep into its territory. Thus, the Euro Martin suspended flights to and from Russia and Ukraine for all its airlines under leasing, Sahara Africa Airlines had to comply with this requirement.

Furthermore, the retaliatory operation by Israel in the Gaza Strip caused a humanitarian crisis with the UN calling for the opening of the roads to allow aid to flow. Again, the air strikes caused the Euro Martin to suspend flights to Israel, Lebanon and Yemen effectively grounding Sahara Africa Airlines.

Chapter 46

Zimbabwe was a member of the Commonwealth. Zimbabwe and the Commonwealth of Nations have had a controversial and stormy diplomatic relationship this controversy was created by the refusal of the United Kingdom to finance the Land Reform program, a key independence deal between UK and the then Rhodesia. Zimbabwe is a former member of the Commonwealth, having withdrawn in 2003, and the issue of Zimbabwe has repeatedly taken center stage in the commonwealth, both since Zimbabwe's independence and as part of the British Empire. There are mixed feelings among member countries over the readmission of Zimbabwe into the commonwealth.

Zimbabwe was the British colony of Southern Rhodesia, gaining responsible government in 1923, the British did not settle well with the locals, their presence was marked with violence, murder, rape and stealing of land from the natives and creating reserves. The Locals were pushed to what were called reserves, areas with infertile land with no nutritional value and areas that received very limited rains. Southern Rhodesia became one of the most prosperous, and heavily settled, of the UK's African colonies, with a system of white minority rule.

The Britons preferred Zimbabwe due to its fertile land, and abundant mineral resources with Gold, Diamond,

Platinum, Lithium, and Emeralds among other mineral reassures. Southern Rhodesia was integrated into the Federation of Rhodesia and Nyasaland. In response to demands for greater black African power in government, the anti-federation white nationalist Rhodesian Front (RF) was elected in 1962, leading to the collapse of the federation. But by then many atrocities had been committed with many founding fathers and mothers of the Chimurenga having been captured and hanged with heads being transported to the UK museum to be displayed and spoils of conquest. Zimbabwe was once the greatest in agriculture earning the name "the breadbasket of Africa" The Country was able to not only supply itself but export food to African countries as well as to European countries. At the time the country was dubbed Little England heralding its vast wealth, cleanliness as well as the orderliness and the level of education that was in place. It is believed that Zimbabwe took time to gain its independence due to the level of investment that the British Government and the Britons had made in their individual as well as corporates.

The RF, under the leadership of Ian Smith from 1964, rejected the principle of NIBMAR that the Commonwealth demanded, and the Southern Rhodesian government, now styling itself 'Rhodesia', issued a Unilateral Declaration of Independence (UDI) in 1965. The United Kingdom refused to recognise this, and the commonwealth was at the forefront of rejecting the UDI, imposing sanctions on Rhodesia, ending the break-away, and bringing about Rhodesia's final independence under black majority rule as Zimbabwe in 1980. However, differences of opinion on how to approach Rhodesia exposed structural and philosophical weaknesses that threatened to break up the commonwealth. After Independence, the commonwealth members could not agree on how the newly born Zimbabwe was to be admitted to the former colony's membership.

In later years, under the presidency of Robert Mugabe the Commonwealth was weaponised and used to beat Zimbabwe into submitting to the demands set before it by the UK, Zimbabwe dominated commonwealth affairs, creating acrimonious splits in the organisations some believed and supported the government of the former president Mugabe while others did not agree on how Harare was dealing with its internal affairs. Zimbabwe was suspended in 2002 for breaching the Harare Declaration. In 2003, when the Commonwealth refused to lift the suspension, Zimbabwe withdrew from the Commonwealth. Since then, the Commonwealth has played a major part in trying to end the political impasse and return Zimbabwe to a state of normality.

Zimbabwe was formerly known as Southern Rhodesia from 1901. It was colonised by the British South Africa Company (BSAC), headed by Cecil Rhodes who now lies atop Matobo hills which he stated as his last wish after making peace with the Ndebele people. Southern Rhodesia first became a central issue in the Commonwealth in 1910, upon the creation of the Union of South Africa. The South Africa Act of 1909 made provisions for the accession of both Southern Rhodesia and Northern Rhodesia (present-day Zambia) to join the union. This was one of three popular options, but actively discouraged by the BSAC, which preferred union with Northern Rhodesia. This was actively pursued by the BSAC administration, under Leander Starr Jameson and Francis Chaplin, as a means of countering an Afrikaner-dominated South Africa.

In the election of March 1914, BSAC-supported candidates (as opposed to supporters of self-government) won twelve of the thirteen elected seats in the Legislative Council. However, when the charter came up for renewal in August of the same year, it was granted only on condition that further political rights were extended: pushing the territory towards self-government. Furthermore, in 1918, the Privy Council ruled that the BSAC did not own any alienated land. Now being unable to sell land, it decided against investing any further in the colony but advocated incorporation into the Union of South Africa, which would be able to compensate its shareholders.

This, however, was unpopular amongst settlers, who, in the 1920 election, elected ten representatives of the Responsible Government Association. Persuaded by its popular support, Colonial Secretary Viscount Milner formed a commission to investigate, and this commission, the Buxton Commission, ruled that the two options – union with South Africa and responsible government – be put to a referendum. Union was rejected by the Southern Rhodesian people, who voted in the 1922 referendum in favor of responsible government, which was granted in 1923.

The European appearance of Southern Rhodesia's capital Salisbury (pictured here in 1930; now called Harare) reinforced the settlers' belief that Southern Rhodesia deserved to be a Dominion, on a par with the Union of South Africa.

Southern Rhodesia had been granted a great deal of autonomy, including powers over defense and constitutional amendment, but falling short of Dominion status. However, observers would be forgiven for thinking that Rhodesia had just become the eighth dominion (as, indeed, reported Time magazine). Southern Rhodesian Premiers were routinely invited to Imperial Conferences of dominions' Prime Ministers from 1932 onwards; and, when the Dominions Office was created in 1925, Rhodesia was the only non-Dominion to fall under its remit, in recognition of its quasi-independent status.

Indeed, the government of Southern Rhodesian itself was under the same misapprehension. Its official position, which it would hold until UDI, was that Southern Rhodesia was already a member of the Commonwealth, albeit not a Dominion. When Robert Menzies, Prime Minister of Australia, found in 1963 that Jack Howman thought that Southern Rhodesia 'is and always has been a member of the Commonwealth', this caused a diplomatic spat that contributed to the Unilateral Declaration of Independence.

Nonetheless, Southern Rhodesia did recognise that it had limits on its self-government. For example, foreign relations were not maintained, nor could the government change the Southern Rhodesian pound from parity against the British pound sterling. The most important derogation was on racial affairs; laws related to racial affairs were to have Royal Assent withheld. However, despite these limits, and the formal supremacy of British statutes under the Colonial Laws Validity Act 1865, a convention emerged that Parliament would not legislate for Southern Rhodesia, nor the Governor withhold Assent, without the Legislative Assembly's permission. The threat of intervention may have achieved some successes, such as when the Rhodesian government attempted to ban native Africans from voting outright in 1934, but these were few and far between. The result is that, even though self-government had been tailored to avoid the creation of a system that subjugated the native population, it happened anyway: directly against the zeitgeist of the rest of the Empire at the time.

Discussions returned to the further integration of Southern Rhodesia with surrounding colonies. Plans to amalgamate with Northern Rhodesia had been rejected by the settler population in 1916 on the grounds that a merger with its less developed neighbour would delay self-government. However, when the Hilton Young Commission recommended in 1929 an even wider union, encompassing both central and eastern Africa, a Rhodesian union became the lesser of two evils and jumped upon.

In the face of this opposition to the recommendations of the Hilton Young Commission, in 1935, Viscount Bledisloe (newly departed Governor-General of New Zealand) was asked to evaluate the future of cooperation and combination of the colonies of central Africa. The government required him to consider the "interests of the inhabitants, irrespective of race." Taking four years to report and acquiring the nickname "Viscount Bloody-slow" for this, Bledisloe concluded that there was a single barrier to political integration: Southern Rhodesia's racist legislation. Under the doctrine of non-interference that had been established, this was seen as insurmountable, putting off any political integration, yet allowing for the economic integration that Bledisloe recommended as feasible.

Southern Rhodesia attempted to show its loyalty to independence from the mother country by symbolically becoming the first colony to affirm the United Kingdom's declaration of war on Nazi Germany in 1939 (like other colonies, as well as Australia and New Zealand, which had not ratified the Statute of Westminster, it had no power to declare war itself). It is often reported that a greater proportion of the population of Southern Rhodesia served in the war than of any other part of the Empire. Even though this has become a part of nationalist folklore, this is to include only the White population (of whom, 15% served), and not the population as a whole (of whom, 2% served). Nonetheless, there developed a nationalist perception that the UK and its empire owed the Southern Rhodesians a debt: which continued right up until the late 1970s.

During the war, Southern Rhodesia benefited from the "lucrativeness of loyalt," by hosting several bases of the British Commonwealth Air Training Plan. Even though there were no established training facilities before the war, shortly after the outbreak, Prime Minister Godfrey Huggins offered to raise three air squadrons, initiating a dialogue that led to the United Kingdom offering a blank cheque to train as many pilots and aircrew as Southern Rhodesia could manage. In total, 10,107 service personnel, including 7,730 pilots, were trained in Southern Rhodesia under the plan. The construction and operation of the bases (paid for mostly by the UK and Canada), as well as the location of thousands of service personnel in the colony, boosted the war-time economy of Southern Rhodesia dramatically. Higgins estimated that the training camps were as important to the war-time economy as the gold-mining industry.

The Central African Federation – incorporating Southern Rhodesia, Northern Rhodesia, and Nyasaland – was designed as a buffer state to Afrikaner-dominated South Africa.

In 1945, a Central African Council was formed as a consultative body for the three British central African territories: Southern Rhodesia, Northern Rhodesia, and Nyasaland (present-day Malawi). This was the limit of the

British wish for integration: fearful for the same reasons Bledisloe had been. However, the conversion in July 1948 of the Northern Rhodesian settler leadership, under Roy Welensky, to supporting federalism (from long-held support for amalgamation) promoted London to reconsider its position.

When Welensky held talks with the Southern Rhodesia leadership at Victoria Falls, he agreed to a wide-ranging agreement that, far from loose federalism, seemed more a plot to amalgamate under white Rhodesian leadership. This would be a recurring theme, firstly in April 1950, as a vicious circle of patently unacceptable Rhodesian proposals were made and flatly refused: potentially alienating the promise of resolution, hence pushing white settlers towards South Africa.

The official visit of Gordon Walker to the region in early 1951 was the turning point for the United Kingdom. Startled by the strength of pro-South African support in Salisbury, Walker's report made it clear that, spurned, Southern Rhodesia could turn to outright revolt, as "potential American colonies – very loyal, but very determined to have their way." This, it was feared, would lead to a cataclysmic war between settler-dominated South and East Africa and native-dominated West Africa: ripping apart the nascent Commonwealth. Coupled with the Baxter report from a conference of officials, the report to the cabinet stated unequivocally: "[federation is] urgently desirable in the interests of the territories (including those of the African inhabitants) and the Commonwealth."

It has been suggested that the main impetus for the British fear of South African domination of central Africa was to avoid South Africa cornering the market in various raw materials: including gold, chrome, and uranium.

The Federation would be "the most controversial large-scale imperial exercise in constructive state-building ever undertaken by the British government."

But for the likely hostile reaction from the rest of the Commonwealth, and hence a threat to its very existence, it is probable that the British government would have accepted an independent Southern Rhodesia upon the death of the Federation in 1963. However, the preservation of the Commonwealth was the predominant concern of the British government and thus persevered with the gradual introduction of black majority rule to Rhodesia to avoid being forced to 'choose between Southern Rhodesia and the Commonwealth' (in Harold Macmillan's words).

The 1964 Meeting of Commonwealth Prime Ministers was the first held after the collapse of the federation, and, even though federal Prime Ministers had attended during the federation, and Southern Rhodesian Prime Ministers had before the federation, this invitation was not extended to Prime Minister Ian Smith. This was seen as the utmost slight, particularly as newly independent Malawi – Southern Rhodesia's former federal partner – was in attendance. Before the federation, the Southern Rhodesian government had attended every meeting since 1932, and its official position was that it was already a member of the Commonwealth, hence entitled to attend as a matter of right.

On 11 November 1965, Smith issued a Unilateral Declaration of Independence (UDI). On the day of UDI, the United Kingdom imposed the most stringent financial and economic constraints it had imposed upon any country (including Egypt during the Suez Crisis) since the Second

World War. In vetoing loans to Rhodesia from the International Monetary Fund, World Bank, and other institutions; imposing a trade embargo on arms, sugar, and tobacco; making it harder for Rhodesians to access London financial markets than the Soviet Union; and removing Commonwealth Preference, the British government was seen to have done everything possible to punish Rhodesia economically, except to impose an oil embargo, which was itself forthcoming on 17 December 1965.

This was not enough to placate some Commonwealth members, who demanded a military response. Two, Ghana and Tanzania, even suspended diplomatic relations with the United Kingdom as a reaction to the United Kingdom's refusal to use military force to oust Smith. An emergency Meeting of Commonwealth Prime Ministers convened in Lagos, Nigeria (the only one held outside London) on 10 January 1966 to address the crisis. At this meeting, Wilson pledged that sanctions imposed by the Commonwealth would bring the crisis to an end 'within a matter of weeks, not months'. However, on 14 January, Wilson stated that military intervention could not be ruled out, and, on 25 January, also stated that there would be no negotiations with the Rhodesian administration except on how to bring about an orderly return to direct rule.

The 1966 full Prime Ministers' Meeting, held in September, saw the Commonwealth as a whole close to collapse, as African members suspected that the UK was on the verge of breaking its pledges not to negotiate over the issue of NIBMAR. Nonetheless, despite Harold Wilson describing it as "by common consent, the worst ever held up to that tim," the meeting passed without cataclysm, but led to a hiatus in PM meetings until 1969 (at the behest of Wilson, and opposed by Arnold Smith). Meanwhile, the UK had been conducting exploratory talks with the Rhodesian government, aboard HMS Fearless (in 1966) and HMS Tiger (1968) which led to Rhodesia declining very favorable terms. Similarly favorable terms were proposed in 1971, but discarded when the British government determined that they were largely rejected by the African population.

However, this movement towards negotiation and appeasement of the Salisbury regime was turned on its head over the following two years, thanks in no small part to pressure from the Commonwealth. The Singapore Declaration, issued at the first Commonwealth Heads of Government Meeting, articulated the political principles of the Commonwealth, including the elimination of racial discrimination. With the incorporation of this implicit commitment to opposing Rhodesia into the Commonwealth's aims and the increasing disparity of British economic interests in Africa, the UK chose the Commonwealth over Rhodesia.

The hardening of the United Kingdom's line came as part of a wave of bad news for the Rhodesian regime. The Carnation Revolution in Portugal led to the end of Portuguese assistance from Mozambique, and, in its place, put an independent Mozambique with a left-wing government, which was eager to aid guerillas from Rhodesia. South African Prime Minister B. J. Vorster attempted détente with the newly independent Angolan and Mozambican governments, and, believing a stable majority-governed country to be in South Africa's interests, persuaded Ian Smith that white minority rule could not continue forever in Rhodesia.

All this brought Rhodesia to the negotiating table with moderate African leaders, leading to the Internal Settlement under which Rhodesia became Zimbabwe Rhodesia. The Commonwealth flatly refused to recognise Rhodesia-Zimbabwe and did not lift its sanctions. At the 1979 CHOGM, the Heads of Government issued the Lusaka Declaration, once again committing itself to ending racial discrimination. The official communiqué of the meeting invited Rhodesia-Zimbabwe's new Prime Minister Abel Muzorewa and Ian Smith to a constitutional convention with the leading guerilla leaders, giving rise to the Lancaster House Agreement in 1979.

The agreement demanded a ceasefire, reverted Rhodesia into the British colony of Southern Rhodesia, with full control from London, and paved the way for an election in 1980. To implement the Lancaster House Agreement, at the behest of Commonwealth Secretary-General Shridath Ramphal and Kenneth Kaunda (and in the face of opposition from Lord Carrington), the Commonwealth created the Commonwealth Monitoring Force (CMF). This included 1,097 Britons, as well as representatives of Australia, Canada, Fiji, Kenya, and New Zealand, totaling 1,548 service personnel. They organised ceasefire assembly places, at which guerillas could disarm and reintegrate into their communities in time for the election. Observers expected the operation to fail, as the composition and swiftness of deployment seemed to fly in the face of convention wisdom. Nonetheless, it succeeded in maintaining peace, demilitarizing the militia and guerillas, and presiding over a peaceful election that election observers deemed free and fair.

The resounding victory of Robert Mugabe's ZANU-PF in March 1980 led to Southern Rhodesia's independence as the Republic of Zimbabwe later that year. Upon independence, Zimbabwe joined the Commonwealth: five decades after Southern Rhodesia's government had mistakenly believed that it had in the wake of its invitation to the 1932 British Empire Economic Conference. The end of the Rhodesian crisis was a victory for Commonwealth principles, and their application to the policies of a member: in this case, the United Kingdom itself. Shridath Ramphal played a vital role in the affair, whilst it was the 1979 Commonwealth Heads of Government meeting that played host to the deliberations and resolutions of the crisis, and a Commonwealth military force that kept the peace.

For its part, Mozambique was recognised as a "cousin state" of the Commonwealth and was rewarded for its opposition to the Rhodesian regime with accession to the Commonwealth in 1995: becoming the only member without direct constitutional links to another.

In recent times, Zimbabwe has dominated the agendas of most Commonwealth Heads of Government Meetings (CHOGMs). President Robert Mugabe's government was accused of abusing human rights, rigging elections, and undermining the Zimbabwean economy. The matters his government is accused of contravene the basic principles of the Commonwealth, as outlined in the Harare Declaration, issued at the 1991 CHOGM in (ironically enough) Zimbabwe's capital, Harare.

After the Zimbabwean people rejected Mugabe's proposed new constitution in a February 2000 referendum, the situation deteriorated rapidly, as violence against opponents increased. To address these issues, in September 2001, Zimbabwe sent a delegation to meet with the Commonwealth Ministerial Action Group (CMAG), which is responsible for upholding the Harare Declaration. Zimbabwe promised to end the violence and defend human rights, as required of them as Commonwealth members but failed to do so. As a result, the United Kingdom pushed to suspend Zimbabwe from the Commonwealth. This has been characterised by Mugabe, and South African President Thabo Mbeki, as a neo-colonial campaign, but this is derided as ungrounded revisionism and racism itself.

The 2002 CHOGM was delayed in the aftermath of the September 11 terrorist attacks on the United States, but Zimbabwe was still top of the agenda.

On 4 March 2002 the CHOGM statement issued at Coolum, Australia implicitly rejected calls by the United Kingdom, Australia, and New Zealand for punitive action to be taken against Zimbabwe for alleged violence and intimidation surrounding the Presidential Election Campaign. CHOGM, instead, "expressed their deep concern," and called on all parties to work together "to create an atmosphere in which there could be a free and fair election." CHOGM also "noted that a Commonwealth Observer Group would report to the Commonwealth Secretary-General immediately after the Zimbabwe presidential election of 9–10 March 2002" and confirmed their agreement to mandate the CHOGM Chairman-in-Office as well as the former and next Chairmen-in-Office [i.e. the Troika] in close consultation with the Secretary-General and taking into account the Commonwealth Observer Group Report, to determine appropriate Commonwealth action on Zimbabwe in the event the Report is adverse...which ranges from collective disapproval to suspension

Shortly after the presidential election had concluded, the Report of the Commonwealth Observer Group was submitted to the Troika. Even the Government of Zimbabwe concedes that its conclusions were "adverse". On 19 March 2002 the Troika, being the competent Commonwealth body, suspended Zimbabwe for 12 months. The Zimbabwe government disputes that there were legitimate grounds for its suspension. Zimbabwe considers that the CHOGM statement only permitted the Troika to go beyond an expression of collective disapproval if something adverse was reported on in the Commonwealth Observer Group Report about the period after the CHOGM statement was issued and ending at the time when the voting in the election ended (7 days in total). The Zimbabwe government considers that although adverse findings were contained in the Report, none of them related to that period and therefore the Troika did not have competence to suspend it from the Commonwealth.

Unlike all other previous Commonwealth country suspensions, Zimbabwe's was for a definite period of 12 months. In the case of a suspension for a finite period, there is no need for such a suspension to be lifted. It automatically lapses unless it is renewed or extended. The Zimbabwean Government and the Southern Africa Development Community contend that this therefore meant that in the absence of a renewal or extension, Zimbabwe's suspension by the Troika would automatically lapse on 19 March 2003. A split emerged in the Troika. Australia was in favor of a further suspension. South Africa and Nigeria (i.e. the majority of the Troika) were not. Indeed, the Zimbabwean Government points to the letter dated 10 February 2003 from the President of Nigeria to the Prime Minister of Australia in which he stated: "that the time is now auspicious to lift sanctions on Zimbabwe about her suspension from the Commonwealth Councils." According to the Zimbabwe Government, the President of South Africa also contacted the Prime Minister of Australia to convey the same message.

Notwithstanding that there had been no Troika decision, on 12 February 2003, the Prime Minister of Australia and the Secretary General of the Commonwealth announced that Zimbabwe would remain suspended until the next CHOGM in December 2003. This "purported" further suspension was disputed by the other members of the Troika and Zimbabwe for the reasons described above. Moreover, the Southern African Development Community formally confirmed its position that Zimbabwe's one-year suspension had lapsed on 19 March 2003. This was reaffirmed at a meeting of the troika of the SADC Organ for Politics, Defence and Security — namely Lesotho (chair), Mozambique and South Africa, with Zimbabwe invited — in Pretoria in late November 2003.

Failing to get Mugabe to meet with the opposition MDC Morgan Tsvangirai, Chairperson-to-be Obasanjo refused to invite Mugabe to the CHOGM.

The rest of the CHOGM's deliberations on Zimbabwe were marked by the same African disunity, foiling Mbeki's repeated attempts to have Zimbabwe readmitted. Ultimately, the CHOGM rejected the Mbeki led minority group and implicitly rejected the views of the majority of the Troika that Zimbabwe's suspension had already terminated. Instead, the CHOGM statement (tabled by Canada and Kenya) treated Zimbabwe as a country that was still suspended and determined to continue its suspension for an indefinite period, appointing a six-member panel to advise on the way forward. The committee, composed of the Heads of Government of South Africa, Mozambique, Nigeria, India, Jamaica, Australia, and Canada, ruled by six-to-one (South Africa being the one) against lifting Zimbabwe's suspension.

Following the CHOGM, the SADC (supported by Uganda) issued a statement in which it expressed deep concern at what it called the 'dismissive, intolerant and rigid attitude' shown by some Commonwealth members toward Zimbabwe. SADC has consistently pleaded for greater patience and understanding of Zimbabwe and cautioned against lecturing and hectoring.

A separate and not directly related matter at the CHOGM was an attempt by Mbeki to oust Secretary-General Don McKinnon, who was up for election but whom the convention dictated should not be challenged. However, only seven (of eighteen) African Heads of Government voted for Mbeki's candidate (along with the four South Asian countries), Sri Lanka's Lakshman Kadirgamar, allowing McKinnon to win by 40 votes to 11.

In an official letter to the Commonwealth Secretariat dated 11 December 2003, Zimbabwe formally terminated with effect from 7 December 2003 its membership in the Commonwealth. This confirmed President Mugabe's decision to leave the organisation following the CHOGM statement issued in Nigeria, which indefinitely suspended Zimbabwe from the Commonwealth. On 19 November 2003, the Minister of Foreign Affairs of Zimbabwe made a detailed statement on the whole affair to the Parliament of Zimbabwe.

The withdrawal marked only the third occasion (after South Africa in 1961 and Pakistan in 1971) that a country had withdrawn voluntarily, although Ireland had voluntarily declared itself a republic in 1949 thereby ending its membership, but in Ireland's case, it was before the London Declaration was enacted.

The next CHOGM, held in Abuja, Nigeria, in December 2003, was once more dominated by the Zimbabwean crisis. Failing to get Mugabe to meet with the opposition MDC Morgan Tsvangirai, Chairperson-to-be Obasanjo refused to invite Mugabe to the CHOGM. At the CHOGM, Mbeki attempted to oust Secretary-General Don McKinnon, who was up for election but whom convention dictated should not be challenged. However, only seven (of eighteen) African Heads of Government voted for Mbeki's candidate (along with the four South Asian countries), Sri Lanka's Lakshman Kadirgamar, allowing McKinnon to win by 40 votes to 11.

The rest of the CHOGM's deliberations on Zimbabwe were marked by the same African disunity, foiling Mbeki's repeated attempts to have Zimbabwe readmitted. To resolve the impasse, Canada and Kenya proposed a committee to resolve the issue of whether to lift Zimbabwe's suspension. The committee, composed of the Heads of Government of South Africa, Mozambique, Nigeria, India, Jamaica, Australia, and Canada, ruled six-to-one (South Africa being the one) against lifting Zimbabwe's suspension. In response, Robert Mugabe announced on 7 December that Zimbabwe was withdrawing from the Commonwealth: marking only the third occasion (after South Africa in 1961 and Pakistan in 1971) that a country had withdrawn voluntarily.

British Foreign and Commonwealth Secretary David Miliband and outgoing Secretary-General Don McKinnon both expressed their approval of Zimbabwe's return to the Commonwealth if the country resolved its infringements of the Harare Declaration, especially under a new government.

Mugabe has stated that Zimbabwe would never rejoin the Commonwealth, calling it an 'evil organisation'. Before the 2008 parliamentary election, opposition leader Morgan Tsvangirai, whose party won the vote, announced that, under his leadership, Zimbabwe would seek a return to the Commonwealth. It has been compared to South Africa's withdrawal in 1961, on the occasion of which Canadian Prime Minister John Diefenbaker said that there would always be a 'candle in the window' until South Africa returned: the reentry of Zimbabwe would vindicate the Commonwealth's moral commitment to the Zimbabwean people and its principles.

Emmerson Mnangagwa, who replaced Robert Mugabe as President of Zimbabwe in late 2017 has indicated that Zimbabwe may return to the Commonwealth in time for the 2022 Commonwealth Games in Birmingham, England, following The Gambia's return to the Commonwealth under Adama Barrow on 8 February 2018, and The Gambia's return to the Commonwealth Games Federation on 31 March 2018.

On 15 May 2018, Mnangagwa submitted an application to rejoin the Commonwealth. In February 2019, Harriett Baldwin, Minister of State for Africa & International Development, said: "As of today, the UK would not be able to support this application because we don't believe that the kinds of human rights violations that we are seeing from security forces in Zimbabwe are the kind of behavior that you would expect to see from a Commonwealth country." In retaliation, Mnangagwa mentioned in an interview with French TV news channel France 24 that: "The Commonwealth has never told us that they are not considering our application. The view of one member is not the view of the Commonwealth".

Many Zimbabweans have long been asking the government to explain why there should be an urgent need to join the Commonwealth nations. In response the government has indicated that being in the Commonwealth, member countries benefit from being part of a mutually supportive community of independent and sovereign states, aided by more than 80 Commonwealth organizations. This means that these nations can form alliances, support systems as well as share economic, social and political and military insights for the well-being of their people. Commonwealth has a total population of more than 2.4 Billion globally, this represents a market that a member nation can do business with. Exports can be bolstered and in the event of disagreements between member states, the spirit of the Commonwealth community allows parties within the community to aid discussions and resolve matters amicably.

The Commonwealth Secretariat, established in 1965, supports Commonwealth member countries in achieving development, democracy and peace. We are a voice for small and vulnerable states and a champion for young people. The Common Wealth also strengthens governance, builds inclusive institutions and promotes justice and human rights. Our work helps to grow economies and boost trade, empower young people, and address threats such as climate change, debt and inequality. Additionally, the commonwealth provides training and technical assistance and supports decision-makers to draw up legislation and deliver policies. We deploy experts and observers who offer impartial advice and solutions to national problems. We also provide systems, software and research for managing resources.

At Commonwealth summits, governments are brought together, by leaders whose decisions will have an enduring impact on all citizens. By uniting member countries in this way, we help to amplify their voices and achieve collective action on global challenges. Best practice regarding sustainability and ESG.

Chapter 47

Captain Smith received a call the day he was to be knighted by the King of England, the call was brief. A hoarse voice came to the crackling phone with thunderstorms and blinding lightning making communication difficult. "You have done well Captain, you need to be proud of yourself, now we are going to be very rich with you holding that diplomatic passport we will be untouchable. Welcome to the new beginning" The Captain held the call deciding not to respond, his phone was on automatic recording but that did not matter as the caller received a message that the call was being recorded. The caller had used artificial intelligence to filter the voice and made the call via a foreign jurisdiction to disguise the true origin of the call.

The event was attended by the Captain's family, after all the formalities the Captain knelt down before the 76-year-old King Charles, the King was dressed in a highly decorated uniform with gold stripes to show his rank. The Captain looked at the sword that the King was carrying and at some point it looked like the King was shaking, the sword, the hilt is 12 3/4 in (32 cm) long and it weighs 5 lb 1 1/4 oz (2.30 kg), without the scabbard. The King had read the exploits that the Captain had performed and this was followed by the tapping of the sword on both sides of the shoulders.

After the King proclaimed Captain Smith a Knight, there was confusion about what to call him as he had his prefix as captain already, a designation that he loved and was passionate about. Sir Smith was a new designation and he was to use it to appease the King. It wouldn't be a good thing for the King's ears to hear that Captain Smith is preferring to be called by his old designation. So a new designation, a new prefix was born, Sir Captain Smith, the names seemed heavy already. So the new world had ended, a new world was to be made, the world of honor and recognition yet in the same code, embarrassment. The new designation brought with it a prospect of shame, and destruction, yet again it was not without wealth. Sir Captain Smith was not a man trapped between good and evil, though he had his weaknesses, he had managed to live a life of decency, managing to look after his family, leaving behind him a legacy of wealth, wisdom, stewardship and love.

***

Sir Captain Smith was at it again depressed in his captain gear for the skies, the uniform that he had done for years had had a new meaning attached to it. As he walked at the Airport approaching the check-in counter, each step was an expression of confidence as those familiar to them shouted congratulatory messages with the captain stopping twice to greet colleagues in the industry. His fame had grown overnight, or shall we say it took him 35 years to grow overnight. The Captain had never felt so in charge of things and the burden of carrying 980 appropriately placed, no one at Sahara Africa Airlines was as fitting as Captain Smith in carrying this burden. The Euro Martin DM747 Max, Flight EMD 1695 was headed for Harare, Zimbabwe.

It was finally happening. Sir Captain Smith took over the mic and without preamble, "Good morning, ladies and gentlemen my name is Sir Captain Smith and I am your captain. We are about to depart for Zimbabwe. Weather forecast, we expect clear skies and temperatures around 24 degrees Celsius. Shortly we shall be taking off, make sure you fasten your seatbelt and sit upright in preparation for landing."

About twenty percent of all yearly general aviation (GA) accidents occur during takeoff and departure climbs, and more than half of those accidents are the result of some sort of failure of the pilot. A significant number of takeoff accidents are the result of loss of control of the airplane. When compared to the entire profile of a normal flight, this phase of a flight is relatively short, but the pilot workload is intense. Sir Captain Smith was aware of this, trained by the finest pilot trainers and having learnt from the best, he knew very well not to take anything for granted. Every step was as critical but on that day everything was critical, the first day a Sir Captain was to fly a plane not any ordinary plane but a euro Martin, not any ordinary plane, a 980 carrying capacity, one of the few orders, an eight engine one with a thrust of 840, 000.

Sir Captain Smith was going through his routine confirmation of the procedures for take-off. Takeoff roll (ground roll) is the portion of the takeoff procedure during which the airplane is accelerated from a standstill to an airspeed that provides sufficient lift for it to become airborne. Sir Captain Smith was clear about this crucial procedure. Lift-off is when the wings are lifting the weight of the airplane off the surface. In most airplanes, this is the result of the pilot rotating the nose up to increase the angle of attack (AOA).

The initial climb begins when the airplane leaves the surface, and a climb pitch attitude has been established. This is considered complete, when the airplane has reached a safe maneuvering altitude or an reroute climb has been established.

Sir Captain was aware that before he went to the pane, he was required to check the POH/AFM performance charts to determine the predicted performance and decide if the airplane is capable of a safe takeoff and climb for the conditions and location of engine and propeller performance, increase takeoff rolls, and decrease climb performance.

It is a requirement that all run-up and pre-takeoff checklist items should be completed before taxiing onto the runway or takeoff area. As a minimum before every takeoff, all engine instruments should be checked for proper and usual indications, and all controls should be checked for full, free, and correct movement. Sir Captain Smith was aware that he was required by safety and flying procedures that he should also consider available options if an engine failure occurred after takeoff. These options include the preferred direction for any emergency turns to landing sites based on the departure path, altitude, wind conditions, and terrain. In addition, the procedure requires that he make certain that the approach and takeoff paths are clear of other aircraft. Engine failure does occur after takeoff and that is the reason why the surrounding area of the airport should be clear of any infrastructure to allow emergency landing and a jettisoning of fuel to avoid explosion of the plane at landing.

At non-towered airports, pilots should announce their intentions on the common traffic advisory frequency

(CTAF) assigned to that airport. But taking off from Heathrow this procedure was an academic point to note. When operating from a towered airport, pilots need to contact the tower operator and receive a takeoff clearance before taxiing onto the active runway. This was an important thing to note and follow religiously as planes take off at Heathrow within fine minutes of each other and following procedure has never been so important, especially at the busy airports. There are heavy penalties for failure to follow take-off and landing instructions.

Taking off immediately behind another aircraft, particularly a large and heavy transport airplane, creates the risk of a wake turbulence encounter, and a possible loss of control. However, if an immediate take-off behind a large heavy aircraft is necessary, the pilot should plan to minimize the chances of flying through an aircraft's wake turbulence by avoiding the other aircraft's flight path or rotating before the point at which the preceding aircraft rotated. While taxiing onto the runway, the pilot should select ground reference points that are aligned with the runway direction to aid in maintaining directional control and alignment with the runway centerline during the climb out. These may be runway center line markings, runway lighting, distant trees, towers, buildings, or mountain peaks.

For take-off, the pilot uses the rudder pedals in most general aviation airplanes to steer the airplane's nose wheel onto the runway centerline to align the airplane and nose wheel with the runway. After releasing the brakes, the pilot should advance the throttle smoothly and continuously to take off power. An abrupt application of power may cause the airplane to yaw sharply to the left because of the torque effects of the engine and propeller. This is most apparent in high-horsepower engines. As the airplane starts to roll forward, ensure both feet are on the rudder pedals so that the toes or balls of the feet are on the rudder portions, not on the brake.

In nose-wheel-type airplanes, pressures on the elevator control are not necessary beyond those needed to steady it. Applying unnecessary pressure only aggravates the takeoff and prevents the pilot from recognizing when elevator control pressure is needed to establish the takeoff attitude.

The pane was in the air flying steadily, a day came to the mine, "Good morning ladies and gentlemen the captain has now switched the lights signaling that it's now safe for you to move, but we recommend that you remain seated with your seat belt fastened"

Back at the language bay for the first time Sir Captain Smith had packed 6 bags, a first in his career. As he always travelled light, only had one suitcase to pack a professional hand-pulled laptop, and an accessory bag. His bags had tags written diplomat, unlike others who received the honor of knighthood, Sir Captain Smith had been blessed with a rare diplomatic passport and was to be asked to have specific government meetings on some of his meetings should the government decide. Whoever had recommended that knighthood was very clear about what they wanted to use it for. So there it was, a Sir with who received a rare honor of a diplomatic passport and was on standby to be asked to perform high-level government business. Yet he was also a high-level accessory and accomplice to drug trafficking spreading them across the world at a scale never seen before.

Sir Captain had been given the four bags each with an undisclosed substance, the Captain was never to open nor was he supposed to know what was inside the bags. He was assisted in dragging the bags and checking in all the bags one by one, the Diplomatic bags and added familiarity led to the airport authorities not questioning the luggage, if that didn't work, there was a gatekeeper, the scanner on shift going by the name Jefferson Macdonald, shift supervisor who oversaw all the operations, if that didn't work five out of the six shift staff in that area were there to make sure things went according to plan.

If there was a problem the shift manager was there to deal with any matter and the Head of security was the last man standing to make sure things went according to the plan. This was a plan made out of Sydney Sheldon's "Best laid plans" The plan was flawless. The operations were based on carefully planned events, risks identified and dealt with, scenario planning as done mathematical tools used to determine the extent of the risk and implications based on case handling and the position of the law.

The planning had both quantitative and qualitative measurements. When a plan is agreed upon, it is stress tested, and conditions of the operational environment change such as key people from scanning or managers being ill. The head of the risk was an MBA holder from Duke University, maters in Physics, MSC in Finance and Risk management. Gerald has more than 25 years in risk management, foreign operations as well as project management.

Sir Captain Smith stopped over in Kenya dropping off passengers, the standard waiting time there was 1 hour, and all proceeding passengers were asked not to exit the plane.

In the cockpit, Sir Captain Smith was accompanied by Donald Gareth from the UK and Norman Roberto from Brazil. It was a men's affair. It was Sir Captain Smith's wish to have more women take up the pilot job for commercial airlines. It was slow progress as with other jobs which required one to be absent from home for extended periods such as the military. These jobs needed women to count the cost between marriage and their professions. Ironically women who were qualified for such jobs had a desire to be in a functional marriage and have children while most women who had fewer demanding jobs did not have any desire for marriage let alone having children. It was an interesting paradox. While those who dared to venture into the profession ended up keeping their marriages, it was not without the heartache of cheating spouses or even the temptation of themselves involved in other relationships. This often created a rift. Sir Captain Smith had been making a lot of noise about friendly working conditions but airlines were not ready to embrace such a policy as it was simply too costly for them. Those who attempted to demonstrate diversity did so but did not go beyond tokenism, with no desire to go any further. Most of these were airlines whose value statements spoke of diversity, etc, and things of that nature.

The boarding time came and passengers started boarding. At the announcement desk, three people were delaying the departure of the Sahara Africa Airlines. "Good morning, ladies and gentlemen, May passenger Kuratwona Masvosve, passenger Tapiwa Mawoyo and passenger Farai Chikwenhere please proceed through boarding gate 6, you are the only passengers delaying the departure of Sahara African Airlines, thank you".

Immediately there was another beep with the lady coming to the mike "This is a security announcement, please do not leave your property unattended, if you see any unattended baggage please inform security immediately, thank you".

Another beep followed announcing the arrival of Air France, another one for Lufthansa German Airways and the Quantas arrived within 30 minutes of each other with the Emirates Airline arriving after the Quantas and so on.

At Exactly 10:30 am Sir Captain Smith completed all the formalities, ground staff exited the plane and it was taxiing time. "This is control tower Flight EDM 1695 come in" the man shouted. "This is Flight EDM 1695" Sir Captain Smith responded almost promptly. This was followed by clearance for take-off. As the Plane was entering the runway there was an urgent call from the tower for the flight to be stopped, the captain stopped the Plane. He had decided to drop the Sir part as it was making him inaccessible to his staff and everyone around him. The captain moved the plane onto the runway after clearance from the control tower. The front wheels aligned with the middle lane before picking up speed for lift-off. In the Blink of an eye, the plane was airborne. The flight was 2 hours 55 minutes, flying at 40,000 feet. The plane was such a sight to be held with seasoned pilots envying the Captain. As soon as Sir Captain Smith had switched the seat belt sign on, folks started moving up and down the aisle, presumably looking to stretch their legs as some of them had left Heathrow at 00:30 am, some removed shoes to allow smooth floor of the blood. Some folks had swollen feet.

There was no shortage of drama in the economy class with some openly talking about their highly paying jobs and how they are based in the UK, others based in the US, yet some were bragging about how they have now found new homes and well-paying jobs in the UAE. The deteriorating economic environment in Zimbabwe had caused many people to seek jobs internationally with doctors, lawyers, engineers, and accountants taking advantage of the point based system in many developed countries. In recent times the.

The crew came pushing trollies stocked with food for the passengers. The curtain to the Business class was closed perhaps to give some privacy to the business class passengers, however there was a thinking in the economy class that the treatment given to the business class is so different from the one in the economy class. For starters folks in the business class could sleep if the wish to or recline. They had cabinets right in front of them and had waiters waiting purposefully to serve. There were many complimentary drinks and gifts that came with being in the business class.

Chapter 48

Mark was nestled on a couch, they had many fights with Solomon over neglect according to Mark while Solomon complained about neglect. There was a tense atmosphere between them. Previously they used to communicate on calls, text messages and they made time to see each other even though they were aware that no one in the family liked their relationship. Jennifer was a vocal critic of Mark, she never wanted to see him close to Solomon, and he was banished from all family gatherings and was seen more as a Pig than a human being, that's according to Jennifer. This was to be expected as Jennifer was born and raised in Zimbabwe, a country where same sex relationships are not only illegal but socially unacceptable. LGBTQs would not survive in Zimbabwe, the stigma is so strong that even walking in the streets in the evening is not easy let alone in the afternoon. So, it was unbearable for Jennifer to see one of her sons in such a relationship. It was disgusting, each time Jennifer thought of or heard about Mark she would become so emotionally charged that she would need some time alone to cool down. Jennifer resented Mark from the bottom of her heart and she wished him death, not an ordinary death but a painful death, she longed for an opportunity to kill him but she never managed to get an opportunity to do so.

Jennifer was working on a case that was so complex that she needed time to herself at least according to her. With the Captain away in Africa it was a moment to get down to work. The absence of the Captain worked as a tacit approval for Jenifer to hatch her wicked plan.

Jennifer jumped out of bed, she stood before the mirror and immediately there was a harp argument within her. Jenny was the nefarious voice in her and was the first to speak to Faye. "Hey Faye, I know you are all about doing the right thing *shani shani* (etc), this time your boy Mark is in the mother of all fuck ups, the kind of fuck up deserving to die, don't you believe me"? Jenny waited for Faye to respond, Faye was trapped in games of moral, spiritual and ethical contest. Being a voice of reason, Faye had expressed concern the relationship between Mark and Solomon stating it as a relationship suited for animals not humans. So Jenny was crafty to keep that conversation to her benefit and was purposefully waiting to pounce when Faye least expected.

Faye was cautious, when she spoke her voice was low but audible. She looked Jenny in the eyes and when she spoke she was firm. "Jenny, the relationship between Mark and Solomon disgust me and there is nothing that will bring me joy than seeing the relationship dismantled you know that's the right thing to do, but I must hasten to say there is no need to kill anyone, Solomon made this decision and approached Mark, he was in charge of his faculties when he did so, hence there is no need to intervene on the matter". The response from Jenny came barely after Faye's last words. Jenny was thrilled, her voice firm but full of disdain and disregard. "Faye, listen here girl, let's talk girl to girl, I am glad you bring out the morality, and ethics about the whole thing but even culturally this relationship is not setting a great example, do you want to perpetuate this relationship and so divide the family? I see a window here, let's use it to our mutual benefit."

"You are unbelievable," said Faye. "No one has power over life you must be out of your mind, it's not our business" she continued.

Jenny looked at her and without blinking she responded "If some bad happens to Solomon and the entire family turns to LGBTQ I will have you to blame, I am inviting you to put an end to this undesirable situation that's unfolding right under our nose. We have the power to do something about it, let's use this opportunity to deal with this situation once and for all."

"Jenny you don't have my blessings on this one" Faye yelled, much to the surprise of Jenny who had always seen Faye as the quiet one.

"Very well then" Jenny responded. I will do this by myself, will do it singlehandedly and there is not a thing you can do about it.

Jennifer was having a headache after the fight between Jenny the evil spirit and Faye the voice of reason. It was very difficult for Jennifer to make a decision, she was inclined to listen to Faye the voice for the good. I suppose that was influenced by the thought of Captain Smith, she was sure that the Captain was going to side with Faye. But as they say, you have to be around to make rules, let alone police them. At that moment the Captain called from the Cockpit, as the phone was ringing, Faye whispered to Jennifer, "Pick the phone my dear this is your chance to do the right thing and the Captain will support you," Jenny interjected with her usual high pitched voice, "Jenny that not your style, you are street smart, make this Mark pay for dividing your family, had he not interfered with your son's marriage you would have saved your Family. Now look at it, Solomon has already submitted divorce papers, Lunela not playing ball and she is willing to go all the way, must put an end to this, If the Captain is too weak then you do it yourself, you have my support."

"Jenny are you sure about this, what are the implications of this strategy", Demanded Jennifer. Look here Jennifer, the Captain is not here and you cannot speak to her if you do not wish to do so. At least you do not have to bear the guilt of looking at him in the eyes and having to explain her mood. He may not understand at this point but he will eventually get it."

Jennifer stood up and started pacing, she was now avoiding the mirror as it normally brings the need to reflect every decision. She switched off her regular phone and seeing this Faye was not intrigued but at this point, the dye was cast, it was a matter of time, the unholy alliance of Jenny and Jennifer was now in charge of the operation. Jennifer took some marijuana from her closet much to the approval of Jenny, she played some reggae songs to go with the air around her and the music was doing the trick, she found herself singing along to Peter Tosh and Morgan Heritage as the marijuana was taking her to a time before creation. She had taken Marijuana each time she was stressed or needed to pump up she used it as "medicinal" She took it each time her conscience was not approving her decisions, actions, or inactions or when she was facing unknown situations and needed the courage and the confidence to overcome.

While Jennifer was still in the mood for reggae music there was a knock at the door. Before she could answer someone had already opened the.

It was none other than Stephen Conley, top max men, a racist assassin with a hit rate of 99%, who carries instructions to the latter. Jennifer handed over an envelope with GBP 45,000 the deal was not yet done, Stephen revealed the flowers he had purchased for Jennifer and insisted that she take them as appreciation. Jenny yelled, "Take the dame flowers girl we are almost there you can't start showing any weakness now we have come a long way." So, it was Jennifer who took the flowers and gave an admiring loot to Stephen who was not in the mood for that. She saw him out and then whispered "Slowly."

Later that night, Mark was in the nightclub in the company of some pimps and prostitutes. Stephen walked to him.

"Hie babe girl, I am Marshall the sailor and I like seafood, you can call me sweetness" Mark was astonished at the kind of greeting. "Sorry honey but seeing from a distance didn't think you are one of those who goes to waste on a woman, babe look at me, the world is of seafood and all you need is grab, you can even eat it with your own scales."

Mark could not resist the dirty flirty talk, they walked past the crowded nightclub. At the Door, Mark stopped. "What's the matter babe girl, you changed your mind" Stephen enquired. "I am paid upfront and my fees are GBP 500 take it or leave it". Stephen was stunned and lowering his head but maintaining his gaze. "Ok then let's make it GBP 600 with a bonus of GBP 400. Mark was surprised and his love for money overtook his reasoning.

They went into the car and drove supposedly to Stephen's apartment. Upon arrival, they went into the house and Mark was asked to prepare himself for what was to be a special night. Stephen cuffed him and Mark could not hide his excitement. At that point, there was a knock on the door and there she was in flesh and Blood, Jennifer. As she entered the house she was ushered into the same bedroom where Mark was and immediately Jennifer whispered to him "I think I need to break his heart first before we break his bones" "And how exactly are you going to do that?" Stephen enquired, his eyes narrowing and hands shaking. "Stephen I want you to sit him off the chair and make love to me while he is looking I want him to watch but before you must tell him that you have found a woman and that you would rather fuck a woman than a man. I want his heart broken.

So, it was. Stephen entered the Bedroom with Jennifer removing and throwing away clothes, at first Mark was not sure what was going on and when she recognized Jennifer he was not pleased. He asked to leave and Stephen asked him to watch. There was an immediate chemistry between Jennifer and Stephen.

"Jennifer, I don't know if you know this but I screw like a demon just saw you know", this confession pleased Jenny who lifted a middle finger at Faye. Jennifer looked at him and smiled, not a smile for one who was in love but for one on a mission. She was all in panties and Bra and they kept kissing as Jennifer moved to the bed, Stephen removed the Bra in one motion, prompting Jennifer to remark, "You are a pro, you know where things are found" Stephen did not respond as he concentrated on kissing Jennifer in the neck, going down to the tender breast, not bad for a granny, Jennifer was a beautiful woman and holding her in his arms,

Stephen had to admit that the woman was hot, he touched her back pressing it towards him and licking the nipples sending Jennifer into wild cries, Jennifer attempted to pull her pant down but Stephen held it up, he lifted her up, Jennifer was thrilled being lifted like a feather and looking at Stephen's steal chest she continued with moaning and groaning. Stephen laid her on the bed, pulled her pants and she lifted her lower body to allow smooth removal.

Wow, you are such a woman he exclaimed. Stephen pulled her towards himself grabbed her by the butt, holding her firmly he started licking her slowly, he pinned the legs with the elbows and reached for the breasts and the tongue worked on the womanhood, Jennifer was in a foreign land, a place he has never been before and there she was moaning and groaning and in an instant Stephen was inside her, she screamed with pain mixed with the pleasure, Stephen was there looking her into the eye and with each stroke there was a follow-up sound of appreciation, he turned her over and the sounds grew louder and louder. Jennifer was pleased and in the hit of the moment, she was glad that she had made the right decision. Stephen grabbed her in his arms and with her legs clipping his waist he made sweet love to her. Jennifer came three times in the whole process.

When they were done Stephen stood there he lifted her and led her to shower. While there it started again and Mark was sick to the stomach when he heard the sounds of pleasure echoing through the walls, clearly the two could not resist each other. Brought together by adversity they now became irresistible to each other.

They came back from the bathroom naked and sat by the bedside, they spoke about life in general and many other top secrets, and in his mind, Mark had mixed feelings. A feeling of sadness yet in the same code, enlightened about many issues and was hoping to paint the city ed, use the information for blackmail purposes.

Stephen lifted Jenifer one more time and he immediately was erect. This time they made slow and sweet love and both enjoyed it. They cleaned up and looked for something to eat. Jennifer had put a fire outside and placed tongs in the Charcoal fire.

Then the time came for interrogating Mark, Jennifer was in her pants and asked Stephen to allow her to handle the matter. She wanted revenge and she was clear about the pain she wanted to inflict on him. Stephen had taken a gun and stood closer to the entrance in case Mark was going to overpower Jennifer.

Jennifer pulled a chair closer to Mark who was still erect. "I thought you were a woman, how did you guys make love when both of you were men" Jennifer asked sarcastically as if she was looking for an answer. "I am the woman in our relationship and I am not shy to be one" Mark responded. "Is that so, that interesting, and how exactly did you satisfy my son, are you going to have children for him, will you have a family" Jennifer enquired her voice increasing with each question that she directed to him as if each came with an increase in tempo.

Mark was quiet for some time and when he spoke, he was shaking with anger mixed with bitterness and regret for ever meeting Solomon. "I do not care about your family, Solomon, or whoever you want to fuck, go ahead and do whatever you want to do. Leave me alone, let me leave this place and you will never hear from me again". "Too late for that". Jennifer curt him in.

Jennifer looked at him, a smirk on her face betrayed her Mischief. She stood up Grabbed his right leg and tied it to the pillar that supported the house, she took the left leg and tied it to the steel bar supporting the superstructure. She held him firm and tied his upper body to the Chair. "Do you want to rap me Jennifer come and see what you will experience, I will take you to paradise. Jennifer looked at him and remarked, Yes honey I am ready she removed her clothes and Mark was pleased, he had thought that he was going to be killed but he was relieved that all she wanted was fuck him. Jennifer was in front of Mark naked, she looked at his manhood and commented "It's a shame that it was gone to waste, might as well use it while it last. Jennifer went and pulled the tongs she could not resist the urge to sit on his manhood, Mark thought it was a game and there he was playing along and when he was enjoying the play, Jennifer stood up and clipped his manhood sending Mark into wild cried. Jennifer rushed to the fire picked another set and in one motion she removed his manhood. There was blood all over. Jennifer took some cotton, staffed the place and poured spirit. Mark was in pain. When Mark had stabilized, he asked for water to drink, he wanted food to eat as well, Jennifer brought him his roasted manhood with salad clean on the side and some water. Mark was disturbed.

Jennifer looked at Mark "You wanted to be a woman didn't you, now you are one, you can be a real woman not what you have been doing all along. Mark pleaded for Jennifer to spare his life, Jennifer loved that part, and it was a part to die for.

Jennifer took pliers and began to remove Mark's teeth one after the other till he was left with a few, he spat on her but Jennifer was not moved. Stephen watched the process and was certainly impressed but perhaps frightened by what women are equally capable of doing. Mark succumbed to his wounds and his body was thrown into the river. The body was retrieved from the river after a fisherman alerted the police.

When the news came through that a man was found dead with missing manhood and several tooths removed, Lunela was sure that it was Jennifer who had done it. But she had not thought that Jennifer would go to that extent. She was extremely scared and left her home looking for the same house away from the house.

Chapter 49

Lunela was shaken, she didn't want to believe what had just happened. She didn't want to wake up from reality. She waited for the next bulletin to see if they were going to reverse everything that was said. She didn't want Mark to die, she wanted to ask him some more questions, and she wanted to know what happened to him. She wanted to redo every conversation that they had and take each one seriously, she wanted a clue if there was any to indicate what Jennifer could have said. Jennifer was filled with regret. She wished she had asked detailed questions regarding Mark's warning earlier on.

Sometimes we find ourselves needing people that we are supposed to hate and hate the ones we are supposed to love. This was Lunel's state of mind at that moment, she was supposed to hate Mark for ravaging her marriage and celebrate his death as a dawn of new hope to save her marriage. Solomon had served her with divorce papers, but Lunela was still to sign, hence the delay in the termination of the Marriage. Lunela feared that terminating the marriage at that point amounted to a death sentence for the children. Lunela wanted the marriage to hold for some time to allow mutual cooperation during parenting. Solomon disagreed that the divorce was not going to change his position. However, Lunela knew that once the termination of their marriage was certified, Solomon's future relationships were going to make it difficult to core parent. There was bound to be some disagreements over the involvement of children and Lunela was fully aware of this and did not want such a thing to happen.

Lunela was anxious, she was passing up and down, her mind racing as she talked to herself. "So why would someone want to kill Mark, what has he done, could it be old enemies, no it can't be." The coincidence of Mark warning Lunela about Jennifer's plot to kill her and Mark being found in the River with parts missing was just too much. Lunela entered the Smith family as a Naïve, peaceful, and happy-go-lucky. She had learned to protect herself, she was now aware that there were deep-seated secrets in the family and that Jennifer if not all the members would do anything to protect that family history and its secrets. Lunela was devastated and took a notebook to make notes of all the things that Mark had told her. She remembered almost everything but none of it seemed to help.

She was back at Mark's case. Mark was found without his manhood, the entire system. If it had been in Africa, we people would have speculated that it was a work of a Sangoma who wanted them for rituals. However, such occurrences were very rare if at all they were recorded. Whoever did that to Mark was loaded for war, from the description in the local paper and people privy to the matter, Mark died a very painful death, most of the teeth were removed from his mouth, and he should have experienced excruciating pain to the point of water and blood mixing caused by deep emotional pain, agony and suffering of the flesh but anguish of the spirit. There were suggestions from some that Mark wanted to finally become a woman and what happened to him was a botched medical corrective treatment from being a male to a female. While this could have been a possibility, there was a problem with this hypothesis. In the UK such operations are permitted and Mark could afford the procedure. There was no reason for such a procedure to be done in a makeshift ward or theatre. Besides, there was no explanation for the removal of the tooth and why the body, why take out body parts. Why kill Mark, Why him? All these were questions that bagged for answer but Lunela did not have any.

As she continued to dwell on it, it dawned on her that while Jennifer resented her, the resentment was not until there were challenges in their marriage. Lunela figured out that the removal of body parts signalled something symbolic, was it a sign that someone out there wanted the world to see? Was it a statement from Solomon's mistress who felt jealous that Solomon was having a sexual relationship with a man? Was it someone who had felt disrespected being dumped for a man, was there another powerful woman who was jilted by Solomon? All there were questions with no Answers. It was a difficult situation that was at play. As she was thinking, there was a knock on the door, she opened the door and without preamble Detective Macmillan brandished his badge, he yelled: "I am Detective Macmillan, please follow us to the police station we have a few questions that we want to ask you." Lunela was stunned, the kids in the tammy moved as if in disapproval of what the detective had just said.

Chapter 50

Solomon's affair with Mark had shaken the foundation of his marriage. What began as a passionate hunt for thrill had morphed into a dangerous obsession. At first, Solomon had felt liberated, and energised, as though he had discovered a new, vibrant side of himself with Mark, the IT guy as he called him at first. He had felt something he hadn't in years.

Solomon had finished his initial consultation about the divorce with Lunela. The news of the twins stopped him cold as he wanted to avoid triggering any undue stress on Lunela for the sake of his babies. He had caused enough stress when she found out about Mark.

Mark, the handsome and charismatic younger man who had turned Solomon's life upside down, wasn't just after a casual affair or a new lover. His motives were far more calculated. As Solomon became more involved with him, Mark's true intentions slowly began to surface. He had a vendetta.

In 2017, Mark had been in a relationship with Solomon's mother, Jennifer. She had lured him with her wealth and power. Her boldness attracted him. At first, it had seemed like a mutually beneficial relationship, Jennifer had the means to spoil Mark, and Mark had the youthful energy and charm she desired. But after COVID-19, Jennifer began withholding financial support and affection and the relationship soured, and Mark's bitterness grew. He was humiliated, discarded, and left with nothing. He felt used and thrown aside like a dirty rug, and he sought to exact his revenge on Jennifer by destroying her son. By seducing Solomon, Mark would not only hurt Jennifer but also destroy the life that her son had built, the one thing she held most dear. That would spiral into destroying her whole family. Mark positioned himself on Solomon's radar and threw hints and cues that worked like magic. Then on that fateful Christmas party, Solomon made his move on Mark.

It was only when they met at the hospital that Solomon's mother discovered he was cheating on his wife with her ex-toyboy. She hid her shock and comforted the shaken Lunela. Since that time, she had threatened Mark countless times but he stood his ground. For a long time, he cowered at her but those days were over. He had executed his revenge and had nothing to lose. She had rented for him and gave him an expense allowance and cut him off without warning. He had to stay in a hostel sharing one toilet with eight grown men. The humiliation and the trauma made him bitter.

It wasn't until Solomon discovered the truth about Mark's past with his mother that everything clicked into place. The fog that had clouded his judgment started to lift, and the sense of betrayal and manipulation hit him with a brutal clarity. He had been nothing more than a pawn in a twisted game, played by someone with a personal vendetta. And to think his mother knew. His own family betrayed him like that. He felt disgusted with himself. Mark's allure had blinded him, but now he could see through the illusion. The passion, the excitement, it was all an act to control him, to tear apart his life for his mother's sins. Conflicted and deeply hurt, Solomon found himself in a crushing position.

He had initiated the process of divorce though he paused it, and Mark had made him feel loved, wanted, and alive again, feelings that had long faded in his marriage. He realised his relationship with Mark had been built on deception and manipulation. His death was a welcome relief. Mark hadn't' been the solution, he had been the problem. His drug dealings created distance with his wife but because of Mark, he lost interest in his wife. He still loved her.

Meanwhile, Lunela, who had been fighting with her sister over being weak, was facing an emotional storm. Emily insisted that she drag Solomon's whole family down. She threatened to reveal the truth instead, but Lunela begged her not to. She had always loved Solomon, despite their years of growing apart. Lunela's grief was raw, but she didn't give up on him. She was hurt, angry, and confused, hence she was prepared to hand his shady dealings to the police. She had nothing to lose. But deep down, she knew that there was something worth saving. She still loved him, and she wanted to rebuild their life together, especially with Mark out of the way forever. Though the emotional scars would never truly heal. Maybe her solace would be the twins.

Solomon made the hard decision to return to his wife. After coming to terms with Mark's betrayal and death, Solomon saw Lunela in a new perspective. They had been through so much, years of growing apart, years of misunderstanding, the drugs, then the cheating, and now the twins. There was still something between them, something that hadn't completely withered away. The affair with Mark had exposed the cracks in his marriage, but it had also highlighted how much Solomon truly had to lose.

Solomon's return to Lunela was not a triumphant homecoming but a humble one like a wounded bull. He came back, knowing the emotional work ahead, the trust he'd broken, the long road of difficult conversations, painful realisations, and slow healing. But for Solomon, coming back to his wife showed his attempt to rebuild the life he had taken for granted. Facing his mother, however, felt like too much work, he had no energy for that.

Chapter 51

With a few weeks away from the trip to Zimbabwe, Susan felt restless though she failed to pinpoint the reason. She tried to pack but she found herself pacing around the house. She shuffled outside and slumped into a bench near the apple tree. For a long time, she insisted on chopping off that tree as it never bore any fruit, but Jack refused as he believed in second chances. Susan gave Jack so many chances yet he seemed to take her for granted. He loved her but he spent little time with her. His work held him hostage. That apple tree reminded Susan of how empty her life was despite enjoying all the luxuries she desired. Her only source of genuine joy stemmed from her kids. She watched them run around their back garden, their laughter forcing her to smile, yet a knot formed in her stomach. It had been eight years since they had travelled as a family, and despite the excitement she had at the initial mention of the trip, a part of her felt awkward. She glanced at her phone, another message from Jack. Another sudden business trip. He claimed his number one love language was quality time and physical touch, yet he dedicated all his time to accounting. To his job and his secretaries and auditors, financial controllers, and the whole so-called finance people. Because of her husband, Susan stopped following love language stuff. Jack only prioritised physical touch but over time that wore off within a year of his promotion. Sometimes she wished he had remained a financial controller. She was happier back then. Now being a full-time housewife with only the kids and gardening to keep her busy plus the domestic chores, her life slipped away. She shook herself back to reading her text message. Jack sent the usual, "Can't make it for dinner, another meeting popped up. I'll join you guys later if I can." She didn't even feel surprised anymore. It had become a routine, an almost predictable pattern in their marriage. Jack's calendar always seemed to be full, his life revolving around consultancy projects, workshops, and month-end financial reports. His office was wherever he was, on a plane, in a hotel room, or surrounded by colleagues at some board meeting halfway across the world. At most, he saw his kids for more than an hour once a month as he chased work deliverables non-stop. The first 15 days of each month were for month-end reporting followed by regulatory meetings the next week. That left only a week and he dedicated that to preparation for month-end reporting. Year-end was a nightmare. It looked like Jack even volunteered to stay behind in case they needed him. When arrived home early he would sip his coffee and pat the kids then hide himself in office work and messaging his parents. When he was home, he was still buried in his laptop, his phone buzzing constantly with emails and updates from colleagues. If the senior guys did so much work, what did the interns and supervisors do? When Susan joked about it with her friends, she said, "Jack's always either in the air or behind the wheel. The man doesn't have an office anymore, he is the office."

The COVID-19 pandemic had done little to change his routine. If anything, he had spiraled beyond reproof. Most of the world had shifted to hybrid/remote working, but Jack's workaholic tendencies pushed further him into work. Susan had noticed distinct differences in the workforce, the two major schools of thought that had emerged post-COVID. On one side, some preferred to work from home, the ones who could wear boxers, a shirt, and a tie and still be productive. Jack had laughed when she pointed it out. He was always the one to joke that those who worked from home were lazy and greedy, constantly snacking and overindulging. On the other hand, there were the officegoers, those who thrived in the community feeling of being in an actual office, swapping stories at the coffee machine, catching up with colleagues in person, and playing darts at lunchtime. Susan teased that married ones were escaping the apparent nagging, whining, and the never-ending list of chores. Funny enough, her husband supported that assertion. They laughed about it then, but in hindsight, he had revealed his true colours. Susan had said it more than once, half-joking, half-serious, that they were escaping from their spouses. They just didn't want to be home." But the single employees didn't really care where they worked, as long as the paysheet came in on time. Susan had laughed when Jack had joked about that too. "At least they don't have to lie to themselves," he'd said. "Work is just a job to them."

Susan rolled her eyes. But she couldn't help feeling a little bitter at times, especially when Jill's 'business trips' were the only times he seemed to feel alive. His eyes lit up whenever he mentioned a business trip. He even packed his bags, something Susan's friends had warned her about. To them, those were clear red flags of promiscuity. She trusted her man. Jack never noticed the randy women who threw themselves at him and ignored the sultry glances of those who tried to flirt with him. He'd always been like that, disinterested, as though their attention didn't even register. To her, it was proof enough, if he didn't care about them, how could he betray her? However, a part of her always wondered—was it really about the work, or was it about the escape? Was he avoiding something here, at home? Was it her? The kids?

"Some trips can't be avoided," Jack had told her once when she asked him why he couldn't just take a break. "You know how it is. I am the key man."

At one time, Susan asked one of Jack's coworkers, a C-suite exec, if all the top accountants had to live on business trips and pull all-nighters at the office. She sought to understand the social side of accounting from someone at his level. To Susan's shock, no one worked harder than Jack, though they all carried the burden of late nights and limited social lives. The man showed her stats from the company: 85% of eligible bachelors and single women worked in the accounts department. There, she had her answer—much to Jack's embarrassment.

Jack scolded her for stepping on his toes. He yelled at her, calling her insecurities ridiculous, accusing her of tarnishing his image with his bosses. From that day on, Susan kept her questions and doubts to herself. Some of her friends sympathized, while others advised her to find a source of income to keep her busy. The more he said it, the more it sounded like an excuse. A way to stay distant. The kids were growing up, and every trip Jack took seemed to take him further away. Not just physically, but emotionally. The distance between them had become tangible, so much so that sometimes Susan felt like she was living with a stranger.

"Well, you're never home enough to make things work," she had muttered one night when he was finally back from yet another trip. And you're never here when you are."

Susan turned her back to him, plugged in her earbuds, and drowned out his words with white noise. Jack's voice trailed off as she stopped listening.

He stared at her, shaking his head. Checking his phone, he murmured he'd make some coffee. Then he trudged out. Always juggling meetings, clients, and pressing deadlines—too busy to be present. The longer he stayed away, the more he was avoiding his role as a husband and father. The kids didn't seem to notice, at least not yet. They were excited about flying, seeing animals, going on safaris, discovering new adventures, and, of course, lots of candy. Ian, the little brainiac, had a serious list of myths to bust. But Susan struggled to keep up. Still, she put on a stoic face and cheered up for the trip. This was supposed to be their break, a chance to step away from their hectic lives and reconnect. But the closer they got to departure, the more it seemed like the trip was just another distraction. She finished the research on local cultures in the Malilangwe area, booked the tickets, and packed all her bags except her husband's. Her husband, being finicky and elusive, packed his bags himself.

As Susan crawled into bed, she heard a message notification and glanced around. Her eyes landed on a basic phone tucked inside Jack's well-worn shoes, hidden behind old boots. She hesitated. The phone flashed a white light, casting a brief glow in the darkened room. Her stomach tightened, and her pedophobia flared. She set up and reached for her bedside lamp, then withdrew her hand. She only had one phone and so did Jack. In any case, she avoided old shoes, and Jack knew that even if he insisted on keeping his for sentimental value. The phone, a classic Nokia 3210, lay still. Its light had gone out, leaving it oddly out of place in the clutter, a blast from the past now silent. Was it another sentimental piece? Then the notification. Susan stared in its direction, sighing in pain and biting her lip.

#

Across town, at the corner of Church Street and 5th, the man in the hoodie lingered in an alley next to the basement parking lot at Jack's offices in Canary Wharf. The area pulsed with the energy of London's financial district, tall glass skyscrapers, sleek cars gliding by, and clean, polished streets. High-end cafés and corporate headquarters were busy while the sharp clang of the DLR trains (Docklands Light Railway) echoed from below. His breath misted in the cold air, a thin wisp of white that disappeared as soon as it formed. He watched cars go in and out as he played a game on his phone. This was the fifth time he'd been here this week.

He knew Jack's schedule by heart. The man, Jack, was working late, as usual. And the woman. Susan, back home distracted, the way she always was. Another phone beeped in his pocket, and he reached for it without taking his eyes off his game. A text from Jennifer. The message was brief, but it was enough to make his pulse quicken.

"Tonight. No excuses."

The man smiled to himself, nodding in silent admiration. True to the arrangement, as Jack drove out of the parking lot, he spotted the man, and he raised the Nokia 3210. With another nod, the man disappeared into the alley, while texting Jennifer. There had been fears that Jack discarded the phone. Mission accomplished. Special cargo confirmed.

Chapter 52

Now with only two weeks left before their trip, Jack's excitement had dwindled, despite it being his idea. His face stayed buried in his phone or laptop, his head angled downward, shutting out the world around him. Susan had tried talking to him, tried nudging him toward family time, but he always responded the same way: a quick nod or a distracted "later." She avoided asking about the secret phone, though it gnawed at her. Why couldn't she just ask? What was he hiding?

On a lazy Sunday evening, Susan paced the house, tidying up and organising stuff for the trip. Her hands worked on autopilot, folding clothes and checking items off the list. She kept darting her eyes toward her husband. He rested on the couch, eyes glued to his phone. Susan couldn't remember the last time he'd looked up long enough to make eye contact. She tried to ignore it, but her frustration bubbled up anyway. She glanced at him again, her eyes narrowing.

"Babe," she said, her voice soft, blending with the gentle notes of *Always Be My Babe* from Google Home.

He kept tapping, glancing at the screen. Susan's patience snapped.

"Jack," she called again, louder now, cutting through the soft music.

Startled, he looked up, his jaw tightening, forehead furrowing as he begrudgingly broke his attention from the screen. "What?"

Nostrils flared, she rolled her eyes, fists clenched, fighting the urge to snap. "I think I should visit my parents before we leave."

Jack frowned. "Why? We're leaving in a few days. We'll do that after the trip."

Susan's friends labelled her "too composed" and "too stoic". She endured a lot in trying to be the ideal submissive wife. At times, her nonchalant reactions puzzled even her. Her stomach twisted. "Jack. You promised we'd go see them, but we keep pushing it back." She felt the anger rise in her chest, but she kept her tone even. "I can't keep waiting around for you to make time. Besides, we hardly talk these days. And since last week, you have been distant. I need to clear my head at my parents' house."

His eyes narrowed, his lips pressing into a tight line. He stood up, setting his phone close to him on the couch. Susan could see the tension in his posture. She knew he was already bracing himself for the same conversation they'd had a dozen times before.

"I don't have time for everything, Susan," he said, his voice controlled but firm. "You know that. I've got work to deal with, things I can't put off."

Susan stood still, her hands now folded across her chest. She hadn't expected him to suddenly change, but hearing the same excuses again felt like a punch in the gut. Work. Always work. Now that small phone.

"I'm not asking for the world," she shot back, her voice rising. "I'm asking for a weekend. Just a weekend to see my parents before we leave. Is that too much to ask?"

Jack swallowed hard, then sighed. He looked past her, then back at the phone on the couch. Susan now stared at him with disdain. Whereas Jack's eyes kept drifting back to his phone.

"What other time away do you need when we are going on holiday? We'll visit them after we return," he repeated, his voice flat.

His words meant nothing. She knew it. They both knew it. After the trip. That phrase had become a lifeline he tossed out to avoid dealing with anything that required real effort.

Susan fought the urge to shout, to make him hear her. Instead, she swallowed hard, a lump rising in her throat. She glanced at the door leading to the bedroom, then back at Jack, her face hardening.

"I'm not doing this anymore," she said through clenched teeth, her eyes narrowing. "You're always on your phones. It's like I don't even exist unless you need me in the bedroom."

Jack exhaled sharply, rubbing his temple. "Phones? What phones? Not this again, Susan. I'm trying to get this work done so we can go on the damn trip. Can't you just—"

"No, Jack," she interrupted, her voice cold. "I said 'phone'. You always say you're trying. But you're not. You talk to your mother, your sisters, what about me, the kids?"

Jack's face twisted. He opened his mouth to speak, but the words caught. Susan turned on her heel and strode toward the bedroom, her footsteps louder with every step. The door clicked shut. For a moment, there was silence. Then, from the lounge, Susan heard the unmistakable sound of Jack's phone buzzing again, his voice rising as he answered a call. She didn't even need to hear the words. She knew it was more work. More business.

She sat down on the edge of the bed, her fingers pressing into the quilt. The room felt smaller now, the air thinner. She could hear Jack's muffled voice getting louder as the conversation went on. Susan closed her eyes, trying to breathe through the pressure building inside her chest. She was so tired of this. So tired of him.

She looked at her phone on the nightstand, and then at the clock on the wall. She could call her parents. She could tell them she was coming for the weekend, take Ian and Tia, just leave, and get away from all this noise. But she didn't want to escape, she wanted to be seen. To matter.

Susan stood up, walked back to the living room, and grabbed her jacket from the hook by the door. She hadn't made up her mind yet, but something inside her was already shifting. She couldn't keep going like this. Jack's voice continued to murmur in the background, as he paced around the living room, his back to her as he made another call. Susan walked toward the door, her heart pounding. Just as her fingers brushed the door handle, she hesitated. She didn't leave. She couldn't. Not yet. The tension in the room thickened, like a storm cloud ready to burst. Susan retreated to the bedroom, leaving Jack now standing in the kitchen.

His hands shook slightly, but it was subtle. He didn't know why his thoughts kept circling back to that summer. The summer his life took a dramatic turn. The phone in his hand felt like a 5kg dumbbell. He couldn't remember the last time he'd been this distracted. He loved his wife. Suddenly, he was 23 again.

That October 14, 2007, Jack stood outside the house in the late afternoon sun, the heat pressing down on him, his shirt sticking to his back. He could hear the distant chatter of kids walking from Tinzi Primary School, a few streets from their home. That showed him it was around 5pm when school ended. He hadn't wanted to fly home. But he had to.

He pulled up to Gatwick Airport at 3.30 am, the terminal dotted with small crowds. The early-morning chill clung to the air as he rushed through check-in, barely having time for a cup of coffee before speeding to his gate. He boarded the direct flight to Harare at 6.30 am, a luxury back then when flights from London Gatwick still ran straight through to Harare without the hassle of connections. The trip to the funeral had felt urgent then, as it always does. It seemed almost too easy, a straightforward flight before they discontinued the route in 2009. Then 10 hours later, he stumbled off the plane, disoriented from the time change, but he pressed on. He hopped onto a taxi to Highfield, Harare, his parents' house.

His parents' house in Highfield was small, and modest, a far cry from the glistening towers and cold boardrooms he had grown used to in London. The air smelled faintly of firewood and dust. It was a smell that reminded him of everything he'd never wanted to be.

His phone had rung earlier around midnight, and again when he left his bachelor flat in Central London.

"Jack, I think you need to come," his mother's voice cracked, as fragile as it was familiar. Her voice was tight as if every word counted, given the cost of the international call. "Your father..."

The words rang in his ears, sharp and jagged. Even though his father had never been there, never showed up to his milestones, and never had time to talk about anything other than business, it didn't change the fact that the man was still his father.

Jack had tried to swallow the lump in his throat as he walked through the wide open gate to allow mourners to come. The wailing inside the house oppressed him, just as it always had. This time, it felt somber. His mother, a gaunt version of the woman he remembered, sat on the floor in the corner, her eyes vacant, her face pale. She didn't look up when he entered. He went to hug her for a good five minutes.

He couldn't say what he felt. He hadn't even been sure what he was supposed to say. There was no emotion to summon, just a cold weight, a creeping sense of inevitability. His father's death had only widened the distance between them. And his mother's unspoken expectations had never been more suffocating.

"You're just like him," she'd whispered, barely above a breath. "Always running away."

Jack didn't answer her. He never did. There was nothing to say.

The memory flickered and vanished. He stood in the kitchen, fingers clamped around the phone, tighter than he'd meant. He blinked hard, shaking himself to the present. That memory never stayed gone for long, always waiting, always ready to burst to the surface when he least expected it. At the time, Jack had believed his father's sudden death would bring closure. But instead, it only made things more complicated. More distant. His father had been distant too, a workaholic who had never seemed to care much for family. Jack had inherited the same cold detachment. He couldn't let go of the past, couldn't stop moving, couldn't stop working. He wasn't sure if it was the death that haunted him or the fact that he had turned out an exact version of his father. And he worked all the time to distract himself from the truth. He had to work. His eyes turned back to his phone. The same message was waiting, urgent, demanding. It wasn't going away. Jack set the phone down on the kitchen counter, the buzzing notifications now low in the background.

The door to the bedroom creaked open. Susan stepped into the kitchen, her expression blank. "I've been thinking about the trip," she said, her voice soft but tinged with hesitation. "Maybe we shouldn't go."

Jack cleared his throat, and clutched his temples, staring at the half-empty mug in front of him. "Why?" He didn't want to ask, didn't want to know the answer, but the words slipped out anyway.

She paused, her gaze turning to the window. "Because you're not really here, Jack. You've never been here. You want to go halfway across the world, but it won't change anything. It's just... another distraction."

Jack clenched his jaw, then turned toward her. "This isn't just a trip, Susan. I won't do any work. This is about us. See how the kids are excited?"

"No," she replied sharply, shaking her head. "You and the kids can go"

***

Outside, just a few houses away from Susan and Jack's home, a man in a hoodie and cap stood at the corner of the street, watching the lights in the windows. On. Off. On again. He tracked the sequence, each switches a signal and a clue. No rush, his focus steady, like a leopard in the underbrush, waiting for the moment to pounce. His face was obscured by the shadows, but his eyes, sharp and calculating, remained glued to the house.

He had been watching them for days.

At first, it had been easy to blend in, casual, unassuming. The car parked down the street, the occasional stroll around the area, the random smiles he threw in the direction of the neighbours when they glanced his way. But now he knew it was time to act.

He glanced at the phone in his hand, the screen lighting up with a single message. It was short, direct. He knew the next step would be the hardest, but it couldn't wait any longer. He held his breath.

"Tonight."

Chapter 53

Detective Macmillan was in charge of the investigation for Mark's Murder. Detective Macmillan had more than 30 years of experience investigating murder cases, and mystery cases. The man required no introduction at all. He was well-known in the medical, legal and even the social science fraternity. He was a cop with the mind of a criminal.

Detective Macmillan took three other detectives with him and took off in a huff to that crime scene specifically to the Thames River. The River Thames known alternatively in parts as the River Isis, is a river that flows through southern England including London. At 215 miles (346 km), it is the longest river entirely in England and the second-longest in the United Kingdom, after the River Severn.

The river rises at Thames Head in Gloucestershire and flows into the North Sea near Tilbury, Essex and Gravesend, Kent, via the Thames Estuary. From the west, it flows through Oxford (where it is sometimes called the Isis). The Thames also drains the whole of Greater London. The lower reaches of the river are called the Tideway, derived from its long tidal reach up to Teddington Lock. Its tidal section includes most of its London stretch and has a rise and fall of 23 ft (7 m). From Oxford to the estuary, the Thames drops by 55 meters (180 ft). Running through some of the drier parts of mainland Britain and heavily abstracted for drinking water, the Thames' discharge is low considering its length and breadth: the Severn has a discharge almost twice as large on average despite having a smaller drainage basin. In Scotland, the Tay achieves more than double the Thames' average discharge from a drainage basin that is 60% smaller.

Along its course are 45 navigation locks with accompanying weirs. Its catchment area covers a large part of south-eastern and a small part of western England; the river is fed by at least 50 named tributaries. The river contains over 80 islands. With its waters varying from freshwater to almost seawater, the Thames supports a variety of wildlife and has a number of adjoining Sites of Special Scientific Interest, with the largest being in the North Kent Marshes and covering 20.4 sq mi (5,289 ha). According to Mallory and Adams, the Thames, from Middle English *Temese*, is derived from the Brittonic name for the river, *Tamesas* (from **tamēssa*), recorded in Latin as *Tamesis* and yielding modern Welsh *Tafwys* "Thames." The Thames through Oxford is sometimes called the Isis. Historically, and especially in Victorian times, gazetteers and cartographers insisted that the entire river was correctly named the Isis from its source down to Dorchester on Thames.

The detective and his team arrived at the scene where the body was found and the homicide team working with Detective Macmillan was retrieving the body.

"Make a whole gentleman" yelled a man leading the team that was retrieving the body. They laid the body for photos, and examination of any physical marks.

"Let them go, I want the fishermen," yelled Detective Macmillan. The Instruction was followed by a "yes sir" barely after the last word from the Detective.

"Good morning Sir, My name is Detective Macmillan, and I am the investigating officer on this matter. Thank you for calling the police, what's your name".

The man looked up and then down, shivering, it was not clear whether he was shivering from the breeze or he was in shock at what he had seen. His fingers were scared, arms strong in keeping with harsh weather that he was accustomed to deal with every time, or shall we say as far as he had been a fisherman.

When he spoke, his voice was barely above a whisper, the detective knew better not to interject or ask him to speak up. "May name Ishmael. I am a fisherman and I saw this man in the early hours of the day."

"Did you see anyone, or a boat around the same time or any suspicious movement?" Demanded the detective.

"No, sir I did not, however, based on what I know this body must have been dumped last night, the people who did this must be good fishermen or well-versed with the river and the tide. I believe nobody can dump a body from a boat. It's too risky, there are too many patrols."

The detective was listening all along, no questions in between, he was busy taking notes and when the fisherman stopped, he looked up and remarked, "Thank you for your opinion on this matter it's so important to us"

The words flattered the fisherman who was feeling an air of sadness yet filled with contentment. "There is another thing, I picked this, it was floating around the same area with the body."

The detective looked at the plastic card holder that contained Solomon's business card and Lunela's credit card. Mark had stolen the card from Lunela's apartment and used it to book rides the previous day leading to the night he was killed.

In the meantime, Lunela had left to look for a safe place to be. Nobody could tell where Lunela was and certainly nobody could vouch for her.

While at the crime scene, Inspector Irene Mecalf approached, flanked by three men and two women you were looking all purposeful and ready for something important. Mecalf could not wait till she reached the scene. Pulling her hair back with one hand, another pulled an ID before she brandished it. "My name is Irene Metcalf, Scotland Yard" she yelled. Detective Macmillan looked around and pulled out a cigarette, he reached for a lighter which was in the lower pocket of his coat, lit the cigarette, pulled hard, and released plumes of smoke in Irene's direction. He looked at her as though viewing underweight cattle at the market, trying to decide the price he might offer. His gaze was impolite yet not intimidating. He kicked a rock into the river and then turned to Irene. "Scotland Yard you say? Well we are clearly out of Land here it's water." remarked the detective sarcastically. He didn't wait for Irene to finish what she was there for.

"It's a matter of national security this matter runs deep" Irene yelled but the detective was already in his car. He just managed to yell back to her "Drop by the office and get the notes and pick it up from there.

The detective got to the office, there was a crisis room and many high-ranking officials were at the office. There was a briefing meeting which was addressed by the detective.

"What we know so far is we have a man dead, killed in the most gruesome manner, something was used to plug off his manhood", explained the detective Mark's photos were paraded on the table and the walls but only a few officers were strong enough to view them.

"We believe that this was done by someone who is a fisherman or at least someone who knows about aquatic life, this is an act of revenge in my view, this was a grave punishment for being caught of adultery. Whatever it is we see rage, craftiness, and anger written all over, this was personal" The detective went on to explain.

"We are however waiting for forensics to determine the approximate time of death, and any other information we can get. We are looking into all the nightclubs, interviewing all the Hawkers anyone with information as well as his phone records, especially the people she has called and talked to" added the detective.

"Detective what about the business card and the credit card that you were handed over by the Fisherman?" A female detective asked in a high voice almost accusing the detective of neglecting the evidence before him.

The detective looked at her and forced a smile. "Honey those are misleading leads but they certainly lead to the real culprit, someone is being framed here. That's what I have seen from experience. Any screaming evidence it's a diversion but I have asked my junior offers to look into it and report to me while I work on something meaty." Responded the detective.

The detective was taken aback, he was not a fan of straightforward, he came from the school of thought that a criminal can be caught at any time but a seasoned one can caught only if they want to. But there were exceptions to the rule. The following day the forensic team had a report. It was a difficult report to read. The report showed that Mark had sexual intercourse before he was killed but DNA could take years to figure out, they pulled out some cobs from the cotton and the team believed from their examination that there could be some female lubricants, this may mean the victim was caught red-handed or asked to enjoy it for the last time before his manhood was cut off. His hands had deeper cuts suggesting he was cuffed his legs had deep cuts suggesting struggle in the process. There were marks at the back and belly, these may suggest the victim was possibly tied to a bed or chair. The nature of the wounds suggests that he may have been burned by hot iron rods or tongs. The same tool was used for extraction. The teeth were removed possibly to cause pain or to extract information.

Detective Macmillan was taking notes, soon after seeing the report he left to attend to Officer Malvern who had been tasked to liaise with the financial crimes division to see if there was anything they could decipher from the credit card for Lunela Smith.

"Boss what an impeachable timing detective", said the overjoyed junior officer. What do "we have here officer," said the detective in response.

"Well say Hello to Lunela Smith married to Solomon Smith, going through a contested divorce, the marriage was rocked by childlessness but while trying Mark got in the way, Lunela killed her in revenge, the removal of the genitals may mean expression that Mark was not a woman after all" explained the officer.

"This is a set-up," said the detective.

The officer went "Easy boss, the credit card that was found was used and again it led to the night club where Mark was. The Video footage shows Mark arriving and sitting with other gays and girls but after that, the footage is blank, well planned, the woman is smart."

"Then what happened after that" asked the detective. "You think he was killed in the club".

The officer looked at the detective smiled and continued "I don't think so boss but we now have probable cause, there is enough evidence to nail her. We went to her house and she was not there. It took us time to find her. She has no alibi at all; she is the master minder of all this."

"I will hesitate to charge her", said the detective. I saw the woman, she was not capable.

There were orders from above she be been charged with the First-degree murder of Mark. Arrangements have been made to place her in a maternity hospital ward where she will have a team of 15 officers armed to the teeth till she delivers.

Detective Macmillan emerged from the conferencing room and right at the door was Irene waiting with two other officers. The detective was removed from the case and suspended for three weeks.

Chapter 54

The plane soared high above the clouds. Susan stared out the window, straining to see past the rows in front of her. The endless azure sky stretched before her, but the uncanny feeling in her stomach lingered, refusing to be ignored. She stared at the endless azure sky, trying to ignore the uncanny feeling twisting in her stomach. She had an inkling something would go wrong. The heated argument with her husband the night before felt like a bad omen. She was submissive, and superstition stuck with her. Her instincts screamed that disaster was coming, yet she couldn't tell Jack. He didn't care. She also couldn't escape the questions that had been haunting her since the moment they booked the tickets, Why now, and why a secret phone?

Jack sat next to her, eyes fixed on the in-flight screen, yet he looked distant. His fingers tapped on the armrest, the faintest twitch of restlessness. The kids sat together across them, window side since Tia only stayed calm on flights when she was holding her brother. Susan cast occasional checks on them, yet her husband remained stone-faced. This trip wasn't going to fix anything.

Across the aisle, at the far end, a man in an oversized coat shifted in his seat, his eyes fleetingly meeting hers. He held her gaze for a moment too long, before looking away. Susan didn't know why, but something about him unsettled her.

Susan glanced across the aisle at their children, Ian playing quietly with his squishy toy, and Tia, watching her brother play. For a moment, she admired their peace of mind and free spirit. They were just children.

Jack, still lost in his screen, was oblivious to the palpable silence between them. He hadn't even noticed when Ian had nudged him for attention.

"Dad, look!" Ian said, holding up a small squishy dinosaur. But Jack didn't hear him, too absorbed in his iPad. Susan watched her son's hopeful eyes drop with disappointment before he turned away, shoving the toy back into his bag.

"Hey," Susan said gently, stretching over to ruffle Ian's hair. "We're going to see some real animals soon, buddy. Don't worry."

But even as she spoke, her own heart sank. She wasn't sure if they were there for the right reasons. The kids had been looking forward to the trip for weeks, imagining the safaris and wildlife, but Susan couldn't shake the feeling that this vacation, like everything else, was a futile attempt to compensate for Jack's neglect.

"Tia yelled. "Mom, why does Daddy look so sad?"

Susan stiffened, her smile barely curling as she turned to her daughter. "He's just tired, sweetie. We'll be landing soon, and then he can rest, okay?" Even as she spoke, Susan doubted her own words."

Susan couldn't help but overhear the couple in front of her. The woman's giggles never stopped, high-pitched and carefree. At first, it irritated Susan. Then the annoyance faded. Her marriage troubles were hers alone, let them have their bliss. They had to be newlyweds, or maybe not yet married. No one else laughed like that. Susan stared and glanced out the window, distancing herself from the couple's bubble. Then her eyes locked with the man in the oversized coat. He looked familiar. His jaw was sharp, his features strikingly handsome, but it was the horseshoe beard that grabbed her attention, familiar, somehow, like she'd seen it before but couldn't place where. A chill crawled up her spine. She leaned toward her husband, whispering, for him to check him out. He barely glanced up. "Could be looking anywhere," he muttered, his eyes still on his iPad. "Just like you." But something in his voice made her pause, his tone sharp, almost too quick. All this time he had ignored the kids and now he jumped to reply. Why was he quick to answer? Had he seen this man before? He sounded defensive too. Ian distracted her.

Time and again, Ian asked his mother questions. "What if we see a lion?"

"Then we'll be sure to take a ton of pictures!" Susan replied, her smile infectious.

The flight from London was long and the brief stop in Lusaka, Zambia relieved Susan who felt nauseous. The leg to Zimbabwe would be a few hours if not 2 and a half at the most. Susan's preoccupation with her kids made the whole trip somewhat enjoyable. Yet, as they neared take-off, she couldn't shake that same feeling of unease.

Flight attendants walked down the aisles for dinner, and Susan watched them in admiration as she suddenly regretted being a housewife to a distant man.

The Captain took off from the Kenneth Kaunda International Airport for Harare. The Euro Martin DM747

Max was the biggest airline that had ever landed at Harare's Robert Mugabe International Airport. This plane's arrival was the long-awaited. From as early as 2 hours before the plane arrived bay was full of taxis waiting purposely while others like In Drive, and Bolt were circling the airport in anticipation of brisk business. The parking marshals at the airport were waiting eager to clamp and tow away cars that were wrongly parked. There was so much effort in maintaining order at the airport due to the sheer size of the plane. But that was not the only reason. There were many dignitaries in the Jumbo and the protocol team was planted in different areas.

The fire safety team was assembled at the usual place save for the fact that this time the entire team was on sight and the head of fire safety was there donning his fire combat gear. This was a reflection of the significance attached to the coming of the plane. It was a great deal, it was a big deal and everyone wanted to do their best. Besides it was time for the SADC summit. The team was not just demonstrating their skill but displaying their loyalty to their nation and creating a positive impact for the nation that had been ravaged by negative International Media coverage following the Land reform program that former president Robert Gabriel Mugabe had initiated. Yet on that day, visitors from all the continents of the world were to be received, boosting the image of the country. This was a golden moment, a rare opportunity to correct the negative narrative and paint a great picture of the great nation of Zimbabwe.

The VIP transport was lined up and all drivers had been trained well with different scenarios being used in the planning of the journeys. The travel paths were marked in advance and software was being used to coordinate the transportation of the VIP and the VVIP. The transportation system was secured with passwords that expired after 2 hours, apart from the password change prompt, there were layers of access requirements such as facial, finger, and voice. This technology was developed by the local consortium of developers.

On arrival queues were being cleared to make way for the Jumbo, and two language bag platforms were to be used due to the large number of people, these were separated based on the seating arrangements. The immigration department was waiting purposefully and launched the e-passport self-scanning machine though it was still under test the speed was good enough to avoid a crisis when the Jumbo arrived.

In the control tower, things were getting heated. The officials were getting overwhelmed with the task ahead of them, but they had received adequate training. At peak air travel times, the Robert Gabriel Mugabe International Airport could have more than 200 airplanes zipping through the sky at any moment. The Control tower is charged with the responsibility to ensure the safety of those flying. Therefore it is the air traffic controller's duty to coordinate the movement of hundreds of aircraft, keep them at safe distances from each other, direct them during takeoff and landing, direct them around troublesome weather, and ensure that traffic flows efficiently with minimal delays. In recent times Control Tower has purchased three Helicopters and six flying cars for the purpose of monitoring the airport from time to time and assessing any risks that may be anticipated. The flying cars were made by a Japanese manufacturer. The car has four propellers on each side, and a ballistic parachute in the front which is connected to the tiny one-man cockpit where one motion can trigger it open and save the car and the occupant. The car has been hand-in allowing areal assessment and follow-up risk assessments being able to alert a ground team of any risks. When taking off the Car does not run to get momentum for liftoff like planes, rather it's similar to a helicopter in that it lands and takes off without running on the runway. The Car weighs 390 pounds with a payload of 200 Pounds. Just like jets, the Car has ailerons. This makes the flying car cheap to operate and suitable for household and small business operations such as access to remote places. The Country has made purchases of a modified version that will be used to carry at least three people in each and will be used for air emergency evacuation during crisis times such as cyclones and hurricane-after-month relief operations. The car is guided by three GPS with signals going up in the sky to triangulate the satellite.

Air traffic control towers are located at over 30 commercial and general aviation airports in in Zimbabwe. These towers coordinate takeoffs, landings, ground traffic, and aircraft in flight within 5 miles of the airport. Their primary purpose worldwide is to prevent collisions, organize and expedite the flow of air traffic, and provide information and other support for pilots. It is ultimately a safety measure-- skies do not have traffic lights!

At smaller airports with less aircraft traffic, the pilots communicate with each other on common radio frequencies. This has proven to be safe at lower volume airports, however, as traffic increases and greater efficiency is required an Air Traffic Control Tower becomes a necessity.

Air Traffic Controllers advise and update pilots about nearby planes and potentially hazardous conditions, Issue landing and take-off authorizations and instructions, transfer control of departing flights to traffic control centers and accepting control of incoming flights. They Monitor or directing aircraft within an airspace or on the ground. As well as compiling information about flights from flight plans, pilots reports, radar, or observations

Areas surrounding airports can rest in knowing that air traffic will run smoothly with very slim chance of disaster. With the help of air traffic control towers, the pilot has a second pair of eyes to ensure safety. Economic developers are more likely to be attracted to areas with air control towers, and companies will have more interest in landing their larger aircrafts in areas with control towers for an added layer of safety.

Captain Smith came to the mic to make an announcement; "Ladies and Gentlemen we shall be starting our descending shortly, weather is cool with clear skies, temperature 25 degrees Celsius. We are estimated to be landing in 15 Minutes. Please return to your seats and fasten your seat belts".

At that moment the plane was lifted abruptly with wings turning violently threatening to send the plane into cigarette rolls. The Captain steadied the plane but there was another problem, clouds had formed and from nowhere it started raining, the plane was tumbling, there was a severe thunderstorm and blinding lightning which threatened to interfere with onboard communication infrastructure. The screams of women and innocent children could heard from the various seating zones. There was panic with some deciding to pray with some folk shouting what seemed to be a prayer in tongues "Zibro Sakata." There was commotion as some hand luggage compartments were swung open with the hand luggage items thrown around hitting passengers in the process. The captain came back to the mike with a firm voice "May we take our seats and remain seated until we have landed. Do not attempt to assist anyone, let the cabin crew do their job. May we offer maximum cooperation to the cabin crew".

At that point there was severe lightning and thunderstorm, the Plane tumbled. As Captain Smith was trying to steady the plane there was panic as the plane violently moved up and down, in some instances going down by 30 feet before the captain regains control of the Beast. Crossing winds made it difficult to maneuver.

The plane was struck by lightning and in the process one of the engines creased with engine 2 catching fire in an instance, Captain Smith was planning to respond to the fire when a swarm of birds flying in the opposite direction accidentally entered the engine, destroying engine number 4. The plane was now flying with only five engines producing a total thrust of 525,000 pounds instead of the 840,000 pounds of thrust. This was still enough to steer the Jumbo but the Pilot needed to max the engines. The captain was battling to control the plane which was no longer stable, the plane started stalling. Another engine stopped working reducing the number to 4 while the other engine was on fire.

Stefano ignored the seatbelt warning, reaching out for Suki. Everyone gasped, frozen. The plane lurched, rattling violently. Stefano staggered but gripped the seats to stay upright. Suki sat two rows ahead, her hand tightly clutched in her husband's. They both faced forward, eyes shut, waiting for the crash they thought was coming. A final moment together.

Then, Stefano was there, on his knees before Suki, pulling her into a fierce kiss. She froze, eyes snapping open in shock. When she saw him, she sighed and kissed him back, her body relaxing in his arms. Tohimo blinked, rubbing his eyes. Was he awake? Was this really happening?

Tohimo's heart twisted. Betrayed. The public façade shattered. With everyone else in panic mode, there were no cameras. He silently screamed for answers, but none came. Maybe it wouldn't matter if none of them survived this. Maybe, in these last seconds, there were no rules anymore.

"Suki, *ti amo*, (I love you). Will you marry me, Suki? I'll die a happy man," Stefano whispered against her lips, his breath shaky, his voice trembling as he pulled her closer.

Tohimo's voice cut through the chaos. "Stefano? What nonsense is this?"

"I was lonely, Tohimo!" Suki snapped, eyes wild. "You were never around!"

The plane's engines screamed as it suddenly nosedived. Stefano lost his footing, sliding down the aisle, crashing into the seats. The sudden drop sent a jolt of panic through the cabin.

Suki's grip tightened around Tohimo's hand, her knuckles white. Tohimo tried to pull his hand away from her grip, but she pinned it tighter. Her eyes stayed shut, holding onto him, believing it was the end. They were dying. They were dying, and yet, here was Stefano, letting their best-kept secret out.

The plane shuddered violently. Jack gripped Susan's hand tightly as his heart raced. "It's just a little bumpy," he said, trying to sound confident.

Suddenly, a loud bang echoed through the cabin, and the pilot's voice broke through the panic. "We're experiencing technical difficulties. Please remain calm."

Tia clutched her brother, eyes wide with fear. "Dad, I'm scared."

"It's going to be okay," Jack said, his throat dry as uncertainty crept in. He shot a reassuring glance at Susan, but her expression was taut with worry.

"Why is this happening?" Ian whispered, his voice shaking.

"Just a malfunction, probably nothing serious," Susan replied, but as the plane continued to shake, she couldn't help but feel the knot of anxiety tighten in his stomach.

The captain was determined to save all the passengers on board and he thought about the recent recognition that he had just received for doing exactly that. The captain contacted the control tower.

"This is Captain Smith requesting emergency landing four engines down two on fire I need emergency clearance" There was no response from the control tower. The Captain decided to repeat the message and this time control tower copied the message.

At the Harare International Airport, it was a hive of activity, all small planes were diverted to Prince Charles or the military air strip neighboring the main airport. Fire safety team was placed on high alert with engines running. Medical staff had been asked to be on standby with some coming from the nearby military barracks.

The UK, and US were all informed by reporters that and plane carrying 980 is on fire and has requested an emergency landing, there were no images of the plane. Global news networks reported that the recently knighted Sir Captain Smith was in charge and it was his first assignment since being knighted by the King of England for great works in the service. There were a lot of conspiracy theories as many tried to explain what could have taken place. There were some who were questioning his suitability for such an honor but each time his CV was read it become clear that there was no one who was more deserving than Captain Smith.

There was panic at the Euro Martin US manufacturing plant as engineers went into the simulation room and based on the information that was trickling in they started making possible impact analysis as to the potential losses. The simulator was fed with three scenarios. The First one was based on plane failing all its engines, which according to the forecast, the degree of losses would be categorized as severely fatal.

The second was based on no further engine loss but failing to control the plane due to imbalance hence landing where ever the plane crashes to, this too had many variables and further analysis done to it. It required the assessment of the whether the plane was to land on water in which case there would be a better chance of survival but that depended on a number of factors including cooperation with the crew in following evacuation orders and the wearing of the jackets. There was an expectation that some people would be injured due to drowning but this option was a better option. However, a much bigger number would be injured due to stampede and injuries from bags coming from overhead compartments.

The engineers were clearly avoiding the option that was more likely, crash landing and explosion. This was a high probability that the plane would crash land resulting in total or near total fatalities. The option did not paint a good picture and was not good for business. The Euro Martin had some five new orders received recently and any investigation that concludes that the plane fell due to mechanical and design weaknesses, was going to lead to immediate termination of the contract of delays in the development to allow rectification of the faulty, the regulators were going to take between 6 to 12 months to conclude the investigations if past investigations were anything to go by.

The CEO and Chairman of Euro Martin had been informed of the situation and agreed with the engineers that they needed to keep working on models and create a plausible explanation to the cause of plane crush. There was need to offer possible explanation and start building the narrative from the word go.

The head of corporate communications and Brand director was called to a crisis meeting and was given a mandate to engage the global and regional media houses to help manage the situation. Their goal was to make sure that despite the manufacturer was seen in good light.

The US regulator was contacted and informed of the impending crisis that was about to happen, the idea was to preempt whatever the outcome of the investigations if not to actually influence them.

Chapter 55

Back in Harare, Thandeka was at odds with her husband's family. She had had enough. He was awaiting trial at Harare Remand Prison on charges of violating the illicit drug laws. Her in-laws pressured her to stand by him, just as they had vowed on their wedding day—through thick and thin. But Thandeka refused to crack under their emotional blackmail. Their son deserved to serve his sentence for ruining the youth of the nation. Dead men tell no tales, but jailed men do. He needed to face the consequences and reform. Had he cheated, she might have forgiven him, but not this. Supporting him now would be the same as endorsing his actions. Besides, what if he still had drug links even while imprisoned?

This case had become a conflict of interest. As a social worker, she couldn't continue in her position in the Harare West area. Her husband had carefully built a network to distribute drugs, what leniency did he deserve? She decided it was time to leave for South Africa, much to her in-laws' disapproval. She had no children with him, so moving to South Africa was easier. Through the police, she learned that Liam had been working with the local drug lords, led by Nancy Blue. At first, the trolling on Facebook during their live session had seemed malicious and unfounded, but they gave Liam an idea: he used them to his advantage. Thandeka found out through police that her husband worked with the local drug lords headed by Nancy Blue in the Avenues area. Although he had cleared his name publicly, behind the scenes, Liam approached Nancy Blue's syndicate and pitched his plan. He also knew the ins and outs of local drug awareness programs, the loopholes in the system, and how the local rehab centre operated, knowledge that kept the drug mafia thriving. When Chief Clemson's grandson and his friends took their lives, Liam supplied them with the dose that likely became their last. Meticulous police investigations, with help from the community, uncovered this. Victor, a key witness, survived because he slipped away with his girlfriend, Jane, just before the boys planned their tragic demise. Victor later tipped the police with information that Liam had supplied those drugs. Apart from the reason of being his wife, police revealed all this to Thandeka as she was a key social worker. This compromised her work. She lived with a monster. She couldn't face the shame so South Africa was her escape plan and so she could start afresh. She phoned Lunela who also shared her drama and the friends cried then laughed at how their lives had almost fallen apart at the hands of men, all for love. Lunela reasoned that maybe Emily was right after all by vowing to remain single. Her longest relationship lasted six months and from then three months was the most she could tolerate men. She joked that she would join the convent one day. On one of her check-in calls, Officer Taylor encouraged Thandeka to keep clear of men while she healed from Liam's mess. She had suffered her own spate of heartbreak too. But lately, she had found love in Officer Ben.

Ben genuinely cared about those he was drawn to. Raised by a single father, he understood the value of relationships and refused to let his parents' separation define him. His father had always told him the split was due to cultural differences when Ben's dad refused to pay *lobola* (bride price) twice. The first payment had gone to the bride's family representatives, but the bride's mother wouldn't inform her husband's side of the family, insisting her uncles take charge instead. When Ben's father found out, he insisted that *lobola* be paid again or the marriage would be considered null and void. Ben's dad refused. That's when her father came to take her away. But Ben's father wasn't about to give in. He fought back, taking little Ben with him, and fled to Harare.

For years, Ben had believed the fable his father told him. But becoming a police officer sharpened his analytical skills. As he investigated further, he uncovered the truth: his mother had been tricked into thinking she was going to work as a maid for a South African businessman, only to be married off to him instead. That was the last time he saw her, he was only five years old. His father was a fitter and turner, a trade that was looked down upon, and his wife's parents rejected him, feeling humiliated by having someone of his status as their son-in-law. Out of frustration and heartbreak, Ben's father had moved from Mutare to Harare.

Ben vowed to find his mother, and he shared his findings with Officer Taylor. That's when he knew he loved her. He had never opened up like that to any of his previous girlfriends. Her sincerity in response was all he needed to confirm it. She was sincere, even when dealing with the issues in the suburbs they patrolled, like Victor' story. It resonated with her own experience of losing a brother to the drug abuse crisis.

Victor felt trapped like the whole world was judging him harshly. Since that day of his accidental live session on

Facebook when he soiled himself, he set to come clean from drugs. His brother's fate was a wakeup call yet it also pushed him into feeling worthless. This sunk him further into the drug dependency cycle. Officer Taylor reached out to him but soon discovered he felt intimidated by her role as a policewoman. She then agreed to swap with Ben who took on the role with a dedicated eagerness. While Ben had no lived experience with drug abuse cases, he had dealt with a lot of such cases at the office and cells. It saddened him that the youth were wasting away over short-term gratification from these illicit drugs and non-medical use of drugs that were legally available such as painkillers and sleeping pills, with fentanyl being Victor's go-to drug. On most days he coped well then on a few days he withdrew from his hobbies, interests and isolated himself. His parents reassured him of how much they loved him in a bid to reinforce good choices. His dad even registered for social soccer with him to redirect him from nasty places. He seemed happier, even engaging in banter, something he had last done when Felix was still alive. Yet, some night those feelings of abandonment wrecked him.

He didn't want to be home, but he didn't know where else to go. Everything felt wrong. His uncle at the cattle ranch had tried to reach out, tried to help by suggesting a change of scenery. However, when he arrived in Gwanda, the place repulsed him. Every word felt like an accusation, a reminder of what he wasn't. Felix had always been the golden child, the one everyone praised, the one going to Yale. But he messed up but they ignored that. His name was always there, floating between them like a shadow. "Remember Felix," they said. "He would've done better, had the demons not possessed him, he would be leaving for Yale now."

It made Victor sick. It made him want to leave, to run from their sympathy-cum-accusations. And that's exactly what he did.

His other uncle in the clergy had looked after him, kept him in the village, away from the noise, away from the mess of his life, away from drug peddlers. But even there, in the quiet, there was no escaping it. The memory of Felix lingered like a dark cloud. Everyone talked about him since he was the pastor's nephew. "Felix was going to Yale on scholarship," they'd say. "He had so much potential. He was bright. He had it all." They never stopped talking about what he could've been.

Felix had been the golden child. The smart one. The one who never struggled. Who didn't fail. Who was everything their parents had hoped for. And now... now Felix was dead. The same drugs ravaging Victor's life had taken him too. But no one could see that. All they saw was the shining, perfect version of Felix, the one who never made mistakes. The one who didn't end up like this. They said the demons had possessed him to take drugs then his ultimate demise.

Every mention of Felix felt like a punch. It wasn't just grief. It was the burden of their expectations, their silent judgments. He could hear it in their voices, in the way they looked at him. As if his brother's brilliance was a benchmark reminder of how far he'd fallen. How worthless he was.

How great he was. How perfect he had been. He couldn't take it.

So, he ran. Again.

Coming back home felt like a trap. His parents, his family, they didn't know what to do with him anymore. His grandfather, Chief Clemson had liaised with Officer Taylor to help Victor. They all wanted to "fix" him and send him to church. The pastors were supposed to help, to guide him through this road to the abyss. But all it did was make him feel worse. Sitting there, pretending to listen, nodding along, watching the time crawl by, or scrolling through social media.

It was boring. It was useless. They didn't get it.

After two sessions, he snapped at the pastors who did home visits. Told them to leave him alone. Told them if they ever came back, he'd end it all.

Maybe it wasn't true. Maybe it was. He didn't know. But the thought was always there now. The heaviness. The dark thoughts that followed him. Every conversation, every moment, every glance from someone who looked at him like he was a lost cause, made him feel smaller, invisible. He had no one. No one understood.

Then there was her. His girlfriend. The one person who tried to stick by him, who listened to him rant about the darkness that wouldn't leave him alone. But eventually, even she couldn't take it. She broke up with him.

"You scare me," she'd said, her voice shaking. "I can't handle this. I need to be safe."

The words sliced him to the marrow. Safe. He wasn't even sure what that felt like anymore.

He went to the clinic, desperate for someone to help him. But they just put another label on him. "Addict." It was the only word they knew. The only thing they saw. A case to diagnose. A box to check.

They didn't see him. They didn't care.

He was tired of being a problem. A burden. A burden to himself, to his family and to his neighbourhood. Tired of everyone seeing him as a statistic. Tired of feeling like a broken record, repeating the same mistakes countless times.

But he had nowhere else to turn. No one to talk to.

The fear settled in again, and he couldn't push it away. The thoughts of running. Of escaping. Of ending it all.

It felt like the only way out.

On a rainy Thursday morning, Victor tossed and turned countless times. His palms sweaty, hands shook as he stared at the small brown bottle in front of him. He knew it was bad for him. He knew it was only a matter of time before he fell headlong. But the craving gnawed at him, like a voice in his head that grew louder each minute.

He glanced at the clock on the wall, 4:45 AM. Too early. No one would be awake yet, and it would be too risky to make the call, but the urge was relentless. He snatched the bottle from the bedside table and twisted the cap off, his fingers trembling. For a moment, he just held it, staring at the little pills inside like they were some kind of salvation. The auditory hallucinations started to quiet. He could almost hear the relief, a soft sigh that came only with the first hit.

The door creaked open.

"Victor dear?"

It was his mother. She had seen the light from his room spilling through the door. His heart dropped into his stomach. He hadn't planned for this.

Her voice was quiet and cautious, but it had that familiar edge of worry. "You are up early. What's wrong?"

He tried to hide the bottle, stuffing it into his pyjama pocket too quickly, his movements were jerky. His face flushed. "Nothing, mum. I'm just—"

"Just what? Victor, my son..." She stepped closer, her eyes darting from his face to the way he was holding himself, the tension in his shoulders. She knew.

"I don't want to do this anymore." His voice was faint, barely above a whisper. He didn't want to say it out loud, but there it was, as raw and painful as ever.

His mother stepped closer and sat on his bed, staring at him with those soft, tired eyes. Finally, she spoke, her voice low but firm, "Then stop, honey."

He guffawed. "If only it was that simple."

"I know it's not," she said. "But it doesn't have to be this way. You don't have to keep going like this."

He looked away, swallowing hard. He wasn't ready to hear it. But it was the truth. The truth that had been staring him in the face for months.

"I'm trying, mum," he said, his voice raw with frustration, but the words didn't sound like they meant anything anymore.

His mother leaned forward, placing a hand on his arm. Her touch was warm, but the pressure of her fingers made his skin crawl.

"Your dad and I will be here. We are not going anywhere, but you've got to decide, Victor. We can't lose you too."

He stared down at the floor, the bottle still sitting heavy in his pocket. The buzz was fading, and the craving was creeping back. It was easier to reach for the fentanyl pills. Easier than facing what came after.

"I don't know if I can stop," he murmured.

His mother squeezed his arm tighter, her voice calm despite the fear in her eyes. "Then let us help. We are in this together. We love you, never forget that."

Chapter 56

The captain struggled to steady the plane, he was sweating and getting overwhelmed by the thought of losing all the lives he was carrying. Arriving safely was every pilot's dream, to see people disembarking and announcing to the cabin crew to open the doors, seeing the people going up the boarding gates and hurrying to see their loved ones. It was a refreshing sight to get people to their destination.

The captain tried several times to connect with the control tower, but it became clear that communication had been lost. There was a tracker that had been giving live feeds about the whereabouts. Radar lost the plane and emergency rescue operations were initiated, the United States of America, Canada, the UK, Germany, and France all offered technical support to track the plane. These countries started offering support while their teams were immediately dispatched to Zimbabwe. It was now a crisis.

The news came as a shock to the hundreds of people at the airport waiting for their loved ones, it was devastating, for many people it was a new experience, nobody knew what to do, how to process it, and how to react let alone what to expect. The nation was gripped with fear and suspense at the same time. The disappearance of the plane left many wondering what to expect. The global networks were now drawing parallels with the Malaysian MH 370 plane that disappeared was never found and till today no one knows what became of the plane and all the passengers that were in it.

The much talked about Malaysia Airlines Flight 370 (MH370/MAS370) was an international passenger flight operated by Malaysia Airlines that disappeared from radar on 8 March 2014, while flying from Kuala Lumpur International Airport in Malaysia to its planned destination, Beijing Capital International Airport in China. The cause of its disappearance has not been determined. It is widely regarded as the greatest mystery in aviation history and remains the single deadliest case of aircraft disappearance.

The crew of the Boeing 777-200ER, last communicated with air traffic control (ATC) around 38 minutes after takeoff when the flight was over the South China Sea. The aircraft was lost from ATC's secondary surveillance radar screens minutes later but was tracked by the Malaysian military's primary radar system for another hour, deviating westward from its planned flight path, crossing the Malay Peninsula and the Andaman Sea. It left radar range 200 nautical miles (370 km; 230 mi) northwest of Penang Island in northwestern Peninsular Malaysia.

With all 227 passengers and 12 crew aboard presumed dead, the disappearance of Flight 370 was the deadliest incident involving a Boeing 777, the deadliest of 2014, and the deadliest in Malaysia Airlines' history until it was surpassed in all three regards by Malaysia Airlines Flight 17, which was shot down by Russian-backed forces while flying over Ukraine four months later on 17 July 2014.

The search for the missing aircraft became the most expensive search in the history of aviation. It focused initially on the South China Sea and the Andaman Sea before a novel analysis of the aircraft's automated communications with an Inmarsat satellite indicated that the plane had travelled far southward over the southern Indian Ocean. The lack of official information in the days immediately after the disappearance prompted fierce criticism from the Chinese public, particularly from relatives of the passengers, as most people on board Flight 370 were of Chinese origin. At various stages of the investigation, possible hijacking scenarios were considered, including crew involvement, and suspicion of the airplane's cargo manifest. Many disappearance theories regarding the flight have also been reported by the media.

The general consensus among investigators is that Flight 370 crashed somewhere in the southern Indian Ocean sometime between 08:19 and 09:15 on 8 March due to fuel exhaustion, although the exact time and location of the crash remains uncertain.

Chapter 57

The control tower from Robert Gabriel Mugabe was worried, the captain had not communicated in more than an hour, and there were fears that the plane had crashed and that if there were survivors, they would have needed support but such support was not going to come on time.

Meanwhile, Captain Smith had battled with the plane and was running low on fuel, he had decided that he needed to have as little fuel as possible before landing while maintaining a flying attitude to be able to manage maneuvers, and he managed to do just that but again the people were anxiously screaming on top of their voices. The Captain used his campus to glide through the rains, he was in Pandamatenga he needed to land either at Victoria Falls International Airport, Hwange, or Bulawayo International Airport. He chose none of the airports.

He fought against the tide going up higher, he was determined to land the plane in Harare as he was sure that the runway was able to accommodate his jumbo. He decided to use a trick that he had learned some time ago, he maxed the Jumbo and went 60,000 feet, he then started decelerating he had a feeling that he was in the right direction, he spotted Kadoma Ranch hotel and continued flying in the general direction his campus was guiding him. As he was getting to the airport there was an explosion as one of the engines exploded sending flames into the air, the plane tumbled the imbalance was now more pronounced. The captain summoned all the power in him, he saw the VASI but as he was about to lower the jumbo it picked up speed, in front of him was a 790 phantom that was landing, the captain lowered the plane, eyes wide open, teeth gritted, the plane released the wheals last minute. The captain narrowly missed the Fly Easy 790 plane with a carrying capacity of 320 passengers.

The jumbo was on the runway, it was in flames, and the last two engines had caught fire, the captain kept that jumbo running till it eventually stopped at the domestic terminal.

Chapter 58

In the meantime, Lunela was brought before the court to answer to the charges of murdering Mark. The Lord Levenberg was in charge, gazing at everyone, the accused and the complainant. As is normal in any jurisdiction, the state was the complainant and the fully blown pregnant Lunela was the defendant. The Lord Levenberg gestured to the clerk of court who moved within earshot. There were exchanges of whispers between the two and after both nodded it was time for the proceedings.

Lunela was being represented by Sir Allan Jewel, a man barely above 1.5 metres whose record of defending clients was impeccable. The man walked with a slight difficulty, his grey hair was there to accompany his long years of practice. He had been knighted for his exploits in searching for and delivering justice for his clients. One particular case made him famous when he represented a man who had been accused of murder and had been sentenced to life in prison the man had served 20 years in prison but Sir Allan took the matter and proved the man's innocence, he successfully sued the state for negligence and wrongful arrest and detention managing to claim GBP 55 million and out of the whole amount Sir Allan claimed GBP 55,000 as legal fees.

Initially, Sir Allan had asked for bail and it had been denied by a lower court and the matter was now ready for hearing. Before the proceeding could take place, there was a scream from the witness stand, it was Lunela, the prosecution frowned and almost made comments but the judge had asked someone to call an ambulance. Lunela was taken to the hospital, it was labour pains.

Back to court, the prosecution had insisted that the matter continued insisting that Lunela could be called for cross-examination when she had delivered the babies. An emergency meeting was held at the judge's chambers and there was an agreement from both parties that save for responses that required Lunela to testify or answer, there was nothing that could have stopped the matter from going on. The judge had read the charge to Lunela and asked her if she understood Sir Allan was there to represent her and answered yes to understanding the charge but pleaded not guilty.

Prosecution was led by Jonathan Greenwood, a seasoned prosecutor, he had a 95% conviction rate and was not about to drop in his rankings. The man was tall and thin, he moved with grace and in some cases seemed like he was about to fall. He got to the stand. He cleared the throat and looked around the room.

"My Lord," he started. "We are living in unprecedented times in which women have become envious of men and have sought to surpass what was previously male-dominated crimes"- "Objection my Lord, the prosecution ought to stay on point this isn't a high school debate where one seeks to impress some girl in the crowd, we are in the middle of a serious matter." Shouted Sir Allan.

"Greenwood stays on point," yelled the Lord.

"What we have here is a pre-meditated murder, Lunela was having problems having children, and when she finally managed to conceive, she realized that her husband was having an affair with Mark. At first, she thought that Solomon her husband was the woman in that relationship, but when she realized that he was the man and that she had been dumped for a man, she could not take it and hatched a plan to kill Mark. The two were united by adversity, Jennifer. Jennifer initially loved Lunela, but when Solomon filed for divorce papers, Lunela threatened to tell all and that's when the rivalry between Jennifer and Lunela started. Lunela resented Mark but she lured him to her house where they had a discussion."

Greenwood stopped and looked around, and then continued. "On that fateful day, Lunela invited Mark to her house, and they went out together till they got to the Bar. Mark even paid for transport using Lunela's card meaning they were together.

"Lunela later Lunela killed Mark, tying him to the chair, his hands were cuffed meaning that she sweet-talked him and tied his legs too. She then used some hot material to cut his manhood."

Greenwood took out photos of Mark without the manhood and circulated to the bench to see. They were all devastated to see with some turning it upside just after seeing it. It was a terrible sight. Greenwood was sure that the photo was going to do the trick.

"In closing, I want this court to search for the truth, and deliver justice to Mark, though he may be dead his spirit will linger to see that Justice is done. After lunch, Sir Allan took to the stand.

My Lord, My client is innocent, the state has narrated a good story with no substance and evidence to support it.

Here are unsubstantiated statements that we as the defense council seek to be stricken off as mere speculation.

1. That Lunela was having a challenge having children, this is a private matter, whether it's true or not, seek to understand how they obtained that information and seek to see it also for our defense response;

2. That the conception of the children coincided with the relationship between Solomon and Mark;

3. Lunela thought that Solomon was the woman in the relationship but turned out to be the man and then hatched a plan to kill Mark, how exactly;

4. That the two were united in adversity, do we have videos, images, phone records, etc. to prove this;

5. That Lunela Lure Mark, how do you know this?;

6. You indicated that Lunela tied Mark to the chair, did you secure evidence to support that?

7. That Lunela cut Mark's manhood, please help us with the evidence for all this.

8. Did it occur to you that the card might have been stolen by Mark, Mark was arrested three times for theft and once for fraud and was convicted for all counts.

"My Lord I submit that the evidence being submitted to the court is weak, unsubstantiated, unverifiable, lacks credence and was collected in a hurry, I believe that someone is framing my client, this probably someone very close to my client"

Jennifer was in the court when Sir Allan was presenting the evidence, she could not help but feel that the prosecution had done a poor Job.

Greenwood was visibly angry, it then downed on him that he had just collected evidence from Jennifer and due to the level of detail he had hoped that the explanations were to add on to the credit card possession and the lack of alibi for Lunela.

Greenwood was unable to offer a suitable explanation to the questions presented by Sir Allan. There were whispers on the judge's bench as Sir Allan went on with his line of questioning.

The following day the court visited Lunela who was in hospital, it turned out that Lunela had given birth to triplets as opposed to the twins as was anticipated, she had tried to contact Solomon but she failed. Solomon was out of the country. After a long time of waiting for him, she eventually named the other boy after him. So it was one Jennifer, One Smith, and one Solomon. This was an unexpected outcome. But nature had its own way of surprising.

The judge was at the hospital to witness the cross-examination at the insistence of the state, the other judges were in the room and Doctors had given a condition that they would be in the room and that if they thought the patient was being overwhelmed then they would ask the court session to end. Papers were signed to that effect.

The Judges listed that the cross-examination was going on. The state had made the biggest mistake of examining a woman who had just given birth, the site was both happy and sad at the same time. Lunela had given birth for the first time yet what should have been a moment of celebration was turned into a time of defending herself from going to prison.

"Lunela where were you the night Mark was killed." Asked Greenwood. Lunela looked at him in the eyes, tears flowing effortlessly, Greenwood looked away. "Mark came to me, and he told me that my life was in danger and that his was in danger too, I dismissed him but later I decided to leave home just as a precaution. Mark came to apologize to me, he complained of ill-treatment by Solomon and while I was angry at him initially, I understood what he was going through."

"Have you ever killed anyone in your life?" Asked Greenwood, Lunela looked at Greenwood and asked him to repeat the question, Greenwood decided not to have further discussion regarding the matter.

Chapter 59

Simangaliso Mthandazo Dube was the man in charge of investigations at Harare Interpol office, Afripol was in attendance. The passengers were all evacuated while the ground team requested the captain to write a report of the incident that had transpired. The passengers refused to leave without seeing the captain and his team. When they emerged, they were greeted with applause cheers, and ululation. The passengers had seen it all and owed the captain a great deal of gratitude.

Dube walked to the captain and whispered, "You did a hell lot of a job there but you have one further task you must accomplish."

"Drink?" the captain responded jokingly. "We have gathered information that you may have been blackmailed and that someone had put a cargo in the plane which is supposed to be yours," explained Dube, "All we need you to do is pretend like all is well and we will take it from there" added Dube.

"You mean you want me to be a sitting duck?"

Dube did not respond but gave him a look that made him understand that the man was not asking him but commanding him to do so. The captain was aware that in Africa human rights were cut to shit size and so he did not even attempt to resist.

The airport transfer bus arrived and picked up the passengers at the arrival gate for formalities, they collected their bags and were taken to the hospital for examination and to be addressed. There were a number of news networks circling the arrival area like vultures following a dying animal.

The cabin crew collected their bags and in an unusual, the captain had more than ten bags, very heavy ones, the crew wanted to comment but the atmosphere was still tense, everyone was trying to process what they had gone through.

The shuttle bus that collected the crew to the hotel arrived and in no time the bus was headed to the city centre to an upmarket seven-star hotel where many airlines normally book. Right at the hotel entrance a BMW screamed to a stop and behind it was a Toyota GD6, six men emerged, three from the BMW and the other from the GB6. They were holding pistols, they pointed the gun at the driver and ordered everyone to get out of the bus, while the other robbers were offloading and loading only captain's bags into the GD6. As soon as the robbers were done, they attempted to flee but there were barricades. There was a full-scale exchange of firepower and, the robbers took out AK 47s, the shoot-out took more than 30 minutes after which the robbers were overpowered. 4 were killed while one sustained injuries while the other one escaped. All the bags were recovered weighed and recorded. In total, she was 120 kg of cocaine.

The captain went to his room, a WhatsApp call came through and it was Euro Martin's Chairman. "What a great flying other there. We have a deal for you and you give no interviews except cooperating with the investigators and we offer you a retirement package of USD 21 million plus—"

The captain cut him. "Please speak to my lawyer."

Within five minutes his lawyer called, "Captain what a hero you have become. The world is talking about your exploits. Now listen, take the money and walk away. It's the best deal or they will make life difficult for you."

The captain picked up the phone and on the other line was the Chairman of Euro Martin. "Ok I accept and I will need this in writing and I need non-sequential cash 25% in Euros, 25% in USD, and the remainder in GBP." The chairman was stunned, but he had a better plan for the captain. The money had been brought to his new home in Borrowdale. It was the wisdom of the Euro Martin CEO that the money be flown to Zimbabwe in cash from South Africa and that a new house be purchased for him. Soon after the discussion, a waiter knocked and gave him an envelope and some keys. They were keys to a mansion in Borrowdale situated at 10500 SM. These were private games.

The captain typed his resignation at midnight after viewing the house and counting the cash as well as having validated the deeds. He owed a great deal of gratitude to corrupt dudes who were able to open public offices at night and perform the search for him. In this life never assume that everyone is asleep when you are. Great things do happen at night.

Captain Smith called Jennifer who was rather cold offering lukewarm congratulatory messages. He spoke to Solomon who was happy to have become a father of three, with Lunela having named the other son after him. He was having a great time. They spoke about Mark's death and how he was killed. The captain asked him to focus on raising his children.

***

Later that day, Lunela was released from prison. She changed her daughter's name to Lunela after Detective Macmillan whispered that he had put the pieces together and found out that Jennifer had killed Mark. The captain was no seer but he had accused Jennifer of Mark's murder in a gruesome manner and Jennifer never refused, she admitted it had to be done. So, it was Jennifer who had killed Mark and was not even questioned. Detective Macmillan had told Lunela that Jennifer was not going to last a year so there was no need to put her in jail.

Sometime after that, Jennifer was now in the habit of meeting with Stephen Conley at the same house where she killed Mark. One day they had a misunderstanding, Jennifer took an extended cable while Stephen was in a bath tab, electrocuting him in an instant. She took an overdose of cocaine, went for a swim and drowned.

Jennifer had a way of making things real. She had drowned and picked up the now deceased Stephen Conley. Save that she was not the Jennifer who was found dead. Weeks after the death of Mark, Jennifer had been displeased with her relationship with Stephen. She considered him too close and she was afraid that when FAYE was in charge, she would be vulnerable and say too much. She was also considered Stephen a threat that needed to be exterminated. It was such a hard decision as she enjoyed making love with him and the way he made her feel young and explode with emotions. But all that was vanity to Jennifer. She valued her family and was determined to do everything she could to save it.

Lissa Hughes was a prostitute ordered through an online platform. Jennifer had created an identity, a fake identity for

Lissa. After Mark died, Lissa Hughes was offered cocaine on arrival to "spice" up things but Jennifer kept encouraging her to take more and more till she was totally spent. Jennifer led her to the swimming pool and Lissa died by drowning.

Back to Zimbabwe, the following morning out of the 120kgs of cocaine that were recorded, only 90kgs could be found. It turns out that there was never 120kgs recorded, the drugs were recorded as 90kgs and there was nobody to ask.

Coming Next!!!

The Land Baron

By

Elliot Chatima and Rumbi Chen

Chapter 1

Engineer Dr Shelton Makaza was driving from his house in Greendale, when an unmarked tinted SUV Mercedes Benz overtook him and parked right in front of him. Assessing the situation, a Hummer blocked his left side while a Toyota Land Cruiser followed closely behind him. The driver holding the steering wheel skillfully with one hand, while the other holding a shotgun pointed at the Engineer. On the left side was an open deep drainage, which could have been easily 15 to 22 feet down. The engineer's heart raced while his mind was calculating the vectors and distances at a speed of Mach 6. As the Engineer was pondering, the Hummer that was on his side suddenly took off at a great speed. The engineer breathed a sigh of relief. However, he could not escape the SUV which, was still right in front of him. At that point, a Toyota GD 6 with a makeshift bumper designed for rugged terrain, hit the Engineer's car sending it rolling into the drainage below. Three men disembarked from the Cruiser behind, followed the wreckage. The Engineer had sustained numerous injuries, the three men ignored him instead they took all the bags that were in the car, searched the bags and after retrieving what they were looking for, they fled the scene but not before the set the car ablaze.

It is 5 July 2010 in the capital city of Zimbabwe, and life seems to be normal. At 08:45 there was a meeting at the

Council of Harava. The meeting was to decide on the application made by a multi-millionaire prominent businessman Mr Micheal Paradzai, a local business tycoon with vast tracts of land across the country. The Meeting was to take place in the Mukuyu Board room. The thirteen member team was seated, save for one Dr Shelton Kakaza, an engineer with vast experience in water and civil engineering. The engineer had communicated that he was coming to the meeting, it was not his habit to be late for a meeting let alone not communicate his position.

British trained ,he was aware that coming to meetings on time was an indicator of how one respected other people. Seconds turned into minutes and minutes turned into hours just like in the "Round and Round" song by Justin Bieber ,yet there was still no sign of the engineer. The chairman of the land committee decided to give the engineer some time till lunch hour. The engineer had prepared the environmental impact assessment report apart from the report normally produced by EMA, the Environment Management Agency. The EMA report was submitted in hard copy and only the chairman of the committee had sight of the report. This raised eyebrows but no one was strong enough to engage the Chairman and demand the report.

By 15:30 Engineer Makaza could not be located and the chairman decided to proceed with the meeting without Engineer Makaza. The Chairman called the meeting to order and since this was a specific matter, there were no minutes of the previous meeting. The quorum was confirmed and Engineer Shelton Makaza was noted as absent from the meeting. The chairman indicated that the purpose of the meeting ,was to discuss the application for land as submitted by Mr Micheal Paradzai through his Native Investments. The Chairman indicated that he had seen the report from

EMA, which he was willing to share after the meeting but was quick to point out that the councillors had not objected to the use of the report. A committee member Mr Changunda raised the matter requiring the chairman to consider adjourning the meeting till the Engineer's Report was heard but he was crushed by the chairman, before other members of the committee could have a chance to consider the proposal. The chairman indicated that there was need to respond to the application in the spirit of maintaining a good relationship with the business community. Another committee member raised a point of order, stating that the land that was applied for was close to some aquatic life which could be disturbed .It was also noted that the land applied for was considered to be wetlands and held some heritage sites and areas of national interest. The chairman informed the quorum ,that a confidential vote was to be used to decide on those in favour of and those against. There was a point of order raised by the chamber secretary who queried the voting methodology proposed. There was a disproportionate and borderline threatening response from the chairman. He insisted that the law talks about voting and does not prescribe how the voting is done and it was up to the councillors to decide. Some committee members were about to leave the room in protest, having realised that there were glaring governance breaches. At that point the chairman indicated that each of the committee members were to apply for one commercial property, one residential property of a maximum size of 2000 square metres.

At that point, there was silence and the members started sitting down one by one. The chairman indicated that the stands were to be paid for and that a 40% discount would be applied. However, the chairman had managed to secure a sponsor and that Native Investments was willing and was standing ready to settle the 60% component. This meant that councillors were not expected to pay anything towards the purchase of land.

"You should have come clean that there were other matters to consider, surely such patriotic and well-meaning stakeholders cannot be punished through lengthy and unjustified processes. We ought to use our influence to reward this at once", one committee member commented with a high pitched voice betraying his excitement, he was clearly elated and did little to hide it.

The chairman indicated that there was a problem with the law ,as there was a requirement that an auction be conducted and the highest bidder allocated the land. Rose Majaya interjected making a point that there was a provision in the Urban Councils Act that the committee could directly allocate land if they believed that the development was in the best interest of the city. The chamber secretary refuted Lisa Rose's position but the chairman was ready to rubbish the contribution from the legal mind. "Find the part of the law that allows the committee to allocate the land without going to tender and fix this," the chairman demanded. "Then you will have to wait till I give feedback" ,the chamber secretary responded.

The chairman looked at the chamber secretary with the look that parents give their misbehaving children when there are visitors at home .Immediately the chamber secretary got the message.

The votes were done and all the members voted unanimously to the awarding of the land to Native Investments. The company had not submitted bank accounts and bankable proposals; they had only stated that they intended to invest USD 2.5 million in Infrastructure that will modernise the city. The market value of the land in question was USD 22,5 million going by similar valuations done for property opposite the 300, 000 SM land. Native Investments was allocated the land at a cost of USD 3.5 million. The meeting was closed and all the committee members went home with offer letters of the land they had been promised in the meeting. These letters indicated that the stands had been paid for in full.

365

Previous books

The Storm

Elliot Chatima

And

Rumbi Chen

Chapter 1

March 2023, Bulawayo, Zimbabwe

On a Thursday afternoon somewhere in the middle of Bulawayo City, the second largest city in Zimbabwe, life is going on as usual; right in the city center, in a Fast and Furious style, a convoy of six Escalade cars in South African Plates emerged in high speed, before long, the wheels screamed to a brisk stop in what used to be Cecil John Rhode's route to Namibia, Ekupumuleni (the resting Place). The road had been intentionally widened to accommodate Rhode's horse-drawn carriage. And being a small town, people had already started gyrating around like vultures following a dying animal, albeit at a safe distance. For ten straight minutes, there was no movement, but the very inaction aroused varied feelings from the onlookers; some felt impending danger, others felt excited, and still others felt livid while others were indifferent.

Their silence was broken by a guy who was passing by selling some cosmetics yelling at the top of his voice, immediately there were some murmurings, and the excitement grew louder as they waited in anticipation. The murmurings were cut short and replaced by complete silence as that of the examination room for students taking an American Bar exam or the Cambridge check point exam as he emerged from the car, the man himself in flesh and blood in the streets of Bulawayo standing beside the third of the convoy of six cars his name, Jonathan Bowman Zuva or JBZ for short as he is affectionately known in other parts of the world. Word had swelled in town that there was something big about to happen not only in town but the country. The adoption of the United States Dollar by the Government of Zimbabwe as a transaction currency had attracted a number of traders, drug dealers and money launderers were no exception.

JBZ was wearing a designer suit made with the finest fabric; a quick glance revealed it could have been Italian style, maybe Corneliani. He was wearing a black Hat with a feather affixed to the center ribbon tucked in a bowtie like style. A horseshoe beard circled his chin and opened atop, making a half-moon like shape connecting with well-trimmed falls from both ears. The horseshoe was in a formation mimicking that of red ants at a barbeque surrounding a big piece of Countrystyle Boerwors sausage from, Colcom Meats.

The chin was distinct, and a scar on the left chic was visibly displayed with pride and perhaps displayed like a Medal of Honor awarded by the President for some good done to humanity. His eyes were blue, and he had a stare that could frighten a pride of lions to the point of giving up their territory. Further down, his Adam's apple protruded and was visible for all who cared to look, and it moved noticeably up and down each time he swallowed.

On closer inspection, the suit was made of the finest material, in the range of USD 3,000 to USD 4,000 per suit. A belt with a head made of two small guns crossed each other and was neatly wrapped around his waist. On the left hand, he wore a wrist watch, a USD 907,900 Patek Philippe made from the finest material and by the finest master craftsman, who have been making wrist watches since 1839. This watch was circa 2017, 41mm taupe brown, platinum, a round face with a baton dial and baton's hands, a perpetual calendar and moon phase indication, screw –down crown, leather strap, a pin-buckle fastening, and an automatic movement. The watch had been evaluated and authenticated by Watch Box, an in-house Swiss-trained watchmaker, and the watch came with a two-year warranty. Behind were small concealed bumps, and these could have been guns, one could speculate, as it turns out it was not any type but a Magnum, possibly a .44mm caliber, the most powerful pistol on God's earth. He had one on each side of his ass. On the right hand, he was holding a Cigar, not any ordinary type but an Inferno by Oliva Serie V Double Robusto, which had been handcrafted since 1886. This one was wrapped in a brown, gold, and purple sticker with a V distinctly marked at the center of the cigar, and it comes in a pack of 24, with each pack coming in at USD 214. On the same right hand was a signature with the letters JBZ printed on the protruding shirt. His shoes were made of real leather, possibly from crocodile skin, with patches of black and white on them to go with the classic suit.

After scanning the city like one viewing his piece of land that was purchased in his absence and for approximately three and half minutes, he had taken his time to satisfy himself of whatever he was looking for, he motioned to the car in front and three men with a 350-meter effective range AK47s emerged from the car. They brought a man in his late twenties, a handsome boy, a well-known boy in the streets of Bulawayo, a promising artist who was also known to be a drug dealer; though he never had drugs on him, he specialized in recruiting youngsters into drug distribution for Manjinji a well-known local drug dealer operating at a very small scale perhaps due to capital constrains and lack of access to key suppliers. For a long time, the streets belonged to Manjinji, and there was not much use of force and violence as there was not much competition. Manjinji personally handled the authorities when arrests and interference became too much. Samson Thumelo Ndlovu was brought to JBZ, and without hesitation and any preamble, JBZ grabbed Samson by the dreadlocks; Samson screamed with pain and fear. JBZ drew a hunter knife and without brandishing it much, he cut open Samson's throat, and as he gasped for breath , blood oozed like a leaking tape, JBZ licked the blood on the knife blade and tucked it back into its position, fear gripped the onlookers and all who were subsequently told of the encounter. As Samson fell to the ground, JBZ kicked his lifeless body. He took a gallon of Gasoline, poured it on him, and burnt the body in broad day light. After that, he addressed the people with a louder voice, proclaiming the start of the new era. The streets were his, and that he would not hesitate to do to anyone what he had just done to Samson. He motioned to the team holding guns, and immediately, they started firing shorts non-stop in the air; at that point as if it were a 21 gun salute following the death of Samson, there was chaos and confusion of the highest level in the small town of Bulawayo. Four men emerged from one car, then another, and another, and there was a massive celebratory shooting in the air; no one was pointed at or threatened, and people failed to make sense of the shooting. It was a celebratory and warning shooting session. The shooting lasted for approximately three minutes, and bullets were raining everywhere while shells were scattered on the ground like Ice cubes falling from the sky on a rainy day. Disturbing screams of innocent women and children could be heard from far and near, and people could be seen running for cover while rivers of cars meandered through the roads, with many colliding and pilling up in a panic-stricken small town. Some pulled off and folded seats in a desperate attempt to avoid being hit by stray bullets, while others left the cars and took off at a speed that could have easily won the 100-meter Olympics, surpassing Usain Bolt's record of 9.58 seconds for 100 meter challenge. Then the shooting stopped, the shooters got back into the cars, and JBZ was still standing there, still like the statue of Oliver Tambo at the welcome gate at OR Tambo International Airport, still smoking his Oliva cigar; he was stable and steady as if nothing had happened. He finally gestured and got into the car, and immediately the cars screamed from zero to 100 miles per hour and hit top speeds of 180 miles per hour, leaving tar marks, smoke, little dust, and a smell of tyres, not bad for a tailor-made Escalade.